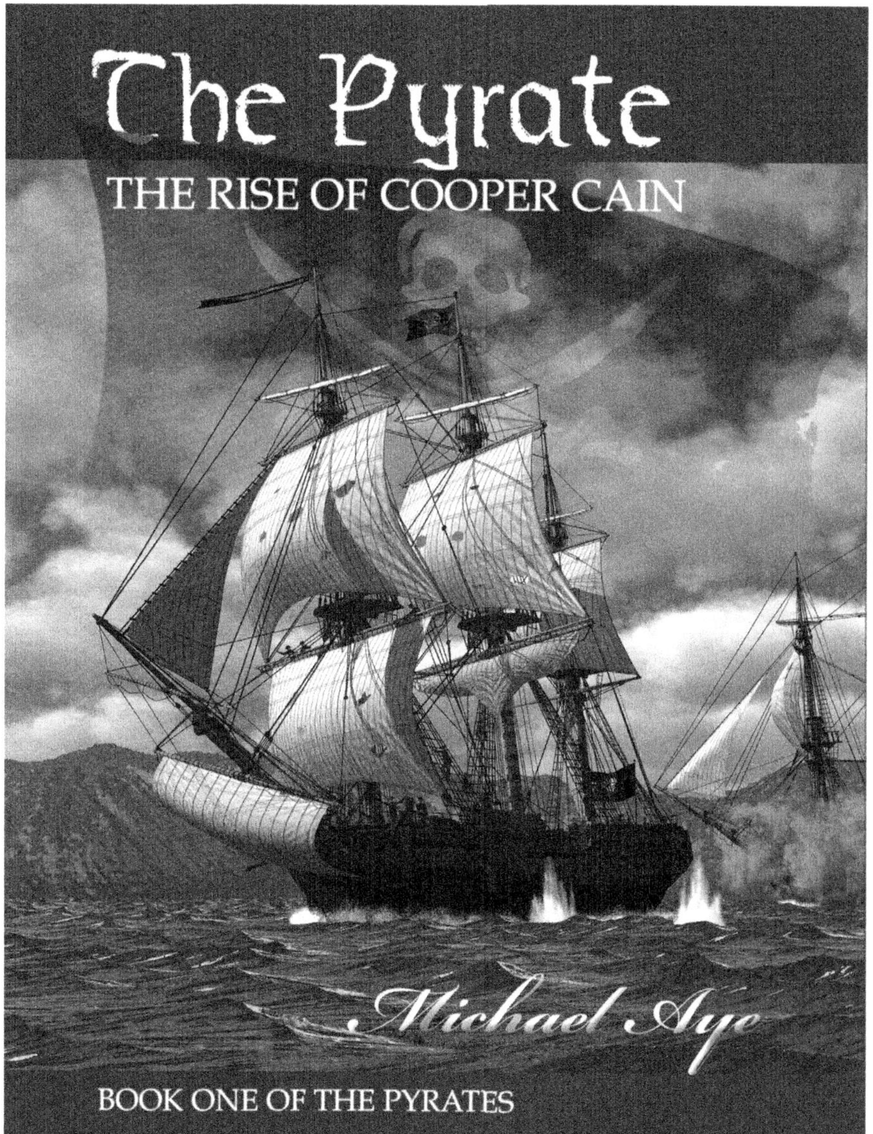
The Pyrate
THE RISE OF COOPER CAIN
Michael Aye
BOOK ONE OF THE PYRATES

The PYRATE

The Rise of Cooper Cain

Book 1

Michael Aye

Published by Boson Books

An imprint of Bitingduck Press
Formerly an imprint of C&M Online Media, Inc.

ISBN 978-1-938463-26-6
eISBN 978-1-938463-27-3

For information contact
Bitingduck Press, LLC
Altadena, CA
notifications@bitingduckpress.com
http://www.bitingduckpress.com
Cover art by Johannes Ewers
Rear cover by Ruth Sanderon

Author's note

This book is a work of fiction with a historical backdrop. I have taken liberties with historical figures, ships, and time frames to blend in with my story. Therefore, this book is not a reflection of actual historical events.

Books by Michael Aye

Fiction

The Fighting Anthony Series

The Reaper, Book One
HMS SeaWolf, Book Two
Barracuda, Book Three
SeaHorse, Book Four
Peregrine, Book Five
Trident, Book Six

War 1812 Trilogy

Remember the Raisin, Book One
Battle At Horseshoe Bend, Book Two

Non-Fiction

What's the Reason for All That Wheezing and Sneezing
Michael A. Fowler and Nancy McKemie

Dedication

To the crew of Allergy & Asthma Clinics of Georgia. It's been a long and rewarding cruise. Farewell and smooth sailing, mates.

PROLOGUE

THE METALLIC CLINK AS blade engaged blade filled the well lighted room. The foes would engage each other; at first, there was a steady feeling out of the other man. A thrust, a parry, and then disengage, a thrust or lunge and disengage again. As confidence built, the attack had increased in intensity and ferociousness. An attack, then a rasping sound as blade slid off blade and then a riposte or counterattack. A loud clank as a blade was beat aside. Respect was evident as the foes circled each other, cautious but not overly so.

Jean-Paul de Giraud was a fencing master. He had been France's greatest maitre d'Armes. He had soundly defeated Italy's best. He had not only brought the championship to France but had kept it there so that French maitre d'Armes was considered the finest in the world. The de Giraud Salle d'Armes in Paris was second to none. Men of wealth would put their sons on the waiting list by the time they were twelve years old. Men would build a piste, a long rectangular room used for fencing instruction and bouts on their property, all in the hopes that their son would master the artistic pursuit of swordsmanship. But that was before Bonaparte. That was also before the guillotine's blade caused panic and fear throughout the country. That was before the nobility of France fled their homeland leaving all their worldly possessions behind. Some of the nobility were living off the generosity of friends, while some of them were living as paupers.

It was the same with Jean-Paul de Giraud. He escaped the guillotine with little more than the clothes on his back and a few of his favorite swords. He also carried his skill. England's nobility and upper class society were no different than the French; men wanted their sons to be trained by the best. The difference was there was no Salle d'Armes. A few piste were built but in place of a school of fencing Jean-Paul would move in with a family, as an honored guest to show off to the local gentry. If the patron had one son it was not uncommon for the stay to last six months or longer. Two sons could mean a stay of a year. At which time the master would have done all that could be done toward turning a pupil into, if not a master swordsman, at least one who was well equipped in the art to defend himself if most honorably. Before long, Jean-Paul found himself so booked up he could not take any more pupils. His bank account had swelled to the point he didn't need to teach ever again. But you could not put a monetary figure on the joy of the sport. This was especially true when a pupil became so apt that it made the teacher work all the harder.

Thus was the case with the young man who faced him, a nephew of Sir Lawrence Finylson. He was a natural, his reflexes matched his instructor. The biggest advantage Jean-Paul had over his pupil was experience. Otherwise, the young man would have bested the master on several occasions. The skill was noted from the start, from the first "engage". The lightning fast blade of young Cooper Cain made Jean-Paul relish the memory of his youth. Maybe it was his sudden distraction of recalling his younger years that cost the master the bout. The pupil attacked in earnest, the foil's blade a blur, Jean-Paul returned the pressure after a gallant parry. But Cain was ready; he beat his opponent's blade aside and with a windmill-like maneuver stripped Jean-Paul's fencing foil from his grip, sending it into the air. Cain touched the nail-like end of his foil into Jean-Paul's chest with one hand while catching the flying blade out of the air with the other. A feat which had been done against the master. Two thoughts came immediately to his mind. One, if this match had been a real battle he would be dead, and two, he was getting too damn old for this.

Bowing to the young man, Jean-Paul addressed him, "M'sieur Cain, the student has become the master."

"Thank you, sir," Cooper responded. "It was but luck. You seemed to be distracted and I took advantage of it."

Shaking his head in acknowledgment, Jean-Paul replied, "But alas you were able to recognize the distraction and you have developed the skill to take advantage of the moment." Then leaning forward, Jean-Paul whispered, "I wish, M'sieur Phillip would show just a touch of interest. I feel my efforts are pointless in regards to that one."

Cooper smiled and replied back in a much louder voice, "He will never do anything that requires he put forth an effort. With Sir Lawrence as a father he may never have to put forth any effort."

Jean-Paul agreed. "But his father has demanded the boy take the lessons. A waste of time I fear, but time in which I'm well paid."

"Well, I'm most appreciative of your time and efforts," Cooper replied earnestly.

Jean-Paul bowed again and turned his attention to Phillip. The windows were open and a cool zephyr caused the candles to flicker. The bout with Cooper had caused Jean-Paul to work up a sweat. The zephyr was welcomed.

"A glass before we start," Jean-Paul said as he wiped his face with a towel. After draining a quick glass of sherry, he used the towel once more and then laid it aside. He doubted that he'd need the towel anymore. It was doubtful he'd do much more than go through the motions with Phillip. He'd never work up a sweat doing that.

THE MOONLIGHT WAS ALMOST as bright as the day. Cooper had walked through the French doors and out the pavilion onto a patio. Burning torches lit up the flagstone pathway to a natural spring pool about a hundred meters away. He could just pick up the sound of water splashing and an occasional giggle. The twins, Jessie and Josie, must be down at the pool, Cooper thought. The girls were no kin to him but liked

to tell everybody they were cousins. They were, in fact, wards of Sir Lawrence. Their father and Sir Lawrence had gone to school together, been in the same Army regiment, and later had each had a seat in Parliament.

On New Year's Day in 1795, their mother and father had been killed in a carriage accident when a careless driver had tried to turn a corner to cross a bridge too fast. The carriage wheels slid on the frozen ground and it toppled over the bridge into the icy waters below. The other driver was killed as well. The twins had been raised by Sir Lawrence since that time.

Cooper made his way down the path and was standing at the edge of the pool watching the girls for a few minutes before they realized he was there. They were not just twins, they were identical. They were also the same age as Cooper and had always enjoyed each other's company. All three of them detested Phillip. The girls were beautiful blond young vixens, and they knew it. Cooper enjoyed walking down a street with a twin on each arm and watching the heads turn in envy. Young or old, men looked, except Phillip.

"He never looks," Josie said. "I wonder if he's a sodomite." Cooper didn't know, he didn't care to know.

However, whereas Phillip never looked, Cooper always looked… and why not? After all, God gave him eyes to appreciate the beautiful creatures he placed on this earth. If Jessie and Josie were not beautiful creatures, he didn't know what was.

Turning, Jessie spied Cooper. Slowly, she backed into the deeper part of the pool so the water rose just above her breast. "Josie, would you look? Cooper has been watching us."

Josie, more forward than Jessie, did not back into the deep water. She, in fact, stepped forward until her entire chest rose out of the pool. Her breasts were pert, like ripe young melons. Taking her sister's lead, Jessie stepped forward. "Do you like what you see, Coop?"

"What's not to like?" he answered.

The girls whispered to one another and then ducked under the water. They then seemed to swirl around and resurface. This time Cooper stood transfixed by the nude tempting beauties.

"Can you tell who is who?" one of the twins asked.

"Sure," Cooper replied. "You have a freckle on the inside of your left breast," he said, pointing to Josie.

"My, you are observant," Josie said.

"Would you like to see more?" Jessie asked, taking a bold step forward so that the pool water was now below her waist.

Smiling, Cooper didn't reply. He watched as little rivulets of water ran down their bodies and drops cascaded down and off their breasts. Damn, they are tempting hussies, he thought.

"Oh, he wants to come in," Jessie said. "Look at his breeches. I do believe we've excited him, Josie."

"I think you are right, sister. Wouldn't you enjoy jumping in with us, Coop?"

Before he could reply, Jessie ducked down into the water pulling a startled Josie with her, the smiles gone from their faces. Cooper heard the footsteps on the flagstones just before a hand gripped his shoulder and snatched him around.

WHAP…a sudden pain shot through him as he was struck across the face and cheek by a riding crop. Warm blood rushed to the surface and ran down his face, dripping on his shirt and pants. Reflex action caused his hand to dive to the small sword at his side. He then recognized his uncle.

"Is this the way you repay my kindness and generosity?" Sir Lawrence shouted. "You sneak up and spy on the girls while they are bathing."

"I was not spying. I was talking to them," Cooper said.

"You were watching them, hoping you would get a glimpse of their nakedness."

"I could see nothing, nor attempted to see anything. I mentioned that once they had finished, Phillip, Jean-Paul, and myself might want to get into the pool." Damn, Cooper thought to himself, how quickly the lie slid off his tongue in his attempt to protect the twins.

"If only I could believe that," Sir Lawrence said, seemingly about to waiver, and then suddenly his anger returned. "You lie," he shouted, rage in his voice again. "You were seen spying on the girls."

"That's a lie, Uncle, and if someone dares to say otherwise let him face me. We'll let our blades show who is the liar."

Sir Lawrence's facial expressions changed suddenly from rage to fear. "Go to your room, Cooper. I will think this over and we'll discuss it in the morning."

Cooper walked back down the flagstone pathway only to be met by his mother and Jean-Paul. The wound to his face was throbbing badly and he felt faint now that his anger and temper had diminished. Seeing the cut dripping blood on Cooper's face, Jean-Paul rushed back for a towel. Cooper walked a few more steps with his mother, Ann, supporting him. He then slumped down in a yard chair.

Jean-Paul quickly returned and blotted the wound with the towel. "You've been cut to the bone, Cooper. You'll need sewing up."

His mother gasped at Jean-Paul's words; she rose and kissed Cooper on the forehead. "I will send for the surgeon."

As she entered the house, Jean-Paul looked at his pupil. There seemed to be an inner conflict for a few moments. When he'd settled it for himself, Jean-Paul spoke but in a hushed voice, "It was Phillip. He watched you go down the path and then he said, 'There goes Cooper. He's going down to play with those sluts of father's. I wonder what father would do if he knew.' Phillip then left."

"I figured something like that had happened. He'll get his, I'll run him through."

"No, M'sieur that you cannot do."

"Humph! I can and I will. It will have to be the right time and place. I cannot do anything to jeopardize mother's situation. But the day will come, I swear it. Phillip will feel my vengeance."

CHAPTER ONE

IT WAS NEW YEARS Day. The year, 1810, had just begun and so had a new life for Cooper Cain. He had spent Christmas, not at his uncle's estate as he had for as long as he could remember, but at Scolfes, a fine inn in Portsmouth. His mother had been with him as had Jean-Paul. The twins had even stopped in for a hurried visit. The flat of rooms could not have been cheap. Cooper was sure it had been Jean-Paul who had paid for them.

In the weeks that had followed the incident at the pool with his uncle, several things had taken place. His uncle had decided he would be sent to Antigua to work either in the clearing house, or if he preferred he could learn agriculture and farming on his uncle's sugar cane plantation. His mother argued that by rights the plantation should be Cooper's as his inheritance from his father. His uncle argued that when Cooper's father had died, the debt owed on the plantation far exceeded its worth and it was only the Finylson stewardship that had kept it in the family. However, should the debt be repaid with the appropriate interest the plantation would be returned to the Cain's ownership.

Jean-Paul had called his uncle to task about the treatment of Cooper based on unfounded accusations. Sir Lawrence was quick to point out the accusations were not unfounded, as Phillip was an eyewitness. Besides, Jean-Paul was an employee and it was not his place to pry into private family matters. Jean-Paul pulled himself erect and said, "When my most prized pupil is so wrongly accused, it does involve me." He also stated he found

Phillip completely without honor and that were he not a guest in Sir Lawrence's home he would demand satisfaction. This sent a bolt of fear through Sir Lawrence. He turned pale and tried to find something to say...to respond. But Jean-Paul held up his hand to silence him and continued, "In regards to employment, M'sieur, be assured that the agreement to teach your son the manly art of swordsmanship is now terminated."

Jean-Paul had called upon Cooper's mother and offered her his support, relating that she need not dwell in her brother's home a minute longer. She agreed to go to Portsmouth with Jean-Paul and Cooper, and await one of Lord Finylson's ships that would transport Cooper to Antigua. Once the ship arrived, the captain let it be known his lordship had said Cooper would be expected to work and pay for his passage.

"Never!" Jean-Paul bellowed, followed by several words in French that neither Cooper nor his mother understood. However, it was apparent that the captain did. After a few minutes, it was agreed that Cooper would be a passenger who would travel in first class. Jean-Paul paid for the ticket and made it plain that should he not hear from Cooper that all was well, then the captain would regret his treachery. The captain assured Jean-Paul that word had gotten out about the incident and while everyone liked Cooper, no one agreed with Sir Lawrence's actions.

Jean-Paul could only smile in regards to the comment about 'the word had gotten out.' All of Sir Lawrence's servants, none of whom liked Phillip, had been quick to spread the word to other servants. Those servants were quick to spread the rumors to their lords and mistresses. On occasion, a coin in the hand here and there expedited the spreading of the incident. When asked personally, Jean-Paul was polite and correct in his refusal to discuss such matters. It was enough he decided, he could not continue in a place where honor was not held in the highest esteem. That was answer enough to those who asked.

Sir Lawrence had sworn to ruin Jean-Paul if he left Finylson manor. To this, the master swordsman smiled and patting his blade, hissed, "Surely no one could be so foolish." The requests for his teaching grew, rather than the opposite. Now he was considering opening a school. The only decision was where to locate it.

After several days in Portsmouth, Cooper had noticed that Jean-Paul had stopped calling his mother, 'my lady.' It was now Ann and Jean-Paul. At first, Cooper felt it was amusing and then realized his father had been dead since he was ten years old. He was now eighteen. During that time his mother had had little more than polite conversation with men. He found himself wishing she'd reconsider staying at Finylson manor. Jean-Paul would not only be a good provider, but also a good husband. He'd be nothing like Cooper's father, who had been a rake and a gambler; he'd been killed in a duel. It was said he was drunk at the time, and he'd called a man out for cheating. Later it was proven that he was right...but being dead right didn't help.

Sir Lawrence had been ready to take in his widowed sister and her son. With his own wife dying, Ann could raise the boys and the twins while she lived a life she'd been accustomed to until she'd married Cooper's father. However, as years passed Phillip had become more and more jealous of Cooper. He was everything that Phillip was not. Phillip could see that his father admired his nephew more than his own son. Now that Cooper was being sent away he'd not have to compete for his father's attention anymore.

COOPER SAT IN HIS private cabin unpacking his things. The *Bonnie Lass* was a merchant ship. She had four first class cabins but as far as Cooper could tell there was nothing first class about them. The lieutenant governor of Antigua had sent for his family now that he was situated on the island. His wife, three daughters, and servants took up two of the first class cabins. A well-to-do planter from Barbados took the fourth cabin, which was next to Cooper's.

It had been a wet, nasty day and seemed like it was getting worse by the hour. The trip from Scolfes Inn to the harbor had not been pleasant. A steady drizzle and a southerly wind had caused the streets to be deserted. The clouds made it difficult to see the fortifications in the distance. Waiting on the dock, as his chests was removed from the carriage and placed in the ship's boat that had been sent to pick up him up, Cooper could see white caps coming alive across the Solent. Rollers were picking up and lapped heavily against the seawall. Heavy, dark clouds hung over the Isle of Wight.

"We best be on our way," one of the boatmen said, as the last chest was loaded. "It promises to be a hard and hellish pull now."

Giving his mom a quick hug and kiss goodbye, Cooper wondered when he'd see her again. He suddenly felt lost and wanted to tell her how much he loved her. But time did not allow a long goodbye. He grasped Jean-Paul's hand and with a firm grip, shook it. "Look after mother please, Master."

A smile creased Jean-Paul's face at being addressed as master. "I shall, Cooper. I will with my last breath. Now be off with you."

The trip had been lively indeed. Cooper was soaked to the skin as he made his way up the slippery battens and through the entry port. He was shown to his cabin and the chest followed. The mate who showed Cooper to his quarters said, "The captain had planned to weigh anchor this afternoon, but I feel like it will be after the weather moderates, which likely means in the morning."

In the silence of the cabin, Cooper wondered what was in store for him. What did his future hold? Would he ever have the opportunity to face his cousin, to call him out? Would there be satisfaction in doing so?

The sounds of rain grew louder on the deck and swells made the ship rise and fall. The cabin grew darker and Cooper became drowsy. He shoved his remaining unpacked chest aside and stretched out in his cot…a swing. Something he'd never slept on before. Sleep soon overtook him. He dreamed of the night his face was laid open. He also dreamed of the surgeon sewing up his face. He dreamed of the twins, how they'd tip-toed into his room and apologized for his getting in trouble. He dreamed of their administrations which lasted half the night and how, if he hadn't have had to leave his mother, he felt maybe the ordeal had been worth it. The twins knew how to soothe one's hurt.

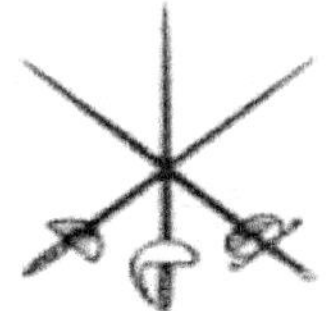

CHAPTER TWO

THE DARKNESS BEFORE DAWN, Cooper had learned, was the most depressing part of the day. The sounds of the watch changing and a ship coming to life made it difficult to sleep through. Cooper had never been an early riser. He had gone to bed at dawn on many a day but getting up, "Gawd."

They were now in the Caribbean, the captain had said. How he knew, Cooper was not sure. Yes, he had his sextant, calipers, divider, charts, and such, but that meant very little to a landsman such as himself.

Throwing the cover back, Cooper felt a chill as he shuddered. Dawn was also chilly and damp. It seemed almost as cold as it had been sitting aboard the ship back in Portsmouth. The mate who'd showed Cooper to his cabin had been right. They had not sailed that day or the next either. It had been the morning of the third day that they'd weighed anchor and got underway. At least, that was how his new friend, David MacArthur, had described it. David had been a navy lieutenant, the second lieutenant on a frigate. He had the misfortune of going to seek his captain as foul weather approached their anchorage in Portsmouth. What he found was the captain sodomizing a cabin boy.

Astounded at the revelation Cooper gasped. "You mean he practiced buggery, right there on board one of his Majesty's ships?"

"Aye," MacArthur confirmed. "I was not seen so I rushed back on deck and collided with the first lieutenant. I grabbed his arm and shouted, 'Follow me quickly.' Thinking it an emergency, Martin, that was his name, followed me through the companionway and into the captain's cabin. The captain had his back to us and was thrusting away like a great bull on a cow. He gave out a great sigh and fell forward just as Martin shouted, 'Captain, God in heaven, man.' The cabin boy grabbed his ducks and fled. The master-at-arms was called and without telling him the charge, he was told the captain was under arrest. Martin called for a boat and had himself taken to the Port Admiral's office. Within the hour, in a driving rain, the captain was taken ashore in chains. Statements were taken from Martin, the cabin boy, and myself. However, we didn't know how strong and politically powerful the captain was. Before the day of the court martial, Martin was told the cabin boy was found floating against the seawall. Lieutenant Martin was then attacked one night by a band of thieves as he left the George Tavern. He was robbed and left with his throat cut. Then, I was awakened and pulled from my cot in the wee hours of the morning, accused of rape by some tavern wench. I was given an option...face charges or resign my commission. Naturally, I resigned. The captain had the power and the money to do away with two witnesses. I think I was left alive just so I could suffer and know I could be next...at any time, at any place. Aye, the captain was ruthless, utterly ruthless. So, here I am a sailor, a naval officer without ever having the prospect of commanding my own ship."

"Why are you going to Antigua?" Cooper asked.

"My mother has cousins there. One of them has a coastal trader and another one is a harbor pilot. I was told they'd get me on somewhere. It's not a warship but it's the sea."

Cooper then asked, "What happened to the sodomite captain?"

"Well, his navy career was over. Even though he was not convicted by the court martial, everyone knew the truth. His family, besides being rich and politically powerful, had a lot to do with the Honest Johns." Seeing Cooper's confusion, MacArthur added, "The Honourable East India Company. It would not surprise me to see him commanding a ship for the Bombay marines." Laughing as a thought came to his mind, MacArthur said, "The Bombay marines, we used to call them, the Bombay buccaneers."

Cooper had heard of the private navy of warships protecting convoys for the East India Company.

"No sir," MacArthur said. "With Captain Buggery Pope's old man a director for the company it would not surprise me to see the sodomite walking his own quarterdeck again."

Dressing in the dark was not hard, as Cooper had fallen asleep in his clothes. The only thing he'd taken off was his boots. Sniffing his armpits, Cooper wrinkled his nose. Damn, what was it they said? When you smell yourself, others have smelled you for three days. No wonder the Williams girls wore so much perfume.

Sir Jonathan Williams, the lieutenant governor of Antigua, had a nice looking wife, Elizabeth. Would her features hold up to the island's mosquitoes, fever, and hot sun? All would take its toll on a woman more used to London's weather. His daughters were something else. Before long, Sir Jonathan could be a rich man by marrying his daughters off to the right planter's son. Lucy was the oldest and she was a ripe cherry ready for the plucking. Cooper was not too sure her fruit had not been plucked already. All three girls had traded their beautiful dresses for sailors' slops. They didn't want to ruin the dresses on all the oakum and tar that seemed to be everywhere on a ship. The sailors were all to ready to donate the slops, which accentuated every curve the girls had, to say nothing of showing off their fine set of breasts.

Lady Elizabeth probably wouldn't have condoned the way the girls dressed. However, she succumbed to a terrible illness the first day out of the channel. Her meals had been carried to her and as soon as she ate, the contents of her meals came back up. MacArthur said he'd never seen such a case of seasickness. So the good lady had been consigned to her cot. The girls had pretty much had the run of the ship, with their flashing eyes, flirting and even making coy comments to the sailors.

Lucy was the oldest, with her and Cooper both being eighteen. On more than one occasion, she had brushed up against him in the narrow passageway between their cabins. Cooper knew she did it on purpose, the little tease. Linda, who was only two years younger, was learning the art well from her older sister, Lucy, who was the master on innuendo and tease.

Only Laura, who was still a child, talked straight and honest. Being a curious girl, one afternoon sitting on deck watching the sunset in the western sky, she crossed over to Cooper. Tracing the scar across his cheek, she humbly said, "That must have hurt terribly." The wound had healed but left a very obvious scar.

"It did," Cooper admitted, feeling again the burn and terrible pain as the riding crop had bit into the flesh.

Laura kissed her finger and then touched the scar. "There," she said in all sincerity. "Now, it won't hurt anymore." Cooper smiled at the girl's words. Seeing him smile, she smiled back and gave him a hug.

Seeing this caused her sisters to laugh and giggle. Laura swung around and stomped her feet. "You two are so mean."

"We're sorry, we didn't mean to be," the sisters said, giggling and whispering together. Lucy rose up and walked toward Cooper, "Likely, a wound over some girl."

"You're wrong," Cooper said with a smirk. "Two girls…sisters in fact. They couldn't keep their hands off of me and I was forced to kill their husbands, in a duel, one right after the other. I was a bit tired in the second duel and the sod got lucky. I had to run him through."

The girls became suddenly silent and pale. "You...your joking," Lucy mumbled.

"There's the scar," Cooper said. The girls suddenly had to go check on their mother.

As soon as they were out of sight, MacArthur, who had been sitting next to Cooper, smoking a cigar stood up and thumped the butt over the side. "What a tall tale. Of course, you gave them cause to stop and think." As MacArthur and Cooper had become close friends, Cooper had shared his story over a cheap bottle of wine one night. "We are both victims of wrong doings," MacArthur had said. "One day we must find a way to right the wrong that has been done us."

"We will," Cooper said. "I vow by all that's holy, Phillip Finylson will rue the day he lied about Cooper Cain."

THE DAYS HAD DRAGGED into weeks. The weather had only been rough on one occasion, with gale force wind and rain coming down in sheets. The next day brought fair winds and sunshine. They had only passed a few lone ships and one convoy returning to England from the Indian Ocean. Cooper, MacArthur, and Clyde Smyth, the planter from Barbados, had finished breakfast and was finishing their last cup of lukewarm coffee.

"Chocolate is much better," Smyth said. "Not as bitter and just as stimulating." Draining his cup, he leaned back and reached for his pipe. Before he could pack it with tobacco, they heard the cry from topside, "Sail ho."

Excited, the men made it on deck just a few steps ahead of the William sisters. The captain was leaning against the weather riggings with a telescope in his hand. What MacArthur had termed a glass. The early dawn chill had already been replaced by a scorching sun. Otis, the William's servant, had stepped on a deck seam where the tar oozed and now suffered with a blister on his foot.

With the sun so bright, Cooper was amazed the lookout could sight anything, but MacArthur hissed, "Lazy bugger. He'd feel the cat on a navy ship."

Shading his eyes with his hand, Cooper said, "From the looks of her sails she's a small ship, not big as this tub, but a sleek lady. A brig or one of the American brigantines, I'd say."

"Deck thar, she's coming about, she be," the lookout called down.

Cooper watched as the blue sea rose and fell with white caps being tossed about every so often.

The captain slammed the glass closed with a snap. "Yonder ship has swung around to run parallel," he said, speaking to the mate. "She'll be up to us before long." Glancing about the deck, the captain spotted the sisters. "You girls there get off the deck and go to your cabin now."

Never being spoken to in such a manner before, the girls realized something was wrong and made haste to their cabin.

"Why is he so upset?" Cooper asked his friend. "We've seen ships before."

"Aye, Coop, but now we're in pirate waters and that ship looks menacing to me."

"Why, we're bigger," Cooper said.

"True, but that one's got teeth. Look at the gunports. I count nine on this side. I wouldn't be surprised if she had two guns forward and aft plus swivel guns on the quarterdeck and in the tops. The captain has cause for concern, friend, we all have."

Cooper watched as the ship closed with its tall pyramid of sails. She was a beautiful ship. Spotting the British flag, Cooper was about to point it out when it came down rapidly and a black flag was run up. The flag had a skull and crossed cutlasses with blood dripping of the blades. Pirates! They were being attacked by pirates.

BOOM...a forward gun was fired on the pirate ship. A splash went up a few yards in front of the bow.

"Reduce sail and prepare to heave to," the captain ordered the first mate. He then grabbed a ship's boy and ordered, "Strike the colors and run up a white flag."

CHAPTER THREE

GRAPPLING HOOKS SHOT THROUGH the air and were pulled taut. Slowly the two ships were pulled together. Cooper looked across at the pirate ship in awe. A trace of fear went through him as he got a closer look at the menacing hoard standing next to the pirate ship's bulwark. The pirates were armed with blades, pistols, boarding axes, and pikes.

"They mean business, don't they?" Cooper said to MacArthur.

"The men are well-armed," MacArthur agreed. "But look up, that man in the tops has a swivel gun aimed at the deck of this ship. One wrong move and a lot of us will be reduced to fish bait."

The two ships bumped and then came together with a grinding noise. They were so close that it would not have been but a large step across if the ships had been the same height. However, with ropes hanging from up top, men swung up and over with ease. They have had a sight of practice, Cooper decided. After several of the pirates landed on the deck of the *Bonnie Lass*, another man swung across.

"That's their captain," MacArthur whispered. The man had no uniform to show his rank but he carried such an air of authority Cooper had little doubt that MacArthur was right.

The man was tall and spare. His features were like a man who hadn't eaten well or who had been ill. His hair was iron gray, very thick and wavy. His face was gaunt; and his hands and face was tanned dark brown and almost leathery.

"I'm Eli Taylor and captain of the *Raven*. You have just fallen to us, sir. However, do as you are told and no bodily harm will come to you."

Cooper's captain bowed and introduced himself, "I'm Ezra Nylinger, captain of the *Bonnie Lass*."

"Former captain," Taylor was quick to point out.

Pirates had continued to swarm aboard from their ship. It now looked like forty or more of the buggers crowded the deck of the *Bonnie Lass*.

"I would be obliged to you, Captain, if you would muster your crew and passengers on deck," Taylor said.

Captain Nylinger nodded and spoke to the first mate. As he went to get the crew and passengers, several of the pirates followed him.

"I must tell you, Captain Taylor, that we have one lady passenger who has been abed the entire voyage."

Nodding, Taylor said, "We will be gentle but we must look for ourselves.

There was no need as at that moment, Lady Elizabeth and her three daughters came on deck.

"Damn," MacArthur hissed. "You would have thought the girls would have pulled a dress over those slops. The way Lucy and Linda look is trouble in the making. Look at those rogues?" As usual MacArthur was right.

Whistles and cat calls filled the air. Lust will make a man do crazy things and Lucy was one lusty-looking female.

"My word," Lady Elizabeth shouted. "Have you men no decency?"

"More than she does," one man called out.

"Humph…I'll have you know I'm the wife of Sir Jonathan Williams. He is the lieutenant governor of Antigua."

"My arse," MacArthur hissed. "She's gone and done it now. They probably would have taken our valuables and anything that might prove useful but now they'll take the girls for sure and use them for ransom. Woman should have kept her mouth shut."

"Have no fear, my lady," Captain Taylor said. "Not a hair on their head will be harmed. I'd say one hundred pounds for these two is a fair price. Until such time as arrangements can be made they'll remain in our safekeeping."

One of the pirates stepped forward and grabbed Lucy. "I'll keep this one safe, ha!ha! Safe for me ownself."

A massacre almost took place. Several of the *Bonnie Lass'* crew members took a step forward including Captain Nylinger. Hammers on muskets and pistols were cocked as weapons were drawn.

"You keep your crew under control, Captain, and I will do the same with mine," Taylor shouted. He then turned to the pirate, who still gripped Lucy by the arm. "Unhand that girl, Finch. She is ship property and her ransom shall be divided into shares." The pirate glared but didn't release his grip. "Now," Taylor roared; as he did so, several of the pirates turned their attention to Finch.

While the *Bonnie Lass'* seamen were on deck, several pirates had gone to survey the ship. "Nothing in the hold but two feet of water," one of the men volunteered. "She's a leaky old sow, bottom is likely rotten. Doubt she'd bring a farthing as a ship. She is worth more as firewood, I'm thinking."

Seeing Nylinger's reaction to the seaman's comments, Taylor could see the captain of the *Bonnie Lass* was of the same opinion. "Probably wishes she was being taken," MacArthur whispered to Cooper.

Two more pirates came on deck carrying a heavy chest. They let it fall to the deck with a thump. "It's full of coin," one of the pirates swore as he straightened up.

Seeing two able-bodied men standing idle, Captain Taylor ordered, "You two grab that chest and take it aboard the *Raven*," speaking to MacArthur and Cooper.

Raven, that's the pirate ship's name, Cooper quickly concluded.

The chest was heavy, almost too heavy. MacArthur didn't seem to struggle with it as much as Cooper. Seeing Cooper's struggle, Taylor called out to a pirate, "Spurlock, if he loses that chest over the side, he'll dive for it and that's a promise."

"Aye, Captain, dive he will," Spurlock replied.

Damn, Cooper thought. *Don't help carry it, just toss my arse over the side*. Peering at Spurlock, his tattooed biceps bulging with muscles, Cooper decided the rogue would relish the idea. Losing his footing as he stepped backwards onto the deck of the *Raven*, Cooper fell to the deck with the chest crashing down between his legs. Two thoughts quickly came to mind, first, *why did I choose this end of the chest*; and second, more importantly, *are my jewels intact and can I still piss like a man*?

Looking up, Cooper could see MacArthur laughing. "Damn Scotsman, what are you laughing at?"

"That was close, Coop, another inch and you'd have had two scars."

"Damn you," Cooper hissed as he got to his feet.

"Over there," Spurlock said, pointing to the mainmast. "Place it there."

After doing as bid, Cooper and MacArthur headed back to the rail to return to the *Bonnie Lass*, but had to pause and give way to the returning pirates and the two girls. That was when the trouble started.

A wave sloshed up between the two ships drenching Lucy and Linda. Soaked, the white shirt Lucy had on did nothing but accent her breasts as the material was now see through and plastered to her skin. Finch was beside himself and couldn't control his lust. Reaching out, he grasped the front of Lucy's shirt and tore it from her body. Lucy's breasts were like ripe, round melons, proud and jutting out. The entire crew, including Cooper and MacArthur, gave a collective sigh at the sight of such beauty. Finch went further; he grabbed Lucy and crushed her breasts with his rough, dirty hands.

Cooper heard Lucy's scream and took a stride to defend her, but Spurlock grabbed his shoulder. It was then that Cooper saw Captain Taylor, his face was fiery red. In two quick strides, he reached out and grabbed Finch, slinging him around to face him.

"Damn you, Finch. You know the rules. Touch this girl or any other and you'll find yourself marooned." Taylor was face-to-face and shaking Finch as he spoke. When he finished, he spoke to Lucy without even glancing her way. "Cover yourself, girl."

The captain then turned to walk away. As he did, several things seemed to happen simultaneously. Finch, who was beside himself with anger, reached in his belt and pulled out a pistol. Seeing this, Cooper snatched a belaying pin from its holder and swung it down with all his might. The belaying pin snapped the bone in Finch's arm but not before he pulled the trigger. It did spoil the aim and the ball smacked into the mast, not a foot from Taylor's head. Wheeling around, Captain Taylor saw a smoking pistol on the deck, where it had landed with a thud. Finch was holding his misshapen arm and Cooper Cain stood by Finch holding the belaying pin.

"I'll see no man murdered, especially from the back," Cooper said, "be he rogue or gentleman."

Taylor turned his attention back to Finch. Seeing the rage in the captain's face, Finch backed up until he was against the bulwark. "Captain...captain," he whined, "I've learned me ways. It...it was that girl, Captain. She's a witch. I was in a spell, Captain, it was her fault."

Taylor stopped about two feet from Finch. "Try to murder me, will you, you piece of whale shat. I'll send you where you belong...to the bottom." With that, Taylor deftly pulled his pistol and shot Finch in the chest. Still holding the pistol, Taylor ordered, "You men, pick that up and over the side before it stains me deck."

Cooper stood in awe. He had never seen justice acted upon so swiftly, or seen a man shot down in such a manner.

"Take the girls to my cabin," Taylor ordered a scrawny little pirate named Rooster, who walked with a noticeable limp. He then turned to the ladies and said, "My apologies, ladies. I'm sorry you had to see that. But no man disobeys my orders and they certainly don't touch a lady, especially one under my protection."

Cooper swallowed hard. *Damned if the bugger doesn't mean it,* he thought. Looking around at the rogues on the deck, he had another thought...*and they know it.*

Once the girls were escorted to the captain's cabin, Taylor faced Cooper with a smile was on his face. "Thank you, sir. It appears I owe you my life."

"It was nothing," Cooper replied. "As I said I'll see no man murdered in such a way.

"Still it took bravery and initiative. I'd offer you a gold bar but they, meaning Captain Nylinger and his bosses, would take it away from you. How would you like to join us, become a free man?" Seeing Cooper thinking, Taylor said, "It's rare you come across one like Finch."

Turning to his friend, Cooper asked, "How about it, David?"

"I don't know, we could get hung," David answered.

"We might, but it might also give you a chance to strike a blow at Captain Sodomite," Cooper replied.

Seeing the look on Taylor's face at hearing the exchange, Cooper said, "I'll tell you about it later." He then turned back to David and asked, "What about it, David, time is wasting."

MacArthur shook his head and said, "I'll do it."

"Go get your chest," Taylor ordered.

Back on board the *Bonnie Lass*, Cooper approached Captain Nylinger, "You hear that shooting?"

"Aye," Nylinger responded.

"The captain shot Finch. I think its best MacArthur and I go along and offer what protection we can to the girls," Cooper said.

"Bless you, bless you," Lady Williams cried. "I will tell my husband of your help. Rest assured, young man, it will not go unnoticed."

"Lord, I better go along and help too. Those girls will need a servant," Otis said.

"Bless you as well, Otis," Lady Williams cried.

As the three descended down the companionway steps, Cooper winked at Otis, "You dog."

"No more than you, sir," Otis smiled.

Cooper quickly got all he cared to take in one chest. Leaving the rest he looked about, it was the start of a new day, a new life for Cooper Cain. "But vengeance is mine," he said. "Phillip and the house of Finylson will know my wrath."

PART II

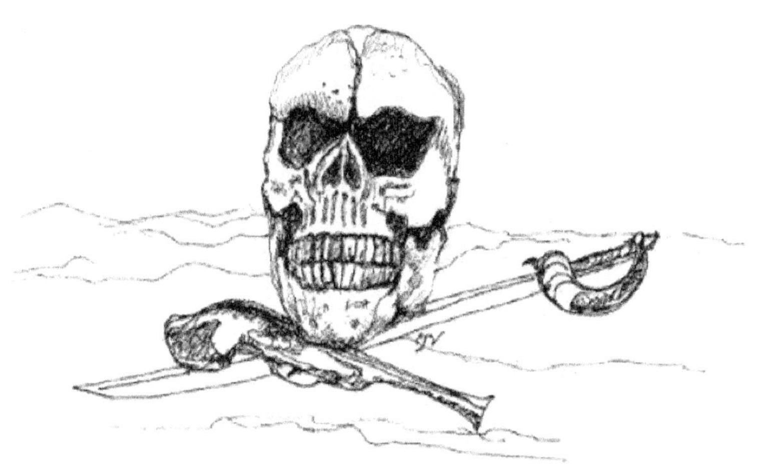

CHAPTER FOUR

COOPER AND MACARTHUR SPENT the first few days of their new life as virtual outcasts. Had it not been for time spent with Captain Taylor, the only other person they had to talk to was Otis. The slave had been a house servant for some years and had been educated. He could read, write, do sums, and seemed well-versed on a number of subjects. Cooper felt that it was because he was so educated that he was not immediately welcomed into the pirate fold, as the two other blacks in the pirate crew seemed to be accepted. The girls had only been spoken to once and that was on the day they were taken.

"We keep 'em segregated," Taylor explained. "Limits the likelihood of another situation occurring like what happened with Finch."

When Cooper expressed his concerns about being accepted as part of the crew, Taylor laughed. "Pirates are a suspicious lot, more so than your average sailor. Once you've been in action together and after you've signed the articles, you will quickly become accepted. Besides, I accepted you, asked you to join us. What more could you want?"

"What are these articles?" Cooper asked.

"Rules to live by…my rules. Every man who would be brethren of the coast signs them. But time enough for that later. Your mate MacArthur…whom I'll call Mac, already is a seaman. Things you've got to learn. You are a man quick to take action, but can you hold your own in a real life or death fight?"

Indignant, Cooper pulled himself erect. "I, sir, have been trained by a master swordsman, Jean-Paul deGiraud. He is world renowned."

"That may be true," Taylor responded smiling, "but a match or a duel between gentlemen is not the same thing. I'd say Mac here," using the nickname again, "could best you."

"Humph," Cooper snorted. "I'll not fight my friend, but I'll take on any member of your crew."

"You will?" Taylor asked, thinking maybe it would be best to prove his point right away. Doing so could save the boy's life and he did like him. "Alright," he said. "Get your blade and come on deck."

As they left the captain's cabin, Mac whispered, "He's right, Coop. There's a big difference between a gentlemen's duel and fighting for your life."

"Not you too," Cooper hissed. "Just you wait, you'll see."

Once on deck, the captain had a number of pirates gathered near the mainmast. "Gentlemen," Taylor called out to the men with an amusing smile. "We have as a new crewman a master swordsman."

I didn't say that, Cooper thought. *I just said I was trained by a master.*

"What we are going to have today," Taylor continued, "is a display in swordsmanship."

Several of the crew gathered. Cooper had learned some of them. Spurlock, the gunner, Diamond, the bosun, Lee Turner, the quartermaster, and a big, mean-looking rogue named McKemie, who Cooper thought was the carpenter. Other members of the crew hearing the voice of their captain gathered. Otis and Mac stood close by.

"Let's form a circle," Taylor ordered, "and watch as two gladiators amuse us."

He's making light of me, Cooper thought just a little aggravated but determined to keep his cool. First rule of swordsmanship, don't let your opponent get you angry.

"Now, Master Cooper, you have your choice of blades."

Several cutlasses filled a barrel that was placed close by. Taking his rapier from its scabbard, Cooper made a couple of cuts through the air making a swooshing sound. "This is my blade," he said.

"Now, sir," Taylor spoke again. "You have chosen your weapon; now choose your opponent, preferably one with both timbers." Meaning not the one-legged captain's servant.

I'll show you, Cooper thought. He looked around and picked the biggest rogue of the lot. "Mr. McKemie,' he announced.

Surprised, but then again not so much so, knowing the young man wanted to make a point, Taylor said, "McKemie, step forward. You have been challenged, sir. Do you accept the challenge?"

McKemie smiled. He couldn't believe he of all the crew members had been challenged. "Sure," he said and without looking reached down and pulled a cutlass from the barrel. Mocking Cooper, he sliced through the air a couple of times and whirled about, causing the crew to laugh.

"Step forward," Taylor called to the combatants. "This, men, is not a life or death battle. It's nothing more than a match for bragging rights. I don't mind a bruise or two, or a little blood. But if one or the other kills his opponent, he will be marooned. If this is understood then the match will go forth." When both men voiced their understanding, Taylor stepped back and said, "You may begin."

"En garde," Cooper shouted and with his hand on his side, he stuck his right foot forward assuming the position for a match.

McKemie looked at his opponent thinking how ridiculous. He did several things at once. He took his cutlass and knocked Cooper's blade aside. He then stomped on Cooper's outstretched foot. As Cooper bent forward in pain, McKemie slammed him in the chin with the pommel of his blade. Cooper never knew what hit him…he was out. Diamond caught him as he fell backwards, easing him to the deck.

"He's got guts," McKemie swore.

"Aye," Spurlock agreed. "He might just make a good mate yet."

THE *RAVEN* SAILED ON toward Marco Island. "It's a barrier island off the southern gulf coast of Florida," Turner explained. "We are supposed to rendezvous with our other prizes there. Some call it Key Marco and others even call it San Marco. Once it was called Horr's Island but they ain't no whores there 'thout you bringing them," he said, laughing at his play on words. When we meet up with our early ships we'll sail on to Barataria. That's Jean LaFitte's bunch but they know's each other well. We can generally sell our plunder and ships there. If not, we take 'em to South Carolina or Savannah, Georgia. If we have any slaves we always can sell them to LaFitte."

"Those places, they're in the American colonies?" Cooper asked.

"That they be," Turner answered.

"They just let you come and go?" Cooper questioned.

"Sure, they does. We don't mess with no American ships. That's one of the captain's rules. LaFitte's too," he added. "Captain Taylor says you got to have a place to rest your head. As long as we don't take no American ships, they got no call to fuss. Captain Taylor says you don't piss in your porridge."

Since Cooper's one-sided sword fight he had become somewhat accepted. Some thought he was next to worthless as a landsman but he was quick and eager and learn.

David MacArthur, former Royal Navy lieutenant, was without a doubt the best navigator in the crew, even better than Captain Taylor. He had assumed all the navigational duties and had started teaching Cooper the art. "What we are doing," Mac explained, "is usually taught by the ship's master in a navy ship. The one that taught me must have been sixty years old and said he went aboard his first ship at nine years old. He truly knew his trade. Bragged that at one time period he didn't set foot on land for five years. Don't know if it was true or not but you didn't argue with the master. Not if you didn't want to kiss the gunner's daughter." Mac then had to explain this meant having to lay over a big gun and have the bosun lay it across one's arse with a piece of rope.

Mac had just taken the noon sights with Cooper when he said, "I think we might be in for a blow."

Cooper had learned what this meant. Looking up, the sky was clear and the winds were favorable. The captain had said they'd likely reach Key Marco on the next day. By late afternoon the sea became very choppy as the wind picked up and it began to drizzle. By dark the rain was coming down in sheets and now the wind was howling. In the distance jagged lightening could be seen.

Captain Taylor came on deck and spoke with Diamond, "We're going to need another man on the wheel."

Hearing this Cooper volunteered. He'd never been in a storm at sea. However, lately he'd been thinking that one day he might like to have his own ship. Therefore, this was an experience he'd need.

Lifelines were rigged and sails were reduced to just storm sails. Before long those men not actually on watch went below decks, all but one. The captain stayed on deck the entire time. Responsibility, Cooper decided, one of those things that came with being a ship's captain.

THE STORM LASTED ONLY a few hours and the next day the sea was normal. The sky was again blue and only a few puffy white clouds filled the sky. It was late in the afternoon when the main-mast lookout shouted, "Land ho!"

Spurlock was on deck when the sighting was called down. He pointed out various landmarks to Cooper and Mac, and then pointed out Sanabel Island. "We used to rendezvous there but it got so that the Dons use the island so much we moved on to Key Marco."

Just as the last rays of sun fell below the horizon, the *Raven* anchored in a sheltered cove. Four other ships were already there. A ramshackle village of sorts was on the beach not far from where the ships were anchored. Several fires had been lit and were blazing, lighting up the night. From the shore, laughter could be heard and the smell of meat being cooked over a spit made its way to the ship.

"Well into a rum keg, I'd say," Captain Taylor volunteered. Cooper hadn't even heard him come on deck. "Go ashore with Spurlock, McKemie, and Diamond if you'd like," Taylor suggest-ed. "Fires will help drive off some of the mosquitoes and from the sound I hear they've got women ashore. Could be you might get lucky. Don't get in any duels though," the captain joked.

"You are not going ashore?" Cooper asked.

"Not with the girls aboard, I'm not. They liable to be gone when I returned if I did, and then there'd be one-hundred pounds gone."

Cooper thought there was more to it than that. The captain didn't want harm to come to the girls. More responsibility, he decided.

"Besides," Taylor said, "yonder ship is the *Tigre*. That's Dominique Youx's ship. He and I have been shipmates before, so he'll find his way aboard before too long."

"I don't want to leave you by yourself, Captain. I'll wait until Captain Youx comes aboard and then I will go ashore."

"Nonsense, Cooper, go ashore. Get a feel for these buccaneers." Laying his hand on his young friend's shoulder, Taylor warned, "They are a rough lot, lad. Otis is more a gentleman than the whole lot. Stay close to our crew members, especially Spurlock and Diamond."

Mac came over to where Captain Taylor and Cooper were talking. "You coming, Coop?"

"Sure he is," Taylor answered, settling it.

Rooster ambled over to Taylor as the men climbed down into the ship's boats. "Your partial to that 'un, Captain," he said, as much a statement as a question.

"Aye, but who wouldn't be. The lad will become a good seaman given time. Besides, he saved my life, what's not to like."

"He's got hatred, Captain. A deep biding hurt and hatred, I'd say. Don't reckon I'd want to be on his bad side."

"Rooster, you talk like you're scared."

"Not scared, Captain, too old to be scared. More like cautious, I'd say."

"I'd agree," Taylor said, "now carry your cautious arse to the galley and fetch something for those girls to eat."

ON SHORE, SEVERAL OF *Raven's* crew were greeted by friends and past shipmates. Kegs of rum had been breached and more than one was well into his cups. Several of the sailors had teamed up with scantily clad women. The women were of various races, and while some of them looked mighty young, others looked old and well worn. A few of them were obviously of mixed race. One such vixen was hanging on to a big, black, fierce-looking fellow.

Seeing Cooper, she squealed, "Look, Caesar, if he ain't the devil, he's the imp's son."

Caesar turned, and seeing Cooper said, "That scar is enough to scare you but stay next to Caesar. I'll watch out for you."

The girl took a step away from her companion. "I don't know, the more I look the more I want to look. Damned if he doesn't set me to breathing hard."

Popping the girl on the rump with his hand, Caesar cursed, "Maybe he is the devil. He done cast a spell on that 'un."

Spurlock and Diamond watched as the pretty little mulatto girl boldly walked up to Cooper and gave him a kiss. After the kiss, she took Cooper's hand and led him toward a row of huts.

"He's got a way with women," Spurlock commented.

"Aye," Diamond agreed, but his eyes were not on Cooper. "I ain't so sure Black Caesar's real happy about it."

"Well, if we have to we can make him happy," Spurlock replied. "We'll keep our wits about us just in case we are needed."

CHAPTER FIVE

HE AIN'T NO PROPER pirate, no ways," Rooster said, "not like Captain Taylor and Captain Youx." He was trying to explain the difference between a real pirate and Black Caesar. "He ain't even got a ship, just a bunch of boats. What they do is hide out among the Keys and when a likely prey comes along, nothing big mind you, they row out, jam a wedge into the rudder so it don't work and the ship can't be steered. They then cast out ropes with grappling hooks and use these to board the ship. Each of the buggars are heavily armed with several pistols, daggers, cutlasses, and such. If the captain or the crew puts up a fight, everybody gets dead for their troubles. Not civil like Captain Taylor, they ain't. Course, he's a gentleman. You saw that when he took your ship."

"What does he do with the ships?" Cooper asked.

"Some he sells to the Dons, others he just sinks. He ain't much of a deep water sailor. If he can't see land he's in trouble."

"What about prisoners?" Cooper inquired.

"Some, like the girls, he'll take to Haiti; that's where he's from. He was part of the slave riots not too long ago. Anyway, he's got a few hellish contacts there so he can sell them outright to, and if they got rich families they ransom the girls off. Most of them though is sold, I expect."

"White girls?" Cooper asked, astonished at what he was hearing.

"Color and race don't make no never mind. If they're pretty or rich, that's all that counts. Of course, some gets used like a bunch of those back there on Marco Island. But you be careful around Black Caesar, Coop. I heard you took his woman. He ain't likely to forget. He's like a cottonmouth they have in the swamps about New Orleans. He's black, mean, and don't usually give you any warning before he strikes. You just get dead."

"Cooper!"

Turning, Cooper saw he was being called by his friend, David MacArthur. Captain Taylor had shortened his friend's handle to just Mac and everyone fell in line. But Cooper found it hard to think of his friend as anything other than David.

David had a sextant in his hand. He'd been teaching Cooper the art of navigation. Once he was able to master the math, which had taken weeks, the rest seemed to be coming along a bit easier. It was time for the noontime sights. The *Raven* had been cruising along under easy sail. Topsails were reefed. Dominique Youx's *Tigre* was off to larboard, and the three prizes sailed along behind *Raven*. They were two days out of Marco Island, well into the Gulf of Mexico. It was a hot and cloudless noon time. The deep blue of the sky overhead seemed to blend in with the blue sea. Grand Terre was where they were headed…to Barataria, the base of Jean LaFitte. Dominique Youx was one of LaFitte's captains.

Spurlock, Diamond, and several others including old Rooster couldn't keep the excitement out of their voice when talking about Barataria.

"LaFitte's got a grand setup there. There is always a market for our plunder and good prices too. Might even sell the ships there," Captain Taylor said.

LaFitte and the captain had known each other for years, and while Taylor was not one of his captains, he provided a ready market for Taylor's goods. LaFitte's only rule, no American ships were to be attacked. Break that rule and he'd see you hanged. Of course, he was a businessman so ten percent of all sales were given to him. This, though, was far better than the twenty-five percent or more that others charged. In 1805, the United States Congress put an end to the slave trade. This did not mean it had ended, Captain Taylor said, it just made it illegal. The Congress passed an embargo act that would forbid trade with foreign countries. By smuggling in slaves and goods from the British, Spanish, and French, a huge profit could be made. Captain Taylor was part owner in a fleet of merchant ships and owned a hotel in New Orleans. One in which LaFitte was treated as royalty and it never cost him a cent. After all, he was the King of Barataria.

THE SUN WAS SINKING low and *Raven's* crew had gathered forward. One seaman was playing a mouth harp, another seaman had a small accordion. Men sang sea shanties, told jokes and seemed a happy lot.

"It's the same," Mac said, "be it on a man-o'-war, merchant ship, or…a pirate ship. Off duty sailors find pleasure where they can."

Cooper had noticed his friend had trouble calling the *Raven* what it was, a pirate ship. Sighing, Cooper could tell that even though David had made the jump, he still hadn't resigned himself to being a pirate. Seeing Otis, Cooper called over to him. When the former servant walked over, Cooper asked, "Did you enjoy your night on Marco Island?"

"Oh yes," Otis replied, his English as refined as any lord or lady.

"Well, tell us about it," Cooper said, wanting to hear of Otis' first evening as a man with no constraints upon him.

"Well, sir," Otis started, still using the etiquette that had been instilled in him since childhood. "I found the woman to be extremely open and sexually forward. I was most amazed that they enjoyed my manner of speech and politeness. In truth, I was amazed when I had not one but three of the ladies ready to check my manly prowess, at one time, mind you. I hope that I proved worthy of their attentions and was able to satisfy their curiosity." Otis paused and pulled a fist full of cigars from a pocket. "Would you, gentlemen, care for a cigar? I smoked one on the island and found it to be of the utmost quality. It burns even, has somewhat of a sweet taste at first, and then turns into almost a spice like flavor with very little after taste. I'm told they were taken from a Spanish ship sailing from Havana."

After lighting up, Otis continued his narrative. "After our tryst, I was engaged by first one then another of the ere...ladies discussing the possibility of a long term arrangement. Two, in fact, said they had no problem if I chose both of them, that way I could choose one or the other depending upon my mood and should I desire a ménage à trios, it was also available. That's when I realized these women were not really the sexually free spirits I initially took them to be. No, their sexual openness is nothing other than a means of survival using the only weapon at their disposal...their looks, bodies, and sexuality. I took time to look at our surroundings. Most of the women offering up themselves were young. Some, I'd not hasten to bet, were as young as the sisters on board this ship. The older women, some not very old at all but looked tired and used up were manning the fires, cooking food and serving drinks. They all had a forlorn look on their face. It was a look of hopelessness if you will. Skin color, language, or race, it was all the same; the lot of them full of misery, just trying to survive."

"You seem to have a good grasp of the situation, Otis."

The three men turned to see Captain Taylor had approached. He obviously had been there some time to make the comment he had. "Tell me, Otis," the captain said, "did you have the opportunity to talk with Black Caesar?"

"I would hardly call it an enlightening conversation, sir, but yes we spoke."

"What did you think of the man?"

Otis took a long draw on his cigar, causing the end to light up and glow in the fading light. After gathering his thoughts, Otis spoke, "I found him to be a brave man, full of raw courage, and certainly he has leadership skills to a point. You can see that by the men who follow him. But it ends there. He is extremely short-sighted and has no desire to rise from the squalor and depravity in which he exists. A man who has led and survived a slave revolt could surely do something more to enhance the plight of others of his race. Yet he raids ships, some with slaves and what does he do? For the most part he sells them into the same institution he escaped from. Captain Youx bought a hundred from him at five hundred dollars apiece. It seems he is more interested in providing himself with pleasures of the flesh than anything else. When I asked what he thought the future held, he said death. Death in battle or the hangman's knot. Until then he intended to live life to the fullest. He then called me an uppity nigger and said I'd be better off as a slave, as I had no stomach to live life as a free man."

Captain Taylor, Cooper, and Mac all were silent. They had felt the passion in Otis as he spoke. Cooper knew Otis would fight for his life and those of his shipmates. However, he'd never be the killer that Black Caesar was.

It was Captain Taylor who broke the silence. "In a way, Caesar was right, Otis. Not in the mean, vulgar way he phrased it, but the point is you are not cut out to be a pirate. You're not a slave either. You are more educated than most people I know. Your speech is better than mine and is as good as Coop's. You are not a pirate either. Not for a moment would I doubt your bravery, mind you. But, if you intend to stay at sea, you'd be better off as a captain's servant or maybe even his secretary. You could make a good living in a hotel or counting house. Those are just a few choices. You need to think on it."

The captain had started to walk off then turned and came back to the trio. "New Orleans is a different town than any of you have ever seen. There are hundreds of free men of color in the city, none though that equals your level of education. Being a free man opens you up to challenges. I don't mean opportunities, I mean duels. Black Caesar called you uppity. There's more that will feel the same way. Men that use the duel as a sport, and men who are deadly with a pistol or blade. A slight, real or made up, intended or not, could very well end in a short life for you, my friend."

Otis started to speak but Taylor stopped him. "You might survive the first duel only to discover a long line of friends to challenge you for beating the first man. That goes for all of you. I can give Otis a paper saying he's my slave. That will protect him. No man of integrity would bother another man's property. It would be beneath him to fight a slave. In that way, Otis is lucky. Cooper, Mac, you're both targets. Your accent alone may be enough. Always identify yourself as free men or brethren of the coast. If any of LaFitte's men are around they will at least keep it fair. Fair meaning one on one, more than that…I cannot help. I took you off your ship to offer you a freedom. You can choose to be a part of my crew. If so, you will be asked to sign the ship's articles. This cannot be revoked but by death. Should you choose to make a life for yourself, New Orleans is the place to do it. You, Cooper, saved my life, I owe you. Should you choose to stay in New Orleans, I will give you one thousand dollars. More than enough to get you started as long as you don't piss it away in some gambler's den or bordello. We will be in New Orleans three, maybe four weeks. I will show you the city so you can get a better feel for what you are choosing between. I'm going below. We will be in Barataria tomorrow."

CHAPTER SIX

THE CRY OF "LAND ho" created an excitement throughout the crew. Even old Rooster seemed to gain a little pep in his lame step.

"We've an hour more before you can see land from the deck," Captain Taylor said smiling. He, too, was ready to reach land and after making sure all was attended to, he could have a few weeks of downtime. First, however, the cargoes had to be unloaded and sold or placed on consignment with LaFitte. This included the hundred or more slaves divided among the prize ships. The girls had to be taken to a safe place until the ransom was collected. There were also the ships themselves that had to be sold. Good merchant ships that would bring in a good price, even putting them up at bargain prices. He needed to see his lawyer, and then there was Debbie. They had been apart too long. She had said when he'd set sail this last time that he didn't need to take the risk any longer; unlike some of his fellow brethren of the coast captains. He had invested wisely in legitimate businesses and, in fact, was now a wealthy man. Still, he did feel that he'd found the right person to take over the *Raven*.

He had several good men, good seamen, but not men who could think and act quickly and decisively if the situation called for it. Maybe that had changed. David MacArthur had proved himself a fine seaman and capable leader. But it was Cooper Cain, who had acted quickly and decisively when action was called for. Not even his most loyal hands had reacted. No, he walked his quarterdeck today because of Coop.

"Captain."

"Aye, Rooster, what can I do for you today?"

"The noon meal, Captain, will we eat as usual or delay it?"

"Feed the sisters, Rooster. If opportunity presents itself, I will come down."

"Should we allow the girls on deck to see this new land, Cap'n?"

The girls had been allowed on deck everyday at noon and just before lights out. They had always been in the presence of the captain and no one else, including their previous fellow passengers, Coop and Mac. Taylor did not want them on deck once they entered port, but he could see no harm in their seeing the land.

"When land can be seen from the deck you can bring them up, Rooster. However, once we enter Barataria Bay, shoo the girls back into my cabin."

"Aye, Cap'n, no one the wiser of our lustful little ladies."

THREE SHIPS WERE ANCHORED in the harbour at Barataria. All of them were three-masted vessels and looked as if they were ready to weigh anchor.

"Those belong to three of LaFitte's captains," Rooster informed Cooper. "The biggest one there belongs to Vincent Gambi. He's a hard man, gives LaFitte the most problems. The others belong to Nez Coupé and Renato Beluche. None are what I'd call good Christian men, but Gambi is the devil himself. I hope they are leaving port. Better for us that way."

The anchor was dropped in the bay not far from those already anchored. By doing this, Captain Taylor was allowing Domimique Youx the preferred anchorage closer to the dock. A boat was put over the side for Taylor to go ashore. Lee Turner, the quartermaster, was in charge of the ship while the captain was away. He would ensure the ship was taken care of before any hands were allowed ashore. They'd drink, gamble, and carouse with the women on Grand Terre, or Barataria as LaFitte called his stronghold, tonight.

Tomorrow, the work of unloading the cargo would begin. Captain Taylor called to Cooper and Mac to accompany him ashore. As they approached the dock a smaller ship, a schooner, was tied up. Several boats, the likes of which, neither Cooper nor Mac had ever seen, were also tied up to the docks. Some were larger than others and one even had a small mast for a sail. But they all looked like hollowed out trees.

"Those are called pirogues," Taylor volunteered. "They are the main form of travel hereabouts. It's sixty miles from here to New Orleans. We'll be going there in a few days. To get there you follow a path of canals through the swamps. The route is too shallow to go by anything much larger. The only other routes are through the gulf or up the Mississippi River. Even then, there's treacherous sandbars. We could make it over the sandbars in the *Raven* if we crossed at high tide. Anything larger would be in trouble."

Gliding up to the dock, Mac stuck out his hand and grabbed a post, effectively stopping the boat. He nimbly vaulted up on the dock and tied the boat off. Taylor and Cooper climbed out and walked down the dock toward the shore. Cooper was not sure what he was expecting but this was not it.

Barataria was a thriving, bustling community. It was nothing like the scattered huts at Marco Island. From the dock, fortifications were visible. They looked to be twenty to thirty feet high, with the black, menacing snouts of cannons sticking out.

However, they were small compared to the big guns at the entrance to the harbour.

Leaving the dock, Captain Taylor took a direct route to Jean LaFitte, the Boss's house. To get there, the men passed through a business district that included a hotel, brothel, and stores for food, clothing, and a ship's chandler.

"That's a gambling den," Taylor said. "If you value your money and your life, stay out of it."

They passed a couple of taverns and a café along the way. Before they got to LaFitte's house, they passed an area of warehouses, one right after another.

"What's that?" Mac asked, pointing to a house-like structure, but with a fence around it and armed guards walking the perimeter.

"That's called the slave barracoon. It's where slaves are kept until they are sold."

"I'm not sure I hold with slaves," Mac said.

"Well, I don't own any myself," Taylor remarked, "but the economy here is built on slave labor. Even free blacks own them."

"Damn," Mac snorted.

By this time, the men had passed a row of whitewashed houses, and just up the way was a two story house made of brick and painted white. Surrounding the house and grounds was a tall wrought iron fence. Before the men got to the gate, two men were walking out of the house and down the steps.

"That's Jean and Pierre LaFitte," Taylor whispered.

The LaFittes paused, seeing their visitors approach. A big smile broke out on Jean's face when he recognized Taylor. "Eli," he said, "are you back to reclaim that beautiful Debbie Russell from my clutches?" The two men shook hands and embraced each other with a hug.

After shaking hands with Pierre, Taylor introduced Cooper and Mac. Pierre took his leave but Jean invited the men inside. Huge open windows allowed a cool breeze to flow through the main room. Fruits were brought out and sherry was offered. The men sat down to enjoy the refreshments. LaFitte and Taylor were talking business, ships' cargoes, and slaves. The discussion then turned to Cooper and Mac.

Afterwards, LaFitte stood up and toasted Cooper, "I will forever be in your debt for saving my friend. Should you ever need anything you call on Jean LaFitte."

A few minutes later, the conversation returned to the slaves and cargoes. "There will be a slave auction at the Temple tomorrow," LaFitte informed Taylor. "You can take your slaves there or I'll give you five hundred each for them now."

This was a good price Taylor knew, as LaFitte could buy slaves in Cuba. However, you had to add the cost of transporting the slaves. Still, some of the slaves would sell for as much as a thousand dollars or more.

Taylor thought about it for a minute and said, "Agreed, provided you send men and boats to unload them tonight." LaFitte stuck out his hand and the men shook on the deal.

"Now about the ships," LaFitte began. "I still have one waiting to be sold. You might find a buyer if you're willing to give them away. Otherwise, I'd send them to South Carolina. Your former navy fellow there could surely sail one there with a skeleton crew."

"I'll think on it," Taylor said. "They still have to be stripped and cleaned." Seeing the look on Cooper's face, Taylor explained, "A man was once hung trying to sell a ship to its previous owner. The man had carved his wife's name on the bulkhead next to his cot. Seeing this, he brought charges on the seller and he was hung. Those are former British ships but they will be stripped and every mark will be removed, so that way there's no incrimination."

"You'll be my guest tonight," LaFitte offered as a servant came into the room. "I have business that needs attending to," he said. The servant must have reminded him of a task that had been forgotten with Taylor's arrival.

"Thank you," Taylor replied, "but I have two ladies I need to take to Grand Isle."

"Ah yes! The lovely Cindy Veigh," LaFitte said with a smile. "Until you return then. I will stop by the barracoon and have Jacques set about unloading the black ivory."

"Another term for slaves," Mac whispered to Cooper.

THE GIRLS' CHEST WAS loaded into one pirogue while Cooper, Captain Taylor, Lucy, and Linda filled up the other, larger pirogue. Taylor gave a running narrative as they made their way in the pirogues. Cooper was unsure about the stability of the craft, but his fears were soon gone as Taylor talked of the island.

"Grand Isle and several other islands are what the French call Cheniers. Rooster pronounces it 'shin ear.' They started with oak groves that rose up from the numerous marshlands. The place where LaFitte sells his plunder, the Temple, is a Chenier. Grand Isle is the highest and rises about six or seven feet above sea level. Since I've been coming to the area these past several years, I've seen significant erosion to some of these islands and a few are all awash at high tide."

As they grew close to the island, Cooper could see wind-bent oaks, a fishing boat with women and two children tugging on a shrimp or crab net.

"Cindy has been able to raise a few cattle on the island," Taylor continued. "One of her slaves came up with the idea of feeding the cattle dried salt grass. LaFitte is a steady customer now that the herd has multiplied. She can't afford to amass to large a herd or she would run out of feed. Another one of her slaves, an old fellow called Gus, makes one of the best wines you've ever tasted. It is made from a type of grape on the island that grows natural and plentiful. His wife, Belle, who has to be twenty years younger than Gus, is the cook. She cooks the best meals I've ever tasted. If I could steal her away, I'd never go back to sea. Humph! I couldn't anyway, I'd be so fat I would sink any boat trying to take me to the ship."

Lucy and Linda, who'd only spoke in whispers, giggled at this. Taking a breath and getting her courage up, Lucy asked, "Are we to be slaves on this tiny island?"

"No," Taylor answered. "You are being brought here for your safety. I'm sure you caught a glimpse of the rogues at Barataria."

Cooper had noticed how elusive Taylor had been keeping the girls on *Raven* until he was ready to depart. He had then quickly loaded Rooster and McKemie in the pirogue with the baggage before bringing the girls out and into the boat. Rooster and McKemie were both fully armed, including a musket a piece. Of course, he, Mac, and Captain Taylor were also armed with blades and pistols. Taylor expertly steered the pirogue into a small creek that led further inland. Cindy's house was almost in the center of the island surrounded by a small stand of sea oaks. They tied up to a small dock that jutted out into the creek. The house could be seen from the dock, it was a two story affair of brick, painted white not unlike LaFitte's house. The roof, though, seemed much different. It looked almost like a masonry roof. The second floor had a balcony that covered the breadth of the house.

Beyond the main house nestled among the oaks, Cooper could see several cottages. For the servants and slaves, he guessed. The main house was set in such a manner that part of the veranda faced the open path to the creek, while the other end was shaded by huge moss filled oaks. A barn was off to one side and milk cows must have been in the barn or a paddock behind the barn, as he could hear lowing.

"Ready for milking," McKemie volunteered, climbing the steps. He could see a square of neatly tilled dirt. A vegetable garden in the making, he decided.

Chickens ran about scratching for some morsel. A faint breeze drifted their way and held the smell of a pig sty. A set of six columns held up the balcony of the plantation house, which sat high off the ground. Ten wide steps led up to the porch.

"Cap'n, is that you done come back from the sea," a voice called.

"Jumper, you rascal, some gator ain't done got you?"

"Nah suh, and they ain't. Had a close call wid a cottonmouth but ain't had no gator come eben close."

"Jumper," Taylor said, speaking to Cooper, Mac, and the girls, "is Gus' son. He is the fisherman in the family. Keep's Belle, his mama, supplied with oysters, crabs, crawfish, gator tail, catfish, and shrimp. Of course, he's always pestering me to go to sea, just for one cruise to see if he likes being a real seaman. I bought him the little fishing yawl you saw tied up at the dock. It has a shallow draft but it's stable enough for the bay."

The next person to see them was Cindy Veigh, a woman Cooper took to be in her late thirties or early forties. Dressed in a plain dress and blouse, the woman exuded sophistication. Her face was striking. The off-the-shoulder blouse showed her skin to be very tan. Not an indoor person. The blouse was tight across a full bosom. When she walked the shapeliness of her hips and legs were evident. A few strands of gray could be seen in her hair when she moved and the sun hit it just right. A widow, Cooper had heard LaFitte say. She was certainly a prize in her day, Cooper thought to himself. If she fixed herself up she'd still turn every head, envious males and jealous females alike, should she walk across the floor of a ballroom.

"I've come to impose on your generosity," Taylor volunteered.

"I see," Cindy said. "Who are they?"

"Lucy and Linda Williams, their father is the lieutenant governor of Antigua."

Nodding, Cindy spoke to the girls. "I have no part in the captain's deeds. I will allow you to stay here solely to keep you safe from the vermin on Grand Terre and in New Orleans. If you do not wish to stay, you may go back with Captain Taylor. If you stay you will remain on the island with me. If you are still under my care when the hurricane season approaches, we will go inland. I have a plantation about twenty-five miles from New Orleans." Turning back to Taylor, she said, "Lord Willoughby played the devil getting his daughter to return. In the end, she married one of the Rigaud boys in New Orleans. He repaid her father his ransom money and now Lord Willoughby is his partner in a fleet of shrimp boats and the Hotel Rigaud. The couple lives on the top two floors. Lord Willoughby says it's the best thing that could have happened."

Those comments had the girls looking at each other with smiles on their faces. "We will be allowed to attend balls and parties?" Lucy asked.

"Yes, dear, properly chaperoned," Cindy replied.

"Oh, we'll stay with Miss Cindy," they eagerly responded.

CHAPTER SEVEN

A YOUNG NEGRO WOMAN, WHO Cindy called Mimi, brought glasses of iced tea. It was sweet and surprised Cooper, Mac, and the girls at how delicious and refreshing it was.

Munching on a ginger cookie, Cooper asked, "How do you keep ice so long?"

"Beneath the house, we've dug down a few feet and store it there, packed in sawdust. It doesn't keep long but it's the best we can do."

"Could you dig deeper?" Mac asked.

"No, we would have ground seepage if we did. I'm sure you noticed the roof. We have lined the ice hole with the same material. We tried wood but termites ate it up in a year."

"What is the material?" Mac asked.

"It's a mixture of crushed seashells really. It was used on forts in Saint Augustine, Florida. We bought a shipload of it, and after experimenting with it came upon a way to make a paste. We brushed it on the roof and that has solved our leaks. Gus is the genius behind it. He decided to cut the material into blocks and then fitted them together and made the ice house."

"You have a smart slave," Mac said.

Cindy took a breath, and with a cold stare, spoke sharply, "Gus and his family are not slaves, and they are free. They live here year round unless a bad storm approaches; they then come to the plantation."

"I apologize and stand corrected, madam," Mac replied.

Cindy smiled, "No need, sir, it would be easy to assume they were."

JUST AT DUSK, JUMPER knocked on the door of the room Cooper and Mac were to share for the night. "Miz Cindy say it time to get ready to eat." Seeing Cooper look at his watch, Jumper continued, "We eat early on the island, not like them folks in Naw Arleans that don't eat until nine o'clock. We usually in bed by dat time. Of course, we usually up wid the sun."

After getting washed up, Cooper and Mac met Captain Taylor in the hall and followed him down the stairs to the dining room. A door was open and Cooper could see a breezeway separating the main house from the kitchen. *Keeps the house cooler,* he thought to himself.

The smells coming from the kitchen had his mouth watering and stomach growling. No wonder Taylor wanted to steal Belle. A shadow in the hall caused Cooper to look up; standing in the doorway was a goddess. The soft light outlined a shapely silhouette. Her cheekbones were high; her skin was a creamy tan. The emerald green thin cotton dress had a neckline that plunged to the top of perfectly shaped breasts thrusting out so that her nipples were outlined through the material. Her moist lips were sensual, her teeth were white. Her hair was the color of a raven and hung down to a waist that was slender and inviting. She had a sexually mature body but also had an innocent, even childlike vulnerability that made her even more desirable. She held a biscuit in her hand and crumbs on her mouth that she licked off, causing Cooper to groan inwardly.

While everyone noticed Cooper staring, it was the braver of the two sisters, Lucy, who spoke out. "God, Coop, close your mouth, you're embarrassing. You never looked at me that way. Of course, she is one beautiful creature."

Cindy started to speak, to introduce everyone but stopped what she was about to say as she looked at the girl. She, too, had stopped dead in her tracks, taking in the man at the end of the table. Not overly tall but not short, a strong pair of shoulders. His nose had a bit of a Roman curve, an almost Nordic face. His ruffled hair was sandy-colored. He also had a scar on his cheek that marred the left side of his face. The scar went from just above his eyebrow to down on his cheek. The sun had tanned his face but the scar stood out white, an imperfection that added character to his face. Not handsome, but not ugly, one that caused a woman to take a second look. In men, it would instill fear.

Clearing her throat to gain attention, Cindy made the introductions. "Sophie Lemoyne."

The goddess is Sophie Lemoyne, Cooper thought to himself. Somewhere in the back of his mind the command to "please be seated" registered.

"Eli, would you say grace."

That had Cooper's attention. Captain Eli Taylor, pirate, saying grace, and a good job of it too. Peeking about, Cooper saw all heads were bowed, including McKemie's and Rooster's. From what Rooster had said, Taylor was a gentleman, unlike some of the rogues he'd heard of and met. Almost on cue, once 'amen' was said, Belle and Mimi came filing in with the food. With so many guests, they used a little cart. While Belle sat down a huge bowl with a ladle, Mimi filled glasses with either tea or lemonade. Cindy surprised Cooper again by asking for half and half. Sophia did the same, so when Mimi came to his side he decided to try it and followed suit. Hot bread was then laid out.

"The corn pone sticks taste better if you smear them with butter while they're hot," Sophia advised.

The bread was a brown crusted and slightly crunchy affair cooked in an iron frying skillet that was oblong and not round. The bread came out in little sticks.

"We like the corn pone sticks better when we have jambalaya," Cindy volunteered as she placed rice in a bowl and passed it to Sophia, who poured the dark, murky, spicy smelling liquid on top of the rice. The bowls were then passed around until everyone had a bowl.

"Belle has prepared an oyster stew for you, Eli. Would you care for it first or the jambalaya first?

Eli responded, "A bowl of the oyster stew first, if you please."

When Mac and Cooper got their bowls of jambalaya, they stared at its contents. They looked at each other, neither of them sure that they wanted to partake of the dish but not wanting to insult anyone either. Taking a quick glance at Sophia, Cooper found her looking at him.

"Have you never eaten jambalaya, Mr. Cain?" Sophia inquired.

So formal, he thought. "No, I, we," indicating Mac and himself, "have never had the pleasure."

"Oh, it's very good. Belle is the best cook in all of New Orleans. She starts with a vegetable soup, and then adds peeled shrimp, crawfish tails, a bit of spice and there you are. Some cooks put too much pepper and spice in their jambalaya, but Belle's is just right." To emphasize this she took a spoonful.

When in Rome...Cooper decided and was delighted at the concoction. Soon a dessert was offered, pecan pie or beignets. Rooster sheepishly asked if any of Belle's café au lait was ready. When she said it was, he chose the beignets.

"Beignets are sweet bread deep fried and then sprinkled with powdered sugar. They go good with café au lait," Cindy explained.

Belle's café au lait was a mixture of French roasted coffee and chicory. This was mixed half and half with milk. The chicory taste complimented the sweet beignets. A heaping platter of the warm beignets was brought out with a huge pot of the coffee. Rooster dipped his pastry in the coffee and swallowed half of it. In two bites it was gone, and he reached out for another beignet. Talk died down as everyone stuffed themselves.

Before he realized it, his belly was full and Cooper felt the need to loosen a button. *Damn,* he thought, for *the first time in my life, food has taken my mind off…well temporarily off a beautiful woman.*

Cindy rose up from the table and said, "If you'd like we can retire to the veranda, where you men can light up a pipe or a cigar. That way, Belle and Mimi can get their chores done."

On the veranda, Jumper was sitting out small pails filled with a yellow fragrant substance. "Citronella," he said, "keeps the skeeters away."

Gus walked up with a box under one arm, a jug in one hand and a guitar in the other. Rooster and McKemie sat on the porch with their legs dangling down. Gus sat on the steps to one side while Mac and Cooper sat across from him. Cindy and Taylor sat in a swing while the girls filled up rocking chairs.

Gus opened the box and offered cigars. "Crooks, I calls them," he said. "After I roll them, I soak them in bourbon." He accentuated this comment by tapping the jug. "I stack them on racks to dry and when I take them off they have little uniform bends, a crooked cigar." He handed the box to Taylor first, who took one and then passed the box around.

"I've been experimenting with rum and cognac," Gus said. "So far I don't have the mixture right. Close but not perfect."

"You still selling the crooks in New Orleans?" Taylor asked.

"Yes sir, every stick as fast as I can make them. This man gives me ten cents a stick at the cigar factory. Of course, he sells them for fifteen cents."

"I have never heard of paying more than a nickel for a cigar," Rooster exclaimed.

"That's because they smell like dog turds," McKemie shot back. "Looks like 'em, too."

Cooper rolled a cigar around in his mouth amazed at the flavor. He reached for the stick Jumper was using to light the citronella wicks with.

Gus reached over and touched his arm, "You don't want to do that. That stick is a sliver of pine lighter. It's full of turpentine. That's why it burns so good. Stick it to the cigar and it'll taste like turpentine. Here, use this," Gus said, passing a small tinder box he built.

It was nothing more than the mechanism for a pistol but when you pulled the trigger it lit small shavings in the box and you had a fire.

"Have you marketed that?" Cooper asked.

"No, folks all over New Orleans got them. Gun maker on Charles Street makes them all the time."

The jug was passed around to the men and a tray with glasses and a bottle of sherry was brought out for Cindy and the girls.

"How old are you?" Cindy asked Linda.

"Seventeen," Linda replied meekly.

"Liar," Lucy hissed. "You're sixteen."

"Well," Cindy said. "You may have one small glass but no more."

"Thank you, madam," Linda replied. She wrinkled her nose and bobbed her head at her sister.

Gus started plucking the strings on the guitar, only pausing to take a pull on the jug before passing it on. Cooper had never seen white men drink after or from the same container as a black man. However, neither Taylor nor his men seemed to mind so he didn't hesitate when the jug came back to him. Besides, once you got a taste you couldn't refuse another. Gus started playing a song. He had a good baritone voice.

The night suddenly reached a height of pleasure for Cooper. Sophia moved out of her rocker and sat on the steps between him and Gus, joining in the singing. Love songs, tearful ballads, up-tempo sassy little songs, one after another. At one point, Sophia rested her hand on the step as she leaned back. Her hand touched Cooper's and caused his heart to pound. Feeling his hand, Sophia turned her head and smiled. Cooper felt like he was floating on air.

All too soon, Gus yawned and put the guitar down. "It's time to turn in," Cindy said smiling as she noticed Linda curled up in the rocking chair snoozing away.

Shocking Cooper, Sophia asked, "Might Lucy and I walk down to the dock and back? I'm sure Cooper and Mr. MacArthur would be glad to escort us."

A hint of a smile came to Cindy's face. "I'm sure they would. Alright, to the dock and back. If you're not back in fifteen minutes I'll send Gus after you."

"It might take a tad more time, should we see anything interesting," Sophia said.

Taking an exaggerated breath, Cindy appeared to give in, "Thirty minutes, but if you're not back then Gus will come with his shotgun." Her statement made Gus smile.

He knew it was an empty threat. Miz Cindy likely had thirty minutes on her mind all the time. They would be back on time though, Gus was sure. If not, it'd be Cindy going to get them as he was ready for bed. The bourbon had made him very drowsy; in thirty minutes he'd be dead to the world.

THE TRIP TO NEW Orleans took three days. Taylor had filled three pirogues with his chests of specie but took six of the boats. Two men in each of the other pirogues were guards, armed to the teeth. They had left Grand Terre at seven a.m. on the morning after returning from Grand Isle. Cooper had never wanted to stay in one place so bad in all his life.

Once away from the house, he had boldly taken Sophia's hand in his. She had not resisted and had even leaned in closer to him, at one point laying her head on his shoulder as they stood on the dock looking at the moon's reflection on the water.

Cooper whispered how beautiful she was and how she made his heart race. Sophia put her finger to his lip to hush him. "Enjoy the moment, my Cherie." The sound of crickets and bullfrogs croaking could be heard.

"How old are you?" Cooper asked.

"Does it matter?" Sophia responded.

"No, not to me, I just turned eighteen," Cooper replied. "But I want to live till I'm eighty and have you with me every day."

As they parted in the hall back at Cindy's house, he said, "I'll see you in the morning."

Sophia did not answer but stood on her tiptoes and kissed Cooper a quick kiss on the lips and then hurried off. He laid awake most of the night, finally drifting off to sleep in the wee hours of the morning. Sophia did not come to breakfast. Cooper finally asked Cindy where she was. "She is not feeling well and wishes not to be disturbed."

As they left, Captain Taylor gave Cindy a small purse. At the dock, a hurt and dejected Cooper asked, "You pay Mrs. Veigh?"

"No, she will not take any money, Coop. She has more than enough. The money is an allowance for the girls while they are with her."

"She lives well," Cooper said.

"She can, she is a rich woman. We recently became partners in a legitimate shipping business. I'm about ready to leave the sea. I've just been waiting for the right person to turn the *Raven* over too."

Suddenly, a thought came to Cooper. Calling Taylor by his first name, he asked, "You think I'm that man, Eli?"

"You could be, son, you could be."

As they neared New Orleans, Mac pointed out the river was higher than the land. This required a dike to keep the plantations from flooding. Tying up to the wharf, two free blacks earning a living with a mule and wagon were whistled up. One of the men recognized Taylor.

"Morning, Cap'n. You headed to the bank?"

Flipping a twenty dollar gold piece out, Taylor said, "We sure are."

The Bank of New Orleans was a big three story building on Saint Phillip Street. It had wrought iron balconies with the bank's sign hanging from the center in front. Turning into the alley, the guards circled the wagon front and back.

"Come with me, Coop," Taylor ordered.

Once in the bank, Taylor, who was now well dressed, was pleasantly greeted by a clerk, who quickly volunteered, "I'll see if Mr. Latrobe is in," knowing good and well that he was. Thomas Henry Latrobe did not make them wait. He ushered his guests into his office and over his shoulder ordered refreshments.

After the men were in Latrobe's private office, Taylor came right to the point. "I have roughly one hundred and fifty thousand in gold and silver coin in the alley. Perhaps you could send out some guards to relieve my men." Latrobe didn't blink an eye when the amount was mentioned, but Cooper found it hard to swallow.

"While your clerks are confirming the sum," Taylor continued, "I'd like to open an account for my young friend here with the sum of ten thousand dollars." The hefty sum mentioned made Cooper feel faint. When the banker stepped out to set things in motion, Taylor whispered, "Only a thousand is yours, except in an emergency. You then can have a loan payable back with ten percent interest. In this town money talks, a thousand dollar account will get you a clerk. Ten thousand and my introduction will see you established. Don't abuse it."

CHAPTER EIGHT

OUTSIDE THE BANK, TAYLOR gave Cooper and Mac one hundred dollars each. "An advancement," he said. "Go see the sites of the city but stay out of trouble. I will have your chest sent over to the hotel. Be there at seven p.m., Hotel Provincial, Charles Street. It's only two blocks from Bourbon Street."

Once the captain had gone beyond hearing, Mac said, "In a hurry to see his woman, I'd say and doesn't want us in the way for the reunion."

What had he done to cause Sophia not to come down and see him off, Cooper wondered. As the friends walked the streets of New Orleans, they were constantly pointing out things to each other. However, Cooper couldn't get Sophia from his mind.

"I've never seen the equal," Mac said, "not even in London, certainly not in Portsmouth or Plymouth."

Everywhere people were coming and going. Women of all races, some dressed very elegantly, while others were dressed to show off their wares…and what wares they had. The women carried themselves proudly, French, Spanish, German, and white. There was also the mixture of race, Creoles, Mulatto, Quadroons, and Octoroons.

Rooster had given Cooper and Mac a quick lesson in these lovely ladies one night after departing Marco Island. Free women of color often became the mistress of a white man; they were not considered whores. They were usually put up in a nice residence and if the man was not married, he would live there with her.

The woman and any children were usually taken care of for life. The woman's children were of lighter skin than the mother and with each successive generation the skin turned almost white, hair frequently straight, but they maintained some of the African facial features to make them very exotic.

"Whatever their race," Mac said, "they are beautiful wenches."

A cacophony of languages was also heard, French, Spanish, and a bastard version of both. Of all the different tongues spoken, American English seemed to be the least.

Saloons, gambling houses and brothels all seemed to be doing a thriving business, as were the normal shops, hoteliers, gun shops, sword shops, and women's boutiques. Dandified men all dressed in top hats, and lace shirts, elegant women in expensive gowns all crowded the streets with slaves ducking around them on some errand or another. Open carriages for the upper class who were too dignified to walk. Yes, New Orleans, the Crescent City, was a delightfully sinful and strange, but wonderful city.

After the two had aimlessly strolled the city they began to get hungry. "It's after two p.m.," Mac said. "No wonder my stomach is growling."

"Aye, but I don't want anything to spicy," Cooper answered. "Look over there, a grocery store with the picture of a sandwich in the window."

The man who waited on them spoke in broken English. "He's a Sicilian," Mac volunteered. He'd sailed off the coast of Sicily and talked with several fishermen. "His name is Mr. Boscoli and he says the sandwich in the window is called a muffuletta. The bread is cut and stuffed with salami, ham, cheese, chopped olives, and with olive oil added."

"I don't care what it is, I'm starving," Cooper said. Taking a bag with the sandwiches and grabbing some bottled beer the men walked a block down the street and sat on a park bench under some huge oak trees. The air was a little nippy in the shade. A large church could be seen at the end of the park.

"Do you know what day it is?" Cooper asked.

"Damned if I do, Coop. Do we need to find out? Is it important?"

"Not really, this is four days since we left Cindy's house and instead of fading with time, Sophia seems to be more on my mind."

"We'll take another trip over to the island," Mac said. "Captain says we'll be here a couple more weeks yet."

"Thanks, David, you really are a good friend, you know," Cooper said.

"Well, I am but that's not all of it. I'd kind of like to see Lucy again."

Smiling, Cooper nudged his friend, "I didn't know the wind blew that way."

Mac said, "I'm not sure it does, but she sure seemed nice the other night. Nice enough that I want to go back and see."

THE HOTEL PROVINCIAL WAS unlike the many hotels the friends had passed on their tour of the city in that it was a low-rise hotel that was somewhat a secluded affair. It was tucked under a group of giant old oak trees, and was about two blocks from what Cooper had decided was the most decadent street he'd ever walked down…Bourbon Street.

"Damn," Mac had sworn, "mutton everywhere I look."

Unlike the outward display on Bourbon Street, the Hotel Provincial seemed more of a romantic and intimate place. It was one of the more desirable hotels for newlyweds or well-to-do lovers. Not like the rowdy crowd they had seen at Hotel de la Marine. Walking inside the light was dim with only candle chandeliers to provide one light enough to see where they were going, but not so many candles burning to make it hot. Jalousie windows were cracked open, which allowed a cool breeze to flow through.

A woman sitting at a small desk saw them enter and rose from her seat. Offering her hand, she said, "Monsieurs Cain and MacArthur."

Bowing from the waist, Cooper lightly touched the palm side of the lady's fingers and kissed the air just above her hand. "Oui, madame."

When the woman turned to Mac, he mimicked Cooper but did speak. "Cooper said you have us at a disadvantage, my lady."

Pleased with the manners she'd not come to expect dealing with the captain's usual guests, she replied, "Renee, Mademoiselle Renee."

"It is our pleasure, mademoiselle," Cooper replied.

"The captain and Madame Russell await you. If you would please follow me," she said.

Deborah Russell was a soft-spoken lady from Georgia with the slightest of accent. Once the captain had made the introductions, Debbie, as she insisted on being called, took Cooper's hand and led the way into a small parlor. It was decorated by a woman but had an overstuffed brown leather chair that was for the captain. Beside the chair, a table stood with a rack of pipes, a tin of pipe tobacco, and a box that looked the right size for cigars. Behind the table was a decorative lantern that could be lit when the captain wanted to read. A man was pouring glasses full of a reddish liquid from a large bowl.

Seeing his gaze, Debbie said, "Rum punch, Mr. Cain."

Cooper smiled, "It's Cooper, Debbie, or as most of my friends call me, Coop."

When everyone had a cup of the tasty but heady punch, Debbie recommended stepping out into the courtyard. "It's cool, there's usually a fair breeze and if you want one of Eli's smelly cigars, I don't mind…out here. I can tolerate the pipe inside but if it's a cigar, the courtyard is the place. Its mint leaves, then, if he wants a kiss." This caused a chuckle from the men.

As they sat down, not surprisingly, cigars were furnished, Gus' cigars. After the men lit up, Debbie sat in a wrought iron loveseat next to her man. "Cooper, I want to thank you for saving my man. I told him he's getting too old for this nonsense."

"Not long now, dear," Taylor whispered.

"Humph, you old sea dog. Next time it could be a blade or a storm," Debbie said.

"Or a jealous lover," the captain interrupted.

"Aye," she said, with a wink.

A NOTE FROM PIERRE LaFitte asked Captain Eli Taylor to please come to his blacksmith shop on Saint Phillips Street as soon as convenient. There was no clue as to the reason for such an urgent request. However, recognizing the handwriting, Taylor rounded up his guests and the trio made their way to the blacksmith shop.

Pierre was sitting on a bench smoking a corncob pipe when Taylor, Cooper, and Mac showed up. Rising to shake the group's hands, Pierre led the way to the back of the shop. Sitting on a barrel was the biggest man Cooper had ever seen.

"Gentlemen," Pierre said, "this is Quang. He is a good man and a good fighter, too good a fighter. He was hired to load a flatboat with cotton bales. He can carry a bale by himself. While carrying a bale, the foreman cursed Quang for a heathen Chinaman and told him to move along faster. That would have been alright had he not emphasized his words with the crack of a whip." This caused Cooper to wince and touch the side of his face. "Aye, brings back memories does it not?" Pierre asked, seeing Cooper's movement. "Then you can understand how it was and why Quang threw…aye, threw the cotton bale he was toting at the foreman, crushing his chest and killing the sod. Now the law is out for our poor friend. You are the only captain in the city right now, so I naturally called on you, my friend. He will make an excellent crewman."

"Aye," Taylor said. "I will take him. We will be here another ten days…two weeks. If you will put him up until then I will pick him up on our trip to Barataria."

"Just send a note when you are ready to leave, my friend. He will be ready," Pierre said.

Feeling a kinship with the huge Chinaman, Cooper found himself coming by the shop daily. Before he knew it, Quang became Cooper's fighting instructor. Not the gentlemanly art like Jean-Paul, but the no holds barred brawler with a few oriental moves thrown in.

"Good, good," Pierre exclaimed, clapping his hands. Cooper had just thrown Pierre's biggest blacksmith. Quang was still the master, but Cooper proved to be a good student. In the beginning, he was frequently thrown flat on his back, with a barrel stave at his throat.

Over the next week and a half, those times of Cooper being flat on his back became fewer. He was an excellent learner, and as such, he noticed how Quang would plant his left foot when he was about to throw his opponent. When the next bout came around, Cooper watched and when Quang planted his foot Cooper ducked, did a side step and slammed the barrel stave into the back of Quang's knee. When the giant went down, Cooper thrust the stave at his friend's neck. He'd won…he'd finally won a round.

After three more days of rough and tumble practice, it came to an end. It was time to head back. Packing up the clothes he'd bought, and a new cutlass he had purchased, liking the way it fit his hand, and a set of good but used navigational instruments. He also purchased Falconer's New Universal Dictionary of the Marine, and The Young Sea Officers Sheet Anchor by Darcy Lever. He bought a book on trigonometry, a must if he was to master navigation, Mac had sworn. With his bags packed full of the things he'd need to be successful at sea, Cooper announced his readiness to the captain. He was not expecting to see what he saw. Otis was sitting with the captain and Debbie in the courtyard.

Seeing the surprise, Taylor spoke, "I sent for Otis. We need someone of his many talents here at the hotel. After talking with Debbie, Otis has decided to be Debbie's next in line. I'm sure he can handle the job after a bit of hands on training."

Smiling, Cooper said, "It fits better than being a ..."

"A pirate," Debbie finished the sentence for him.

Chapter Nine

At Pierre's blacksmith shop, the group picked up Quang and was leaving when Mac noticed a handbill that was tacked on the door.

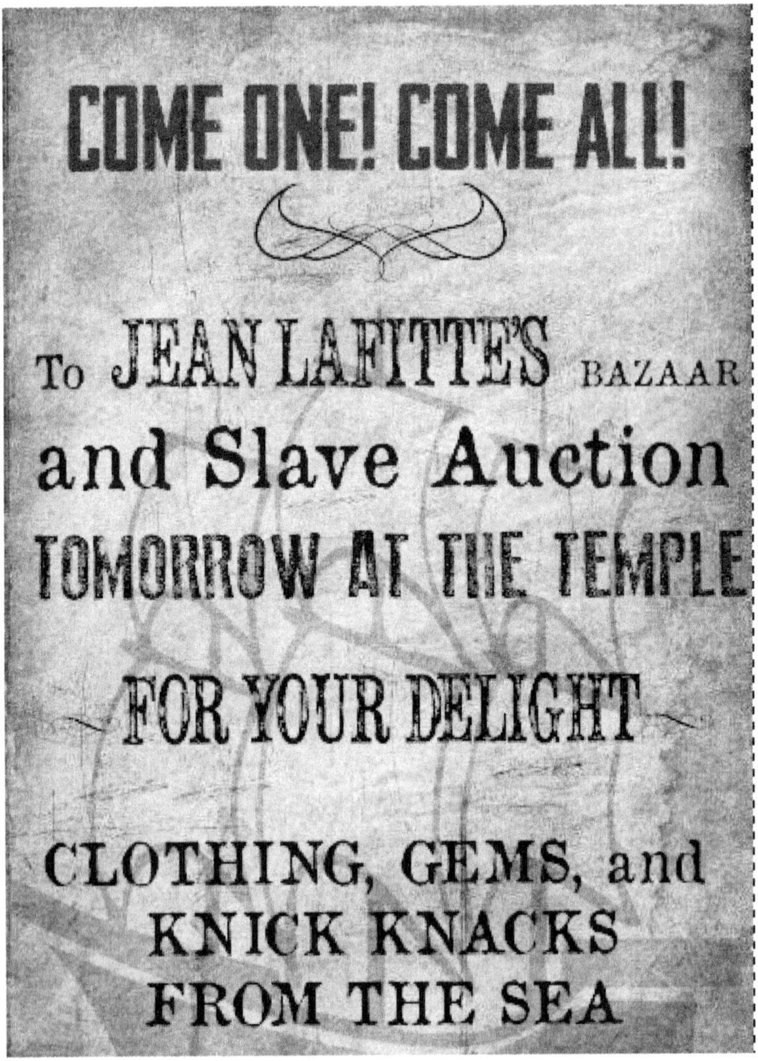

COME ONE! COME ALL!

To JEAN LAFITTE'S BAZAAR
and Slave Auction
TOMORROW AT THE TEMPLE

FOR YOUR DELIGHT

CLOTHING, GEMS, and
KNICK KNACKS
FROM THE SEA

"Could be it might still be going," Taylor volunteered, noticing the interest in Cooper and Mac as they read the notice. The bayous and waterways that led to the Temple and Barataria beyond were an impenetrable mass of flora, fauna, and pest, unless you knew the way. More than one man had died trying to find the right waterway. Even if you knew the route, as did Captain Taylor, the murky waters were floored by quicksand and undertow. The bayou was walled by low hanging moss, cypress trees, and knots all along the waterway. Tall marsh grass could bring a traveler to a sudden halt. You didn't dare get out of the pirogue, as the swamp was alive with eyes and all of them looking at you. Cottonmouths hung from low lying limbs and would strike before you even knew they were there. Alligators, lizards, mosquitoes, and rodents were also out there waiting to dine on human flesh. The bright rays of sun rarely made their way through the tree tops. The croaking of frogs would damn near drive a man crazy.

This was the path to LaFitte's kingdom. It was also the path LaFitte's barges, some one hundred feet long, made on their way to the Temple or New Orleans. Taylor's group made it to the Temple by noon the next day. The public was there in droves. Everything you could think of was on sale. Canisters of Cuban cigars, snuffs, jewelry, dresses, parasols, cookwares, furniture, fine weapons, and slaves, of course. Cooper had noticed all the large pirogues and barges tied up on the crunchy sand and shell beach when they arrived. LaFitte, no doubt, provided a ferry service to the Temple and back. He also had a means of transporting goods and slaves for the buyers.

A cheerful LaFitte walked about in a suit of green with a small sword at his side. His hat had feathers bristling to one side. He greeted one and all, the perfect host. He shook the hands of the men, passed out cigars, made humorous comments to the ladies and even had a mock sword fight with a lad about six years old.

Servants were toting purchases for the buyers, children bounded about eating sugar cane, pralines, and taffies made by the pirate's women. Most of the men loitered about the slave platform drinking free rum or wine. Glancing over their shoulders to see if their wives were looking, they inspected some young female slave suitable as a house servant or other like uses. Big, strong male slaves were sold. Prime field hands and they could also be used as breeders to improve the slave stock already owned.

One of the auctioneers lifted a black's breech cloth exposing his manhood. "Built like a stud horse, he is. You could offer his services for a hundred dollars a whack," he claimed.

Cooper suddenly felt bile rise up in his throat. He spit and said, "I've seen enough." He walked away from the slave platform and saw Lucy, Linda, and Cindy Veigh.

"Isn't this just something?" Lucy cried excitement in her voice. "Cindy and Gus brought us over. Oh, there's David. David MacArthur!" It was obvious where Lucy's attentions were. Cooper bought Cindy and Linda a pecan praline.

Cooper was about to ask if Sophia was there, when Cindy, guessing his thoughts, said, "No, she isn't here." Cooper's heart sank. *Would he ever see the girl again?* Noticing Gus had a few boxes of his crooks, Cooper bought three of them. After a while, Taylor showed up and said he was ready to shove off.

Cooper found Mac and Lucy behind a stand of oaks holding hands. The sight made him even more morose. He was glad for Mac, but doubted he would ever obtain the hand of Lucy Williams. Lord Williams would never approve of a pirate for a son-in-law. Saying their goodbyes, Mac promised he'd see Lucy in a few days. Getting into their pirogue, Cooper turned just in time to see Cindy give an envelope to Taylor, who quickly placed it in his coat pocket.

Quang was the last to return. He was carrying a wrapped up package. He stowed it at his feet as they shoved off. Looking back at the sand and shell beach, Cooper noticed a fierce looking pirate looking their way. Catching Cooper's eyes, the man cleared his throat and spit. He then walked back up the trail toward the stage where the slave auction was being held. Two days later, they arrived at Barataria.

Tying up at a small dock, Captain Taylor said, "I'll see how many of the crew are here. I want to meet on the ship tomorrow morning. You men take your plunder out to the ship and get squared away. If you see any of the mates, pass the word along. If the quartermaster is aboard, tell him to call upon me at Hotel Mayronne for supper." Looking up at the sky, he absently muttered, "Mid afternoon. No wonder my guts grumbling. If you men desire one last really good meal before we set sail, come to the hotel tonight." With that he turned and shuffled off.

"Well, that puts paid to seeing Lucy again anytime soon," Mac said.

Feeling sad for his friend, Cooper said, "David, I was with the captain when he went to the lawyer, whose name is W. Edward Meeks, to set the ransom demands in motion. I heard him say it would take upwards a year for the documents to find their way to Antigua and a rendezvous set up. You know, we will be back in time for you to see Lucy before then."

Once aboard *Raven* Lee Turner, the quartermaster, was found. Cooper gave him the captain's message and Turner put Quang in the mess with Cooper and Mac. As the men unpacked their possessions and placed them in their chest, Quang handed the package he'd bought at the Temple to Cooper.

"You very good friend," Quang said. "You make good warrior. Warrior need good blade."

Tearing the wrapping open, Cooper was aghast. He could not help but be amazed. It was a knife, no a dagger would be a better word. The handle was whalebone carved to look like a stallion horse. It was intricately carved; ears bent backwards, eyes open, nostrils flared and teeth bared, a war horse. The blade was twelve to thirteen inches long with just a hint of an 'S' curve. The blade was double edged and had a rib down the center to add strength. Where the handle fit the shaft was an oriental emblem inlaid in gold…a warrior's knife indeed. A leather scabbard came with the weapon. Cooper unbuckled his belt and slid the scabbard over his belt.

"Thank you, my friend. I am honored. But I have nothing to match to give in return." Realizing this, Cooper started to unbuckle his belt to remove the gift.

Seeing this, Quang said, "No! You good friend. You don't turn up nose cause Quang not white."

Almost tearing up, Cooper said, "Aye, we are friends, until the death."

"Until the death," Quang repeated.

Hotel Mayronne was a white, wooden two story building set in the middle of Barataria's business district. A large sign painted in red announced the hotel. When you walked in the hotel, a clerk sat at a large desk with a ledger and ink stand. Behind the desk was a shelf with cubicles. They were numbered one to sixteen. At either end of the desk, a set of curving stairs that reached the second floor rooms. To the left of the desk was a restaurant, which was said to have the island's only chef. There were several cafés on the island, most of them open air establishments where you sat on built in benches and shutters were propped open.

At Mayronne's you sat down in style. To the right was a bar and tables for cards and games, gentlemen games. The hotel was not for the average pirate. It was for the captains and guests of Monsieur LaFitte. Planters, lawyers, and city officials were not uncommon. A huge Quadroon named Benard set by the entrance of the hotel to ensure riff raff didn't enter. Benard was a fierce looking man with cream-colored skin, a bald head, a gold earring in his left ear and a tattoo on his bicep. The tattoo was of fighting snakes. As fearsome as Benard looked, it was the old-fashioned blunderbuss held across his lap that held rogues in check. He once fired the blunderbuss at a wooden crate to demonstrate the effectiveness of the weapon. All that remained of the crate was splinters for firewood. There had never again been a question in regards to what the weapon could do.

The Mayronne was named after the owner of Grand Terre, Francois Mayronne. LaFitte leased the entire island from him but it was rumored that he was engaged in most of LaFitte's smuggling activities. At seven p.m., Cooper, Mac, and Quang entered the hotel and turned left into the dining room. The captain, Lee Turner, Diamond, and Spurlock were sitting at a table with Jean LaFitte. A table was open next to theirs so the three sat down at it. A pretty little waitress was making her rounds and motioned she'd be right there.

Across the room the pirate captains, Vincent Gambi and Louis 'No-Nose' Chighizola sat at one table while Renato Beluche sat with two very attractive women. Rooster had said Beluche was a cousin of Pierre and Jean LaFitte. At another table a man and his son sat. Cooper had met the man in New Orleans at the lawyer Meeks' office arranging a land sale. His name was

de Marigny and he was said to be the richest man in New Orleans. *He certainly knew how to stretch his dollars if he traded with LaFitte,* thought Cooper. When the waitress came around, the men ordered their meal. All three of the men wanted fried channel catfish, grits, and honey glazed biscuits. They were also served ice cold sweet tea with their meal. Strong drink was not served in the restaurant. It was tea, hot or cold, lemonade, coffee made half and half with chicory, and a fruity wine called sangria that came with a slice of orange floating on the top. Dessert was a choice of crepes with orange marmalade, pecan pie, or beignets.

Not too quietly, Gambi scrubbed his chair back on the wooden floor as he rose from his table. He haphazardly tossed his napkin on the table, the corner landing in a half finished bowl of gumbo. As he came around the table he leaned over and whispered to one of his men, who turned toward Cooper's table. It was the rogue on the beach at the Temple.

No-Nose Chighizola sat for a moment and then quickly rose and left the dining room, making eye contact with Captain Taylor and shaking his head as if to say, "I'm not involved," as he walked by.

The rogue at the table turned his chair as he faced Cooper. "The air in here has turned foul with the stench of some British bastard." Mac made to rise, but Cooper put his hand on his friend's arm. Not getting the rise he intended, the man continued, "Are you Taylor's little arse licking British puppy? I heard what you done to Finch. He was my friend. You hit him when he wasn't looking. I wonder if you have the nutmegs to face a man."

"That's enough, LaRoche," Spurlock retorted.

"Humph! Just as I thought no nutmegs," LaRoche continued.

Cooper had had enough, his words were not yelled but the coldness carried his words across the room. "It sickens me to have a killing before supper, it ruins a man's appetite. It was a handsome meal I had ordered."

"Killing!" LaRoche threw back and rose so fast that his chair slammed to the floor with a loud bang.

Through the swinging door Benard came and his stare brooked no lip. "Outside," he ordered. "Carry it outside or die where you stand. We can repair the place from your accounts."

Knowing he meant it, LaRoche took a deep breath and challenged Cooper, "Will you meet me outside?"

Realizing the man would grow angry with waiting, Cooper said, "After I eat. If you're still waiting I will send you to hell with your friend." LaRoche stormed outside.

Jean-Paul had always taught Cooper an angry man makes mistakes. He would say, "Fight on your grounds, not his."

"You don't have to do this," Taylor said from across the way.

"Yes, I do. I have to establish myself or I will always be challenged," Cooper replied.

"We will see there's no interference," Diamond said.

"Aye," Spurlock agreed.

Quang said, "You will win, I have no doubt. He's big and strong but does not know what you have learned. You will win."

Cooper poked around at his food when it came. He had lost his appetite but wanted to make LaRoche wait. Finally, after twenty minutes he pushed back and stood up. He reached for his purse but LaFitte spoke up, "Tonight it's my treat."

Taylor, Diamond, and Spurlock went out the door and down the steps first, followed by Cooper, Mac, and Quang. A man made to put his foot out to trip Cooper only to find Quang's blade at his throat.

"You may want to live long enough to see the fight," Quang said in his broken English. The man gulped and shrunk back.

Torches had been lit and a circle had been created as men rushed to see the fight. LaFitte walked down the steps and raised his hands. The crowd became quiet for the boss. "This is to be a fair fight," he announced. "Any man who interferes will be shot instantly." LaFitte's words were law. Everyone knew that to step out of line meant death for certain. "A sash," LaFitte called.

A filthy, foul-breath man stepped forward to remove his sash. LaFitte held up his hand to stop the man and took a step back, turning his face from the man. "Whew! If your sash tastes like you smell, we will have two dead combatants before the fight starts."

The man initially looked hurt but smiled as the crowd roared in laughter. Wagers were made as LaFitte untied his sash. He turned to Cooper, "Each man puts an end of the sash in his mouth. That limits the distance you can separate and to a degree takes away the advantage of a man with longer arms and greater reach."

"Will the fight be till first blood or…to the death?" LaRoche threw out before LaFitte could finish his statement.

Turning to Cooper, LaFitte looked as if to say do you agree? Cooper answered the unasked question, "As he wishes." Putting the ends of the sash in their mouths, the men pulled their blades and began to circle each other.

"I'll have that pretty blade before you know it," LaRoche hissed.

"You sure will, but not the way you expect it," Cooper retorted.

The sash grew tight in Cooper's mouth as LaRoche tossed his knife back and forth from hand to hand, trying to confuse Cooper; the hand being quicker than the eye. Realizing his foe's ploy, Cooper moved his gaze away from the hand to LaRoche's eyes. He was just in time as the man's eyes widened as he struck. Cooper's training with Jean-Paul kept him from a blade through the gut. He quickly sidestepped the attack and deflected LaRoche's blade, he then countered with a backhand slash that caused a crimson line across his enemy's chest, drawing first blood.

"Is that all you have?" Cooper taunted LaRoche. "I surely thought you had more than that."

The taunting did the trick. LaRoche charged like an angry bull. Again, Cooper sidestepped and tripped LaRoche. What Cooper didn't do was let go of the sash between his teeth. LaRoche's weight pulled Cooper to the ground with him. LaRoche swung his knife backwards impaling the blade in Cooper's deltoid muscle. Sensing victory, LaRoche swung around again but Cooper was not there. The pain made Cooper react quickly, so he was up on his feet. He had an open target to LaRoche's back so he lashed out making a cut from shoulder blade to shoulder blade. LaRoche was fast…fast and nimble he spun around on his heels and faced Cooper. Again it was instinct and reflexes that saved Cooper as he batted the blade aside and was able to deliver a nick to LaRoche's cheek.

The crowd was hollering, bets were being made and odds were changing. No one had expected the British kid to last more than LaRoche's first attack. Not only had he lasted but except for the wound on the ground, a lucky wound, it was LaRoche, not Cooper, who was getting carved up. LaRoche was supposed to be a sure bet. He'd carved up several men foolish enough or drunk enough to accept his challenge. Now it was LaRoche bleeding from several wounds.

He might have gotten the most nicks in, Cooper knew; but LaRoche had inflicted the most severe wound. His shoulder hurt…hurt like a burning hell, much like the riding crop across the face. Blood ran down Cooper's arm to his hand and dripped on the ground. He'd held back from fighting his uncle. There was no restraint now. LaRoche suddenly became the target of all of Cooper's anger and pain. Not an uncontrollable anger but a controlled, deliberate anger. LaRoche's face suddenly changed and it was Phillip standing across from him, sash in his mouth.

"You've had your time," Cooper hissed between clenched teeth, "now it's my turn to play."

It was all LaRoche could do to parry the first couple of advances. Fear filled his eyes as Cooper laughed a loud laugh. "You said to the death so be it." Using every trick he'd learned by a master swordsman, Cooper attacked. His blade moving so fast LaRoche couldn't keep up. LaRoche felt a sharp burning pain as the war-horse blade made a circular motion around his wrist, severing veins, arteries, and tendons; his blade fell to the ground from useless fingers. As he looked up, he saw the face of death. Had it been this way with his victims? Had he caused them to realize their last breath was upon them, that their time had come? Did he look to them like the blonde haired demon with a scarred face looked to him?

"Oh God!" LaRoche cried. Looking up toward the moon filled sky; he sunk to his knees just as Cooper made a final swing severing the man's throat with blood spewing from severed arteries.

The crowd was quiet. No one had ever seen such a display as Cooper Cain had just put on. Nor were they likely to again. Who would be so foolish? Cooper was heaving as his friends walked up. He was trying to get his breathing under control. Someone handed him a tankard filled with rum. Looking up, Cooper saw that is was the rich planter that had given him the drink. The rum was a strong heady rum. It helped to get rid of the nausea and bile that filled his throat.

"He asked for it," he muttered. "He said to the death."

"Aye, he did at that," Spurlock said, "and he got his wish."

"Now he's in Hades, no doubt," LaFitte spoke. "Let's get our victor to my house and let the surgeon see to his wounds. It's the ill humours that come after the fight that you have to worry about."

Cooper was feeling faint from blood loss and only halfway remembered being carried to LaFitte's house where warm hands and cool cloths were applied to his body.

CHAPTER TEN

IT WAS AN UNCOMMONLY cold morning for the south. It felt like the contrary winds that whipped across Barataria Bay were full of ice. Captain Taylor had thought to weigh anchor and sail with the tide. However, having no schedule to keep, he looked at the sullen sky with its dark, heavy clouds and quietly declared they'd put off setting sail until the weather moderated.

"A captain with some common sense," David "Mac" MacArthur swore. That would be a rare finding in the navy he was used to.

In the days that had passed since Cooper had killed LaRoche, he seem to become more withdrawn while his acceptance with the *Raven's* crew had been totally given, with little reserve and few exceptions. The man had proved his mettle. He had faced what most felt was certain death and done it with the dignity of a gentleman. His skill with a blade was tested and not found to be wanting. Now the blackhearts knew to step gently around "killer Cain". Not a name he was called to his face. It had demonstrated to everyone that Captain Eli Taylor was justified in bringing the boy aboard a man's ship.

The hands had put forth an effort to have the ship set to right and made ready for sailing. The holds were filled with casks of fresh water, barrels of salt pork and beef, barrels of rum, a few cases of wine, chewing tobacco, pipe tobacco and cheap cigars. Bags of ship's biscuits, chests of extra clothing, shot and powder replenished, several new muskets and pistols, a few boarding pikes, a barrel stuffed full of usable cutlasses, new ropes, tackles, and an extra set of sails were also put in the holds. Anything else they would procure from prizes taken.

Worn out from loading supplies and his arm still aching from where LaRoche had wounded him, Cooper sat down to rest with his mates. Quang fetched a tankard of rum for the group.

"Damn if this ain't a shitten job," Cooper swore.

Mac laughed and replied, "It's nothing compared to what a Royal Navy ship brings aboard when they are ready to set sail. The officers don't do much other than supervise. Of course, we have to be more self-sufficient and we are out much longer. Captain Taylor must not be planning on a long voyage as there's no livestock or chickens on board, and only a few fresh fruits and vegetables."

Quang volunteered, "These men not much on vegetables or fruits. They want mostly meat, potatoes, and rum with a liberal helping of women and gambling."

"Humph! I thought I was a wastrel and a rogue," Cooper snorted. "I doubt one in ten could rub two schillings together after a month on shore even if his life depended on it."

"Forget schillings, you are not in England now," Quang said, and then added, "but it's been one damn good time they've had. It's the life they've chosen."

A rumble of thunder was heard and the men rushed below decks to their mess. Of the three, only Quang was used to living in such close quarters. In truth, because of his experience Mac could have joined the likes of Spurlock, Diamond, and Turner in a four-man cubicle below the captain's cabin. That group ate in what Mac thought of as the gunroom.

The mess had four thick deck prisms that lit the space up fairly well. The headroom between the thick beams allowed a man to sit but not stand. Cooper had butted the beams enough to finally learn to stoop. The below deck odors were better now that the ship had been in port for a while. However, when Cooper was first showed the hammock where he'd sleep, he had almost vomited on his chest. The smell of the bilges was bad enough, but the added smell of unwashed bodies and sour clothing had almost been more than he could bear.

Cooper, and as far as he could tell, Mac, were used to regular baths. Some he knew subscribed to the myth it was unhealthy to bathe too often. He was not one of those men and had been chided for dumping cold sea water over his naked body, soaping up and rinsing off. Hopefully, he could persuade a few more to take up the practice. Quang, as with most orientals, was a very clean person.

THE NEXT DAY THE early morning looked like someone had painted a reddish swath over the sky, across the bay and Grand Isle. After a breakfast of strong black coffee and biscuits, the order to set sail came down. On deck, Captain Taylor called Mac over and surprised him with his formal speech, "Would you care to get the ship underway, Mr. MacArthur?"

"Aye, Captain," Mac responded, easily slipping back into his naval ways.

"The anchor is hove short," Quartermaster Turner volunteered.

"Thank you, Mr. Turner. Hands aloft, loose topsails; stand by to hoist foresails."

Cooper had spent hours reading his books and had learned the basics of each evolution. Yet, he knew himself to be a lubberly sort compared to the way the true seamen streamed about, up the shrouds and ratlines for the mizzen top. Men stood by the braces to angle the sails so as to catch the wind.

"Stand aside, Mr. Cain." This was from the captain, who sensed Cooper's hurt. He then added, "There's a time to watch and learn and then there's a time to do. Now's your time to learn, so watch and learn well, young sir."

The topsail was soon set. The ship moved but seemed to be moving sideways. Neither Mac nor the captain seemed alarmed. Taylor stood still and very stoic and Mac barked out more orders. The clank, clank, clank forward could be heard as the anchor was raised. Forward, the stay sails and jibs were set. Now the ship seemed to pay off and gain headway.

"Course, Captain?" Mac asked.

"Make steerage for the mouth of the harbor, Mr. MacArthur."

"Aye, Captain. On the mizzen, aloft, set the spanker."

Cooper watched at how quickly the evolution was carried out and he gained a new respect for *Raven's* crew, and for David MacArthur. *I'll be a seaman before long,* he swore to himself. The mass confusion he'd witnessed was in actuality a display of professionals.

"Mr. Cain, do you wish to go forward and watch the anchor being catted home?" Captain Taylor asked.

"Do I wish, indeed," Cooper said.

"What he means is get your arse forward and watch real seamen so that you might prove to be more than a passenger at some point," Mac replied.

THE *RAVEN* WAS SAILING along easterly, with Barataria having long been lost from the stern. It was a cool evening and the Gulf of Mexico was content to produce no more than a rolling sea of gentle swells. It was a peaceful dusk; men were enjoying a tankard and a smoke. Rooster found Cooper, Mac, and Quang sitting with a group of older seamen. Cooper was listening intently as sea stories were being told, each more lewd and bizarre than the previous.

"Captain wants you," Rooster said, motioning to the three.

Reporting to the captain was the same regardless of Royal Navy, merchantman, or free ship. You always wondered why you were sent for. Entering the cabin, Taylor nodded to Rooster, who poured each a glass of rum. As the men sat down in straight-back chairs in front of the captain's desk, he produced a leather binder. "Here are the Articles of the Free Ship *Raven*. After reading them, you must decide to sign on or be put ashore."

"Quang sign." With that he had the captain write his name – Quang. The Chinaman then pulled his knife out and stuck the tip of the blade on his thumb so that a spot of blood appeared. He then pressed it down next to where his name had been written. "There Quang chop," he said.

"Means his signature," Taylor volunteered. "See the print of his thumb? The Chinese swear everyone has a different print or as Quang said, his chop. Means just as much as a signature to him."

Nodding he understood but really not comprehending a bit of it, Cooper said, "I'll sign."

"Read the articles first," Taylor advised. "You need to know what the articles say. It's how you will be governed. You need to know what your rights are, what's against the rules, what punishments are, what your share of prize money will be. It's all in there. Mac, you will be rated as a first mate."

"Thank you, Captain," Mac said.

"You proved yourself at every turn," Taylor responded.

"What about me?" Cooper asked.

Taylor smiled, "You are rated as other. That means you are lower than whale shat. But you have promise so I don't think you will be there long. Now, read the articles and sign or I'll put you off my ship."

"Fine time to tell us that with no land in sight," Cooper whined in mock despair.

"Read the damn articles," Taylor replied with a grin.

These are our articles, we swear by them to the last man

I. Every man shall have an equal vote in affairs and movement of the ship's company. He shall have equal share and title to all the provisions and liquors unless a scarcity makes it necessary to ration these items for the common good of the ship's company.

II. Every man shall be called upon fairly and in turn for the safe sailing, operation, and up keep of the ship. The quartermaster shall draw up a watch, quarters, and station bill. Each man will be fairly called upon to go aboard any prizes and act as prize crew.

III. If any man is found "guilty of cowardice" in time of engagement, he shall suffer death by hanging. If any man shall offer to run away, shirk his duties, or keep secret from the "ship's company" he shall be put to death or marooned. If any man shall steal from any man of the "ship's company" he shall be put to death or marooned. If the thief is marooned he shall further suffer his nose and ears to be split.

IV. None shall game for money, rat catching, dice, or cards.

V. No man shall strike another on board ship. But every man's quarrel shall be ended on shore by sword or pistol in a civil manner, should a man commit or attempt to commit murder the punishment is immediate death.

VI. No boy or woman shall be allowed to be a member of the "ship's company." No woman shall be brought on board the ship for the purpose of sex.

VII. Every man shall keep his arms clean and fit for engagement. Failure or neglect will result in punishment as the captain or the "ship's company" shall think fit.

VIII. No man shall Snap his Arms, or Smoke Tobacco in the Hold or carry his Pipe without Lid or carry a Candle lighted without Lanthorn. Punishment will be as in the former article.

IX. If any Gold, Silver, or Jewels be found on board any Prize, the Finder must deliver it to the quartermaster immediately. Failure will result in the same punishment as in Article III.

X. If at any time a prudent woman is brought aboard the ship, no man shall meddle with her. The penalty is death.

XI. All plunder and prizes including collected ransoms shall be divided as soon as feasible with the profits shared as set forth in the table attached to these articles. The cost of keeping the ship fit, found and capable of engagement at sea shall be first deducted from the gross sum of prize money. This includes but is not limited to the arming and fitting out of the ship. When possible all materials necessary for the operation of the ship will be taken from captured prizes. Compensation for death and disability shall be listed on the same table as shares.

XII. If the "ship's company" includes a first officer for the purpose of navigation, he will be awarded the same shares as the quartermaster. The sum to be deducted from the gross sum of prize money to be placed in the ship's fund.

XIII. If a doctor is part of the "ship's company" he is to receive from theship's funds the expense of the chest of medicine. The doctor shall receive for himself the same shares as the quartermaster.

XIV. Any person who first spies or provides information, where a prize is taken and proves to be worth one hundred dollars a share, that man shall be given an extra fifty dollars.

Punishments:

Marooning – Any man who is to be marooned has the option of being keel-hauled for a period of not less than three minutes time. If the person decides to be marooned he shall be set ashore with one bottle of water, one small flask of powder, one small firearm, and a few shot.

Death – If a man is to be put to death, he shall be hanged from the mainmast yard arm at sunrise the day following his trial. He may also choose to be shot or cast over the side shackled to a ball and chain.

Table One

Shares

Captain	15 shares
Quartermaster, doctor, first officer	10 shares
Boatswain	5 shares
Gunner	5 shares
Carpenter	5 shares
Sail maker	5 shares
Ship's purser	5 shares
Armourer	5 shares
Able seaman, 2 years experience	2 shares
Ordinary seaman, some experience	1.5 shares
Ship's cook, captain's steward	1.5 shares
Others	1 share

Death and Disability

Death: If a man dies, his share goes to his wife or children. If he has neither, it is divided among the gross shares.

Disability:

Loss of an eye or joint	Fifty dollars
Loss of an arm or leg	Three hundred dollars
Loss of both eyes, loss of either both arms, both legs, or an arm and a leg	Five hundred dollars

The loss of use due to severe injury is the same as a loss.

CHAPTER ELEVEN

While it was not officially announced, everyone seemed to know the crew had three new members. Articles were signed, and they were bound together to face what came their way. Diamond spent much of each day teaching Cooper the names of each sail and mast. He discussed the running riggings, explained how yards could be maneuvered to catch the wind for optimal sailing. Diamond also explained how the yards were raised and lowered, each block and tackle, and also the purpose of the shrouds, the main chains, and the anchors. Cooper had purchased a small notebook in which he took many notes and made several sketches. At night, he'd look over his notes and review them and read his Falconer's. Diamond had told him to put the Young Sea Officers sheet anchor away for now. "That's for later," he said. "The best topman or seaman I got couldn't tell you cat shit about that book but they know how to handle this ship in calm or a blow. Learn the ship first and then we'll look toward the quarterdeck." *Good advice*, Cooper thought.

He'd gotten confident enough that he scampered aloft with the sail handler when Captain Taylor wanted the sails trimmed, taken in, or to make more sail. A tattooed, toothless, wizened topman always seemed to be around Cooper when they went aloft. "Remember lad, one hand for the ship and one hand for thyself." The topman was called Banty by the crew. The nickname having to do with his resemblance to a smallish, fighting fowl called a banty rooster. Cooper had never seen one but planned on having one pointed out to him when they went back to Grand Terre.

One day when the wind was a bit brisk, Banty took Cooper aloft, higher than Cooper had ever ventured. Normally, the heights didn't bother Cooper but with the wind tugging at his shirt and pushing at his face he felt queasy as they climbed. *God, I hope I don't fall, or worse shat my britches,* he thought. Up they went until they reached the topgallant yard. Giving a heave Banty grabbed a small yard and pulled himself up on the cap of the mainmast. He grinned his toothless grin and danced a little jig.

Horrified, Cooper knew the wind would sweep the idiot into the sea at any second or else he'd make a splat on the deck. "Damme, man, but have you been into the rum?" *Was he in his cups? How would he get the lunatic down*, Cooper wondered. A voice from below made Cooper look down. One glance and he grabbed hold of a line, he suddenly felt dizzy.

"Banty," Taylor yelled through a speaking trumpet. "You daft bugger, get your arse on deck instantly or by all that's holy I'll shoot you myself. Get my long rifle, Mr. Spurlock."

Grinning like an ape, Banty grabbed the small cross yard and did a handstand and then came down by Cooper. "Skylarkings over," Banty said. They climbed down to the top platform and grabbed a backstay and slid to the deck, Banty much faster than Cooper.

On deck, Quartermaster Turner grabbed Banty by the ear and led him forward for a tongue lashing. "If he was aboard a man o' war, he'd taste the cat for that trick," Mac snorted.

Taylor eyed Mac but didn't respond. Instead he placed a hand on Cooper's shoulder and handed him his handkerchief. Cooper's face was drenched in sweat and his hand burned. "Now, you know what not to do," Taylor said. "In truth, Banty has taken a shine to you and felt he was showing you a joy. Just don't let someone cause you to lose your sense of good judgment."

Cooper continued his on the job training. He soon got to the point he shunned the lubbers hole when making his way to the top platform. He spent time with the carpenter, the sailmaker, as well as the gunner. Every noon he took sightings with David MacArthur. "Bless me, Cooper, but you're now at least on the right continent." Cooper's first undertaking had them in the Black Sea. Having a very elementary knowledge of math, the noon sightings were the hardest to understand. His friend spent at least an hour after the evening meal going over problems.

"Hell's half acre," Mac swore one evening. "Damme, Cooper, but you got one right." After that things seem to come a little easier until all his problems were correct. His noon sightings were closer and closer and soon matched Mac's.

THE DAWN WAS BREAKING. You no longer needed the candles in the wheel binnacle to see. You could recognize people's faces as individuals instead of just shapes and shadows.

"It will be a warmish day I fear," Turner said. No one disputed him.

Aloft, a lookout yawned, stretched, and took his glass to scan the horizon. He swept past an area, and then quickly backtracked and focused his glass. Excited, he called down, "Sail ho." This was the first sail sighted since putting to sea.

Captain Taylor ordered *Raven* to be put about. It was nine o'clock by the time they drew within a mile or so astern of the chase. "She's British, a three masted freighter," the lookout called down.

The distance between the ships was closing fast. Everyone that had a telescope seemed to be focused in on the ship. "She's a merchantman," Taylor said, "low in the water so she's heavily loaded."

"Fourteen guns, seven a side," Spurlock advised.

"I don't like it, a ship that big, heavily laden and no escort," Taylor said. Taking his speaking trumpet, Taylor called up to the lookout, "Do you see another set of sails?"

"Nary a one," came the quick reply.

"Look about damn you, look about."

It was a full minute before the lookout called down again, "Horizon is clear all about."

"Very well," Taylor said half to himself. The ship was now a mile away. "Mr. Spurlock, I want all but the forward gun loaded with ball and grape. Load the swivels in the tops with grape. Something just doesn't set right with this fish."

Spurlock was soon back, "Guns ready, Captain."

Cooper didn't miss the difference in the way Taylor was addressed. Always with respect but generally much less formal. Spurlock was very formal in his reporting to Taylor. This was a time the men knew that the slightest error could cost lives if not the ship. The captain was now the law. His word was to be carried out without question, without a vote. *Damnation, what a change*, Cooper thought.

Taylor nodded to Spurlock, "Put one across her bow, Mr. Spurlock, but be ready. Any monkey business, give 'em a broadside."

"Aye, Captain," Spurlock replied.

"Damn! Of all the luck," Cooper said.

"What is it?" Taylor asked.

"See that flag, Captain, the yellow flag with a blue "F" inside the shield. That's a Finylson ship," Cooper said, excitement in his voice. "Same as what you took us on."

"Well, that's good to know, Coop, but why is she not sailing in convoy?" Cooper could only shrug.

BOOM...the forward gun fired. Immediately the chase lowered her sails. Raven trailed behind until the other ship was almost at a stop.

"Do you surrender," Taylor called across.

"Aye," came the reply.

"What ship you?" Taylor asked.

"A Finylson ship, the *Sea Rose*."

"Ask who's the captain," Cooper whispered, "it was John Lamb when I last heard."

"Who's your captain?" Taylor called.

"Captain Lamb."

"That ain't him talking," Cooper whispered again.

"Are you Captain Lamb?" Taylor asked.

"No sir, Captain Lamb is in bed."

Taylor gave Cooper a questioning look. Cooper replied, "He is old."

"Stand by to receive boarders. I will warn you that I have you covered with swivels loaded with grape," Taylor said. *That ought to put the fear of God into them,* Cooper thought. Turning toward Turner, the captain gave a slight nod.

"Grapnels away," Turner barked. Grapnels flew through the air and then men hauled taut as the two ship's hulls were pulled together. Boarders swung across from *Raven* to the *Sea Rose*. Finally Taylor, Diamond, and Turner went across. Spurlock staying aboard *Raven* to watch and have the guns fired if all was not as it seemed.

The young-looking mate, nervous with sweat dripping from his face spoke to Taylor, "You got a doctor with you?"

Taylor replied, "Sorry, lad, we don't carry one."

The mate gave a deep sigh, "I was hoping."

"Let's go below and see your captain," Taylor said.

Below in the captain's cabin, a smallish black woman shook her head when they entered. "That's Henrietta," the mate said. Walking over to the swinging cot, Taylor saw the ship's captain lying in a pool of sweat. His skin was ashen gray and he had a pulse but his pupils were fixed and dilated.

"He's almost gone," Henrietta said softly.

Tears came to the mate's eyes. "He was like a father to me. Damn their eyes. I hope Phillip rots in hell. The captain wanted to retire, to live out his days at home but Phillip, the black-hearted ass, said if he did he'd get no retirement. He'd signed a contract to make this voyage and he meant for the captain to honor his contract. Serves him right having this ship took."

"Sounds like Phillip," Cooper said.

"Why are you alone?" Captain Taylor asked.

"We sailed first to Halifax. There the captain took sick and so the convoy sailed without us. We wouldn't, we couldn't just leave the captain, you understand. After a week the captain seemed much better but soon he was looking bad again. I wanted to stop at Bermuda but the captain said it was better to hurry on to Antigua."

"What's your cargo?" Taylor asked.

"Mostly military supplies for the army garrison at Antigua. That and a few casks of wine, some odds and ends, ship supplies for English Harbour, and the rest is dry goods for merchants in Antigua."

"Is that all?" Taylor asked with a stern look. The mate swallowed so that his Adam's apple went up and down. "We will tear the ship apart if we have to," Taylor growled.

"There is a locked chest under the captain's desk. You pull up a few planks. It's in a between space," the mate replied.

Captain Lamb gave up the ghost by noon. Captain Taylor read from the prayer book and both crews stood by to give a good seaman a proper burial.

The two ships got underway then. Once Grand Cayman Island was sighted the crew that didn't wish to become free men were put into two longboats with their personal belongings. Captain Taylor gave the mate fifty guineas. "This should tide you over until you all get home."

"Thank you, Captain, for everything," he said.

A COMPLETE INVENTORY WAS carried out. There were bales of military uniforms that had little or no value. One bale was military cold weather coats.

"They were going to Antigua, didn't they say," Diamond asked.

"That's what they said," Cooper answered.

"Well, it's like the military to make a shitten mess of things. Who needs a winter coat in the West Indies? Maybe we can sell them, maybe we ought to just throw them over the side," Diamond said.

"Farmers will buy them," Taylor said, "them and the boots if we can't sell them to planters for their slaves."

"Bet don't nobody will want these damn brass buckles," a pirate named Harry said. He was bald all over.

"Well, those cannons, muskets, pistols, swords, powder, and shot will bring a nice profit," Turner said, joining the conversation.

Spurlock intervened saying, "Captain, those English cannons are good nine pounders. I'd like to use them and replace these old six pounders."

"Will *Raven* stand the recoil?" Taylor asked.

"May have to brace up the timbers a bit, Captain, but she'll hold," Spurlock answered.

"The extra weight might cost you a knot or two," Mac said, speaking for the first time.

"Tell me, Cooper," Turner asked, "do you think those sailors will tell, you were one of us that took their ship?"

"I don't know, but in truth, I don't give a damn. I want to ruin the Finylsons," Cooper replied.

"Well said," Spurlock declared. "Now, Rooster be a good mate and get us a bottle of rum while the captain counts the specie."

CHAPTER TWELVE

RAVEN AND HER PRIZE cruised for a month along the normal trade route without spotting another sail. They had decided to head back to Grand Terre when a small lugger was sighted. It was a small costal trader and she was heavily laden, sitting low in the water.

Captain Taylor had Spurlock put one across her bow and she hove to immediately. She only had ten crewmen: the captain, three sons, and six cousins. They were from Jamaica. The hold was full of good Jamaican rum and Spanish wines. From the looks of the ship, the captain and his family were not poor.

"How much were you to be paid for delivering your cargo?" Captain Taylor asked.

The man took off his hat and told the captain, "Twenty five guineas."

"For delivering a load of rum," Taylor snorted, giving the little captain an evil eye. It was not that far from Jamaica to Grand Cayman, which is where the invoice said the cargo was headed.

"Well, there is our personal items we were going to sell and what we would have carried back to Jamaica."

Not liking the idea that he was being duped, Taylor called for Mr. Diamond. "Put these men over the side with a cask of water. They can rig a sail with an oar. You can also throw in two bags of ship's biscuits."

Damme, Cooper thought, *I've seen a most generous and humble side to the captain, now I'm seeing the hard side.*

"Getting soft he is," Rooster declared. "Time was, he'd put them in a boat and drop the water cask in the boat."

It took a moment for Cooper to realize the significance of Rooster's comments. Dropping a water cask over the side meant it would go right through the boat's planks. They'd have to swim for it or drown. The captain decided they'd head back with the hopes of picking up a straggler in the Gulf of Mexico. Surprisingly to Cooper, Captain Taylor sent David MacArthur aboard the small island trader as prize master with a small prize crew. This showed his faith in Mac's abilities.

THE SUN WAS SINKING over the horizon and the sky had a reddish tint that seemed to merge with the Gulf waters.

"Grand Terre tomorrow," Quang said as he sat down to share a bottle of rum and cigars with Cooper. The ships were moving along with a soft breeze that was just enough to fill the sails.

"Not if the wind don't pick up," Diamond said as he walked by.

"It will be brisk before the night is over," Quang replied. "Storm to the east of us, we'll get some wind, maybe rain from it." Diamond eyed Quang but didn't dispute him.

Rooster walked up and greeted the two, "Captain wants you, Coop."

Cooper had lost some of his earlier anxiety when the captain called him but he couldn't help but wonder the reason for the summons. Entering the captain's cabin, Taylor pointed to a chair. "Yes sir," Cooper said as he was seated.

"Care for a glass of hock?" Captain Taylor asked.

"Aye, Captain, that would be nice." Private stores, Cooper decided.

"Rooster keeps a bottle in the bilges to keep it cool," Taylor said, as he poured a glass.

Cooper had started to develop a taste for rum since they'd set out on the voyage, but the hock went down well, arousing old taste buds used to the finer beverages. Rooster brought in two plates of roasted kid with a tangy sauce, sweet potatoes that were sliced thin and topped with butter and cinnamon. A loaf of bread that was not to stale was offered. There were no vegetables.

"Top your glasses?" Rooster asked. The captain nodded the affirmative. After topping the glasses, Rooster left.

So this was to be a private conversation. *Damnation,* Cooper thought, *am I about* to be *cast ashore*? The captain said only a few words during the meal. When he finished, he pushed his plate back and belched. "Hits the spot, does it not?" he asked.

"Aye," Cooper replied. "Not near as good as Belle's cooking or that in New Orleans but for sea fare it's not bad."

"Do you have any questions about the voyage thus far, Coop?"

Taking a last bite of the kid, Cooper thought as he chewed. "Is Barataria the only place we can sell our plunder?"

Taylor smiled, "Why do you ask?"

"I've always been told it's not good to put all your eggs in one basket, as it were," Cooper relied.

"Good Cooper. No, Barataria is just convenient for the time being. I also sell our products in Savannah and Charleston. Barataria has a good market for now. LaFitte is a good businessman; he doesn't try to cheat you and it's close to New Orleans."

"Meaning Debbie? I wondered if that might be an influence," Cooper said.

"To be successful you have to have the minimum of three things; product, market, and a place to rest," Taylor said. "You noticed we passed an American merchant trader our first day heading out to sea."

"Aye," Cooper said.

"We are pirates, Cooper. The penalty is death, usually by hanging. But no American can ever accuse us of taking one American vessel. I've gone out of my way a few times to help some American ship in distress. My name is well thought of in the southern states. I own, in partnership with a Colonel Jedidiah Lee, a small fleet of traders. I am a partner with two gentlemen, Mr. John Will and Mr. Brett Randle, in a group of warehouses and merchant ships in Savannah. So I have a place to lay my head when I need rest. We prey upon the British, the Spaniards, and to a lesser degree the French. I try not to kill anyone and I also try to be fair with the ship's master and crew if they behave. If not, we show no mercy. It's a risky game we play but one that is most rewarding. To be truthful, Cooper, it's one of which I begin to tire. I think another year and I'll pass this hellish game on to someone else."

"One of your crew," Cooper asked, picking up his glass. He was not ready for Taylor's response.

"Those rogues? Hell no. They are good men as blackhearts go, but we've argued more than once over how to run things. It comes down to whom they would rather have as a captain. If it's me, we do things my way. They've all been paid a King's ransom over the years by keeping me as captain and most have lived to enjoy their gains. Therefore, I'm still the *Raven's* captain. But I'm getting long in the tooth. They know it and accept it. Now, Cooper, let's get down to why I asked you here. Every since you met Sophia, you've been mooning over her like a lovesick cow. She took a shine to you as well. But the truth is, Cooper, she is not a free woman."

"Is she married?" Cooper asked.

"No…no, she's under contract." Seeing the puzzled look on his friend's face, Taylor topped their glasses with the rest of the hock and said, "Let me explain. First you will have to admit

New Orleans is like no other place you've been, probably not another place like it in the world. There are lots of free women of color in New Orleans. A good number of them have mated with whites. Plantation owners frequently bed their slaves. The result is often a child of mixed blood. Over the years these offspring have further mated until the black lineage is reduced and they have more white features than black. This has made for some beautiful women, as you have seen. Almost every man of substance has one of these women as a mistress and provides his sons with the same enjoyment. I know that you heard Pierre talk of the upcoming Quadroon Ball."

"Yes sir," Cooper replied.

"Well, when the females turn of age, a mother finds a suitable, might I add a wealthy, benefactor. A contract is negotiated where the girl becomes the man's mistress. It usually includes a place to live, an allowance, and recognition of any offspring along with provisions that they be provided for, including an education until they are of a certain age. Now, the lighter the skin of the girls, the higher the price. A mulatto, which means one black and one white parent, doesn't bring much unless someone takes a particular fancy to her. A quadroon is the designate for a person with one black grandparent and three white or Caucasian grandparents; another way to look at it is she's one quarter black and three quarters white. An octoroon is one eighth black and seven eighths white, and so on. The mothers of the girls start at an early age, by the time they have their first monthly I was told, to teach the girls how to pleasure a man. I have it on good word these mothers teach their girls to be virtuosos in the erotic arts. These arts are mentioned at the time a contract is negotiated."

"How long are these contracts?" Cooper asked, feeling almost as dejected as he did when he was forced to leave England.

"The arrangement usually ends if say it's for a planter's son and he gets married. However, it's not unheard of for it to last a lifetime. Marriages are sometimes arranged for financial benefit and therefore the man keeps his lover forever."

"Is Sophia a quadroon or an octoroon?" Cooper asked his voice barely audible.

"Sophia is a mustefina, Cooper. She is only one sixteenth black. With her beauty she is a prize indeed. I would not doubt she brought in ten thousand dollars."

"Why was she at Miz Cindy's?" Cooper asked.

"Ah…there lies the problem. Her contract was with a planter for his oldest son by the name of Henri d'Arcy. Henri got married but he must have bragged to his brother how skilled and pleasing Sophia was as a lover. He came home to Sophia's house to find his brother, Paul, trying to force himself on Sophia. A fight ensued and Paul was killed. Cain and Abel if you will. Sophia was sent to Cindy until things could be sorted out. So you see, Coop, she is not a free woman."

"Would Mr. d'Arcy sell her?" Cooper asked Taylor.

"I'm not sure," Taylor admitted. "If you like I will have Lawyer Meeks test the waters. But remember, Cooper, and I don't mean this to hurt you, Sophia must be some kind of lover for a man to kill his brother. If the father decided to sell her contract you'd better be prepared to defend your purchase, because I'm sure you will be challenged to a duel."

"So be it," Cooper said. "Let's see Mr. Meeks."

"Humph…," Taylor snorted, "you are forgetting one thing, Cooper. Do you have ten thousand dollars or more?"

Cooper's response didn't take the blink of an eye. "No, but you do. You can have every schilling I make until you are paid back."

"Cents, Cooper, in America it's dollars and cents. But just to ease your mind, I will have Jean LaFitte deliver a message to Mr. Meeks before we sail again."

Cooper looked at his friend, "Eli, do you mean it?"

"Aye, I do. So learn all you can, Coop, so you can increase your shares. Right now they don't amount to…as the English say, a fart or a farthing."

CHAPTER THIRTEEN

It was Sunday afternoon and a freshening breeze blew across Barataria Bay. Coop and Mac sat around the stern of *Raven* with several other crew members. Since signing the articles and having been a part of the recent voyage the last of the barriers had tumbled down. Men who had previously given a cautious acknowledgement now sat down with the newcomers, shared a tot of rum and engaged them in conversation. It was like a series of test that they had to pass. Cooper thought he'd become accepted when he fought LaRoche. He had in some quarters, but now no one kept their distance and the hands had taken him under their wings determined to make a seaman of him. A rum bottle was being passed around and cigars and pipes were being smoked.

One of the men, a man from Georgia named Moree, was trying to light a cigar and was having a devilish time of it. Mac handed his cigar so Moree could use it to light up. "This wind is something," Moree remarked.

His comment caused a little laugh and grin to break out on Johannes' face. Johannes was a German with a natural gift at painting and drawing sketches. Smiling, he looked at Moree and Banty and said, "Speaking of the wind made me think of Rooster and the captain's parrot." The mentioning of this incident caused the men to break out laughing. Banty laughed so hard, he cried.

"Must have been something," Cooper remarked. The three men were so hysterical, he found himself laughing with them.

Taking a swig from the bottle, Banty still laughing, was able to get out, "Tell 'em, Johannes."

It took a couple of attempts but Johannes got control of himself and told the story. "The captain was playing poque with Joseph Gaspiralli. He's a pirate who hangs around off the Gulf coast of Florida. Well, Joseph had some good cards but was short so he couldn't make the pot. He thought the captain was bluffing. So Joseph says, 'Eli, you're bluffing but I ain't got the coin to call you, unless you're willing to let me use this parrot to even up the pot.' Well, they'd known each other for a while and had always got along and were on friendly terms. So the captain allows Joseph to use the parrot to make up what he was short in the pot. Now, the captain had four of a kind and that beat Joseph's two pair. So, the captain now had a parrot. Thought it made him more seaman like to own such an exotic bird. The parrot's name was Salty. He was a nasty mouthed, umgh...who ever taught that bird to talk was a foul mouthed something. Captain wouldn't even take him around Miz Russell. Damn bird would see a woman and say, 'Mutton, fine piece of mutton.' He'd also say, 'Damme, what catheads, look what catheads.'"

Banty interrupted and said, "Catheads means tits."

"Hush Banty," Moree said. "They know that. Ain't everyone who's dumb as you."

Johannes waited for the others to hush and then he continued, "That wasn't all the bird would say. He had Turner hopping one time squawking out, 'Weigh anchor, weigh anchor', and then he would follow that with 'Move your arse.' It happened on a night like this but we were underway, the captain's door was flung open with a bang and the captain came running out just a cussing Rooster. Right behind the captain, Salty come flying out and landed on a ratline. Fact is, Banty was about to go up to take his watch. As Salty flew out the cabin he was just a squawking, 'Who shat, who shat, awk…who shat.' He landed on the ratline and his little claws closed around it and one more time he squawked, 'who shat.' He no more got who shat out of his mouth than he twisted his little head around and said, 'I'm dead' and damned if he didn't just fall still holding on to the ratline but his head was pointing to the deck. Banty took hold of him and the captain looked at his parrot and shouted at Rooster, 'Damn you, Rooster, damn you. You have the vilest wind of any human I've ever met. Now your stinking winds done killed my bird. I ought to keel haul you.'"

"He died," Mac asked.

"We thought he was dead, but Banty was rubbing on the little bugger's chest and he came around. "

"What happened to him?" Cooper asked.

"We were right here at Barataria one night when Gambi yelled at some wench. She was petting Salty and when Gambi shouted like he did; the bird flew up in a tree. We couldn't coax him down and the next morning Salty was gone. Captain said if Salty didn't want to be around Gambi that was reason enough for us to keep away from him and his kind. Of course, the captain told Gambi face up if he found out he'd done mischief to his bird he'd get him another parrot and its first meal would be Gambi's liver."

"Strong words," Cooper said.

"Aye," Johannes replied, "but the captain meant it. He figures it was Gambi who sicked LaRoche on you, Cooper. Of course, he was a dead man time he stopped at your table, he just didn't know it. Had you not run him through, the captain would have blasted him."

"But I would have been just as dead," Cooper said.

"Aye, there's that," Banty acknowledged for the others. "But your ghost would have rested well knowing your killing had been revenged."

Grabbing the rum, Cooper took a long pull and swallowed hard. "Well, that's right comforting, Banty, I'm sure my ghost appreciates it."

BELLE HAD FIXED A lunch of fried catfish, warmed over breakfast biscuits that were served with butter and honey. Fish, shrimp, and crawfish seemed to be a staple around Cindy's place.

"It's cheap and there's plenty of it," Gus said smacking his lips over the honey and biscuits.

When there weren't a lot of guests, Belle, Gus, and Jumper would eat at the kitchen table with Cindy. Cooper and Mac had become more like family or at least like regulars so nothing special was laid out. That morning Cooper had accompanied Gus as he took care of the small grove of orange trees he had planted.

"It ain't no regular grove," Gus admitted, "but it was worth a try. Our weather ain't that much different than Florida; only it's a might colder in the winter. I'll put out smudge pots if it's likely to freeze. No bigger than this grove is that ought to keep them from freezing."

"It's a lot of work," Cooper said.

"Yeah it is, but fresh oranges and orange juice is good. Belle can make marmalade and put up preserves. Umph…makes my mouth water thinking about it," Gus said.

On the way to the kitchen for lunch, Gus related that a produce man on Market Street had offered to buy all the oranges Gus brought him. As they neared the house, Mac, Lucy, and Linda were walking up. "Jumper's got himself a big ole gator," Lucy exclaimed.

"Has to be four feet long at least," Linda added.

"Well, that's big enough for the boy to handle," Gus said, "but it ain't no big 'un. Some of these gators are eight to ten feet long and I've heard of big ole granddaddies that are over twelve feet long. Jumper better stay shy of the big boys."

At the lunch table Cindy put down her glass of tea and asked, "Cooper, have either you or David written to your mother or family?"

Cooper looked down at his plate and mumbled, "I have been meaning to. I've never been a good hand at writing but I guess I need to just do it."

"There's a desk with writing materials in the den," Cindy said. "I expect at least a page before the evening meal. That goes for you as well, David."

"I'm not sure if I should address it to mother at the Finylson's manor or where," Cooper said.

"Don't worry," Cindy told Cooper. "Lawyer Meeks will send it to a friend in Portsmouth. He will get the letters to where they need to go. Return mail will follow the same procedure, unless you tell your mother where you are, she'll never know. She will have a means to correspond and that means a lot to a mother."

"Thank you, madam, that was very thoughtful of you to think of it," Cooper said.

"Aye," David added.

After lunch, Cooper was able to talk with Cindy alone for a few minutes. "I'm sure you know the captain is trying to buy Sophia's contract." Cindy nodded yes.

"The captain said it was you who suggested it. Thank you," Cooper said. "Do you think it wise that I visit her?"

"No, not at this time, she is away from it all and while she would love to be with you, she realizes it would only bring trouble down on you," Cindy said in a sincere voice. "We have not told her of the negotiations," Cindy added.

"Why not?" Cooper asked.

"What if they refuse, Cooper? There's no need to get her hopes up only to be dashed if negotiations fail."

A determined look came over Cooper and his voice was harsh. "I'll steal her if I have to and they can all be damned."

Cindy placed her hand on Cooper's arm. "Don't you know, my dear friend, she'd never go. Her mother made and signed the contract. She has been paid. Sophia would never dishonor her mother by running off. It would ruin the family. They'd have to pay back the money received and if there's another daughter she'd never be able to receive a good contract. The family would be tarnished."

"Damn it all," Cooper hissed. "She has been the one hope of happiness since...since this," Cooper said, touching the scar on his face. He had tanned from being at sea and in the elements, but the scar hadn't. It stood out, a very white line that was the width of a person's small finger.

Unable to think of a reply, Cindy stood on her tiptoes and reaching out pulled Cooper's head down and kissed him on the scar. "My brave buccaneer friend," she said.

CHAPTER FOURTEEN

R*AVEN* SAILED WITH THE tide the following Friday. The weather was clear and fair. Captain Taylor had decided to change to a different hunting ground. With all her canvas raised, *Raven* seemed to fly across the ocean.

"Twelve…fifteen knots, I'd swear," Turner volunteered. Within a few days they'd left the Gulf of Mexico and were plowing through the Atlantic.

"Fine sailing weather," Captain Taylor swore as Mac and Cooper took the noontime sightings. Not a cloud in the sky. When they finished with the noon sights, Mac compared his figures with Cooper's and danced a little jig.

"Damnation, Coop, you are spot on. I've finally got you trained. Cooper's got it right," Mac yelled. The crew roared in response, whistles, cat calls, and good-natured jibs.

"That felt good, Mac," Cooper told his friend.

"Now iffen you can find your way into some whore's drawers you'll be a true pirate," Banty quipped.

A peaceful night followed but just before Cooper got ready for his hammock, the lookout called down, "Lights off the larboard bow, Captain. Might be stern lights."

Taylor slung a glass over his shoulder and tugged at the leather strap, making sure it was properly secured. A good night glass didn't come cheap and you couldn't get another in the middle of the ocean. Grabbing hold of a shroud Taylor climbed up the ratlines about ten feet. Looping his arm around the shroud he took the glass off his shoulder and focused in on the sighting. Without saying a word he backed down to the deck and called Mac and Turner over.

"Its stern lights, I'm sure. I think the ship was tacking the way the lights were there one minute and then disappeared. I think we'll change course and follow. It might prove to be a suitable prize, if not all we've lost is a few hours."

Sail handlers were called to tack and *Raven* swung around on her new course. The crew was excited and several bets were secretly made on what the dawn would bring. Sleep seemed to elude Cooper, as he, like the rest of the crew was anxious and excited to see what the morning would bring. When sleep finally came, it was filled with dreams of Sophia. She was on the ship they were chasing. She stood on the stern waving and calling to him but the ship continued to outdistance *Raven*. Every inch of canvas was put on *Raven* but still the ship with Sophia grew further and further away.

Cooper woke up in a sweat. Someone was shaking his hammock. "You alright, Coop." It was Johannes. Rising a bit, Cooper wiped his face with a shirt sleeve. "I was dreaming," he stammered.

"Must have been a bad one," Johannes said. "You were screaming like the imps of hell were after you."

"Sorry mate, I think I'll get up," Cooper said.

"It's almost dawn anyway," the German told Coop as he stood back so Cooper could rise.

MAC TOUCHED COOPER'S ARM as he came on deck. "Bad night?"

"Aye, bad enough," Cooper told his friend, wondering how Mac knew. "Was I that loud?" Cooper asked.

"Loud enough you woke the whole mess," Mac said with a laugh, trying to make light of the incident. "They think you're chasing demons. You know how superstitious sailors are," Mac said.

"I was dreaming of Sophia," Cooper whispered.

"I figured," Mac replied. "But don't tell the men. It's better that they think otherwise."

"Sail ho!" the lookout called down.

"Where away," Captain Taylor shouted, more than a little aggravation in his voice.

The reply came back quickly with a full report. "Straight off the bow, Captain, I make it a small convoy. Six sets of sails. Indiamen they be."

"That's more like it," Taylor snorted. "It's a good day for it," he said.

"Aye," Diamond agreed.

The wind was favorable and the sky was clear. All sail handlers were called again as Taylor ordered all canvas clamped on. Within the hour it was obvious they were overtaking the last ship in the convoy. The hands went about their morning routine as usual. Breakfast was cold biscuits and cheese and a small beer. It was not much but the men were too excited to care.

"We'll have that 'un before noon," Spurlock predicted.

"Or sooner," Mac joined in.

"Ten dollars on it," Banty said.

"No betting," Taylor growled. "You knows better."

It was eleven o'clock when Captain Taylor called to Spurlock, "Put one across her bow, if you please."

"Aye, sir." Spurlock already had his crew ready, anticipating the order. As soon as the word was passed the starboard forward gun boomed. There was no reaction from the chase ship, however.

"Put one through her jib, Mr. Spurlock, this 'un is a bit stubborn."

"Aye, Captain."

The gun crews quickly sighted the gun in. Another boom was heard and a hole was seen in the jib sail. A gunport opened on the Indiaman and a gun was run out and fired. Cooper didn't see where the ball landed but it was nowhere near *Raven*.

"That was for his honor," Taylor told Cooper and Mac. "The rascal can now say he resisted."

"What if he'd hit us?" Cooper asked.

"He'd be a dead man," Taylor replied in a stoic voice. "Mr. Diamond, let's let him have a moment of honor and then run up the red flag."

Cooper turned to Mac and asked, "No mercy?"

"Aye," his friend replied. "The captain has played the game now it's time to heave to or pay the consequence."

"Trouble is while we are playing the other ships are getting away," Cooper swore.

"Can't be helped," Mac said.

A squeak was heard as the red flag was run up. "Truck needs grease," Diamond said, thinking aloud. Once the red flag was run up the sails came off the chase. The name across the stern proclaimed the ship to be the *Cambridge*.

"She's an Honest John ship," Mac said. "She's returning from either India or China and she's heavily laden. We might have struck upon a fair prize here."

Grapples shot through the air as the two ships closed together. Soon after, the Indiaman's deck swarmed with the *Raven's* crew. Taylor called for the captain, and a man who'd been standing behind the first officer came forward.

"Hell's bells," Mac swore and moved up to confront *Cambridge's* captain. "If it ain't Captain Sodomite. This is my old captain," Mac said to all those within hearing. "He had Lieutenant Martin's throat cut, drowned our poor little cabin boy and had rape charges hanging over my head so I had to resign my commission or face trumped up charges. Now, you are at my mercy, you buggering bastard."

"Please," the captain begged as fear gripped him, "I made a mistake. I've changed, I swear."

"No, he hasn't," a young voice squealed. "He's used me most violently. I can barely hold my bowels at times. Says he'll have my mum and sisters turned out of their cottage if I tell. He even said he'd put me over the side one night if I told."

Slap! The captain backhanded the cabin boy, who fell to the deck. "Don't listen to Hector, he lies."...the last word was drawn out as a look of pain filled the captain's eyes and he cried out as he crumpled to the deck. Hector had grabbed his knife and stabbed the man, severing his spine.

"I...I can't feel my legs," the captain cried.

"Good," Hector replied and spit in his tormentor's face. "I may hang but you'll never bugger another boy," Hector blurted as tears streamed down his face.

"At last," Mac said, "revenge is mine. Cast him over the side," he ordered without consulting Captain Taylor. Two of *Cambridge's* own seaman picked up the crumpled man and walked toward the rail.

"Wait," the captain screamed. "I can't swim."

"If I thought you could, I'd run you through first," Mac retorted and then made a motion to continue with his hands. Over the side, Captain Sodomite went screaming, even as he splashed into the Atlantic, the scream turned into gurgles as he sank and disappeared.

"Are you alright, lad?" Captain Taylor asked Hector, who still had tears in his eyes.

"Aye," the boy sniffed.

"Well, what to do with you," Taylor said. He called Bond, *Cambridge's* first officer, and Mac over to the lee rail. "The boy has suffered enough," Taylor said as he and the men talked.

A decision was made soon, and Taylor called Hector over. "We have talked and the first officer has agreed to say pirates took the ship, killing the captain in the process. This will leave you free of charges and you can go home to England. The other choice is to come with us and the likelihood is you'll never see your family or England again."

Looking at the *Cambridge's* first officer, Hector spoke, "If I won't be charged I'd like to go home."

"You won't be, lad. We've had a suspicion you were being abused but couldn't prove it. We'd also heard our captain had been cashiered from the Navy. There's not much that will put a captain on the beach so we all suspected something was amiss."

THE PRIZE DID PROVE to have a valuable cargo: silks by the bale, jade, Oriental china that was hand painted, and tea of the highest quality. The captain's cabin was searched and only a small amount of coin, both gold and silver, was found. "Most of the captain's money was tied up in personal ventures," Bond advised them. All of which made its way aboard *Raven*. A case, almost like one dueling pistols came in, was found in the captain's desk. In it was six pipes made of meerschaum and intricately carved. One was an elephant, another a tiger, the third pipe was a ship's bow, the fourth one a ship's wheel, the fifth was an anchor, and the last pipe was crossed swords.

Mac went to Turner, the quartermaster, and Captain Taylor. "I found these," he said, "and I'd like to buy them if I may, either in coin or taking it from my shares."

"We'll put it to a vote," Turner responded. "But I see no reason why the crew will not approve it."

"They are beautiful," Cooper said to Mac after the ships got underway. "What are you going to do with them?"

"Gifts," Mac replied. "They'll be gifts."

CHAPTER FIFTEEN

AFTER TAKING THE *CAMBRIDGE*, Captain Taylor clamped on all sails but by dark they still had not sighted the convoy. Therefore, Taylor had the *Raven* put about and resumed their original course. They were off Cape Verde when the next sails were sighted; a large convoy with escorts.

"A frigate and another large ship, Bombay buccaneers," Taylor snorted.

"That's the *Cornwall's,*" Mac volunteered, lowering his glass. "I've seen her in Portsmouth. The frigate might be the *Bombay*. They sailed together the last time I saw them."

"Buccaneer ships, they sail with the convoy?" Cooper asked.

"*Bombay* buccaneers are what the Navy dubbed them," Mac said smiling at his friend's confusion. "The real title is *Bombay* marines. They are a fleet of private warships owned by the Honourable East India Company. A tough lot they are too. I'd recommend letting them pass."

"Aye," Taylor agreed. "No use losing what we got. Prepare to come about, Mr. Turner. Let's show them a fair set of sails."

Nothing else was spotted after a week of traversing across the Atlantic. They were off the coast of Africa when Turner and Mac approached Captain Taylor. "Do we round the Cape of Good Hope or put about, Captain?"

"Put about, I think," Taylor decided.

It was noon and *Raven* was off the northern coast of Africa on a course for Cape Verde with a fair wind when a sail was spotted dead astern.

"She be overreaching us, Captain," the quartermaster advised. By four o'clock the ship could be seen from the deck. "She's a frigate," Johannes called down from the tops where he had lookout duty. "Looks British made, Captain, but I believe she's flying a Spanish flag. Wind ain't right to get a proper view."

Captain Taylor spoke to his quartermaster, "Let's feed the hands, Mr. Turner, and then prepare for battle. Mr. Spurlock, once we've been fed I'd admire you take the larboard side, and Mr. MacArthur, you the starboard side."

We must be in for a fight with the captain being so formal, Cooper thought. After the crew had been fed, Taylor had the hands put to battle stations. The order was repeated by Turner and the hands began to scurry to their assigned stations.

"Raise the American flag," Taylor ordered. The ship kept coming and was bearing down on *Raven*.

"Not a good wind," Turner mused. "Fair winds all day and then when you need it, its contrary."

Cooper had been assigned to the quarterdeck as messenger. "Walk about when the firing starts, Coop. No need to give them a good target," Turner said.

"Aye," Cooper replied, glad someone was thinking about him.

Puffs of smoke could be seen from the frigate followed by a boom; a ball splashed one hundred yards astern.

"Put your helm down," Taylor called to the helmsman. The next shot was far off the mark but the following one was closer. "Up your helm," Taylor called. "Hold it for the count of one hundred and then go back to our original course."

Cooper realized Taylor was making it hard for the enemy to get a good target. Taylor was doing for *Raven* what he told Cooper to do…move about.

"Mr. Spurlock."

"Aye, Captain."

"Do you reckon we are within range with our stern guns?" Taylor asked.

"Close, I'd say, Captain."

"I'd admire you show yonder ship that we are not toothless."

"Aye, Captain." Spurlock soon had the stern guns ready. The first shot created a water spout about twenty-five yards off the frigate's larboard bow. The next time both stern guns roared, causing twin clouds of white smoke to drift back into the ship.

"The winds have shifted in our favor," Taylor commented, looking up at the sails. Cooper was sent down to the cabin where Spurlock had the stern guns hauled in and they were being sponged out. "Captain says you have straddled her," Cooper relayed.

"Aye," was Spurlock's only response. "Prime your guns," Spurlock roared as the guns were made ready to fire again. "Aim 'em," Spurlock snarled. "Damn it, aim the bloody guns you idjets. That's it, that's it, me hearty's, on the up roll fire." Again *Raven's* stern chasers fired, with the smoke causing the men to cough and their eyes to burn.

"Sponge out," Spurlock shouted, "that's it. Handsomely now, times a wasting, load 'em with shot and a measure of grape. If we don't get a direct hit maybe we can sprinkle a few of the sods." Once again Spurlock gave the order, "Fire."

Grape and round shot erupted from the hot muzzles of the guns and flames belched forward to drive the shot home into the frigate's bow.

"Lovely shooting, mates," Spurlock said just before a ball crashed into *Raven's* stern. Men shrieked in agony as a second shot slammed into the stern. The larboard gun was overturned and all but one of its crew was dead. The enemy's guns had found their target.

Cooper winced in pain as a sharp object struck his chest. One of the gun crew's severed arm had hit Cooper square in the chest. Looking at what had been the gun crew, bile rose up in Cooper's throat and he feared he would vomit. Blood was spurting from one of the downed men. The rest of the men lay in a heap under the overturned gun, torn and bleeding as the last of their blood pumped out onto the deck planks by dying hearts. The gun captain, the only one who had survived, was sweating profusely, his face a pasty white color, with his leg caught under the gun carriage.

"Move yourself, Cooper. Tell the captain we need more men," Spurlock barked.As Cooper rushed off, Spurlock was rising from the deck apparently unhurt. He got his surviving crew members together and lifted the gun carriage from the trapped man. He then had the starboard gun loaded and run out. He sighted the long nine himself and fired on the up roll. The crew shouted as the ball hit the frigate's bow sprit. Hanging by ropes the shattered bow sprit acted like a sea anchor as the frigate came almost to a stop and slewed around to starboard.

Maybe it was the sudden stop, maybe it was a lucky ball, but the forward mast followed and came down with a crash almost as loud as a cannon firing.

Seeing the ship come to a stop, Taylor called Mac and Turner over. "I intend to cross the frigate's bow and pour a broadside into her. I'll teach the whoresons to fire on me ship. Mac, I want you to fire every gun into the bow. Aim each one and fire as you bear. If we've not sunk her after the first pass, I'll try to come about and give her another dose. Mr. Turner, make sure we don't allow the frigate's broadside come to bear. Those are twelve pounders at least on the frigate and the *Raven* will not stand to their punishment."

Raven came about and Mac shouted at the gun crews. "Direct your fire to the bow. The bow is your target. Punch a hole clear through to her arsehole. Double shot, double shot, you idiot, not shot and grape. There you are. Now, gun captains, direct your fire and make sure you aim true." Mac watched as the gun captains directed each crew and raised their hands signaling they were ready.

A voice from the quarterdeck called out, "Be ready, Mr. MacArthur." Mac bent over and looked out of the gunport. They were no more than two hundred yards from the frigate. "Ready," he called out. "Gun captains, fire as you bear."

BOOM...BOOM...BOOM, *Raven's* guns fired one after another until the entire broadside had spewed out its fiery hell. The swivel guns barked out their loads of grape spraying a lethal swarm of lead balls cutting down a number of men trying to cut away the wreckage. The double-shotted nine pounders tore through the bowels of the frigate. Shouts and screams floated across the water. Curses of mad, wounded, and scared seamen could be heard. The wounded ship then leapt up from the ocean followed by a large explosion as flames engulfed the frigate.

"Hit the magazine," Taylor said, speaking in a low soft voice now that the battle rage was off him. Men watched, awed at the horror and destruction before them.

As the frigate sank, the men turned to righting the *Raven*. The gun captain's leg was so bad the carpenter had to amputate it. However, the gun captain died just as the leg was removed. One of the helmsmen had had a ball pass thru him. "Shot clean through," the carpenter swore. "No ball to fester, nothing in the wound to cause ill humors."

"Thank Gawd," the man said, and then yelled as rum was poured on and through the wound.

"Told by a surgeon that helps," the carpenter volunteered.

"Well, you could have given me a tot first," the helmsman cursed.

"Could have been worse," the carpenter shot back.

"Aye, and it could 'ave been better," the wounded man shot back, determined to have the final word.

Later that evening the crew puzzled over who it was that chased them and why. "Possibly a ship sent out to make us pay for our past deeds." Taylor mulled the thought over for a while. "Could have been. We've hit the British convoys hard of late."

"Some not hard enough," Cooper said.

"I think we have," Taylor answered in a stern voice. "Let's be burying our dead and putting *Raven* back to rights.

"Captain," Mac called. "Nothing against the carpenter but why don't we have a surgeon? Wounds like that happen in the Navy and the surgeon saves most of them."

Taylor nodded. "I'll not dispute the need, Mac, but I've yet to see a surgeon volunteer on his own accord to be part of a free ship. But if you find one, we'll welcome him. He wouldn't even have to sign the articles; being a man of medicine he'd be exempt."

Well, it's worth thinking on, Mac decided to himself.

At sundown, the dead were given their last farewells. In canvas shrouds, with round shot at the feet and a last stitch through the nose, the dead were buried as was a sailor's right.

CHAPTER SIXTEEN

On deck, Diamond had the hands hard at work. The channels were cleaned, the decks holystoned, and the sides washed off with fresh water. Hammocks were stowed away. Awnings and wind sails had been brought up from below. The hawse-bucklers had been removed and the anchors had been taken off the bow, anchor-buoys had been rigged; all in preparation for anchoring. The damage that the frigate had inflicted upon the *Raven* had mostly been repaired. It stood out from lack of paint, but that would be taken care of in the safety of Barataria Bay.

Cooper's knees were sore from holystoning the deck. Banty had been next to Cooper earlier that morning when preparation for entering the harbor and anchoring had started. "Captain ain't no slouch when it comes to the *Raven*," he said. "He runs a tight ship 'e does, unlike Black Ceasar and some of his like. Time you get within hailing distance the stench hits you square in the face. Man with weak innards would cast his bout over the side before he could board." Banty always amused Cooper. One time he'd say he and the next time it would be 'e. The more excited the little man was the more slang he used. "'Em buggars wouldn't last a day wid the captain, they wouldn't. They feel deck work is beneath 'em."

Cooper was smiling at Banty's talk when the seaman caught his smile. "You thinks it's funny," Banty snarled.

Thinking fast, Cooper said, "No, I could just imagine one of the rogues telling Mr. Diamond he wasn't going to do his part."

"Aye," Banty smiled. "It'd be fun to watch only it wouldn't last long, that is unless the bugger could swim, cause Mr. Diamond would throw 'is arse over the side." Cooper thought, *Whew, got out of that one.*

Robinson was climbing onto the fore-chains with a lead-line in his hand. They had anchored here many times but Captain Taylor took nothing for granted. He'd play it safe and take soundings. Cooper looked about and realized just how much he'd taken for granted and overlooked. It was easy when you were a passenger. A lubber as Mac put it. Both Mac and the captain said the trip to the quarterdeck started forward, meaning you had to learn to be a seaman before you could be the captain.

Mac said he'd been a midshipman for four years before making lieutenant. "I was given every shitten job that could be found," he swore. "No matter how good a job I did, there was always someone that would find fault in it. You have to start at the bottom, Coop, as it should be, but at least the captain and crew have taken to you and are willing to teach you. In the Navy, most of the snobbies, that's slang for a midshipman, are jealous and afraid you'll catch the first lieutenant or captain's eye before they do, so they'll screw you every chance they get. Of course, the captain's usually got some toady willing to put a knife in your back." The surprised look on Cooper's face caused Mac to laugh. "Figuratively only, Coop. Figurative of speech."

THE ENTRANCE OF THE bay was just off the bow when Captain Taylor called to Mac, "Mr. MacArthur, you took us to sea, would you care to bring us to anchor?"

"Aye, Captain, it will be a pleasure," Mac replied.

Cooper stood envious as Mac took to the quarterdeck and picked up the speaking trumpet. He turned his head and had a private word with the captain. *Probably asked where he wanted to anchor,* Cooper thought. Coop had learned Captain Taylor did not like getting too close inshore so that weighing anchor might prove difficult.

"All hands, prepare to bring ship to anchor."

Cooper was proud of the trust and responsibility his friend had been given. He watched intently, thinking one day that'll be me.

"Stand by to take in flying jib, royals, and studding sail," Mac barked.

"Haul taut! Shorten sail!"

"Come on, Coop, move your arse," Banty said, grinning like some fool. "It'll be a warm whore ashore tonight."

"What whore'd have you, Banty?" Looking over, Banty saw Moree had spoken.

"Oh, they's plenty," Banty said and then crowed like a rooster.

"Man topgallant clew lines."

"Sounds like 'e's on a man 'o war," McKemie grunted.

"Aye, trained right he was," Robinson responded.

"Haul taut!"

"In topgallants!"

"Up foresail!"

The ship must appear to be mass confusion to a landsman, Cooper decided, remembering when the *Bonnie Lass* first sailed. *But they don't know what I do…or as Banty might say, 'What I does.'*

"Helm alee!"

"Main topsail clew lines!"

"Haul taut!"

"Let go topsail sheets!"

Breathing hard from exertion, Cooper shouted, "You is right, Banty, thinks 'e's still in the bloody navy, 'e does." *Damme, now I sound like Banty, God I love this,* Cooper thought.

"He's yer mate," Robinson said with a grin. He too was breathing hard.

"Aye, I'll claim him," Cooper replied.

"Haul taut!"

"Let go topsail sheets!"

"Top bowlines!"

"Clew up!"

"Down jib!"

"Haul out the spanker!"

"Settle away the topsail halliards!"

"Square away!"

"Stand clear the starboard cable!"

"Stream the buoy!"

"Let go the anchor!"

At last, Cooper thought, then remembered he had to be part of the party to rig awnings and wind sails.

THE THREE DAY TRIP to New Orleans had been a miserable one. Misty, wet weather that had increased to a steady drizzle. At times, you were fighting a wind that drove right into your face, making the pirogues difficult to pole. Repairs had been completed on *Raven* including a new color scheme. This was to disguise the ship if there were indeed pirate hunters after the successful *Raven*, who had probably done more than any other ship to raise the insurance rates levied by Lloyds of London. Had it been a ship Lloyds had sent out to sink or capture the *Raven*? Captain Taylor mused this possibility over, time and time again. Or... was it some rogue who wanted the *Raven* and felt that due to the ship's size, the smaller *Raven* would be easy prey. Well, if that was the case they paid dearly for their mistake.

Captain Eli Taylor was not a man to give up all so peacefully. He was a fighter, a leader, and his men were alive with healthy purses because of his leadership.

"Aye, he's a man to follow," Mac had said. "Not a cruel man but one that can be as hard as the situation dictates."

Quang had decided to stay in Barataria. He was not sure his transgressions in New Orleans had had sufficient time to be forgotten. Rooster and Diamond were in the captain's pirogue and Robinson and a new seaman, Bridges, were in Cooper's. Mac had decided to go to Cindy Veigh's house in the hopes of spending time with Lucy. He had bought a few gifts, silk and jade for Lucy, Linda, and Cindy. He also had a nice knife for Jumper, a long rifle for Gus, and a nice bolt of cloth for Belle.

Cooper wanted the best for his friend but was sure his heart would be broken in the end. It was unlikely that Lucy's father would ever let his daughter's hand be taken by a commoner. If the knowledge that Mac was a pirate became known there wouldn't be a chance in hell. But, why speak about what both the lovers surely must know. Let them enjoy the time while they had it.

When the pirogues tied up in New Orleans, the men all went separate ways. Rooster, Banty, and Bridges made for a bordello on Conde Street. The establishment had a doctor on staff who examined the girls on a weekly basis and any not passing examinations were put on leave until she proved to be symptom free. Any girl who was unwell after a month was turned out and the money put up for retirement was given to her.

The upscale bordello was run by Madam Toussaint, who was affectionately called Dutchess, and was a fair hostess. Only men who had the means entered the doors of her parlor. Fewer still made it to the backrooms where high stake card games went on Friday and Saturday nights. Admittance was by invitations only and a new guest had to put up ten thousand dollars prior to admission. If, at any time, the sum was reduced the player had to replenish the account by the following Friday or he was not eligible to resume play. More than one fortune had been lost and won in the Dutchess's rooms without any ill behavior. The Dutchess received five percent from the winnings and this was split with her silent partners, Captain Eli Taylor and lawyer Edward Meeks. The men each received one and a quarter percent each. Just that small percent had made for comfortable living and had in fact purchased Hotel Provincial.

Cooper accompanied Captain Taylor to his hotel, where he was fondly greeted by Otis and later Debbie Russell. Supper that evening was in the hotel's main dining room. Both Cooper and the captain had steak cooked medium rare, succulent shrimp that had been grilled and then glazed with a sweet sauce, potatoes that had been sliced and chopped and cooked with the peelings on them with a cheese melted over them. A fine wine was served with the meal and later for dessert, egg custard and coffee. The coffee was fine roasted but without the chicory. After the meal, cigars were lit as the group made their way out to the small courtyard. A chocolate drink, a liqueur was served and while Cooper's taste went to straight alcohol or wine, he enjoyed the drink.

"It's called an Irish Crème," Debbie said when asked about the drink. "It's becoming the fashion for New Orleans where couples or ladies are served." The drinks were finished and cigars were down to a nub when Debbie broke the news. "We have a note from lawyer Meeks in regards to Sophia. He said the transaction looked promising and requested he be called upon when next you were in town."

"Damme, but that's good news," Cooper swore, and then apologized for his language.

"No apology necessary, my dear. Remember I've come to overlook such language from my dear sailor." Taylor feigned hurt but Cooper insisted he was out of order.

Sleep was difficult that night. At six a.m., Cooper was up. He called for hot water to fill the tub in his suite and took a bath and shaved. He decided to put on a fresh set of clothes. He had put on fresh clothes before dinner the previous evening but they smelled of tobacco smoke. After dressing he went downstairs. Otis was headed to the dining room to eat. It was just seven a.m., most people in the crescent city would not be up for a hour and the banks and lawyer offices would not open until nine. Heading to the dining room, they passed Mademoiselle Renee. She gave Coop a coy look.

"That's one more woman," Otis whispered. *I wonder if that's experience speaking,* Cooper thought to himself, smiling at Otis.

"I don't expect Miz Debbie until ten a.m.," Otis volunteered, changing the subject.

"The captain will be dressed and ready long before that," Cooper responded. Years of getting up before dawn to see what the horizon offered made it unlikely for the captain to be able to lay in bed for long.

Otis called for scrambled eggs, grits, bacon cooked crisp, and black coffee. Cooper had never eaten scrambled eggs to his recollection so he tried them. He was even more surprised when not only did Otis put butter on his grits, he stirred the scrambled eggs into them and then added salt and a heavy topping of black pepper.

"Oh well," Cooper said, in for a penny in for a pound. The concoction was very tasty, as were the fig preserves that were liberally applied to the still warm buttered biscuits.

"Miz Russell has a regular chef for the evening meals but a free black woman does breakfast and lunch. She's near as good as Belle, not quiet but almost," Otis told Cooper. He then leaned over and whispered, "But don't tell her Belle is better or she'll quit."

Cooper was right. Captain Taylor walked in while he and Otis were having their second cup of coffee. Like Cooper, Taylor had finished his toiletry and put on fresh clothes. As he sat down by Cooper, the faint air of perfume could be picked up. Miz Russell must have snuggled close for him to still have her perfume on the captain. That or they had had an early morning

tryst.

Looking at Cooper, Taylor snarled, "What are you looking at?"

"Nothing sir, just amazed at how cheerful you look and… ahem…smell this morning," Cooper replied.

"Go to Hades, Cooper. If you don't shut your trap, I'll have Otis tell the livery man to put the barouche away."

"I'll mind my manners," Cooper said.

"You better," the captain said with a smile as he opened the Louisiana Gazette.

CHAPTER SEVENTEEN

THE MEETING WITH THE lawyer Edward Meeks was not what Cooper had hoped it would be. Henri d'Arcy was most interested in selling Sophia's contract and ten thousand dollars was an agreeable price. However, there was the flat he'd purchased in which Sophia had lived. He would have no further need for it if Sophia's contract was sold. The flat bordered on the line between a modest white neighborhood and one for free blacks. If the sale of the flat for an additional two thousand dollars was agreeable then the transactions could go forth. If not, he would shop Sophia's contract at the next Quadroon Ball.

"Tar and damnation," Taylor spewed. "The whole row is not worth that amount. What did he furnish it with…imports from China?"

"More-than-likely they are discounts from LaFitte's sales," Meeks answered with a smirk. "But regardless, Henri d'Arcy has a point. I dare say I know no less than a dozen young men who'd pay the twelve thousand and that'd be for Sophia alone."

"Not just young men," Taylor responded, with a raised eyebrow at the lawyer.

"She's tempting indeed," Meeks replied, "but I'm a one woman man, Eli, and Carolyn has my heart and soul."

Thus far, Cooper had kept quiet. He was about to speak up when Taylor said, "Tell the damn skin flint he has a deal. Cooper will have a place in town when we're in port. It will be a damn sight safer than her staying on Grand Terre."

"You've made a wise choice," Meeks volunteered, as he took some papers from his desk that had already been completed. "Just sign here, Eli."

"Humph!" Taylor snorted, as he took the pen. "Damn sure of yourself, I'd say."

Meeks smiled, "We have been friends too long, Eli, for me to not know when you'll agree to something and when you won't. I had the contract drawn up in Cooper's name with you as guarantor."

No sooner had Taylor signed the contract than Cooper said, "When will Mr. d'Arcy sign the contract and I can see Sophia?"

"Just as soon as he returns from a horse buying trip in Tennessee," Meeks said.

"What damn luck," a deflated Cooper groaned.

"It should not be more than a month…maybe sooner," Meeks said. Besides I've always heard absence makes the heart grow fonder."

"I don't want to hear it," Cooper said as he helped himself to a glass of bourbon from Meeks crystal decanter.

Eli and Cooper were saying their goodbyes to Meeks when a secretary announced another lawyer, the district attorney in fact, Mr. Edward Livingston. Because both men were named Edward, they greeted each other using their last names. Cooper had heard Livingston was an ally of LaFitte, some said a well paid ally. However, this was their first meeting. After introductions were made and beverages offered, Livingston came to the point.

"We are down two at our card table tonight. My wife will be most disappointed if the tables are not full." Livingston looked at Taylor, "Captain, would you and your young protégé care to dine at my house tonight and stay for a game of whist or pogue?"

Taylor looked at Cooper, "Do you play cards?"

"I have played whist but I'm afraid I only have a rudimentary knowledge of pogue," Cooper replied.

"No problem, you can sit at the whist table until you are ready for the other," Livingston said.

Back in England, Cooper had been quite the whist player when he had either of the twins, Jessie or Josie, as a partner. They had emptied many a young blades purse when the young man spent more time looking down at bosoms than at his cards. Most were so lovesick and enamored they scarcely paid attention to their losses.

Once they agreed upon a time and the address was given, Cooper and Taylor left. In the barouche, Taylor asked, "You any good at cards, Coop?"

"Better than average, I'd say. With the right partner I should hold my own," Cooper replied.

"Well, it will not be me," Taylor advised. "It's not done that way. You will be teamed up with another guest."

"Are these card players good?" Cooper asked.

Eli was lighting up a cigar. When he finished he exhaled a cloud of smoke and replied, "Most brag more about what they have lost than what they have won. Still I'd not be surprised if the buy in is not a thousand dollars," a sum which caused Cooper to raise his eyebrows.

THE DINNER THAT EVENING went well, better than Cooper would have imagined. Captain Taylor introduced Cooper as a friend from England whose family owned a shipping fleet, properties in the West Indies, and a large estate in Kent.

Once, Cooper caught a couple of women looking at his scar. He smiled and touched the scar with his finger and said, "One jealous husband too many." This caused the women to smile and wave their fans even quicker. It was not long before Cooper found himself surrounded by middle-aged women showing enough cleavage to put the doxies on Grand Terre to shame.

With the house bright with candlelight and so many bodies close together, Cooper could feel the perspiration bead up on his head. He'd not thought to bring a handkerchief. He was about to excuse himself when a lady handed him her hanky. "I'm Caroline Meeks," she said by way of introduction. "We are to be partners at the whist table tonight."

"Thank you, Mrs. Meeks," Cooper said. Wiping his forehead, he spoke to the little group, "With so many heavenly bodies I find myself absolutely flushing."

"So many heavenly bodices you mean," Carolyn whispered.

Once the tables were set up and the cards were dealt, Cooper looked at his hand. Hearts were trump, and he had eight. He had no clubs. Soon as the cards began to play out, Carolyn had the ace and king of clubs. She was smart enough to notice he lay off her high cards and played another suit. When she came back with a low club he used his trump. The player after him did not seem to notice the trump was played and wasted a queen. Carolyn and Cooper's gaze met, they each knew they had a partner that knew their cards.

By the time the evening was over, Cooper was tired and ready to stretch his legs. He walked out on to the courtyard where several men were smoking pipes and cigars. Captain Taylor's banker was there, and a plantation owner was talking to him. Noticing Cooper, the banker made the introductions. "Villere, Jacques Phillip Villere, he owns the plantation next to Cindy's."

"I know your neighbor," Cooper said, "Miz Veigh."

"Yes, a most handsome woman," Viller's said. "I have tried to buy her holdings but alas, she has no interest in selling."

"She is a most capable woman," Cooper volunteered.

The banker looked to make sure his wife was not in hearing distance and whispered, "I have to agree with you both, a most capable and beautiful woman. Knows her affairs, she does."

Captain Taylor walked out, and seeing Cooper said, "Mrs. Meeks is looking for you, I believe she has your winnings."

Cooper walked back in and immediately found his partner. "A most rewarding night, young sir, we shall have to do this again. Not often enough though, to scare away anybody but enough to keep us in spending money." Cooper was surprised at the size and weight of the heavy leather purse. "Put it away and wait until you get home to count it."

"But I need to half it with you," Cooper stammered.

Carolyn gave him a quick peck on the cheek and whispered, "That is your half, Cooper. We skinned some folks tonight."

Cooper raised his eyebrows and smiled, "We are good partners. Better than the twins I played with in England."

"But not as pretty, I bet," Carolyn said.

"No, madam, you are absolutely beautiful," Cooper replied.

Carolyn laughed. "The weight of that purse has affected your eyesight, my gallant young sir."

"Who's your gallant young sir?" Mr. Meeks said, overhearing his wife's words.

"Who do you think?" his wife asked.

Mr. Meeks said, "He must have filled your coffers."

"Overflowing," she replied.

"Damn sir, but there'll be no stopping her now until the two of you have fleeced every windbag in New Orleans."

"No need to worry, sir," Cooper responded. "Between Sophia and the sea I'll not have much time for cards."

Meeks leaned close and whispered, "Sophia is like most women, so you better find time for the cards. I have clients whose wives can spend it with a spoon faster than their husbands can bring it in in a wheel barrel."

"Hush," Mrs. Meeks hissed. "The boy is in love, let him have his honeymoon."

Gathering their things the Meeks left as a servant brought up the barouche. Taylor was waiting for Cooper at the bottom of the steps. "It's cooler out here."

"It is," Cooper said, "but I'm ready for bed. I'm tired, mentally and physically."

"At least your purse is full," Taylor said.

Cooper took the bag from his pocket and hefted in the air liking the weight and the sound of the clink. "I have to count it when we get home."

"No need, its five thousand dollars," Taylor said.

Cooper was dumbstruck, "Five thousand. That's a winning of four thousand after subtracting the stake you advanced me." He hefted the bag again. Smiling, he handed the bag to his friend. "Now, I owe you eight," he said, meaning eight thousand.

Taylor gave a little nod and pocketed the bag. "Remember Cooper, this was a friendly game with people who could afford to lose the money. I don't want this little success to entice you into the gambling dens with the thought of quick dollars."

"No sir, I know the difference. Unless it's like this or with me mates…off the ship, that is, I'll not get involved in cards. I'm looking forward to a long life with Sophie," Cooper said.

"I wish you luck, son, I truly do."

LATER THAT NIGHT, Eli lay next to Debbie. "I don't think I could have done better if I'd had Cooper for a son."

"I think he feels the same toward you, Eli, I think he sees you not just as his captain, but as a father, certainly a friend," Debbie said.

"Aye, a damn pirate for a friend."

"A pirate you may be," Debbie said as she cuddled closer, "but I'd wager you've been one of the best influences he's had in his life."

"So far, he's only had a master swordsman and me. From what I gather his father squandered away a plantation, his uncle is a cheat and miser, and his cousin a liar. He did…does have a good mother," Taylor said.

"Shh, Cooper will be fine, you've taught him well. Now close your eyes and come closer. Oh!! That's closer than I meant," Debbie said.

"Do you want me to move?" Taylor asked.

"No, I kind of like it, like that," she said.

"Kind of, you wench, you love it," he said.

"Aye," Debbie replied, "now less talk."

"It's not talk I've got on my mind," Eli said.

"I can tell," Debbie replied, "now hush."

CHAPTER EIGHTEEN

HOTEL DE LA MARINE was considered a somewhat rowdy establishment at times. Men did not bring their wives or young ladies of society here as they would Café Mesparo's, Hewlitts, the restaurants d'Orleans, and LaVeau Qui, or Hotel Provincial. Men did on occasion bring their mistress or some lady of the evening. However, more often than not the hotel and its lounge was where men of reasonable means gathered, played cards, drank better than average liquor and wasted away the evening in camaraderie. The son of a plantation owner, a sailor of rank and the odd young man making his way up the ladder as a professional. Young lawyers, doctors, and sons of men with shipping interest. In general, it was men who had reached their majority, and had the where with all to avoid the lower class taverns and ale houses but had not made it to the upper class establishments. Several of the *Raven's* men that would have been considered lieutenants or warrant officers were gathered around a table playing friendly cards. A rule book had been acquired by Cooper and a penny ante game of the latest card sensation, Pogue, was being played.

Diamond, Spurlock, David MacArthur, Cooper, and the quartermaster Lee Turner, were playing cards. Sitting at the table next to Cooper, learning the game but not an active participant was Bridges. The game had been friendly with lots of good-natured taunts jabbed at others at the table. The men, as a group, had consumed a bottle of rum.

Looking at the empty glasses, Cooper rose and picked up the empty bottle, announcing that since nobody else had volunteered to replace the empty bottle, he'd do it. "I realize the advanced age and ailments of my older comrades make me the likely choice to wade through the sea of boisterous young men exuding piss and vinegar."

It had indeed grown louder as the evening wore on. A thick fog of tobacco smoke drifted in layers across the room. The various scents of different types of tobacco, alcohol, and sweat assaulted the nostrils and burned one's eyes. The table that *Raven's* men had claimed was at the end of the bar and next to a window. It provided a degree of relief from the heat given off by the late summer sun and provided an exhaust of sorts for the tobacco smoke and mingled scents that attacked one's nostrils. If one was in a hurry to leave, it also provided a quick exit as the door was on the other side of the crowded room.

Cooper glanced over at Bridges, "Take my place while I'm gone, Tracy, but watch Mac. I've seen the way he tries to look at one's cards."

Mac's reply was less than pleasant. Bridges moved into the empty chair and Cooper made for the bar with his empty bottle. Reaching the bar was not the easiest course he'd ever set. Once at the bar, he sidled up to a tall, dark haired gent. "It was nip and tuck, but I see you made it," the man said.

"Aye," Cooper agreed, "but not without sore toes." They both laughed at Cooper's admission. Placing the empty bottle on the bar, he waited until he got one of the bartenders' attention. Since he couldn't be heard, he pointed at the bottle and held up a finger indicating one. The bartender nodded his understanding. Waiting for the delivery of the bottle, Cooper dug out coins to pay and reached out his hand to the man. "Cooper Cain," he said by way of introduction.

"Beau Cannington," came the reply. "You're a sailor, I take it from the tattoos, and get-up of your friends."

"Aye," Cooper acknowledged, but didn't elaborate any further. "And you sir, what's your profession?"

"I am a physician and surgeon. I just arrived from Georgia hoping to build a practice where I can stand on my own skills."

"I'm from England," Cooper said, suddenly interested in the young doctor. "I'm recently new to the area myself. Do you come here often?"

"Couple of nights a week, usually for a nightcap before going to bed. I've hung around longer tonight hoping the crowd would thin out a bit," Cannington said.

"I don't blame you," Cooper responded. The bartender was now there with the new bottle. He picked up the coins and set the bottle on the table. "Keep the change," Cooper said. Turning to the doctor, he said, "Nice meeting you. Maybe we will meet again soon." The two shook hands and as Cooper turned he found himself shoved back against the bar. The bottle of rum was knocked from his grip, shattering as it hit the floor, rum splashing everywhere.

The young man who'd shoved him made no apology, and ignored Cooper as he got right in Beau Cannington's face. "You sir, are a scoundrel, a low life and are not fit to call yourself a physician." The way the man said it was more like 'phyzecician'.

Cooper was livid. The rum had ruined a new pair of breeches and silk stockings. It had not done his shoes and toe a lot of good either. On top of that, he was being ignored like some servant. "I do not know you, sir, nor do I know the reason for your rudeness and ill behavior but look what you have done to this bystander," replied the doctor.

The man angered Cooper even more with his retort. "He will be dealt with later."

Cooper was livid; his hand went to his small sword. Cannington put his hand on Cooper's sword hand and said, "Wait." Turning back to the angry man, Cannington spoke in a controlled but firm voice, "Would you do me the honor, sir, of letting me know whom I'm addressing?"

"Robert Jochum," the man snorted.

Cannington nodded and asked, "What offense have I supposedly committed to cause such an inflamed attack upon my person."

"You know," the man hissed, spittle spraying the taller Cannington's clothes.

"Obviously I don't, sir, otherwise why would I inquire?"

The room had gotten very quiet and still. Chair legs scrubbed loudly on the floor as Cooper's comrades rose and in single file made their way to the bar.

"You've forced yourself on my fiancé," Jochum replied loudly.

Cooper was amazed at Beau Cannington's restraint. He would have already run the lout through.

"Again, I must ask of whom are you speaking?" Cannington asked.

"Kimberly Johnson. You have forced yourself on Kimberly."

A voice in the crowd said, "I know Kim, probably didn't take much forcing."

Jochum didn't turn his head but retorted, "I'll deal with you next."

"I'm sorry, sir," Cannington said to Jochum, "the young lady has never mentioned that she was betrothed. Otherwise, I would not have called upon her."

"She doesn't know it," Jochum said.

Cannington was fuming, "She doesn't know it. You dare to confront me with such slander and then admit that the lady in question does not know you are engaged."

"She knows, everybody knows. she just forgets sometimes."

"Well, sir, I did not know, so it's apparent that not everybody knows. You should inform Miss Johnson. Now, if you will apologize for your slander and compensate my new friend, we will then consider the matter closed," Cannington said.

Swat…Jochum slapped Cannington with his gloves. "How dare you tell me what to do you…you quack." All pretense of civility was gone.

"You pitiful excuse of a human being, I will kill you. But first you must know I tried to avoid your little Miss Kimberly but I got tired of running." Then with a cruel smile, Cannington said, "She proved to be a most experienced lover."

Now it was Jochum who was on the offensive. "This is Mr. Bordeaux, he is my second." With that he turned and hurriedly left the room.

"My apology to both of you," the man said. "I have tried to explain to my cousin that the lady in question is…how do you say it? No lady. I will try to talk sense to him. Would the apology need to be in writing or would a spoken apology be acceptable?"

"Either would be fine, sir," Cannington said.

"Thank you," Bordeaux said. "I can't promise it as Robert is a rash young man. His father is most rich and so he has provided his son with everything except a judgment in women and a means to control his anger." Facing Cooper, Bordeaux rolled out several bills. "This should pay for the suit and shoes. Please accept my apologies and know nothing was meant in regards to your person. You could do me a favor and chalk it up to a lovesick idiot."

"Now sir," the man said after Cooper had taken the money, "one thousand dollars for a hundred dollar suit." He was indeed trying to ease his cousin's rudeness. "Would you be so kind as to give me the name of a second?" Bordeaux said, speaking to Cannington. "Someone I can either issue an apology or set the time, place, and choice of weapons. Should you have to go through this nonsense, you are the one who has been called out so you have your choice of weapons."

"I will be his second," Cooper volunteered. "With your permission," he said to Cannington, who consented with the nod of his head. "Should it be necessary we will choose pistols," Cooper stated.

Bordeaux nodded his head. "An address?"

"The Hotel Provincial, my name is Cooper Cain."

After Bordeaux left, Cannington said, "Why pistols? I'm not the best with blades but I'm little better with pistols."

"Because he is an expert with blades, I think. The rapier at his side was a Gills from London. Generally, a man who can carry one of those is a man of substance who has been trained in the manly art. I would venture to say that with a rich father, the son has had training by a master swordsman. I know, I have been trained by the master of masters, Jean-Paul dé Giraud. I would also say it was a master who either awarded the blade to Jochum upon completion of his training or recommended it to be purchased." After a pause in which Cooper took a drink of rum the bartender had set up for *Raven's* men and Cannington, he continued, "I have been in New Orleans for months and that's the first time I've seen one of those blades."

"I trust your advice," Cannington said.

"You should," Spurlock said. "I've seen Coop in action. He's the devil himself with a blade."

Cooper knocked on Captain Taylor and Debbie's quarters upon arriving at the hotel. After apologizing for the intrusion, Cooper related the events, leaving nothing out. A messenger arrived the next day and sadly reported no apology would be given.

The time was to be at dawn the following morning, if agreeable. Captain Taylor produced a cherry wood case with two of the finest dueling pistols with ivory handles that Cooper had ever seen. Cannington had arranged for a surgeon to accompany them.

The site was the dueling oaks. Many 'affaires d'honneur' had been settled under the giant branches of the majestic trees. The grounds belonged to the Allard family and were a popular location for duels. Sometimes multiple duels were fought, one after another.

Cooper introduced the captain to Dr. Cannington. "Let's do away with the Dr. Cannington, call me Beau."

"Then I'm Cooper or Coop as most of my friends call me." With a smile, Cooper said, "Everybody calls the captain, captain."

"I can see that," Beau responded.

THE SOUND OF THE barouche's wheels and harness as the driver drove to the oaks was the only sound as the men grew silent. A deep silence created by the weight of the upcoming duel, a needless fight. One in which one or both men might be killed. A grave situation to ponder, to create the somber silence.

Arriving first, at dawn, the men dismounted. Two small portable stands were set up; one to hold the case of pistols and the other to hold the surgeon's bag and instruments. When Jochum's carriage arrived it was followed by two more carriages full of friends, all drinking and carrying on as it if were a circus they were attending and not a duel.

Jochum was dressed in a white ruffled silk shirt as was Beau. They both wore capes to ward off the early morning dew and chill that was in the air.

Another coach pulled up and a M'sieur LeClair stepped out. An unbiased referee who would make sure the duel was conducted in a honorable fashion. Stepping from his coach, he heard the laughter and boisterous language from Jochum's group and a look of disapproval came over his face. "Seconds," he called. Once Cooper and Bordeaux attended him, a purse of twenty-five dollars was given, the fee for his professional service.

Pocketing the money, LeClair looked at Bordeaux and said, "I do not like the atmosphere coming from your principal's side, sir. The duel will not take place until the affair can be conducted with proper respect and honor."

"My apologies, M'sieur LeClair. I will attempt to bring order to the occasion." After a few moments of heated conversation a carriage filled with Jochum's cronies too drunk to behave drove away. Bordeaux returned and again apologized.

Looking toward Jochum's side, LeClair said, "The situation seems to have been taken care of. Are you satisfied, M'sieur Cain?" Cooper gave a slight nod. "Gentlemen, are we sure that this 'affaire d'honneur' must continue? Are there not other means to settle one's slight?" This was a standard attempt that was asked each time there was a duel.

"I'm afraid not, sir," Bordeaux said, a slight tremble in his voice. "I have just tried once more to get my party to think about his actions. Alas he persists in his demands. Regardless of the outcome, I hope Mr. Cain and Dr. Cannington know I have tried and take no pleasure in the situation."

"Well said, M'sieur. Is there any ill feeling on your behalf toward this gentleman?" LeClair asked Cooper.

"None, sir, he has conducted himself most honorably. I know not the rules of etiquette but unless it's not appropriate I would shake Mr. Bordeaux's hand," Cooper said.

"Not at this time," LeClair said. "It might upset Mr. Jochum. Now if you will, kind sirs, have your principals meet with me. Captain Taylor," LeClair called, "the weapons please."

Taylor picked up the case off the small stand and walked to LeClair. The case was opened and one at a time the weapons were loaded and primed. The hammers eased back and the pistols were laid back into the case. Captain Taylor then looked at LeClair, who gave a slight bow with his head indicating he was satisfied with the loading of the pistols. Taylor then stood back.

Since Cannington had chosen the type of weapons, Jochum was given first choice of the pistols. They were a perfect match so Jochum reached in and took the one with the handle turned to his side. Beau then took the other pistol out of the case. LeClair had the men stand back to back.

It was sunrise. They held the pistols at their shoulders with the barrels pointing up toward the sky. Both men were lean and muscular. Beau's hair somewhat longer that his opponent and he was taller by nearly a head.

Clearing his throat, LeClair called so all could hear, "Gentlemen, at the count of three you will both advance ten paces, then at ten you will halt. On my command you will turn and fire. One, two, three you may advance."

The combatants took ten paces each and LeClair called, "Halt, you may..." before he could complete the sentence, Jochum turned and fired. The ball whished past Cannington's head.

Eyeing the man with hatred and disgust, Beau aimed his pistol and then at the last second swung his arm slightly so the ball would miss. As Canninton pulled the trigger, Jochum panicked and instead of standing still as required, he moved a step sideways, walking into the ball by doing so. The ball struck him in the forehead, creating a third eye. Jochum fell instantly to the ground, dead.

Angry men swarmed on the field of honor. They were all shocked at the outcome of the duel. One of the men braver than the others pulled his pistol and aimed it at Beau. Many things happened at once. Captain Taylor gave a shrill blast on his bosun's pipe and half a dozen men appeared from behind trees where they had been waiting. Cooper pulled his blade and rushed to Beau's side.

Before he could get there, LeClair, stood in front of Beau holding up his hands. "Please, please," he said. "Let's not turn this into a melee. Honor has been served but what happened was an accident. It was in no way deliberate."

As people continued to rush forward, LeClair took out two pistols and fired one into the air getting everyone's attention. "I will personally shoot the next man who moves before I'm finished with what I have to say." The crowd grew silent. "A foul was committed on the part of Mr. Jochum. He turned and fired before the word. Dr. Cannington then pointed his pistol directly at Mr. Jochum but then moved his arm so as to miss his opponent. It was Mr. Jochum who unfortunately panicked and took a side step as Dr. Cannington fired. Had Mr. Jochum stood his ground as honor demanded he would not have been harmed. Embarrassed by his foul perhaps, but not harmed."

Bordeaux stepped forward, "M'sieur LeClair is an unbiased and honorable man. I trust his word and abide by it. This duel is done. Someone load Robert into a coach so that I can carry him home." Turning toward Beau and Cooper, he said, "We could have been friends had the situation been different. I hold no fault with either of you. But, Dr. Cannington, Robert's father is a very rich and powerful man. Robert was an only son. The father knows his son was a hothead. I was given the task…unattainable task I might add, of keeping Robert out of trouble. I had sent word to his father that he needed to intervene. It was my misfortune that the father was away at Natchez. He was to return today. He will not bring personal harm upon your body,

Doctor, but he will ruin you otherwise. I would consider it wise if you should move your practice from New Orleans."

"Thank you for your advice, sir, I will consider it," Cannington said.

Bordeaux turned and walked to his coach. Spurlock picked up the captain's pistol that Jochum had dropped and wiped it with a cloth and put it in its case. Without thinking, Beau handed him the pistol that still hung at his side.

"I had started to kill the lout," Beau said. "I then decided he wasn't worth it."

"If only he had stood still," the referee shook his head, and then said, "you are without fault, M'sieur. Jochum proved a coward in the end. It is a good thing you chose pistols however. I have seen several men fall to his blade."

"It was Mr. Cain who chose. He recognized the man as a swordsman."

LeClair looked at Cooper with new interest. "You have knowledge of such things, M'sieur?"

"I was a student of Jean-Paul dé Giraud, sir,"

"The best of the best," LeClair said. Turning back to Beau, he said, "You fought with honor. However, it is as M'sieur Bordeaux said. You would do well to leave the city." Hands were shook and the referee returned to his coach and left.

Walking toward the barouche it dawned on Beau that the captain had staged men so as to respond if needed. "I must thank you, Captain, for your foresight, and your assistance with the duel. It's my first and hopefully my last. Now I guess it's back to Georgia."

"Not necessarily," Cooper said. "Have you ever considered being a ship's surgeon?"

"No, I haven't," Beau admitted. "What type of ship do you have?"

"A pirate ship," Cooper responded boldly. Beau looked very surprised and coughed.

Spurlock said, "Damn Coop, you've given the man apoplexy."

"Aye," Taylor agreed. "It's not the way I would have said it but it does make the point. Accompany us back to the hotel and we will discuss it. The decision will be yours without hard feelings if you decline the offer. If you agree, you will have a more rewarding practice than you would on St. Peters Street."

"Who treats your men now?" Beau asked.

"The carpenter," Captain Taylor admitted.

"Humph… it does sound interesting," Beau admitted.

"I think you will find your skills will be put to good use if you decide to join us," Taylor said.

"I agree, it's something to discuss," Beau said.

"Good," Taylor replied. "Let's be on our way."

PART III

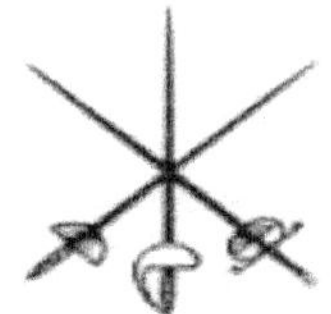

CHAPTER NINETEEN

RAVEN LAY HOVE TO in a gentle sea with a slight land breeze. Captain Eli Taylor stood on the quarterdeck, with Cooper Cain and his new bride, Sophia, standing before him. On the quarterdeck also stood the best man, David MacArthur, and the maid of honor, Cindy Veigh. Guests included Debbie Russell, Lucy, Linda, Jean LaFitte, Dominique Youx, and the *Raven's* crew. Due to Sophia's previous circumstances, Cooper knew a wedding in the traditional sense was not very doable. He also knew a ship's captain could perform the ceremony at sea. Therefore, after a brief conversation with Sophia, the two asked the captain to marry them, which he readily agreed to do.

Cooper had wanted the contract burned but Lawyer Meeks had felt this not wise should legal matters arise. Sophia had whispered, "What does it matter? We have each other."

Once the ceremony was over, the *Raven* sailed back to Barataria. Robinson, Bridges, Johannes, and Quang acted as an honor guard of sorts and rowed the newlyweds to Grand Isle. Gus, Jumper, and Belle, with the help of Millie, had decorated the dock with sweet smelling gardenias. The path up to the porch was strewn with rose petals and a rose was on each side of the steps leading up to the porch. The inside stairs also had roses on each step and the couple's bedroom had vases filled with roses.

Once in the bedroom the flames of passion were quenched. Sophia kissed Cooper in such a manner that drove him wild with desire. He kissed her mouth, face, eyes, and neck; then their lips found each other again. She unbuttoned his shirt and kissed his chest. When Cooper sat down to remove his boots Sophia tugged them off, giggling as he pushed on her rump. He stood up and they moved away from the chair and toward the bed. She then shoved Cooper back landing him on the bed. She grabbed the legs of his unfastened pants and pulled them from his legs tossing them over his head. Cooper tried to rise but she pushed him back on the bed. He watched in awe as this beautiful creature, his love, his wife undressed. Her body was taut and trim with a flat belly and cream-colored skin. Her breasts were firm and jutted out and upward.

Lying prone on the bed, Cooper watched as his little vixen shook her head and let her hair fall across her shoulders. She leaned over causing her breasts to dangle slightly making him grow with desire. She placed her hands on his thighs and joked, "Your blade is unsheathed. I think it's ready for action." She then crawled up and over her husband, lowering her womanhood upon him, and then leaning forward brushing her breasts against his chest and kissing him with all the fiery passion a woman in love could give. Their lovemaking was a frenzy and afterwards they lay exhausted, a contented exhaustion with their hearts beating together as peaceful sleep overcame both of them.

It seemed New Orleans entire population of twenty thousand filled the street as Cooper Cain took his new bride shopping in Debbie's barouche. Cooper had never fully realized the Mississippi River nearly circled the city. As they went from one type of shop to another as recommended by Debbie or Cindy, the river was never far from sight. The streets were narrow and unpaved, though a few private entrances had brick or stone laid down.

Most of the houses were two stories, and had beautiful wrought iron balconies and flat roofs. *Must not get any snow,* Cooper thought to himself. He soon found that volunteering to accompany his wife shopping was probably a mistake. She looked over everything she saw and couldn't decide what to buy. She then went somewhere else only to double back and purchase the item in the first store. The last couple of stores he had been content to sit in the barouche and smoke a cigar. When Sophia returned, she wrinkled up her cute little nose but didn't say anything about the cigar. She just sidled up to Cooper and told him about the cutest little outfit the she really shouldn't have bought but it was such a bargain. Her face went blank, it was almost like it dawned on her the amount of money Cooper must have spent buying out her contract.

"Oh, Cooper, I really shouldn't have, should I? Can we afford this? Doesn't matter, I'm taking it right back."

He put his finger across her lips to shush her and then gave her a kiss. It was a good thing he'd teamed up with Carolyn Meeks at another whist game. It had not been as high of stakes as the previous game but still at the end of the night, he walked away with two thousand dollars. He'd not looked at the purse when Carolyn had given it to him but after counting the money, he couldn't help but think that she, knowing about Sophia, had padded his take somewhat. At the tables the recent duel was still the main topic of gossip. It was common knowledge that Cooper had been Beau Cannington's second. It seem dueling was only done among gentlemen so the conversation was not taboo at such a gathering.

"How long had you known Dr. Cannington?" a gentleman named Kirk asked.

"I'd just met the man."

"Why did he ask you to be his second if you'd just met," the lawyer Livingston asked.

"I think he knew I had been insulted as well and being new in town he had no one to ask."

"How were you insulted?" Kirk asked, not letting the subject drop.

Somewhat warned by a look from Carolyn, Cooper told the truth and then said, "But I must say apologies were made as well as restitution for the damage to my suit."

Kirk seemed to accept this and his demeanor changed. "You still consented to be the second."

Cooper took a drink of brandy to collect his thoughts. "Being a gentleman and not knowing the local customs I didn't know there was an alternative. Besides, Mr. Bordeaux was such a nice man I didn't see the harm…of course, no one could have predicted the outcome."

"Do you think there was a foul committed?" Kirk asked.

"In truth, sir, I do not know the full rules of the affair. The referee declared there had been one and I'm told Mr. LeClair was an unbiased man."

"Most unbiased," Livingston said.

"Tell me, sir," this was from Kirk, "do you think Cannington meant to kill his foe?"

This time Cooper was very direct. "I do not, sir. I doubt the man could hit a man-size target at twenty feet. While I do not know enough of the rules to make a statement one way or another about a foul being committed; I do not believe the man meant to kill his opponent. In fact, he seemed most nervous to even hold a pistol and I personally saw him move the gun out as such," Cooper said, demonstrating with his arm. "I did not think he was doing anything but pulling the trigger to say honor had been settled. Mr. LeClair said as much the same at the oaks. A most unfortunate accident if you ask me." Meeks and Livingston both nodded their agreement.

"Well, it's too bad for the young doctor," Kirk said. "His reputation ruined before he was settled."

As the crowd drifted away, Carolyn had a moment to whisper, "A very smooth and wise rendition of the events. I see you did not say anything about the good doctor being a part of your ship's company."

Cooper grinned, "Aye, some things are better left unsaid."

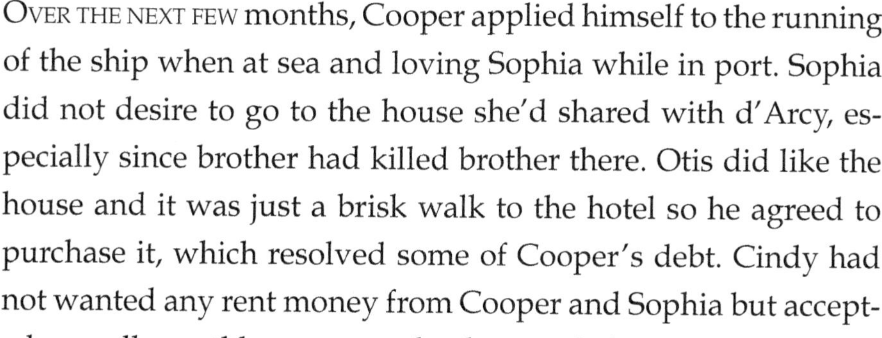

OVER THE NEXT FEW months, Cooper applied himself to the running of the ship when at sea and loving Sophia while in port. Sophia did not desire to go to the house she'd shared with d'Arcy, especially since brother had killed brother there. Otis did like the house and it was just a brisk walk to the hotel so he agreed to purchase it, which resolved some of Cooper's debt. Cindy had not wanted any rent money from Cooper and Sophia but accepted a small monthly rent to make the couple happy.

The *Raven's* cruises had not been particularly profitable. Captain Taylor and Dominique Youx decided to sail together toward Africa and see if they could pick up a few prizes. It was Cooper's first time to get the ship underway as the officer of the watch. He managed with only a couple of hints from Diamond, who made the hints with gestures. Mac said he was not sure who was the most nervous, Captain Taylor or Cooper.

Cooper now had the noon sightings down to where they were almost identical to Mac's. After three months, the *Raven* and *Tigre* returned with fifty slaves and a shipload of furniture taken from a Dutch trader. A coastal trader was taken off the coast of Tobago that had several cases of good French wine that was being shipped from Martinique.

"LaFitte will buy this for his own stock," Youx swore.

They kept the coastal trader, as Taylor was sure the Rolands would buy it and use its shallow draught as a fishing vessel in the bay. Tired of empty seas and growing short on supplies they headed home. They were midway between Aruba and Hispaniola when British warships were sighted. The sun was hanging low in the sky but it'd still be an hour before it grew dark.

"Run up the Spanish flag," Taylor ordered.

Mac was on the little coastal trader and seeing what *Raven* and *Tigre* had done, he searched and finally found a ragged Spanish flag.

Taylor called Cooper over and asked, "What do you think yonder captain sees when he looks our way?"

"I hope he sees three Spanish traders," Cooper answered and added, "however; if he has any eye at all he'll know *Raven* and *Tigre* are not Spanish made but American. Regardless, I would expect him to be curious and decide to see for himself. He may even decide to search for British tars."

"Aye, you are thinking right. Now what type of ships are those?" Taylor asked.

Cooper answered without looking since he had done that once the ships were sighted. "The larger ship is a frigate, a thirty-six if I counted right. The smallest one is a brig and I believe the one between those two is a ship-rigged sloop. It has three masts and looks like a frigate, only smaller." Before Taylor could ask, Cooper added, "The brig has fourteen guns and I couldn't see but would guess the sloop to have eighteen, maybe twenty."

"And what do we do if they alter course?" Taylor inquired.

"We haul arse," Cooper said matter-of-factly. "What about Mac and his mates?"

"We pull alongside and let them board and leave the prize," Taylor replied. "What course would you lay?"

"We have the weather gauge and it will be dark soon. We could probably make it through the Yucatan Channel and into the Gulf of Mexico if we cast the prize adrift," Cooper said.

"They could possibly overhaul us and we'd have to fight," Taylor responded.

"We could run for it until dark and then change course. We could even pull into some port," Cooper replied.

"Those are all options," Taylor agreed. "What do you think the British captain will do?"

"I think he believes we'll run for it and change course in the dark."

"What are your plans then, Captain Cain?" Taylor asked.

"Run for the Yucatan Channel and keep running. If I guess wrong, then we fight if we must. That's not to say if some other opportunity presents itself I won't take it," Cooper said.

"Deck thar, British ships have changed course to intercept."

Cooper took the speaking trumpet, "All hands, prepare to make more sail."

CHAPTER TWENTY

LUCK WAS WITH THE *Raven, Tigre,* and the prize. When the sun came up the British ships were gone from the horizon. Turner had the watch when Barataria Bay was sighted. Calling Cooper over, Captain Taylor gave his quartermaster a wink and said, "I believe you've stood your watch, Mr. Turner. I believe Mr. Cain is anxious to bring us in."

Turner, who was usually very stoic and no nonsense, replied, "Aye, Captain. He's so anxious; I do think he's slobbering."

Cooper had just gulped down a swallow of lukewarm coffee when his name was called. He spilled some of the coffee and then missed a spot when he wiped his face with his sleeve. A drop was still on his sleeve.

"Wipe your chin, Mr. Cain, and relieve Mr. Turner," the captain ordered.

Once he assumed the watch, Cooper took the speaking trumpet and bellowed, "All hands to shorten sail and prepare to bring the ship to anchor."

Taylor stood back; arms crossed and watched his young protégé go through the drill. Not as smooth as Mac or Turner but done nevertheless. By the time Cain ordered, "Helm a lee," even he had gotten over his jitters. The order 'stand clear of the larboard cable' was given in a clear, crisp voice with no hesitation or tremble to it.

"Let go the anchor," Cooper ordered. A splash was heard and as the slack was taken up the ship swung slowly on her cable. Smiling, Cooper turned to his captain, "Ships at anchor, sir."

"Passable," Taylor replied. "You'll get better in time."

Well, damme, Cooper thought. Seeing the flush on his friend's face and having heard Taylor's comments, Mac spoke, "What were you expecting, Coop? You brought us to anchor safely. It was not the best I've seen. It was certainly not man-ò-war fashion, but it was as good as, if not better than some grocery merchant."

Cooper started to get control of his sudden anger. "Think I'll ever get it, man-ò-war fashion?"

"We'll see," Mac joked.

On the bow several men were pointing and talking about a new ship in port. The ship had swung on its cable so the stern was not visible. However, most any sailor worth his salt could recognize a ship without reading the name across the stern.

"That's the *Floridablanca,*" Banty was swearing. "That's Gasper's ship. I'll lay ya odds on it."

"Looks like her right enough," Johannes agreed.

"I didn't say it wasn't," Moree retorted. "All I said was it looked like a Don's ship. Now, what is Gaspar, if he ain't a Don?"

Quang was next to Cooper, "That's Gaspar, him bad man. Put the ax to men's head, ransom or make whores of the women."

"I heard he was a friend of the captain," Cooper replied.

"Friendly, no friends," this was from Captain Taylor. "We get along and trust each other to keep his word. We are pirates."

"How can you be really good friends with a pirate?" Thinking after the fact, he should have kept his mouth shut, Cooper asked, "What about LaFitte and Dominique Youx?"

"Different all together…and if you can't see the difference I've wasted a lot of time and effort," Taylor said.

"My apologies, Captain," Cooper responded.

Taylor merely nodded his head and then said, "Come on back to my cabin once the ship is secure and I'll tell you about yonder pirate."

It took the better part of the watch to get the ship satisfactory for Quartermaster Turner. The sun was sinking and the captain had to meet up with Dominique Youx and Jean LaFitte to discuss the prize and contraband that they'd brought home. It was not the best cruise they'd ever had but when all was settled each member of the two crews should have six to eight hundred dollars; all depending upon the market, of course. The slaves that were captured were all aboard *Tigre*. Cooper was grateful for this. He'd never been fond of slavery but recognized it as part of society and figured it would die out one day. He had been very shocked at the number of free blacks in New Orleans. The Crescent City was like no other place in the world when it came to its racial diversity. *Would it last, would people continue to get along*? For some sad reason, Cooper didn't think so. A lot of the newcomers tended to look at the free blacks differently. Many of whom were much like Otis and very well educated. They were also very good businessmen.

"Ahoy! From where do you come?" someone of the watch inquired.

"Captain Youx, with a message for Captain Taylor." The note was taken by Bridges.

Seeing Cooper, he asked, "Would you be taking this to the captain?"

"Aye," Cooper replied. He and Mac made their way aft. After a knock, they were told to enter.

Taylor took the offered note and read it. "LaFitte's at the Temple and not expected back until Thursday or Friday. Well, there's nothing to do but wait. Dominique will send the slaves ashore. Rooster!" Taylor called. "I know your blasted hide is about. I heard you fart, and then giggle. Pour us a glass of hock, you mangy bilge rat." Taylor winked at his guests. "Don't be sampling the wares, Rooster, I can hear the glass clink."

"Aye, they do that when you charge a glass," Rooster replied with a snarl.

The wine was good but a bit sweet for Cooper. Mac downed his glass, which Rooster refilled. "Do you want your pipe, Captain?"

"Cigars, I think," Taylor said and then looked at his guests. They shook their heads indicating yes. "Make that three, Rooster. No make that four," Taylor looked at his guests and said, "He'll take no pleasure from a cigar that's been given. He likes to think he steals them without my knowledge." Thinking of a time or two when Rooster had offered them a good cigar, Mac and Cooper looked at each other and broke out in a laugh.

Cooper looked at Taylor, who was amused but not sure of the reason for their laughter. "I believe, sir," Mac said, "we have on occasion been on the receiving end of contraband."

Taylor pushed back in his chair and laughed, "It means he likes you, others he won't give a dried dog turd too." Once the cigars were lit, Taylor cleared his throat and said, "Let me tell you about our pirate from yonder ship. His name is Jose Gaspar but he goes by Gasparilla which I've been told means Gaspar, the outlaw. Rumor is that at the young age of twelve he kidnapped a young girl from a wealthy family and demanded ransom. He was quickly captured. The judge felt the boy was just feeling his oats so he gave Jose a chance…he could enter the Royal Spanish Naval Academy…" Taylor paused, letting his words sink in. "Or he could go to jail. Naturally, the young man took the Naval Academy. This was the right choice…to a point."

Taylor dipped the tip of his cigar in the wine and took a puff. "Not bad," he commented, and then dipped the cigar again. "Once in the navy, Jose demonstrated superb skills in weapons and tactics. It's said his cunning and bravery are second to none. I've seen the man in action so I can attest to his skills. Now, sometimes you can be too cunning and it catches up with you. Jose Gaspar rose like a shooting star through the naval ranks. He went from lieutenant to captain to admiral of the Atlantic Fleet. Because he was at sea a great deal of the time, his romantic affairs, and there were many I'm told, did not catch up with our friend. His naval career was so shining, much like your Lord Nelson's, Mac; that at the young age of twenty-seven or so he was made a naval attaché to the Court of King Charles III."

"Damme," Mac responded, "that's fast. I never thought that I'd have a chance at admiral and here's some gutter snipe making it pretty as a Saturday night whore. Cooper and Taylor smiled. Mac didn't usually get so worked up.

"Being at court was Gaspar's downfall. He became involved with several women at once. They began to catch on and there was no sailing away on the tide. Now, listen closely my boys. Not only did Jose like to dip his wick in numerous holders, one of the holders was the King's daughter-in-law. Let this be a lesson to you. There's a lot of women that will tête-à-tête with a married man, but when it's a court full of them…sooner or later it's 'flagrante delicto.'"

Mac and Cooper raised their eyebrows at this. "He must have had a set of bullocks the size of six-pound cannon balls," Mac swore.

"It's said the lady in question was so outraged and spiteful she conspired against our quim monger and accused him of stealing the Spanish crown jewels. Jose caught wind of his predicament and barely escaped. He went aboard the *Floridablanca* and sailed away."

"Well, he might not have gotten the crown jewels but at least he kept his jewels," Cooper said.

"Aye that he did, but Jose is not a forgiving soul. He has constantly sought revenge on Spain. Juan Gomez says he knows Jose has taken thirty-six ships since he's been a crew member. Others say he's plundered four hundred ships. Who's to know? The biggest haul I've ever made was when we had stopped over in Charlotte Harbor, that's his base. He has a dozen or so palmetto log houses where he keeps his captured women." Taylor paused a second, lighting his cigar back up and collecting his thoughts. "I don't believe I've ever seen a captive male."

"Cause he murders 'em," Rooster shouted.

"Hush, damn you. I'm doing the telling," Taylor returned.

"Then tell it right," Rooster responded.

Taylor raised his eyebrows and shook his head. "Getting back to where I was before being so rudely interrupted."

"Wasn't nothing rude 'bout it," Rooster said.

"Damnation, Rooster, do you want to tell the story?"

"No, you're doing a passable job."

Taylor took a breath but didn't respond to Rooster. "There's this burial mound and it's high."

"'Bout fifty feet high," Rooster added. Cooper and Mac couldn't hold back their laughter. Cooper laughed until he cried and Mac fell out of his chair which made Taylor and Cooper laugh more.

When Taylor was finally able to stop laughing, he shouted, "Bring us that bottle, Rooster."

Rooster replied, "Sounds like you have had enough."

"Damn you, Rooster, hold your innards. I'm coming."

Mac got back in his chair and Taylor continued, "On top of this fifty foot high burial mound Jose built an observation tower that he keeps manned. When a likely prize is spotted they ring a bell, the ship is manned and they set sail. He has his spies now, on both Cuba and Puerto Rico. Some say he's not particular and will stop an American ship as well as a Spanish one. That has caused a rift between the two, he and LaFitte, that's why I'm somewhat surprised that he's here."

"He's raided United States ships?" Cooper asked again.

"Aye, he raided the ship, *Orleans*, and took over forty thousand dollars in goods and specie. He has a sense of humor that one does. After taking the *Orleans*, he sent a note to her captain that read:

> At Sea, and in Good Luck
>
> Sir:
>
> Between buccaneers, no ceremony; I take your dry goods and in return I send you pimento; therefore, we are now even. I entertain no resentment.

"There was more to it than that, but that's all I remember," Taylor said.

"What did you get when you were together?" Cooper asked.

Taylor got up and went to the stern window and tossed the nub of his cigar out. He sat back down and said, "Rum and spice. Good rum, Cruzen Rum from Saint Croix, and spices from the Orient. How the two ships sailed together I don't know. Rooster was a topman back then and Spurlock had just come aboard. We boarded the one and left a prize crew and took the other."

"LaFitte was happy, I bet," Cooper offered.

"Didn't take the ships to Jean, I didn't know him that well back then. We took the ships and cargoes to Savannah. Back in those days as long as it wasn't a United States ship, they'd buy them, cargo and all. We made a bundle that day, didn't we, Rooster?"

"Rooster! He's done found a corner to curl up in," Taylor said and then added, "damn his worthless hide. I'd be lost without him."

"I'll remind you of that one day," Rooster responded. This caused another bit of laughter.

"Had we needed something, he'd have sworn he was asleep and we'd have had to fetch for ourselves. That's right, ain't it, Rooster?"

"What's that?"

"Never mind. That was a good day," Taylor said again. "Cargoes and hulls fetched us better than one hundred thousand dollars. I think back on my share and wished I'd quit then and there. I ever make another such haul you can bet I'll spend the rest of my days on a front porch in a rocking chair, drinking sweet tea and smoking my pipe or a good cigar."

The cabin was suddenly quiet. Cooper looked at Taylor, his receding hairline, tough, weathered face with crow's feet at the corner of his eyes, gray showing through at the temples; big, hard calloused hands and rough voice. Cooper saw the man in the brief moment. A man who is ready to pass the command on to somebody else. *Am I that man? Will I ever become the leader he is? Will I have the tactical ability and cunning that not only Gaspar possessed but also that of Captain Eli Taylor*? A man who'd plied the sea for over two decades and never got caught. He'd outsmarted them every time. A game where to win could mean almost anything you could want. And if you won enough, a degree of acceptance and legitimacy. But to lose…it meant only one thing… death. Death in battle, a hangman's knot or a watery grave if you preferred it to the hangman. What would Jose Gaspar do, what would Eli Taylor do? What would he do? A chill ran down his back and he gave a shudder. Now was not the time to think on death. It was the time to think of life, life with Sophia. A long happy life where they could love away the night, sleep late and love again. Why think of anything but life?

After a few minutes they bid each other goodnight. Tomorrow he'd see Sophia. Cooper walked on deck and heard a curse and laughter from across the anchorage. It came from the *Floridablanca*. Gasparilla, he ain't no gentleman like the captain, they said.

CHAPTER TWENTY ONE

A LARGE CROWD WAS GATHERED at Hotel Mayronne. Several plantation owners had made their way to Grand Terre to look at the slaves rather than wait on an auction at the Temple. In addition to these wealthy planters, the notorious Jose Gaspar sat at a table. His presence was frowned upon by LaFitte. This was due to his any ship, any flag attitude in regards to piracy. Yet it was his notorious reputation that attracted the planters to stop by his table, buy drinks and offer cigars. Later, they would brag to their wives, children, and even their mistresses, "I shared a drink with Gasparilla, the famous pirate."

Several of *Raven's* men entered the hotel with the idea of something better than ship's fare. Walking past the bat wing doors leading into the lounge, Cooper got a good look at the pirate before being pushed along so others could peek at the legendary figure. His Spanish heritage was obvious. His hair was combed back on top showing a receding hairline, but he had a full head of black hair with only a trace of gray at the temples. His eyebrows were thick and bushy as was his moustache. His nose was rather large. He wore a full beard sprinkled with gray and was trim, and his neck was clean shaven. He wore a large gold earring in his left ear and had a red neck cloth. His jacket appeared to be a blue naval officer's jacket with gold buttons, no other gilt or embroidery was noticed. Rumor had it that he was born in 1756, which made him fifty-four years old. He did not look or act his age. His nose, on closer look, seemed bulbous.

Was it from drink? There were certainly a lot of empty glasses on the table.

Beau Cannington, who was taller than all his friends, asked, "We going to go eat or stand here and stare?" This moved the men along.

Seating themselves in the dining room, their orders were soon taken. Sitting at a table halfway across the room was Mr. Mayroone. Sitting with him was a man and what appeared to be his daughter. Beau's eyes were constantly on the small group.

"You want some jalapeno in your tea?" Cooper asked.

"Sure, one or two pods will be fine," Beau replied. Mac, Spurlock and Johannes were barely able to hold their laughter.

Finally, Cooper said, "Beau…Beau Cannington!"

"What, what is it?"

"Your eyes are going to pop out of your head. My goodness, sir, a learned man, a physician, no less. Where are your manners?"

"She's looking this way, Coop."

"So is her daddy and Mr. Mayroone," Cooper replied.

"Uh oh," Beau said.

"Wipe your mouth, Beau, you're drooling."

"Damn, Coop, you got to pester me so?"

"I'm trying to keep you from embarrassing yourself."

"Here's our food," Mac said as Peggy, the serving girl, brought an armload of plates. Tell me, Peg," Mac asked, "who is that sitting with Mr. Mayroone?"

"His brother-in-law and niece, so no groping or tiddley winks," Peg said.

"Peg, you wound me."

"Eat your food, you rogue."

"I'm going to marry her," Beau volunteered.

"Not tonight, you're not. Eat your steak, it's getting cold."

Before the meal was finished, Mayroone and his guests left. Passing their table, Mayronne nodded and spoke, "Evening, doctor." Before any of Raven's men could rise they were out the door.

Once the meal was finished, Spurlock asked, "Anyone for a walk over to Tammy's? I hear she's got some new girls. She's got one, Che Che, I think is her name. She's short but a looker. She has a tattoo on arm that say's Tom."

Johannes said, with a smile, "I'll stick with Brandy or Frog."

"Frog?" Cooper asked.

"Yeah," Diamond said. "When she sings, she puts on like a frog. It kind of stuck. She's pretty now, regardless of her name."

"I like Brandy," Spurlock said. "She's a wild one."

"Fire your cannon does she?" Mac asked.

"Aye, a whole broadside at one time," Spurlock responded.

As the men rose, Johannes asked, "You coming, Mac?"

"I think I'll find out what the captain's got planned. If we are to be here long enough, I might go over to Cindy's with Coop."

The men left, dragging Beau with them. *One of Tammy's girls will put his mind to sorts,* Cooper thought to himself and smiled. *I don't know; I must have looked just like Beau when I saw Sophia for the first time.*

A TRIP TO CINDY'S was not to be. Captain Taylor had his crew gathered on the main deck of *Raven*. He stood on the top step of the ladder leading up to the poop deck. "We have been asked to go on a cruise with Captain Gaspar. He has been informed a convoy will be leaving Cuba for Pensacola. It is said to contain the payroll for Fort St. Michael and Fort Barancas. Governor Gonzales Manrique is said to be expecting a large shipment of personal valuables from Spain."

Gaspar was not a trusting man as most of his crew was new. If he was asking the captain to come along he must be expecting a large convoy of valuable prizes. Valuable prizes meant warships as escorts. The risk would not be slight but the reward, if the right ship was taken, would keep the men in wine and women for a year.

"Even if you only get Coop's share," the captain joked.

"What about the spoils, Cap'n?" one of the crew asked. "Do we divvy up and shares split between the two ships or is it keep what you take?"

"It will be share and share alike. Bad if we get the payroll ship. But good if all we get is food stuff for the fort."

"What about captives, Cap'n?" This was from Banty. "I don't mind taking the valuables but I ain't about murderin' the lot just because they are Dons, nor raping the women. Tammy's got plenty of willing wenches."

"You ought to know," Johannes shouted. This caused the entire crew to laugh.

The captain waited until the laughter subsided. "I have stressed my concerns in that regard to Gaspar. He has promised to control his men as best he can. That's all I can tell you. Mr. Turner, I will go below. Take a vote and let me know the results. We have to decide soon. *Floridablanca* sails on the tide." With that, Taylor went to his cabin followed by Rooster.

Mac whispered to Cooper, "First time we've voted on whether to make a cruise."

"The cap'n don't want this to be on his shoulders alone," Banty whispered back as he'd heard the two's discussion. "Truth is, I expect the cap'n would turn it down, was it left strictly up to him. However, the promise of a big purse is something he feels the men must decide. Most realizing there's a few who ain't likely to be coming back."

"What if a lot don't want to go?" Coop asked. "I know majority rules, but what if they just don't feel it's the right thing to do."

"Cost 'em a thousand dollars," Banty said. "Thousand dollars and they walk away. Listen now."

There was a lot of discussion among the crew for a good fifteen minutes. Turner answered a lot of questions with most them being "Your guess is as good as mine." One asked, "Where in the convoy do you think the payroll ships will be?"

"Tar and damnation, Butler," Turner swore. "Where do you think it'll be? Next to the escort ship with the biggest guns would be my guess."

"They'll likely have some guns with some weight as well, would be my guess," Spurlock volunteered. "I can't see that much coin loaded on a ship with nothing but swivels."

"Enough talk," Turner said. "Let's vote. All in favor hand up."

It was going to be close, Cooper could see. The first vote was a tie. Turner then asked Beau to do a separate count and then once again all in favor raised their hands. Turner and Beau both got the same number, those in favor won by a mere five votes.

"Heaven help us," Johannes said.

Cooper glanced around at *Raven's* crew members. Unlike the jovial mood they usually exhibited when starting out on a cruise it was very somber. No laughing, no good-natured jibes at each other, no bragging of last night's escapades and of one's prowess with the wenches at Tammy's or in New Orleans.

Rene Belsche and Luis "cut nose" Chigizola passed to larboard headed for shore in a long boat with several other sailors.

"Probably to discuss some venture with LaFitte or possibly to just have a bit of carousing ashore. Cap'n's alongside *Floridablanca*," Quang said.

Cooper had been so deep in thought he hadn't even heard Quang approach. Captain Taylor had gone over to Gaspar's ship to inform him of the vote. When he returned, they'd up anchor and get underway. The conversation didn't take long as Cooper spied Gaspar and Taylor at *Floridablanca's* entry port. They shook hands and Taylor made his way down the battens and into the waiting boat. The man rope must have had something on it as Taylor looked at his hand and then wiped it on the leg of his breeches.

"Cap'n never allows a dirty man rope." This was from Robinson. "Dirty man rope would cause a man to slip and take a dunking or worse."

"Aye," Cooper acknowledged, taking a last look at Grand Terre and hoping it was not his last.

The island was inaccessible except by sea or boat from the mainland. Brown pelicans flapped their wings and fussed with a neighbor over on the beach. Out from the beach palm trees stood, and further inland was huge oaks and oleanders. Some of the oaks had branches that hung down and touched the ground and then curved upward. More than one drunk sailor had woke up lying under one of those trees; often itching to high heaven from the red bugs that lived in the moss that hung from nearly every limb. Not long ago Moree had gone to see Beau, his skin covered with red spots from the itchy pest.

"Captain alongside," Quang announced.

"Rooster," the captain shouted. "Get me something to clean my hand. Mr. MacArthur," he continued, "get us underway if you will." The captain then headed to his cabin muttering he'd wear gloves if he went aboard that ship again, and it'd be old gloves in the bargain.

"Call all hands, Mr. Diamond," Mac said. "Prepare to make sail."

Jumper's little boat was in the bay as *Raven* and *Floridablanca* headed out to sea. *I wonder what he's fishing for,* Cooper thought. Flounder, maybe even snapper or dolphin. Not shrimp or crab, as no nets were visible. He might be headed to one of the bayous to fish for speckled trout or catfish. Belle fried up some damn fine catfish last time he was there. Fact was Belle fixed up something good every time he was there. Last time she'd fixed collard greens with ham cooked in with it and cornbread. There was a pepper sauce she put up that could be added to give it a tad more flavor.

Robinson walked up and asked, "Thinking of Sophia?"

"Thinking of Belle's cooking and my stomach," Cooper admitted, with a touch of guilt.

"Always heard the way to a man's heart was through his stomach," Robinson said.

"I heard if you're looking at his stomach you're looking to high," Bridges said, causing all of them to laugh.

As they were looking at Jumper's fishing boat, the boy stood up and waved; most of *Raven's* crew waved back. Cooper shouted, "Tell Sophia I'll be back soon." Jumper nodded. *Did he understand what I was saying,* Cooper wondered. Back at Grand Terre one day and then at sea again. That played hell with one's love life. Maybe he should have just paddled over, even if it had only been for a few minutes.

"Cooper!"

Hearing his name, Cooper turned to see Rooster. "Cap'n wants to speak to you."

"Aye," Cooper answered and headed for Taylor's cabin. Turner was leaving the cabin as he entered.

"Sit down," Taylor said and poured an empty glass half full with rum from a bottle sitting on his desk. "I've talked with the quartermaster and he feels you can now be rated as a topman. He also felt you could have been rated before our last cruise so your shares will be awarded as such. I now want you to spend time with Spurlock. Learn everything you can about the guns. Time will come when it will serve you well."

"Thank you, Captain, I will," Cooper said.

Taylor nodded and said, "Finish your drink and then be on your way. I've got paperwork that needs tending."

Cooper gulped down the hard rum, feeling the burn as it went down, making him shudder.

Taylor who was watching smiled, "One more thing, Coop. With your share from the last cruise you're off the accounts with me. Paid in full you are, boy, including the tab of money I sent to Cindy for the girls' upkeep."

"Thanks Eli," Cooper said, using the captain's given name. "My account may be paid but I will forever be in your debt."

"Nonsense," Taylor replied and then paused for a second. He had been packing his pipe, now he lit it. "You may want to tell Mac that word has come and the girls should be on their way home soon."

"Thank you again, Captain. You know he is very much in love with Lucy and I believe she feels the same way for him. Not that anything will come of it. He lacks the social standing for any type of permanent relationship."

Taylor nodded, "It could be this cruise will make him so rich that he can quit the sea and set himself up proper."

"Do you really believe this cruise will be that successful, Captain?"

"It has the potential, Coop, but I have my doubts. This is a lot of effort based on some spy's word. Of course, it has always been good in the past. Jose's coffers will bear that out."

"But the risk," Cooper said.

"Aye, there's that, but no risk no gain. Now be off with you, boy, but have a care. The Spanish are out for Gaspar. He has punished them hard, so I've no doubt they'll be expecting some devilment on his part."

Cooper thanked the captain for the drink and promotion. He'd made his way to the cabin door when he stopped. "Had it been a tie, Captain, and you had to break the tie, would you have voted yea or nay?"

Taylor eyed the young man who was the closest thing he'd ever have as a son. "What do you think, Cooper?"

"Nay, sir, too much risk voting yea."

"You are a very perceptible young man, Cooper Cain. You will be a captain if you live long enough. Now be gone, and when the time comes don't take any unnecessary chances. Remember, luck is a fickle lady at best."

CHAPTER TWENTY-TWO

FIRST LIGHT CAME LATE due to dark clouds that filled the early morning sky. A drizzling rain had been with them most of the night. There was a brisk wind from the south and the sea was choppy. It would be a miserable day. Turner was on deck clucking to himself, which usually meant he didn't like something. Moree was in the main tops, "Deck thar," he shouted, proving he was not dozing. "Convoy off the larboard bow."

Taylor was now on deck and nobody had noticed his arrival. "Where's our cohort?" he asked.

"To starboard, Captain."

"Send up the signal convoy sighted."

"I doubt he'll see it, Captain, not with the weather as it is."

"Try anyway," Taylor ordered.

"We could send up a flare, that'd get his attention," Banty remarked.

"As well as the Dons," Johannes said, answering Banty's comments.

"We'll wait a bit," Taylor said. "Mr. Diamond, send another pair of eyes to the tops. I want his eyes on Gaspar while the other lookout watches the convoy."

"Aye, Cap'n."

"Shall we go ahead with the morning meal?" Turner asked.

"Aye, men fight better with a full belly," Taylor responded. "Any change in Gaspar's tack?" Taylor called up.

"Not as I can tell," the lookout said.

"Damn the man and damn his lookouts," Taylor swore.

"Probably expects the convoy to be closer to the coast," Rooster volunteered.

"Well, he expects wrong. With foul weather and knowing Gaspar'll be on the lookout, I'm surprised they are not further out than they are. Mr. Spurlock!"

"Aye, Captain."

"Break out the damn flares. If he's not changed tack by the time we've finished our breakfast, we'll send one up."

"Aye, Cap'n."

Gaspar had still not acknowledged the signal when the meal was finished and the galley fires put out. Cooper felt a queasy feeling when he broke his fast on just ship's biscuits and coffee.

"Deck thar, the convoy is clamping on more sail."

"That means they have a better lookout than our friend yonder," Banty smirked.

"Fire the flare, Mr. Diamond."

Spurlock nodded and then sent up a red flare. After a moment one of the lookouts called down, "They've changed tack, Captain. Gaspar is bearing down on us."

"About time," someone snorted.

Even though the merchant ships were cumbersome and had to tack back and forth, it was near noon before they closed with the convoy. A big, two decker warship had put about and was now almost at the back of the convoy.

"Bring her up two points," Taylor ordered the helmsman. If they want to come to the rear we'll pick out a prize a bit more to the center of the convoy." Seeing what Taylor had done the Spanish two decker tried to follow.

"He'll never even get close," Quang said. "She's lubberly if you ask me."

Gaspar seemed to be doing the same as Taylor on the starboard side of the convoy. Closing fast, Turner alerted his captain.

"Mr. Diamond, get a crew ready to board that ship," Taylor ordered, using a cutlass as a pointer.

Diamond saluted and went about gathering his men. They'd board and if there was no fight, *Raven* would move on to the next ship that looked promising.

"Where's the two decker?" Taylor shouted to the lookout.

"Far behind in our wake," came the reply.

"A Spanish eighty gun, lots of firepower but old. No longer the sailor she once was," Bridges volunteered. "Probably thought her size would scare us off," he added.

"Ready Captain," Diamond shouted.

"Put one across her bow?" Turner asked.

"Let's see," Taylor said, and then added, "show yourselves and make some noise."

That did it, seeing a hoard of blood-thirsty pirates, the Spanish captain dropped his sails and *Raven's* crew soon swung over on lines. Watching for a moment, the *Raven* made for the rest of the convoy as Diamond had the prize put about and headed for the rendezvous.

The next ship was a bit more stubborn. "Spurlock, put one across her bow, and then put one through her mainsail. Run up the red flag, Mr. Turner."

"Aye, Captain, leave it to a Don to be stubborn." Once the red flag was run up the prize's captain ran up a white flag and lowered his sails.

"Take fifty men, Mr. Turner. The signal for all clear is a crossed pistol and blade. The sign that all is not well is a pistol shot. I hear that and you'd better duck, as all standing will likely get a piece of grape up the arse from the swivels."

"Aye Captain. You heard 'im men, make sure your weapons are not cocked."

Over the fifty men went, some slipping on the wet deck. A ship that size should only have a crew of twenty-five to thirty-five. A quick count showed thirty on deck, including a woman and young girl. Probably the captain's family. Taylor was starting to get impatient when looking through his glass he could see his men go on deck, speak to the quartermaster, who then sent the message all is well with a crossed pistol and blade. It had taken more time but Turner had sent men below to make sure all was as it seemed.

All sail was bent on as *Raven* attempted to overtake the convoy again. Much as Diamond had done, Turner had the prize put about and headed to the rendezvous point.

"We got a straggler it appears," Banty said. "Not the sailor her cohorts are."

"She was alongside the ship we just took," Robinson advised. "Lucky we didn't cross over and take her at the same time." It did not take long to overtake the Spaniard. Across the stern "*Senora Inez*" was painted.

"A Spanish brigantine," Johannes offered as they closed with the ship. "She could mount fourteen guns but probably not the crew to man them."

"Put one across her bow, Mr. Spurlock," Taylor ordered.

"Aye, Captain."

The bow gun boomed out but to Cooper it seemed the sails were coming down before the gun was fired. A white flag went up the mainmast. *Raven* was only slightly taller than the *Senora Inez* and standing on *Raven's* poop he could see down into the other ship. Thirty or so men approached the rail with hands up.

"I've never seen anybody crowd the rail like that before," Banty said.

One of the Spaniard's men jumped back a bit bumping the man behind him. Captain Taylor had reduced sail and was almost up to the stern of the prize.

"Captain, Captain Taylor," Cooper shouted. "Smoke, Captain. I saw a tendril of smoke from behind the rail of that ship." He kept looking, "There is several wisps all down the rail."

"Hard a-lee," Taylor shouted. "Down, men down."

Fourteen gunports on the Spanish ship were thrown open. Orange flames spewed forth as over eager gunners fired to soon. Most of the guns were firing into empty air where *Raven* would have been but two of the guns found their mark, hitting just in front of the main chains. The balls ripped out the bulwark and overturned a cannon, killing at least four of the gunners. The other shot that hit cut through the jib sail and spanker boom. Around *Raven* slewed, its deck canting so that seamen had to grab hold of something or fall. Once around, Taylor luffed up.

Spurlock was at the quarterdeck in a flash. "Carronades, Captain, the whoreson tried to lure us in and let fly with those beasts."

"Aye," Mac said. "Lucky you figured it out before they could get a broadside into us."

"Wasn't me," Taylor acknowledged. "It was Coop."

"Bastards blasted away flying the white flag, and killed several of my mates," Johannes said.

"They'll pay," Taylor said. "Mark my word on it. Those carronades pack a lot of weight but give a lot in range, am I right, Mr. MacArthur?"

"Aye, Captain, you are correct."

"Johannes, run up the red flag. I'll not let that ship swim. The forward guns, Mr. Spurlock, are they serviceable?"

"Aye that they are, Captain," Spurlock responded.

"Go with him, Mr. Cooper. Banty!"

"Yes sir."

"See about getting our wounded down to the surgeon. Robinson, is the two decker closing?"

"Not that I can see, Captain."

"Get aloft with you and watch for her approach. Tell Moree to watch ahead of us in case an escort heads this way. Bridges, clear away the damage forward. Rooster!"

"Here, Captain."

"Get below and make sure there's no damage below the water line."

"Aye."

Picking up the speaking trumpet, Taylor called, "Commence firing at your pleasure, Mr. Spurlock."

"Aye, Captain. They're almost in range now."

The Spaniard, having failed in his surprise had hauled his wind. But *Raven* had a clean bottom and was a fast sailor. It was not ten minutes when the forward nine pounder on the starboard side boomed and shortly after that the larboard gun followed suit. The crew members were shouting and jumping up and down. Spurlock must have already scored a hit. The gunner knew his business, he did.

The rain had lessened and now wasn't much more than a mist. *Raven's* guns were equipped with flintlock firing mechanisms. The gun captain had only to pull the lanyard to fire the weapon. Did they not have those on the chase? Was the captain worried the flint wouldn't spark with the rain and had slow match lit just in case or did he have the older carronades that used slow match. Regardless, it was the slow match and Cooper's good eyes that prevented wholesale slaughter.

Raven was not built to stand up to such weight. What was it Mac had speculated, twenty-four pounders. The forward gun continued to boom. Smoke drifted back toward the quarterdeck.

"Above," the lookout called down. "The Don has hove to, Cap'n."

Raven hove to just astern of the prize. A full broadside was trained on the Spaniard. "Go aboard, Mac. Signals the same. I don't see you or the signal in five minutes after you board, get down and I'll blast her."

"Aye, Captain."

Taylor had not ordered Cooper to go over but he hadn't forbade it either. Seeing him in a ship's boat with the rest of the crew almost made him call out. "I can't do that," Taylor said to himself. That would be sending the wrong message to men he might one day command.

The carnage was sickening. Dead men lay sprawled everywhere, wounded men were groaning. Stretcher barriers were made to pick up a man and he screamed out. The deck was awash with blood, which ran down the channels and out the scuppers. A uniformed officer stepped forward holding out his sword in surrender.

"Where is your captain?" Mac asked with a snarl. "He fired while he flew the white flag. The man is without honor. I demand to see him at once."

Cooper was not sure the Spanish understood all Mac said but he got some of it. When Mac demanded to see the captain, the officer gently took Mac's arm, turning him around. There was their captain. A rope around his neck, dangling from the mainmast spar in the air, his face was blue and his neck was at a grotesque angle. He'd been hanged. His body swung in rhythm with the sea. The Spainards had satisfied honor in their own way.

Overall the cruise had been a dismal failure. They had taken five ships including the one who'd fired upon them while flying the white flag. "If Cooper had not spied the smoke we would have been taken," Taylor told his crew once they had rendezvoused. "The *Raven* would never have withstood a broadside from those big bruisers, but even if she had, they'd had enough men to overpower us. This was an attempt to get Gaspar. The Spanish lieutenant told Mac that they thought we were him."

The governor's treasures turned out to be embroideries, dinnerware, enough wine to replenish his cellar if there was one, and various food delicacies including cocoa. Another ship had two cases of muskets, powder and shot, wheat, corn, and tar. In the *Senora Inez,* the dead captain had a small cache of silver.

"A failure," Taylor swore.

Jose Gaspar was fit to be tied and swore he'd see that his informant would die a terrible death. On board the *Raven,* several had died and more would have been dead had it not been for Beau Cannington. He had had to amputate one leg but the man survived and laughed about spending his retirement on a small tavern. Several of the crew had splinters from where the rail had been blasted away. Only one of those was still in bed. A splinter, a foot long, had impaled the man in the groin. "At least, it missed my wedding tackle," Norris said.

"Might have been better had it took it," Banty chided. "It didn't do you any good anyhow and at least you wouldn't limp."

"I'm amazed at how the crew can be in such spirits after such a poor take," Cooper remarked.

"Cause they're alive," McKemie said. "They've cheated death yet again. The takings were hardly worth the trip, but the possibility had been there so they took it. Had they not given it a try, they would have always wondered what if."

Cooper could see the logic in McKemie's words and wondered how many would make the same choice if they had it to do over again. Five would never know. They played the game and it cost them. We'll head home tomorrow the captain had said. He was taking the loss of life hard.

"That's how it is when you're the captain," Mac said. "It's a terrible thing to see men you laughed with, faced hard times with, beat the odds time and time again with only to see them killed for no profit. To see your ship pounded and had it not been for a freak wind that showed the smoke, to know the ship you love might now be at the bottom of the sea. All of this is going through our captain's mind, Coop. And I'll tell you something else, mate. Don't take it wrong but everybody saw what they expected to see. What they've seen time and time again… except for one person. Not the quartermaster, not an old navy gunner, not an ex-navy lieutenant, not even the captain, not one seasoned seamen; but the person with the least amount of experience in the whole crew. Someone said that was easy and you thought too easy. So you looked and because you looked you saw the smoke and you sang out. The captain realized the trap when the smoke was seen but nobody knows better than the captain, Coop, that we are alive tonight because some young wannabe, who has barely got his sea legs saw what all others missed. Would there be five dead and sixteen wounded if any of us real seamen had not taken things for granted? That's what is on the captain's mind, Coop. He's thankful for you, but he's hurt and feels like he's let his crew down, that he's responsible for those deaths and injuries. Not a man aboard would fault him. Most would say but for his quick actions more would be dead. But they ain't the captain. That's the loneliest job aboard this ship, any ship in truth. You'll see one day when you are a captain. Don't laugh, Coop, you will be a captain and sooner than you know, I'm thinking."

CHAPTER TWENTY THREE

RENE BELUCHE AND LOUIS 'Cut Nose' Chigizola sat at a table enjoying a tankard of rum at Grand Terre's largest tavern. They were listening to two other sailors argue over one's intentions toward the other's sister. Cut Nose, also known as Nez Coupé, had lost his nose in a knife fight. Some said it was over a woman, others said it was in battle. Regardless, he wore a leather cover to hide the deformity. Seeing Cooper, Mac, and Banty walk in, Cut Nose motioned them over to the table he and Beluche were occupying.

Pulling out a bench, the three took a seat and Cut Nose raised his tankard and motioned to a wench to bring rum for his friends. The exchange between the two seamen was becoming more heated and voices were raised.

Mac nodded with his head at the two and asked, "Why the commotion?"

"A sister," Cut Nose replied as if that was all the explanation that was needed.

Banty nodded and then said for Coop's benefit, "Never heard of a sailor disrespecting a mate's mother. On the other hand, it ain't wise to let on you got a sister. 'Specially if she's a looker." This brought a smile to Cooper and Mac.

Cut Nose had just asked about the venture with Gaspar when a shot went off. One of the sailors grabbed his abdomen and was bent over while the other stood with a smoking pistol. Blood oozed between the fingers of the gut shot man as he buckled to the dirt floor on his knees and then crumpled down.

"He better get gone before the dead man's mates get him or LaFitte hangs him," Cut Nose volunteered.

The pirate must have been thinking the same thoughts. He dropped the pistol and turned toward the entrance but stopped and headed toward the bar and out the back.

"He'll go to New Orleans and will sign aboard the first ship sailing," Banty said.

"Aye, if he makes it that far," Cut Nose added.

Captain Taylor and Turner came in soon after. He inquired about the commotion and then said, "The ship should be refitted and Turner will be in charge of seeing what all is needed." As the last venture had been unsuccessful, he was going to New Orleans to get some money out of the bank for the crew. Most all of the crew had money put up for just such situations.

Taylor told Cooper to go get Sophia and in the morning he, along with several men, would accompany him to the bank in New Orleans. Taylor gave a list of men to make the trip to Mac so that he could round them up and have them ready in the morning. He then bid the two good-by and took his leave with the quartermaster, Turner, following.

"Taylor is a rare one," Cut Nose said. "Most Cap'ns pays up and a man's got nothing after a fortnight ashore."

"Aye," Banty agreed, "but there's them that don't have money on account." Looking at the list Mac held, Banty continued, "Most of them whoresons are at Tammy's place dipping their wicks. I know that wench, Che Che, has got some of the sod's tongues hanging out."

"Wait here," Mac said to Cooper. "I'll be right back and then I'll go with you to Cindy's." Cooper nodded, Mac no doubt wanted to spend as much time with Lucy as possible.

THE TRIP TO NEW Orleans took the usual three days. Each night when they camped, Cooper and Sophia found a spot away from the others and loved the night away. On occasion, a blanket would be hung between two trees to offer more privacy. Each morning the men would grin or poke fun at Cooper, but Sophia was treated like royalty. The group was falling all over themselves to do for her on the trip.

Cooper had his thoughts on Sophia when he realized someone had shouted his name. Captain Taylor was looking at him with a stern look and Sophia was giggling, while the rest of the men were grinning. Cooper had been thinking of the lovemaking he'd enjoyed since returning from the ill-fated voyage with Gaspar and hadn't even noticed they were already at the wharf in New Orleans.

"Now that I have your attention," Captain Taylor was saying, "I want you to take Sophia to the hotel, and tell Deborah I'm in the city, and if you can keep your thoughts together meet me at Lawyer Meeks office."

"Aye, Captain, Lawyer Meeks office."

"I expect to see you there in no more than an hour and a quarter," Taylor added in a firm voice.

Well, no time for dallying, Cooper thought with a grimace. He still had the look on his face when he eyed Sophia. Seeing the downtrodden look on his face, she giggled again. Cooper lost the grimace and smiled as he helped Sophia out of the pirogue and onto the dock. If he could catch one of the many cabs now plying the city's streets, he might find time to dally.

TAYLOR WAS ALREADY AT the Meeks' office when Cooper got there. He was out of breath and sweating in spite of the cooler than usual fall. He'd not found a cab, therefore he had to rush to get Sophia settled in. He had taken a few moments to speak with Deborah and Otis and then legged it to the lawyer's office.

Captain Taylor would not watch the clock but he did not tolerate a laggard person. Meeks' secretary greeted Cooper, and told him he was expected and showed him back to where Meeks and the captain waited. Meeks took one look at Cooper and ordered a glass of tea.

Taylor explained that he had a bill of sale for one of the ships they'd captured. LaFitte had been able to sell the other but this ship, being larger than the others, had not found a buyer willing to lay out the coin for it. Taylor had decided to purchase the ship and add it to the merchant fleet in which he held a partnership. The bill of sale was from a firm based out of the Port of Spain in Trinidad.

"This looks very official," Meeks volunteered.

"It is," Taylor said. What he didn't say was that Dominique Youx had sailed it to Trinidad, sold it for one hundred Spanish dollars and then repurchased the ship. The firm had only to fill out the papers and make not only the purchase price back but a profit of five hundred dollars.

Meeks would now take the official bill of sale and transfer it to the firm of Taylor, Will and Brett. After deducting the cost to obtain a bill of sale, Taylor would pay the crew the purchase price minus his share as captain, for when the ship was taken as a prize.

Cooper sat and listened, not opening his mouth. He was amazed at how smart the captain was in hiding the ship's history. No one would ever know her original origin. Meeks' part was all legitimate in his transfer of the ship's ownership. Something he did on a regular basis. The secretary brought the tea in as the legal transaction was being completed.

"The reason, one of the reasons, I asked you to meet us here, Cooper, is LaFitte gave me a message that Mr. Meeks has a letter for you. The other was for you to witness these transactions. The knowledge may prove useful at some point," Taylor said.

Cooper was not exactly sure what the captain meant. However, he'd paid attention and was sure the captain would fill in the blanks at some more private time. Cooper was asked to sign as witness the transfer of the ship's ownership.

When that was done, Meeks took a letter from his desk. Handing it to Cooper, he said, "There's a spare office where you can read the letter, young sir."

Taking the glass of tea and letter, Cooper moved into a small office. The room was full of books stacked on shelves from floor to ceiling. It smelled musty. A small desk and worn chair sat next to a window. He was able to raise the window a few inches to let in some fresh air. After staring at the envelope for a minute, he opened it only to find another envelope inside. The outside envelope merely had Cooper Cain written on the outside. The inside envelope was addressed to Edward Meeks, Barrister, and had the address of the New Orleans' office. Sighing, Cooper took a sip of tea and then removed the letter from the envelope and started reading:

> My Dearest Son,
>
> A considerable burden was lifted from your mother's aching heart when I received your letter. I was surprised in the manner in which it was delivered and the man's instructions not to mention to anyone that we have corresponded. I have kept this a secret from all except Jean-Paul, whom I will soon wed. He was as relieved as I was to hear you are alive and doing well. When Jean-Paul and I wed, I will move from Lawrence's and not look back.
>
> Nothing is as you remember it. Lawrence has become almost impossible. He has even snapped at the twins on occasion.

Doctor Bryan has been called on numerous occasions for one ailment or another. On one visit, the good doctor related, "Many of Lawrence's ailments have to do with his treatment of you and Jean-Paul." He is for the most part excluded from the hunts and games at his club. I'm told he's been shunned at the tavern as well.

The twins miss you and speak of fond memories. Phillip has become somewhat of a dandy. His dress is most distressing to Lawrence. Phillip now has a male guest who has taken your old rooms. The twins heard Lawrence criticizing the way Phillip behaves, and saying at least Cooper was a man. Phillip replied, "Well, Father, you certainly have no one to blame but yourself. Lawrence snapped back, "But you told me..." Phillip answered saying, "Perhaps I was mistaken."

This caused Lawrence to go into a fit of coughing. I question if my dear brother is long for this world. I tried to entice him to write you a letter of apology but he said what's done is done. When he does go on to meet his maker, I wonder how long it will be before Phillip squanders all of Lawrence's fortune. He has already sent letters that he will no longer assume responsibility for Phillip's gambling debts. He had to mortgage your father's property to do that, we are told.

In your letter you mentioned you had met the dearest girl. I hope things have progressed to your liking. I would love to meet the girl that's able to steal my son's heart. You must keep me informed about her. I'm not young anymore (though Jean-Paul makes me feel girlish at times), so it would not disappoint me to know you were married, settled down and I was a grandmother.

Son, I am concerned about you. We have heard of your gallantry to keep the governor's daughters safe but lately we've heard rumors that you are a buccaneer yourself now. The twins jumped with glee when it was said you have raided the Finylson Company ships. I understand your desire for revenge, but I can't help but worry about your safety. I take solace in Jean-Paul's words when he says you have a good head and can take care of yourself. He still tells people you were his most prized student.

I fear I have rambled on like the old woman I'm getting to be. Please stay in touch. You and Jean-Paul are all I have. Jean-Paul has said a trip to America is something we can do. While not the man of wealth your uncle is, Jean-Paul has done well and says we can live comfortable the rest of our lives. This means a lot to him but I'd be happy just being in a small place of our own. With you being close enough to visit.

I shall always be your devoted and loving,

Mother.

Cooper folded the letter and sat staring at the wall. He was glad to hear from his mother but her letter made him realize how much he missed her. He'd never taken time to consider what it would mean to her to hear he'd become a pirate. He'd skirt around that in his next letter. He'd tell her that Sophia and he were married. He'd offer to bring her and Jean-Paul to New Orleans.

So Phillip had turned into a popinjay, a fop. Well, it didn't surprise him. Looking at the date on the letter, it had taken three, almost four, months to reach him. Had Mother and Jean-Paul married yet? Jean-Paul would be a good husband. He'd have to get something for them as a wedding present.

Cooper's growling stomach reminded him that he'd not eaten yet today. He downed the last of the tea that had grown tepid. He started out of the room, remembered the window and went back to close it. The captain was laughing at something Meeks had said.

Seeing Cooper, Taylor said, "All is well I hope."

"Aye," Cooper replied.

"Good, let's go get the ladies and break our fast. Edward, you are welcome to join us."

"Sorry, Eli, but other clients await me," Meeks responded.

CHAPTER TWENTY FOUR

CAPTAIN TAYLOR, DEBORAH, COOPER, and Sophia sat in the little courtyard behind Deborah's quarters at the hotel. They had dined well and retired to the courtyard where a slight breeze whisked away the smoke from the men's cigars. Taylor and Cooper had a glass of brandy each, while the ladies enjoyed a glass of sherry.

"What do you think of a trip to Savannah?" Taylor asked Deborah. "I have to take the ship there. Cooper could bring Sophia. I want to look at some land I've been told is for sale. We could spend a couple of weeks or even a month there and then return overland. I want Cooper to get a feel for his adopted country, at least the southern aspect of it."

"The hotel, should I leave it for that length of time?" Deborah asked.

"Why not, Otis can take care of the day to day events, and the bills can be run through the bank. I talked with both the lawyer and banker today. All you have to do is sign a couple of papers and Edward Meeks will see that everything is taken care of. Should Otis have any questions or concerns, he can just call on Meeks," Taylor said.

"It seems that you have already thought this out, Eli," Deborah responded.

"I have. The season is upon me to make a change. Cooper is just about ready to take over so there's no time like the present," Taylor said.

Cooper had his mind on a fresh bed, clean sheets, a soft mattress, and Sophia. So when Taylor had said taking a month or so off he was ready. But for the captain to say he was almost ready to take over the ship…that was a different story. One he'd need to think on. Mac, was the sailor, the one with experience. With Mac at his side…maybe. Still, there's a lot he'd need to know. But that would come later. The brandy and full belly was making him sleepy. He was ready to call it a night. Yawning, he put out his cigar and swallowed the last bit of brandy. The honey colored liquid burned as it went down. He could feel it all the way to his stomach. That would be good for cold nights at sea, he decided. Holding Sophia's hand, they made their way to their room.

"Young love," Deborah said.

"Yes, and I want to keep it that way," Taylor said. "Meeks told me young D'Arcy had been asking around about Sophia. I don't want Cooper to have to kill the sod over Sophia, so I think it best to get them out of New Orleans for a while."

Deborah took her man's hand as he rose from his chair. "You really like the boy, don't you, Eli?"

"Aye, like a son."

"Then let's be on our way to Savannah," she said and then added, "Put that cigar out before you come inside. It stinks to high heaven."

Taylor grinned, "You sure are sexy when you fuss."

THE NEWLY NAMED MERCHANT vessel, *Dashing Debbie,* set sail on a Friday afternoon in a fresh breeze. Captain Taylor had asked for thirteen volunteers to sail the ship from New Orleans to Savannah. Half of *Raven's* crew volunteered. To keep it from looking like anyone was being shown favoritism, sailors pulled beans from a jar. The jar held thirteen white beans, the rest were black. The only exception was for Rooster, who was the captain's servant.

One of the men drawing a white bean asked Taylor, "You don't hold with the sailor's tale that changing a ship's name will bring bad luck, do you, Captain?"

Taylor knew a lot of sailors believed in the myth so he chose his words carefully, "Aye, Johnson, there was bad luck to be had…for them we took the ship from."

Several of the sailors had been listening. Hearing the captain's comments, they set up a roar of laughter.

Raising his hands to quiet the crew, Taylor added, "And good luck to us'n's. Did you count the coin *Dashing Debbie* has put in your purse?"

Another roar went up. "Well said," the quartermaster whispered to Taylor. Turner had offered to volunteer but Taylor wanted him to stay with the *Raven*.

The ship needed an overhaul but did she need to be placed in a dockyard. As the ship's quartermaster, Turner would stay behind and see to the ship, and hopefully keep the crew together and out of trouble. A sailor, in port with money in his purse, was bound to find mischief. Hopefully, it could be kept to a minimum. It would take most of the crew to help beach *Raven* and careen her. *Raven* had lost a couple of knots and Taylor wanted to know the reason why.

Cooper was standing near the fife-rail looking down into the waist of the ship. Spurlock was lighting his pipe and having a difficult time of it with the breeze. His mate, Diamond had stayed behind to help the quartermaster. As the bosun, he'd be needed, whereas the gunner had little to do.

Sophia came up and placed her hands on top of Cooper's. "I can see why I shall never have to fear another woman, my husband. But the sea! How can I fight such a devilish mistress. She has a lure I could never match."

"Not so, my love. While I have come to love the sea it pales in comparison to the love I hold for you."

Sophia turned to Cooper, a tear running down her cheek. "You, my love, are the dearest of all men. Others may have bought my contract and expected to reap…certain benefits, but you bought it out of love. Now that I'm a free woman, I shall love you in ways you can't imagine, for I truly love you. I fell in love the moment you walked into Cindy's house. I knew then and there that you were the man I wanted to spend the rest of my life with."

"And I you, my love. You have quelled my desire for vengeance so that it's only a small ember, while my love for you is a roaring blaze," Cooper said.

"Speaking of a blaze, dear husband, look at the horizon, the sun is setting and the glow reminds me of fire…a sea fire."

Cooper grinned at Sophia's words, "What an imagination you have."

Sophia looked hurt, "It's not an imagination. When I was a little girl our house burned down. I was on a hill with some of my friends playing when we saw this red glow that filled the sky. Trees blocked the view of the house so we couldn't see the burning house, just the red glow that filled the sky. It was just like the glow on the horizon, a sea fire."

Caring naught for those who might be watching, Cooper pulled Sophia to him and kissed her long and hard. When the embrace ended, Spurlock shouted, "Hurrah for Cooper and his missus." The crew all shouted up cheers and clapped their hands.

"It appears we have an audience," Sophia said, her face blushing.

"I don't care if the world watches," Cooper said, giving his wife a quick peck on the forehead.

As the sun set, a ship was seen on the horizon. Banty was in the tops and called down, " A frigate she be, flies a British flag."

"Is there cause for worry?" Debbie asked, not wanting anything to spoil their voyage.

Not wanting to alarm his woman, Taylor hid his true concerns. "Nothing to fear, Debbie. Our papers are intact. We have enough cargo to look legitimate with proper invoices." He did not mention that with Mac and Cooper being British that some captains would take them away and press them into the Royal Navy.

This occurred so much that Edward Meeks said Congress had complained to the British government and demanded the practice be ended or expect another war. Seaman's rights, they called it. Being at war with France, England could ill afford another war. However, it was that war which created such a need for seamen that it caused British captains to stop ships and impress seamen. LaFitte had hinted Letters of Marque or as the French termed it, "Lettres de Marque" issued by the governor at Martinique could be had for the sum of five hundred dollars.

However, it was only good for a period of six months and then it had to be purchased again. The British Navy seldom recognized the letters but Taylor had agreed to purchase one and the dates should be omitted. LaFitte would know the answer by the time Taylor returned to New Orleans.

The weather held and as the sun sank the wind was favorable. The frigate disappeared from sight.

"Do we change course, Captain?" Johannes was acting as the master. He had been a master in a German merchantman but a disagreement with his drunken captain caused the ship to run aground entering the harbor at Kiel. The captain had influence and his shifting the blame upon the ship's master was upheld. After leaving Germany, Johannes found billets on several ships before he wound up in New Orleans and aboard *Raven.* His first days were difficult, as he only spoke a little English. One of *Raven's* crew, a man called Harvey, thought him a Fin and wanted him removed from the ship.

"He's a wizard," the seaman claimed. "He has the power to conjure up wind and storms. He can wreak supernatural vengeance on those he doesn't see eye to eye with, I tell you."

However, two things happened. A fight broke out in a tavern and the poor sailor had three men on him at once. Johannes busted a chair over one of the foes' head and then took a busted chair leg and bounced it off another of the attackers. Now the fight was even and *Raven's* man won out easily. Harvey thanked Johannes but was still wary until another German came aboard. This man spoke English well. He assured Harvey and other crew members that Johannes was truly a German and not a Fin.

IT WAS TWILIGHT AND the stars were beginning to flicker overhead. The evening meal had been eaten and except for the few sailors on watch, the men, Deborah, and Sophia gathered in the waist of the ship enjoying the songs being sung by Mac. He had a rich baritone voice. He sang several Scottish folk songs. Some so sad it brought tears to your eyes, while others were lively tunes. Sophia danced with several of the crew while the others clapped and tapped their feet upon the deck keeping time with the music.

Mac claimed to be from the clan MacArthur from Argyll. His family was the pipers to the clan MacDonald. The MacArthurs, MacDonalds, and several other Scottish kin were rivals to the clan Campbells, who historically sided with the British, to the detriment of their Scottish kin. One of the songs David sang was about the daughter of a MacDonald, who fell in love with the son of a Campbell, but with the war between the two sides their love could never be. He also sang a song called "Daddy's Little Girl," which told of a man watching his daughter grow up and marry before he knew it, realizing time had flown by. However, even though she was grown and married she'd always be Daddy's little girl. It was getting late when the little crowd broke up. The ship's bell rang indicating it was time to change the watch.

Looking over the larboard rail, Sophia was taken in by the way the moon shown down on the water, which was smooth and almost like glass. Looking aft, the ship left a luminous phosphorescent wake that was fascinating.

"It's almost like the lightning bugs we used to catch and put in a jar," Sophia declared.

Captain Taylor and Deborah were standing next to Sophia and Cooper. Deborah leaned over and whispered to Taylor, "In spite of how she's been raised, she has the innocence of a child."

"Aye, a woman child," Taylor agreed.

THE DAWN ROSE WITH an empty horizon except for a red sky. Otherwise, the weather was clear with a brisk easterly wind. All hands were called to trim sails as the ship was passing through the Straits of Florida. Johannes stood next to Johnson, who was at the helm. He had an uneasy look about him.

When Taylor approached, Johannes said, "I've an uneasy feeling, Captain. The air's not right and the sky is red."

The Captain looked at the sky and thought he'd never seen such a fine day for sailing as the day promised thus far. However, he'd learned never to question his master when they spoke of the weather.

"The sea is too smooth," Johannes volunteered. "There's a different sound to the riggings."

"You think we have a squall in the making?" Mac asked. He and Cooper had walked up and heard the exchange.

"Nay, worse than that, a full storm, a hurricane I'm thinking," Johannes said.

Cooper looked at the cloudless sky and wanted to question Johannes but refrained. If the captain and Mac didn't doubt Johannes, he surely wouldn't.

"Let's look at the charts," Johannes said. "See if we can find a likely island to take shelter in."

The chart was unrolled and spread out over a table in the captain's cabin. The ends were weighted down with a pistol and an empty tankard at the top. The captain held one side and Johannes the other at the bottom of the map.

"Bimini appears to be the most likely safe port, Captain. I've never been there but if the chart's right, the harbor's deep enough. We can anchor forward and aft and hope for the best. The land mass should offer all the protection we could hope for without coming about and finding a safe harbor off the Florida coast or one of the Keys."

"Do you think Bimini will be the best, Johannes?" Taylor asked.

"Aye, Captain, that I do."

"Very well, Alice Town it will be. Set a new course, Mr. Ewers," Taylor said, speaking formally, using Johannes last name.

The hands had just finished their midday meal when the sky began to darken. Soon large drops of rain began to spatter on the deck.

"I guess Johannes was right," Cooper said to the captain.

"A lesson to you, Cooper. Regardless of what the sky looks like never argue with the master. If he feels it in his bones, then it will likely happen."

Mac walked up. The wind was rising so he had to shout. "Do we reduce sail, Captain?" The ship was under full canvas.

"Not yet, Mac. We will have to later, I'm sure, but for now we are in a race with the elements," Taylor replied.

Deborah and Sophia came on deck. Seeing the rain, Deborah said, "I could smell the rain and the air was sticky."

Taylor only nodded. "I will come below to get my tarpaulin, but it's best if you and Sophia stay below."

"You'll not come?" Deborah asked.

Taylor shook his head. "Nay, my place is on the quarterdeck."

Deborah acknowledged her man but couldn't help but worry. She and Sophia went back below. On deck the sky continued to darken until it was almost black. Hatches were battened down and deck gear secured.

"At least, we don't have to worry about the big guns," Mac volunteered.

"Aye," Spurlock agreed.

"Land ho!" the lookout called down.

"We should be within fifteen miles or so," Johannes volunteered to Captain Taylor.

"And not too soon, I'm thinking," Taylor answered. "Mr. MacArthur."

"Aye, Captain."

"Time to shorten sail," Taylor replied.

"Aye, aye sir. All hands," Mac called.

The bosun's pipe shrilled and the hands gathered, and then went aloft one mast at a time to shorten sail.

"In Royals, stow flying jib and main royal staysail," Mac ordered.

The evolution went smoothly if not fast. Had the *Raven's* full crew been aboard the act of shortening sail would have taken no time at all.

"In topgallants," Mac ordered.

Grinning, Cooper looked across to Spurlock, "Been a while since you've been aloft, gunner."

"Aye, Coop, but I ain't forgot, one arm for you and one for the ship." The men grinned at each other as they completed their task.

The wind tugged at their shirts and pulled the skin on their faces back until their eyes watered. Finally, when the ship was reduced to storm sails, the island could be seen from the deck. The smooth, gentle sea had changed until huge rollers with white caps slammed into the ship's hull. *We got the sails shortened with little time to spare,* Taylor thought. The ship was starting to heave as it bucked over one wave, fell into a trough and climbed out again, only to plunge back again into the deepening trough. The sky was now almost dark as night.

"Another man on the helm, Captain?" Mac asked.

"Aye," Taylor said, agreeing with Mac.

Hearing the exchange, Cooper stepped over to the ship's wheel, taking one side. The helmsman gave an appreciative nod. Waves now crashed over the bow and water came flooding down the channels and out the scuppers. Life lines had just been strung up when a wave crashed down, knocking Bridges from his feet. Holding to the life line with one arm, Robinson stretched out his six feet plus wing span and grabbed Bridges and held on until the wave had sloshed on. He then pulled Bridges to the life line.

The wind increased until it was almost impossible to see. Waves grew until they appeared to be higher than the ship's mast. The rain came down in sheets, a hard driving rain that felt like hammers against the skin.

"We should be getting close," Taylor said. What he didn't say was *I hope we don't run aground and cause the ship to flounder.*

Mac slung a glass over his shoulder and managed to hold on to the shrouds as he climbed several feet up the rat lines. "Land dead ahead," he bellowed.

"Time to rig a sea anchor?" Johannes asked the captain.

"Aye, it wouldn't hurt," Taylor replied.

A spare boom was being rigged when suddenly the weather moderated. As the wind died Cooper asked, "Are we in the eye?"

Mac shook his head, "I think we are now feeling the shelter from the storm that the island is providing." The sky was still dark but the sea was less violent and the force of the rain was less.

"Mac, if you will get a lead line and take soundings," Taylor requested.

"Aye, Captain."

"Banty, get into the bow and form a good lookout."

"Aye, Captain," Banty replied.

From the chains, Mac called out the soundings as Banty kept his eyes open for shoals and breakers. When the sounding started to show less and less water under the keel, the storm sails were furled and Taylor ordered the helm put down.

When headway was lost, Taylor ordered, "Let go" and the best bower was let go. Looking at the lead, Mac called to the captain, "Bottom is mud and sand."

"A bit of luck, Mac," Taylor said.

"Aye, Captain, more than we deserve if you asked me."

"What did the captain mean by the mud and sand being a bit of luck?" Cooper asked Quang.

"A rocky bottom could cause the anchor to wedge in a crack and we'd lose her," Quang said. "A good anchorage is one where the ship is protected from the prevailing winds and not too deep.

Good ground is when the bottom is blue clay, that's the best with mud and sand next. The mud will hold the anchor."

As the ship swung Taylor dropped the second anchor. "That should hold her," he said speaking to Johannes.

"Aye Captain, best we can hope for," Johannes said.

The wind could still be heard and the rain fell. Two men at a time stood anchor watch and were changed every two hours. Everybody from the captain down to Rooster took their turn. But the anchor held and the island offered good protection. A sleepless but uneventful night.

CHAPTER TWENTY FIVE

"AHOY ON DECK, I sees a ship," Banty called down. *Damned if he doesn't spend most of his time in the main top as lookout,* Cooper thought aloud.

"Lazy, the bugger is," Spurlock answered. "Not much expected if he's up there. But he's got a set of peepers so the captain lets him stay aloft long as he wants. Nobody else likes the tops like he does, be it a sea calm as glass or coming on a blow. He sings to himself at times if he gets to bored."

The sea still held a moderate chop and the wind was brisk, but the sky was clear with puffy white clouds, as Sophia was wont to say.

"Where away," Taylor called up."

"Two points off the starboard bow," Banty called down. "No sails, took me a minute to make her out."

"Probably lost his sails and rigging to the storm," Mac volunteered.

"Set a course to bring us in close," Captain Taylor barked to Johannes who spoke to Johnson who was at the helm.

As they closed with the ship it was easy to understand why she didn't carry a spread of canvas. The ship was little more than a floating hulk. Her mainmast was a stump about six feet off the deck and the mizzenmast looked like a bare pole. There was nothing of a forward mast. Captain Taylor and Mac each had a glass on the ship. Mac was standing on a ratline holding to a shroud while Taylor stood on the poop deck.

Deborah and Sophia were at the rails when Deborah exclaimed, "God, what is that smell!" Holding their noses they ran to the other side of the ship, with Sophia gagging.

"We are upwind and you can still smell the shitten ship," Taylor said. "Do you have a good stomach, Coop?"

"I thought I did, Captain, but I don't know. I've never smelt anything so foul."

"Were I sure there was no one aboard and we were in *Raven*, I'd hole her twixt wind and water. But since we're not in *Raven*, we better send a boat over. McKemie, Quang, Johnson, Robinson, and Bridges see Mr. Spurlock so that you can collect pistols and cutlasses; and then come back and get ready to go across with Cooper." After a pause, Taylor added, "And Mr. Spurlock."

The wind shifted a bit and more than one of the crew squinted his eyes and turned his head.

"Wouldn't hurt for you men to get a handkerchief or something to go around your nose," Taylor said.

Cooper went below deck and grabbed a handy scarf. He then went over to Sophia's chest. He rummaged around a bit and took out a bottle of perfume and liberally splashed it on the scarf. Returning to deck, Spurlock handed him a brace of pistols and a cutlass. The men climbed down into a ship's boat and headed for the disabled ship.

"Damn, Coop, you smell like a French whore," McKemie said.

"Better than that," Cooper said, pointing with his blade toward the slaver.

"He's right there," Bridges said, but Robinson gave his mate the eye like maybe he wasn't sure.

By the time they got to the side of the ship the stench was almost unbearable. "God," Johnson said as he vomited over the side.

"It smells worse than ten outhouses," Spurlock said.

The foul odors of urine, feces, rotten flesh, and alcohol all mingled. "Smells like death," Quang said. "A battlefield just after the battle is over."

Latching on to the man rope at the entry port, McKemie held the boat while everyone went up the battens.

"Captain's cabin first," Spurlock advised. "The rest of you stand guard over the hatches."

The moans and groans of slaves could be heard. "Some are still alive," Quang said.

Inside the captain's cabin three men were found, all passed out drunk. Wine bottles were rolling across the deck. In the corner of the cabin a young black girl was curled up. She was light skinned, possibly a mulatto. She, too appeared drunk. Spurlock called to Quang and asked him to fetch a couple buckets of water.

"Crew members," Spurlock said. "The captain and most of the crew probably deserted the ship. They left these four, and fear got to them so they swilled away at the captain's wine stores."

Cooper looked about and felt Spurlock was right. Quang returned with the water, and Spurlock said, "Stand back, Cooper. He then drenched the drunken sailors. Rousted out of their stupor, the men looked up wild-eyed and afraid. Quang poured the remainder of water on the girl and she blinked, coughed, and stood on wobbly feet.

The men were soon able to focus and one of them, an older man, finally managed to speak, "Thank God, we are saved." The other two spoke but in Spanish, so nobody was able to understand anything but a word here and there. The English speaking sailor confirmed much that had already been guessed. They were carrying a cargo of slaves to Bermuda from Santiago, Cuba.

"Any other cargo?" Coop asked.

"Only some small things the crew was allowed to sell," the man said.

"Quang, escort these gentlemen and the girl on deck." Once gone, Cooper spoke quietly to Spurlock, "Captain once said slavers always carry a contingency fund. Let's keep the cabin off limits until we can do a thorough search."

"Aye," Spurlock agreed. "The captain's little pet might know where it's kept but I wouldn't trust her to be out of my sight. We are going to need keys to the slaves' chains and shackles. The mate would have a set but so would the captain. Let's look for the keys and if they are not here, we will search the mate's cabin." The keys were easy to find. They were lying in the captain's desk drawer.

"Now for the hard part," Cooper said.

THE SLAVE TIERS WERE a horrible sight. The slaves were packed like sardines. "A short run," Spurlock said. "Otherwise, there would have been more space."

There were men, women, and older children, all naked as the day they were born. They were chained together with shackles on their ankles and lying in their own filth.

"We have got to get these people on deck, cleaned up, and fed," Cooper said, not believing his eyes. "We can't bring but a few on deck at a time, otherwise, they may go berserk and run rampant."

Cooper called the men together once they got back on deck. "Send a signal for the captain to close within speaking distance. Then have the slaver's men rig the deck pumps. We will bring twenty-five at a time on deck, wash them down and clean their tier as well as possible and feed them."

"Aye," the men replied.

Once Taylor closed, he sent two more men over. Mac was one of them. The evolution was carried out. The mulatto and a crew member cooked a watery oatmeal that was cooked with butter and sweetened with sugar.

"In the Royal Navy, we called that skillygalee," Mac said.

A bucket of water was brought on deck. The slaves took to the food and water like there was no tomorrow. However, they let up a cry when an attempt was made to wash them off with the deck pump. Had McKemie not been quick on his feet, one of the poor devils would have jumped over the side.

"They are afraid of the pump," Coop said to his group. "Have one of the ship's crew washed down so they can see we don't intend to harm them. Besides they reek almost as bad as their human cargo." After showing the slaves what the deck pump was all about, they took right to it.

"What do we do with the dead un's?" Banty asked.

"Over the side with them, that's our only option," Coop said.

"Aye," Banty replied. "That was my thinking as well."

As Banty turned, Cooper called him back, "Find out if that mulatto girl speaks these people's language."

It was obvious they didn't understand English. As it turned out, she could speak enough to get by.

"What's your name?" Cooper asked the girl.

"Rosita," she replied.

"Rosita, I want these slaves to bring the dead on deck and cast them over the side. And then, they need to wash down the tier so they won't have to lie in their filth."

The girl spoke to the slaves and soon bodies were being brought up and without ceremony cast over the side.

"Don't seem right, not speaking any words over them," Mac said. He looked grim for a bit and then said, "I guess they wouldn't know what was being said anyway. Most of them coming out of Africa are heathens, anyway, so they don't believe like we do."

Seeing everything being carried out in an orderly manner, Mac spoke again, "Captain sent me over to see if the ship has got any extra spars or anything we can use to jury rig a mast of sorts and get some canvas on her."

"Moree," Cooper called to one of the *Raven's* volunteers. "See to our English speaking sailor and find out if they carried anything that would be useful in getting this ship underway."

"Aye, Coop, but just so's you know the whoreson is called Orville."

Coop gave a mock salute as Moree headed off. While Spurlock was watching, keeping everything in order; Cooper followed Mac as he made a thorough inspection of the ship.

"Need to pump the bilges after washing down the slave tiers but the ship seems sound, apart from having lost all her mast and rigging. We may have to tow her to Savannah," Mac said.

"How far are we from there now?" Coop asked.

"Had we not come across this ship we'd been off the coast tonight. Now, I'm thinking two maybe three days," Mac replied.

A shout was heard, a woman's voice, so Mac and Coop ran back toward mid ships. Rosita was standing there; hand in her mouth obviously frightened.

"What is it?" Coop asked.

The girl didn't speak, she just pointed over the side. There must have been close to one hundred dead slaves thrown overboard. Now the sharks were among them, gray fins everywhere. Mac and Cooper both gasped. No wonder the girl was frightened. It was a feeding frenzy.

"I wouldn't put a boat in the water with that going on," Cooper said.

"Me either," Mac said.

Cooper looked across the way to where the *Dashing Debbie* lay hove-to. He was glad Sophia was not on deck to see this. In fact, he wished he hadn't and said as much to Mac. *Will they drift away*, he wondered but didn't ask.

Moree was soon back, "Orville said this was his first voyage on this ship so we asked his Dago mates. They said the captain didn't waste space for such on a short voyage. So we can look but I doubt we find anything useful."

"You speak Spanish," Cooper asked.

"A little but Orville speaks it good. That's what got him the job," Moree replied. He had a chew in his mouth so he walked a few steps over to the rail to spit. "Jesus, sweet Jesus," the man from Georgia exclaimed. "Don't reckon I ever seen such a sight as that." Hearing Moree, several other men came over to look. "Stay away from the bottle and the rails tonight, mates... otherwise!"

By the time the slave tiers were cleaned and the rest of the slaves fed, the sun was going down.

"Might as well get some lanterns lit and set about. I'll make a signal to the captain and let him know we're staying aboard this tonight," Mac volunteered.

"Think he'll guess why?" Cooper asked.

"He's an old hand, Coop. He's bound to have seen at least some of the sharks and he's sure to have seen the bodies go over the side. He knows why we are staying," Mac said.

Cooper called to Spurlock and had him set up a watch. "Don't know that I trust our new hands," Cooper told Mac.

"No, they're probably like most sailors, full of mischief and bear considerable watching," Mac replied. This caused Cooper to grin.

"Let's go search the captain's cabin. Could be if we promise a little reward Rosita might be helpful," Cooper said.

"I'll give her a reward," Mac teased. "No wonder the captain kept her close. She's a pretty little wench. She'd definitely keep the bed warm on cold and damp nights. Bet she'd stir a few at the quadroon ball in New Orleans. Cream colored skin, brown eyes, and a body made for pleasure. She looks more Spanish than not."

Cooper listened to Mac ramble. "Aye, she was a pert little something but compared to Sophia...well, there was no comparison. Call the wench, Mac, and if need be I'll volunteer for the first watch."

"Well, Coop, you are a good mate, damme if you ain't."

CHAPTER TWENTY SIX

IT WAS A NEW day. The sun came up over the horizon revealing an empty sea as far as the eye could see. The sharks had had their fill and swam on looking for another meal. The slaves moved on deck, twenty-five at a time, and were hosed down gently with sea water. Only one more slave had died during the night. Like the others he was cast over the side. Rosita and the two Dons cooked up more of the skillygalee. The slaves filled their bellies.

"It won't take long before we are out of food. I never knew you could pack so many humans in one ship. I heard once a man named Brooks carried six hundred and nine from Africa. Almost that on this tub," Cooper snorted.

"It was supposed to have been a short cruise," Orville explained, only to get glared at by Cooper and Mac.

Boats put out from *Dashing Debbie* with a new crew to relieve the men from the previous day. Cooper went over for a visit and to inform Captain Taylor of his and Mac's discovery. He was welcomed aboard warmly by Sophia, who, after a warm greeting backed off and exclaimed, "You need a bath."

"Time for that later," Taylor said, shooing the women away.

"We have four hundred and nine of the pitiful buggers," Cooper said very bluntly. "How the slavers put up with such is beyond me. I'm no saint, Captain, but to treat a human in such a way is more than I can understand."

"Not much we can do about that, now is there, Coop?" Taylor asked.

Eying his captain for a moment, Cooper looked down, shaking his head. "No sir, there's not. The ship's register says she's the something *Inez*. She's out of Santiago, Cuba bound for Bermuda."

"Not any more she's not," Taylor said. "She's now destined for Savannah. We need to get a tow on her right away and put as many miles behind us as possible. Every day will mean more slaves lost."

Cooper wondered if the captain was thinking from a humane point of view or of profit but he did not ask. "We found the captain's funds with the help of his little mulatto. Mac promised her one hundred dollars if she could help us find it. She led us straight to it. Two boards near the stern come up and there are several bags of Spanish coin. About seventeen thousand, Mac figures, before her finder's fee."

"She take any persuasion," Taylor asked.

"Well, she and Mac were alone for an hour or so." Cooper had made his way to the entry port as he spoke. Reaching it, he turned and smiled, "I'm not really sure who was persuading who, Captain."

"Be off with you, Coop, before you get Sophia stirred up."

RIGGING THE TOW WAS simpler than Cooper realized it would be. A boat was rowed over with a rope attached to a line. Quang took a boat hook and pulled the rope up and fed it through the hawsehole. By pulling this way a heavier towing hawser was gotten on board and fastened around the capstan.

Mac then set the men working so that the hawser would not chafe. Cooper looked on, learning and making mental notes. *I would like to see how it's rigged on the other end,* he thought. When he mentioned this to Mac, his friend promised to draw schematics demonstrating a couple of methods but related there were illustrations in the book on seamanship he'd purchased in New Orleans.

Prior to getting underway Taylor came aboard with several lanterns. "If we have a soldier's wind we may continue the tow through the night." Three vertical lanterns from either ship meant 'cut the tow line'.

"Do you want to take the extra cargo back with you, Captain," Cooper asked. "It might lessen the temptation from the ship's original crew if they see it leaving the ship."

"Good idea, Coop, I'll divide it with Sophia if we lose you somewhere." Cooper stopped and stared at Taylor.

"Close your mouth, Coop, he's kidding," Mac said, and then added, "we won't cast you adrift while I'm on board."

"Bloody arse," Cooper hissed, "both of you." He then let a smile creep onto his face. "I've no worries. Once Sophia had a real man she'd not look twice at the likes of you."

"Disrespect...disrespect is what it is, Mr. MacArthur, and to think I've took him under my wing like I have."

"Aye, Captain, it's his youth I'm thinking," Mac said.

Shaking their heads as if in deep quandary, Mac walked Captain Taylor to the entry port with Cooper following close behind. As Taylor started down the battens, he grasp the handrope and shouted, "Sophia was right, Cooper. You do need a bath. You stink, lad, you stink."

All of the crew started laughing at Coop. "We'll rig the deck pump before you go over again, Coop," Mac said gently slapping his friend on the shoulder.

THE WEATHER AND THE tow held and aside from it getting tricky a few times when they tacked, the voyage was uneventful. At noon on the third day, they arrived at the mouth of the Savannah

River. Just inside Tybee Roads, the *Inez* was cut loose from the tow and anchored.

"I'd not want to tackle Horseshoe Shoal with a tow," Captain Taylor admitted.

"What fort is that?" Mac asked.

"Fort Pulaski," Taylor advised. "I will send a boat over to tell them what we are about. Still, don't be alarmed if a guard boat comes over."

"Humph," Mac snorted. "Anchored under the lee of a fort's big guns, what's not to be alarmed over?"

Taylor smiled, "A British sailor no doubt would be anxious in such a situation. Bring the slaves on deck and sluice them off. We will ferry them into Savannah and put them in the barracoon. I need to see my business associates and our Savannah lawyer. We will have a set of rooms at the River Street Inn. The men will be put up at the East Bay Inn. You may want to clean up there before going to the River Street Inn. I'm not sure they'd allow you in …as you are now."

"So I'm not fitting for the River Inn?" Cooper asked, acting hurt.

"Let's just say you'd not be out of sorts at the East Bay Inn. It's been around since 1762, and the River Inn is brand new. I would imagine their patrons would be a little sensitive for you to enter reeking as you do," Taylor said.

"They should smell the slaves that have been cooped up in the hell hole then," Cooper snarled, not joking this time.

"Yes, well there is little either of us can do to change society. I can see a change coming, mind you, Coop, but it'll take another fifty or sixty years," Taylor said.

SAVANNAH WAS A DIFFERENT city all together compared to New Orleans. Cooper and Mac had just seen the last of the slaves removed from the ship when a boat carrying a number of men showed up with a note from Captain Taylor. They would relieve the crew and go about washing the *Inez* down and fumigating the ship with brimstone.

Now that they were presentable, having been scrubbed clean in flower of lilac water; the men hailed down the only cab they saw. Flyers were posted on store fronts and on the sides of buildings. Each one letting the good citizens of Savannah know a play was to be held at the coffee exchange. The golf club was giving lessons and a horse race was scheduled on Sunday at the Jockey Club Race Track. There were bills advertising slave auctions everywhere as well.

"Damme," Cooper said. "We traded one odor for another."

"Stop whining, Coop. You heard the lady, 'If it was good enough for King Louis of France, its good enough for the likes of you'. Besides," Mac added, "we may get some stares but they aren't holding their nose and running away."

"Well, there's that," Cooper admitted. A change of clothes had been left at the East Bay Inn. "I guess we do look presentable even if we smell to high heaven," Cooper said, not letting the subject die.

"Just for that," Mac informed his friend, "you will pay the cab fare."

Cooper had his back to the driver, so he didn't know they had reached their destination. Mac briskly jumped down from the cab and waited by the inn's entrance. They inquired at the desk as to their rooms. The clerk was a pleasant, busy man who obviously had been expecting them. "We have a note for you, gentlemen, I believe," he said.

"Who from?" Cooper asked.

"A Captain Taylor, I believe," the clerk said.

Mac looked at his friend, and then at the clerk. "You know or you believe?"

"I'm quite sure it was the captain, sir. I believe he's in the tavern, sir, with some other gentlemen." The clerk now looked nervous and was not sure how to take this sweet smelling British sailor.

Cooper and Mac walked through a doorway into the inn's tavern, or as a sign decried, Ye Ole Public House. The tavern was dimly lit but each table had a candlestick holder with three candles. A huge fireplace smelled of a recent fire. Seeing his men, Taylor called over to them. As they approached the table, three other men stood up.

"Gentlemen, meet my two finest officers, David MacArthur, formally of the Royal Navy, and Cooper Cain. Cooper is just learning but has the makings of a good ship's captain. Mac, Cooper, meet Gregory Clark, he's one of my lawyers. He will be asking each of you a few questions about the *Inez*. How we found her, her state when we came upon her, any crewmen or passengers left aboard and the state in which they were found. Also, please inform Mr. Clark as to the live cargo, the condition they were in, the number dead and so on including how we were able to bring the ship into the Tybee Roads."

Cooper and Mac were both quick to pick up on Taylor's comment about live cargo and not valuables found. Taylor then introduced his Savannah business associates, Mr. John Will and Michael Brett. Pleasant conversation was had over a round of ale. Will and Brett took their leave with the promise of a fine dinner and a play the next evening.

Clark apologized about detaining the men but felt certain statements and affidavits had to be completed before the ship and cargo could be considered salvage and disposed of. An hour later, he advised the men that that was all he needed for the time being. He would now make his way to the East Bay Inn where Spurlock had the three sailors from the *Inez* under close watch.

As Rosita was nothing more than a traveling companion for Inez's captain, it was doubtful they would need any testimony from her. "Indeed, what information could she possibly have," Mac repeated to Coop when they were away from the lawyer.

Chapter Twenty Seven

Sophia and Cooper nestled together, spent from their passion but too excited to sleep. Sophia lay in Cooper's arms. "I had a good time tonight, my love," she said.

"I'm glad," Cooper yawned.

"I was a little anxious when I was told we were going out with the captain's friends," Sophia said.

"Why?" Cooper asked.

"I wasn't sure what they'd think of me," she replied.

"They thought you were the absolutely most beautiful creature. That's what they thought," Cooper reassured his wife.

"Coop, have you ever been to a play before?"

"No," he answered.

"Me neither. What was the name of the group?"

"Why," he asked.

"I'd like to see them again," she said.

" Are you worth the dollar a ticket?"

"Hmm," Sophia whispered. "Only you can answer that," she said, taking his hand and laying it on top of her breasts.

"I guess you are worth it," he said, feeling her nipple harden. "The company was Charles Gilferts Charles Town Theater Company."

"Did you think they were good, Cooper?"

"I enjoyed it."

"I loved it," she told Cooper.

"I'm glad," Cooper replied as Sophia's hand traveled down his abdomen.

"Did you like Tondee's Tavern?" she asked.

"Yes, I thought the food was excellent."

"Did you like the wine?"

"Uh huh," he said.

"It made me a little tipsy."

"I think you're always a little tipsy," he replied. "Ouch, don't pinch so hard."

"Then be nice or I'll move my hand."

"I'll be nice."

"Would you like to live in Savannah, Cooper?"

"I'm not sure yet. Eli is going to look at some land that's for sale. I think he's trying to talk Debbie into making a move from New Orleans."

"Why love?" Sophia asked.

"To put his past behind him. Here, he's only known as a sea captain and not as a pirate," Cooper said.

"Does the men he does business with know?"

"I'm sure they do, but it's customary for merchants to turn their heads. Look at all of them doing business with LaFitte and his brothers." After a pause, Cooper whispered, "Sophia?"

"Huh," she said.

"You don't have any more questions, do you?" he asked.

"No…well, just one. Are you sleepy?" she asked.

"No, are you?"

"Yes, goodnight."

Savannah Import, Export Merchants and Ship Chandlers sat on a bluff overlooking the Savannah River. Looking out the windows of the company's office, Cooper could see two warehouses, but beyond the warehouses it looked like a forest of ship's masts reminding him of Portsmouth back in England.

The hustle and bustle of sailors, warehousemen, porters, and merchants was the same as Portsmouth. A carriage had been waiting on him, Mac, and the captain that morning. Cooper noted that Savannah sprawled out while New Orleans was laid out in a more confined manner. Tall, huge pine trees towered above the road leading down to the wharf. Huge two story red brick houses lined Reynolds Square, and Cooper noted three churches.

Carpenters, masons and other craftsmen were busy at every turn. The smell of fresh bread wafted from a bakery and Mac pointed out no less than three houses where a doctor or surgeon had hung out his shingle.

Mr. Will and Mr. Brett welcomed the trio and arranged a tour of the warehouses for Cooper and Mac. "We are right now in an export boom," John Will said. "Savannah is leading the way, with rice, indigo, timber, tobacco, and skins."

"We are also starting to do a fair amount of exporting cotton as well," Michael Brett threw in.

Noticing both a flyer for horse racing and golf, Mac pointed at the flyers. "Do you enjoy those?"

John Will smiled. "I like the horse racing. Michael is the golfer."

"Savannah now has a golf club," Michael said proudly. "We play on the East Commons, just beyond the city."

"You can sign up for the Jockey Club at Brown's Coffee House," John said, putting in a plug for his sport. Greg Clark has all the papers signed transferring the ownership of the deserted ship *Inez* to you, Captain," John Will informed Taylor.

"Ah yes," Michael Brett said, and then added, "We paid a fee to expedite the transactions. I think the fee was cheaper than feeding the slaves the extra time the usual process takes. We can now start repairs on the *Inez* and either put the ship up for sale as a slaver or make changes and sell her as a merchantman. If you approve," he said, "we will send the ship to Yamacraw Shipwright Robert Watts."

Taylor nodded his consent. "Gentlemen, it's almost time for lunch. Shall we proceed to Gunn's Tavern where they put on a sumptuous noontime meal?"

RIDING HORSEBACK MADE THE trip faster, which meant Cooper would be back with Sophia sooner. While it was a pleasant thought, it did not do anything to lessen the discomfort he was feeling. Seamen did not belong on a horse's back, saddle or not. Captain Taylor was riding out to Thunderbolt to look at a plantation that Mr. Logan Cates had decided to sell. It was highly recommended by Michael Brett. A place where the captain could retire and enjoy his autumn days.

His closest neighbor would be the Lee's. Colonial Lee made a name for himself in the Revolutionary War and the son, Jonah, had been a scout for Mad Anthony Wayne. Just south of Cates place, was an additional two hundred acres that was for sale. A good percentage of the land was located near the Wilmington River.

Once out of the city, the land was cultivated with huge fields for planting crops. "I was told Cates' Place had good earth for farming," Taylor volunteered.

Mac and Cooper had yet to find a comfortable position in the saddle. Taylor, on the other hand, seemed at ease and even lit his pipe as his horse clipped along at a good gait. The road was lined with live oak trees, maples, and giant pines. Toward the river marsh grass grew, and in the more wooded areas the ground was covered with palmetto. A small herd of deer darted across the road, momentarily taking Cooper's mind off his aching arse. Taylor was making comments about the land and how a man could do worse than settling here about.

Bang!! Taylor pulled up his mount abruptly and the other two horses stopped as well.

Bang!! Another shot and shouts of anger could be heard. "Something's amiss," Mac volunteered. The men tied their mounts to nearby trees and moved forward, keeping just inside the wood line. The voices grew louder.

"Highwaymen," Taylor guessed. He motioned for Mac to cross over to the other side of the road and then they crept up closer. A carriage was stopped in the road. One man lay on the ground; another had his hands in the air as a rogue had a blade pointed at his gut. Two women stood beside the carriage. One of them was young, and the other was older, likely mother and daughter.

So intent were the three highwaymen, they failed to notice they had company until Taylor pulled the hammer back on his pistol, filling the air with the telltale click.

Ever the cool head, Taylor spoke, "May we be of service, Madame?"

"Be off wid yew, old man, before I run yew through," spat the trio's apparent leader.

"I'm doubtful of that with him holding a cocked pistol and you've only got a rusty blade," Cooper said.

"There be three of us," the leader said.

"Which means three fresh graves," Taylor threw back. Thus far, Mac had yet to make his presence known. "Use your head," Taylor said, trying to avoid bloodshed.

A shot rang out and then a second. A muffled shot, as one of the rogues fell to the road. Mac spoke out, "Sod was using his mate to cover him while he tried to get a clear shot at you."

"Well, now its three to two, only it's now in our favor," Taylor said. "Be off with you and you can live."

"Be damned," the highwayman with the rusty blade shouted. He moved quickly, raising his cutlass to chop down on the man.

Taylor casually pulled the trigger, causing a spot to blossom on the man's chest. The spot grew in size as the man crumpled and fell. As the rogue coughed, blood came from his mouth.

"Now there is only you," Cooper said to the last of the three.

The man was wild-eyed, sweating and nervous. A trembling hand held a dagger. "I'll cut her throat, I will, if you don't back off. You want this wench to live, don't you?"

"She's all that keeps you alive," Cooper hissed. "Look at your friends. I know you are smarter than they were. Drop the blade and you can live. But, you so much as scratch this lady and I will make you wish you were dead. This has gone on long enough. Run or die."

Common sense took hold. The villain threw down his blade and ran. For a moment no one spoke and then the older woman broke the silence, "Thank you, gentlemen, we are lucky you came along."

"The pleasure was ours," Mac said, before Taylor or Cooper could respond.

"I'm Faith Anthony, this is my son, James, and my daughter, Madelyn."

"Maddy," the girl interjected.

"Let's see about Morris," James said, walking to the driver.

Morris had a scalp wound but came around. A cloth was wet using water from a canteen and the wound was cleaned.

"He should mend," Taylor said.

"Are you sailors?" Maddy asked.

"Aye, you've a good eye," Taylor replied. "I'm Eli Taylor and these are two of my officers, Cooper Cain and David MacArthur."

"Are you two British?" the girl asked.

"Maddy," her mother said. "You don't ask questions like that."

"Well, they sound like British to me," the girl responded. "Those two anyway. My daddy is an admiral," the girl continued. "His brother was an admiral and so was his father. Now, Uncle Gil is the Governor of Antigua."

"My, but you come from an impressive family," Taylor responded. "You, sir, are you in the Navy?"

"No sir, I'm afraid the chain was broke with me. I'm a farmer. I look after my mother's side of the family. My brother is in the Navy, however."

"James just inherited a big farm," Maddy said. Not sure what to say, the men didn't say anything.

"My Uncle Gavin Lacy died," Faith said. "Since he had no living sons, he gave the farm to James. It's near Thunderbolt."

Smiling, Taylor said, "I'm considering buying a farm near there myself, Logan Cates' place."

"Why that's next door to Uncle Gavin's farm," Faith said. "You and James will be neighbors."

As Faith, the captain, and James talked, Mac and Cooper eyed Maddy, who was a younger image of her mother. She had blonde hair, blue eyes, a pert little nose and a woman's figure.

"Are you from Georgia?" Taylor asked.

"No, Beaufort, South Carolina," Faith answered. "James still runs the plantation there but Uncle Gavin's place is larger so we may sell our land in South Carolina. I hate to though, that's where my mother and father are buried and where I was born."

"It's where Nanny and Lum are buried too," James offered.

Without knowing why, Cooper offered, "I wouldn't sell it. I'd keep it forever."

"Thank you," James said. "I think there are too many memories there to sell."

"It's where mama met father also," Maddy said.

"What do we do with the farms so far apart?" Faith said with a sigh.

"Find a good overseer and let him take care of one of the places," Taylor recommended.

"Mama, we're never getting back tonight," the girl whined, looking at the sun.

"Hush, Maddy." Faith then turned to their rescuers, "I thank you again, gentlemen for your kindness. May God be with you in your travels."

"If any British captain stops you, you tell him you're mama's friends and daddy will have them flogged if they don't be nice to you," Maddy said.

Faith shook her head, "Such talk, Maddy." Again, they all shook hands and said their goodbyes.

CHAPTER TWENTY EIGHT

"YES SIR, THAT'S SOME of the finest pipe tobacco I've ever packed a pipe bowl with," Captain Taylor declared.

"I'm glad you like it," Colonel Lee said proudly. The two men sat on the colonel's side porch in the shade of a big oak tree. Colonel Lee had pointed out that the reason for the wraparound porch was to find shade from the hot Georgia sun, regardless of the time of day.

"Mama Lee's idea really," the colonel admitted. "So's you can always find a shade."

Drinking ice cold tea and smoking their pipes, the men talked about growing tobacco, rice, indigo, and cotton.

"The Cates' place is a nice farm," Colonial Lee advised. "He's got a man, David Gill, who runs the place. If you buy the place, Captain, you would do well to keep David on. He's smart, a good steward of the land and honest. Not many around with all his qualities. The slaves work well for him without use of the whip."

"I noticed you have a boy…a mixed breed, Colonel, how does he respond to your slaves?' the captain asked.

"I don't own any slaves, well not many. When I buy a slave, I make him or her indentured servants. I set up a wage scale and if they meet it in seven years, I set them free. After that, they can stay for wages or leave, most of them stay," the colonel replied.

"How does that set with your neighbors?" Taylor asked.

The colonel removed his spent pipe from his mouth and bumped the bowl on the heel of his hand, knocking the ash from the pipe, then tossed the ash off the porch into some azalea bushes. He blew through the pipe stem and then set it on the small table. "Not so well at first," the colonel admitted finally. "We had a period when we were not invited to many shindigs. I was not surprised and discussed it with Mama Lee. Her response was she had the answer to God, not man. After a time or two when a neighbor needed some help with crops or sickness, we came to their aid and soon things were back to normal."

"What about the Oxford place?" Taylor asked.

"Two hundred acres, I understand. Run down, run down bad," Lee said. "Man's wife and son came down with the fever and died. Oxford hasn't been the same since. He's got river frontage but other than that it's nearly surrounded by the Cates' place. Cates has always been good about egress."

Cooper, Mac, Jonah Lee, and Moses walked around the side yard to the porch holding up a string full of catfish. The four had been fishing and returned with supper. Taking in the big, half-black, half-Indian, Taylor could not help but think of him as a pirate. *He'd be a terror*, he thought. Nothing more was discussed in regard to the land or slaves until the following morning when Taylor, Cooper, and Mac got ready to leave.

After a fried catfish supper with grits, biscuits, honey, and ice tea, the group settled back while Mac played the guitar and sang. The following morning they had fried eggs, more grits, biscuits, blackberry jelly, and strong black coffee.

Once when the two were alone for a moment, Cooper whispered to Mac, "If you didn't like grits you'd starve."

"Aye," Mac replied with a smile.

Getting in the saddle to ride back to Savannah, Cooper moaned, "Oh God!"

"We have a wagon," the colonel volunteered with a smile.

"Many more trips and I'll need it," Cooper replied. "I'll be laid out in the back of it." This caused a chuckle.

"Colonel," Taylor said. "I want to thank you for your kind hospitality. I will have my lawyer make an offer to Cates and Oxford. I will also take your advice in regards to Mr. Gill and the…farm hands."

Colonel Lee nodded. "I don't think you will go wrong, Captain, and I welcome you as a neighbor."

THE SLAVE SALE TOOK place the following Saturday. Due to the size of the sale it was held at the race track just outside of town some three miles. Four hundred slaves were to be auctioned. Taylor's only rule was women with children were sold together. It meant less money but his heart wouldn't allow the sale to take place any other way. The slaves walked the three miles from the barracoon to the race track. The men were all fitted in heavy cotton or denim work breeches and a lighter cotton shirt. The women were dressed in colored clothes.

Once the stage was erected for the sale, the men were arranged by age and size. Buyers arrived in carriages early and a few arranged for private sales. These sales brought in top dollar. Eleven slaves had been sold directly from the barracoon. A handler was assigned to a buyer, who wanted to inspect the slaves he was interested in.

The auctioneer who was handling the sale and would get ten percent for his services saw Taylor and called to him. "There are over two hundred buyers here, Captain. You stand to make a good profit today."

Taylor smiled and nodded but didn't feel the excitement he had a days before. "Thank you, Mr. Grimes," he said to be polite to the auctioneer. Seeing Mac, Taylor told him to find Spurlock and keep him and the crew close by. "I don't think anyone would be foolish enough to attempt a robbery but you never can tell."

"Aye," Mac agreed. "We will position ourselves around the pay tent."

Unlike many auctions, today's sales were cash only. The sale started at nine a.m. and by four p.m. only a handful of slaves were left; mostly mothers with children.

A man approached Taylor introducing himself, "I'm David Gill, Captain Taylor." Taylor was glad to meet the man who might soon be his overseer. "I understand you are purchasing the Cates and Oxford places," he said, getting to the point. Taylor nodded his affirmation. "Mr. Cates told me you were very interested in keeping me on."

"That's right," Taylor responded.

"Then my first recommendation is you keep that lot," Gill said. "There's plenty they can do and it's cheaper to keep them and use them than to let them go for almost nothing. The young boys will soon be big enough for field hands and the women and girls can work around the house and garden."

Seeing the wisdom in the man's words, Taylor quickly called to the auctioneer to cease the bidding. A few who had been bidding low immediately tried to increase their bids but Taylor said, "No, I am keeping them for personal use." He then added, "Don't worry Mr. Grimes; you'll still get your ten percent." Everyone laughed except the auctioneer, who finally smiled, thinking he'd made a good profit this day.

THE SLAVE SELL BROUGHT in far more than Taylor could have imagined. Even after expenses and a generous share to the crew, he had made four hundred thousand dollars. Of course, over three hundred of the slaves were prime males, bringing top dollar of twelve to fifteen hundred each. He had kept twelve women with fourteen children, in which most of them were males. The women were all young of child bearing age. That was important to David Gill, as he thought slaves born in America tended to be stronger and healthier.

The land purchase had been agreed upon and the lawyer, Greg Clark, was handling the last minute details. A trip to the land was made in a wagon with Debbie and Sophia coming along.

It was with Sophia present that Captain Taylor told Cooper the two hundred acres from Oxford was a wedding present. "You have been very lucky for me," Taylor explained. "Debbie and I talked and we want you next door."

Sophia was very excited and gushed with happiness. Cooper couldn't help but think getting away from New Orleans was part of it. The Oxford home needed repairs and cleaning but there was plenty of room at the Cates' house until their house could be brought up to standard. Most of the crew would go back to New Orleans via a company ship. The captain, Debbie, Sophia, Cooper, and Mac would make the trip overland.

Sharing a midday meal with their new neighbors, the Lees, Jonah and Moses decided to accompany Captain Taylor, Cooper, Mac, and the women on their overland journey back to New Orleans. They agreed to be ready on Saturday morning and have the supplies needed for the trail ready. Mac wanted one more night in Savannah but was not interested in the dining and evening concert that had been planned by John Will, Michael Brett and their wives.

Mac would meet the group at the Lee home on Saturday. He'd bring Rooster, Banty, and Quang to help out on the trail and add to their numbers in case trouble showed up. "Who knows," Mac whispered to Cooper out of the women's hearing, "I might even bring Rosita if I catch up with her."

"You do and there's sure to be trouble, my Scottish friend," Cooper replied.

CHAPTER TWENTY NINE

NEW ORLEANS WAS BRISTLING. It was Christmas Eve and people were rushing about. Cindy had invited everyone including Mac to a Christmas dinner. A week before Christmas, Jumper and Gus had cut down a fir tree, and every night they added decorations to the tree, some of them all the way from Germany. Belle popped some popcorn and made a garland of if to wrap around the tree. She also made a treat, calling her concoction, sticky corn. It was a sweet mixture of butter and syrup poured over the popcorn.

"Belle has outdone herself again," Cooper declared licking the tips of his fingers. Looking up, he realized everyone was smiling. "Sorry," he said, about his bad manners, "but it is too good to waste."

"I lick my finger every time mama cooks," Jumper declared. This made everyone laugh.

"Belle makes good peppermint candy canes too," Gus said. "They are my favorite."

Seeing Cooper and Mac's look, Cindy asked, "You've never heard of peppermint candy canes?"

"I'm afraid not," Cooper said.

"Me neither," Mac admitted.

"Eli, have you had a candy cane before?" Cindy asked.

"I have got to admit I haven't," Taylor said.

"You want to tell our guests the story, Jumper?"

"Oh yes mam," the boy said, excited that he knew something his worldly friends didn't. "A long time ago in the 1600's in Cologne, Germany. That's right ain't it, Miss Cindy?" When Cindy nodded, Jumper continued, "The man in charge of the choir wanted the church to hear his choir singing so he figured to keep the 'chillins' hushed up he'd give them something. He talked with this man who had a candy shop and they decided to make peppermint sticks. So the younguns would keep their mind on Christmas he had the candy man put a crook at the top end of the stick so it would make them think of the Shepherds who came to see baby Jesus when he was born."

"Ain't that so, Miss Cindy?"

"You are right, Jumper," Cindy said.

"I'll be," Taylor said.

"Yes, you will, Eli, once you've had some of Belle's peppermint."

Christmas was a great event. Belle, who was the best cook any of the men had ever met, outdid anything she'd done so far to Cooper's way of thinking. The guests spent the night and left the following day after the noon meal, which were mostly leftovers from the night before. Lucy and Linda were gone. The entire group had missed the lively girls, especially Mac. Lucy had left a letter for Mac, which he'd read in the privacy of his room. Cooper felt a tinge of guilt over his happiness and seeing the downtrodden look on Mac.

When they got back to Debbie's hotel the men risked the evening chill to smoke cigars. In a few minutes Otis came out bearing a large box followed by Debbie and Sophia.

"While you men were off gallivanting in Savannah, we found this," Sophia said. "It's for you, Mac."

Opening the box, Mac stood back. It was a set of bagpipes. "A wonderful gift," he exclaimed. Mac then produced four small packages. Perfume for the ladies and pipes for the men. The ones he'd found and purchased. The one with the ship's wheel went to Eli, and the crossed swords to Cooper.

"What did we get?" the captain asked the ladies.

"Humph…you got us," Debbie responded, and then squealed as she was slapped across the rump. "Eli!"

Sophia only snuggled closer to her man. He knew the look at this point; his reward would be waiting when they got upstairs.

Turning to Mac and Cooper, Taylor spoke, "I've made no secret that I'm ready to give up the sea. Well, I'm done. The *Raven* is my ship. I can do with her as I wish. She is now your ship, Coop. Not free, you will pay for her but you will be able to afford it. While I can give you the ship, I can't guarantee the crew will vote you their captain. If they don't, you may have to find your own crew. Turner plans on retiring as well. But you've got good hands that will stay. Make Mac your first officer or navigator as I did. They trust his seamanship and they trust you. Together, I can see a bright future for the two of you. If you want to continue, things are changing for free men but it's not over yet. There's still time for you to make your fortune. Just stay away from ventures like we had with Gaspar. When you rely on yourself and not somebody else other than your own crew, you will find things usually turn out better in the end. And both of you remember you have to have a country; a place to lay your head in peace. Make not war on your own country."

Later that night, long after Sophia had gone to sleep, Cooper thought of Eli Taylor's words. He also felt the scar on his face. *I've yet to settle with the Finylson flag but I will. Phillip and his father will feel my wrath.*

That night with Sophia in his arms, Cooper thought about the last month, most of it having been spent with his wife. The trip from Savannah to New Orleans had been a grand leisurely adventure. Jonah Lee and Moses were not only good scouts and excellent hunters; they were also good traveling companions. They were quick to point out things of interest and of danger including coming on a band of Indians, the first ones that Cooper or Mac had ever seen. The trip was over and now he was being thrust into command of a pirate ship. Would he stand the test? Did he have what it takes? Eli thought so. He had a good friend in Mac to offer advice and good seasoned crewmen. But still there was this lingering doubt. What about Sophia? Eli and Debbie would watch after her but it was not the same as the two being together. Together, something he liked, something he'd grown accustomed to and something he'd miss. He'd take command and go pirating but only long enough to provide for Sophia.

THE VOTE WAS AS Taylor predicted. Most of the hands put their support behind Cooper. Those that didn't were allowed to leave without paying their account. A handful left, but some decided to wait and see. Johannes was voted in as the new quartermaster, the voice between the captain and the crew. He would also second Mac as navigator should the need arise having once been a master's mate. The only bad news was the ship's bottom. She needed new copper and was due for an overhaul.

"She needs much more than we can take care of here. The *Raven* needs to be taken to the Tidewater," Turner said, relating his findings after careening the ship while Taylor and his group were in Savannah.

Knowing Cooper was clueless, Taylor told his friend, "Tidewater is what Turner calls the docks in Norfolk, Virginia. There are monies in the ship's fund to see the repairs done but some of the guns are old. We've replaced a few but we should replace them all and use the same size guns. "

Cooper knew the wisdom in his former captain's words. "LaFitte will likely buy the guns we have now," he said.

"Aye," Taylor replied smiling. "You're thinking like a captain already. After the first of the year we will load up our personal belongings and you can take us to Savannah. There I will have a home waiting for you when you need rest."

"Aye," Cooper said, shaking his head. "It will be better for Sophia as well, though we both will miss Cindy."

"We will all miss Cindy," Taylor admitted, "but we can visit."

"Did Otis like taking on the hotel for half shares," Cooper asked.

"Yes, and if all goes well in seven years it will be his," Taylor replied. He had pulled that thought from Colonel Lee.

"Did you notice the free blacks in Savannah?" Cooper asked.

"Yes, but they don't seem to be accepted as well," Mac said.

"They intermingle in the sporting clubs," Cooper said.

"Aye, men with the appetite and the means usually find pleasure. But that don't mean they'd have Quadroon balls to find either themselves or their sons mistresses. No, Coop, for all its good, bad and ugly, New Orleans is a city you're not likely to see the likes of again. I'm not even sure we'll see the degree of acceptance in New Orleans much longer," Taylor said.

"Aye," Cooper acknowledged. "The new governor has got different ideas."

The men sat for a few minutes, each with their own thoughts. Cooper then spoke, "You know what you need to do as your last act of piracy, Captain?"

Seeing the devilish grin of Cooper's face, Taylor couldn't help but ask, "What my young friend?"

"Steal Belle," Cooper replied.

Taylor laughed, "Damme, boy, but that is a good idea."

PART IV

CHAPTER THIRTY

THE BREEZE BLEW SOFTLY as gulls floated in the air, diving at a small school of fish. The Chesapeake Bay sky was full of lazy clouds that looked like puffs of cotton.

"That's Sewell's Point to larboard, Captain," Johannes said, who knowing these waters was bringing the *Raven* into the crowded port. "Bring her up a point," he ordered the helmsman.

The James River was crowded today. They were under reduced sails but the ship seemed to be moving too fast for Captain Cooper Cain's comfort. Not that he didn't have every confidence in his quartermaster, it was just everything seemed to be moving so fast.

Otis had taken over Hotel Provincial, Debbie's belongings plus what few Sophia had, had been loaded aboard *Raven*. Bankers and lawyers were visited and everything was put in order for the move. Jean LaFitte threw a big party for Captain Taylor and then goodbyes were made to Cindy, Belle, Gus and Jumper. They had become family to Cooper, Mac, and Sophia. Cooper had gotten *Raven* underway while Taylor spent most of his time in the captain's cabin.

In Savannah, everything had been unloaded. David Gill had met up with Taylor and said the house was ready. *Raven's* crew was given the weekend to visit the taverns and sporting houses. Beau Cannington warned the crew about bringing back from the sporting houses more than they paid for. John Will and Michael Brett had arranged a set of rooms at the new Washington Hall

Hotel. After a huge meal that caused the men to loosen their pants one button, they bought one-dollar seats and watched a play at the Exchange Building.

Mac and Beau Cannington then took their leave from the couples to do a bit of carousing on their own. The next two nights were nights of passion for Cooper and Sophia. The time ashore was then up and *Raven* put to sea. For the first time, Cooper felt like a captain. Sophia had gotten him a captain's coat with big pockets and Taylor had given him his hat. "You need to look the part," he'd said.

Now, with the pipe Mac had given him in his coat pocket, Cooper stood on the quarterdeck as Johannes brought the ship in and moored across from Tidewater Shipyard and Dry Dock. A boat from the shipyard put out to meet them.

A man came aboard introducing himself, "I'm Roger Nobles. My father still runs the place but he's up in age so I meet the ships now." He recognized the *Raven* as she moored but was expecting Captain Taylor.

Cooper was still staring at the man who'd not given him a chance to speak. Johannes spoke up, "This is Captain Cooper Cain, and he has a letter for you from Captain Taylor."

"Yes," Cain said and reached for the letter he'd put in his coat pocket that morning. Cooper, Mac, Johannes, and Diamond rowed over to the shipyard office where they met the senior Nobles. Arrangements were made for the crew to be housed and fed if they were around at meal time.

"There's room for you as well, Captain," Nobles advised and then added, "but most captains and officers find their own lodging closer to town."

"We'll stay tonight anyway," Cooper advised. Looking across the harbor after finishing the business in Nobles' office, Cooper commented, "That looks like a large shipyard across the way a bit. I can see ship masts."

"Aye, you've a good eye, young man," Nobles senior said. "That's Gosport, used to be private but now the federals have taken it over, so it's mostly for Navy ships now, what few they be."

"I see," Cooper replied, as he and Mac strolled off to find the Fouled Anchor, a tavern that catered to sea captains and officers. Cleaner than most and ship shape, Nobles had sworn.

"Probably gets a cut for every sailor he sends their way," Mac whispered.

It was the most mournful tune they'd ever heard. The sound poured from the open doorway. Without looking at the sign, Cooper and Mac entered, drawn by the music. The place was packed. A table by the fireplace had one patron. The man looked up as the two walked over. Using his hand in a quick motion, he invited them to the empty bench on the opposite side of the table. No words passed.

The musician, if that was what you could call him walked the aisles between the tables playing a scarred fiddle. The bow had so many frayed horsehairs Cooper wondered if it was down to bare wood. The man playing was little more than a skeleton, his skin ghost white, pale and his sparse hair hung down to his shoulders. Cooper looked about the room to see more than one dabbing the tears from their eyes, men and women alike. When the old fiddler finished playing he picked up a sack and put the instrument away. He then picked up an empty tankard and walked around; coins clinked as they filled the pewter tankard. When he got to their table he said, "That one was for you, old friend." The man smiled and placed a coin in the now nearly full tankard.

Smiling, the fiddler looked away and then turned back and looked at Cooper, "You're a marked man. Have you paid your dues? Let me tell you, friend, it's a long hard road. That goes for you too, my Scottish friend. Careful, as death awaits you." The man wheeled and walked away leaving Cooper and Mac spellbound.

"He's daft," a serving girl said. "The owner lets him play cause he packs the place but every once in awhile he comes up with a scary something.

Cooper and Mac ordered and told the girl to refill the gentleman's tankard as he so willingly shared his table.

"Thank you," the man said. "My name is Dagan, Dagan Dupree." The men all shook hands with Cooper and Mac introducing themselves.

Dagan, Cooper could see, had once been a seaman. His face was weathered, with crow's feet at the corner of his eyes from squinting in the sun and hard leathery skin on the back of his hands.

"You're an old tarpaulin," Mac said, more a statement than a question.

"Aye, and you two are British, I take it," Dagan replied.

"We're British, still are I guess, only we make our home in the southern United States now," Cooper said.

"Aye, much as I have, met a woman from here in Norfolk so after the war I left the Navy and came back. We had a good life."

Without thinking, Cooper said, "Had?"

The old man shook his head but did not speak for a beat or two, "She died this past summer. Our doctor said her heart wore out. It was a happy life we shared though. She was afraid I'd miss the sea, but I didn't. She gave me more than the sea ever did. I have thought about going back to the sea for awhile; maybe visit some family I haven't seen in years."

Cooper felt a kinship with the old man, without knowing why. "Our ship is here for an overhaul. When she gets out of the yards you are welcome to sail with us if you've a desire to sail south."

Dagan smiled and his eyes narrowed so much Cooper wondered if he could see between the lids. After a moment of silence, he spoke, "Your friend has the look and ways of a seaman. But you're the captain. I think, my friend, your ship could be a raider. Gooley felt it and I feel it. You've a good heart and I'm pleased at your offer. I will consider it."

The maid was back with the food and drink. Dagan asked the girl for a pipe and a long stemmed while clay pipe was brought to him. He opened a pouch he'd had laying on the table and packed the pipe bowl with tobacco. The girl reached in the fireplace and lit a piece of straw she'd snatched from a broom.

Mac was facing the girl as she bent over so that he had the pleasure of a glimpse of her ample breasts. She held the burning straw over Dagan's pipe until the tobacco was lit and then threw the remnant into the fire. Looking at Mac, she said, "He's a gentleman, that one, unlike some." Mac blushed knowing he'd been caught eyeing her wares. Dagan and Cooper chuckled.

"The fiddle player, is he really crazy?" Mac asked.

Dagan puffed on the pipe a time or two, sending little plumes of smoke into the air. "Gooley's a lost soul alright. Claims he sold his soul to the devil on the fiddler's green so that he could play like he does. Legend has it any fiddler or violin player worth a bloody damn got that way by swearing allegiance to Lucifer. But Gooley's lost his mind. He was away on a privateer during the war of 76. When he came home much of Norfolk had been burned. Some say by the British Navy. Gooley's house had burned down and his wife and child were never found. People say he just went crazy, maybe from a broken heart. My father-in-law was General Manning. He found Gooley nearly frozen to death. He brought him home and warmed him up. Betsy, my wife, fed him and I gave him some warm clothes and a coat. He got better and left. He'd show up from time to time after that. Gooley stood outside the church and played when Betsy died, said he wasn't allowed to come in. He plays sad, mournful songs. It's like you can feel his pain when he drags the bow across the strings. It's a rare jig he'll play, and then only after he's well paid. "

The men had finished eating and each had another round when Mac yawned. "It's been a long day. Let's go find the Fouled Anchor and see if there's a room left. Could you give us directions, Dagan?"

"Aye, it's easy. See that door across the room?" Mac nodded. "That's where you get your room. You've been in the Fouled Anchor these past two hours," Dagan said.

"Well damme," Cooper said.

"You have your bag with you, I see, so you can check on a room if that's your desire, or you can come to my house. There's room enough so you can each have your own bedroom. Maggie's the cat, she won't trouble you none. I have a woman and her daughter to do the cooking and cleaning. They'll wash for you as well," Dagan said.

"We wouldn't want to impose," Cooper said.

Dagan replied, "You're not, I asked you. It's good to hear a British accent. I want to know how things were when you were last in England and why you've come to be a raider."

Cooper noticed the old salt said raiders, not pirates. But he knew. How, Cooper didn't know, but he knew.

THE TIME PASSED VERY quickly, not one month but two. The ship was now newly coppered, and she had been rearmed with twenty-two nine pounders, eleven per side. She also had new swivels, forward, amidships, in the fighting tops, and on the quarterdeck. The mainmast and foremast were new, as were the spars and rigging. Dagan had gone down to the ship with either Cooper or Mac at various times. He seemed to quicken his step as they toured the ship. He missed the sea, that was plain to see.

Lodging with Dagan had been more than Cooper or Mac could have hoped for. It was almost like family. Maggie, the cat, had even started hopping up on Cooper or Mac's lap after supper, purring as they scratched her ears. Mac was beside himself when at the breakfast table; she brought in a freshly killed mouse.

"She likes you," Dagan swore. "Never knew her to offer anybody a mouse but Betsy." He showed the two men a painting of Betsy, one of General Manning and then one of his nephew and his wife.

Looking at the painting, Cooper swore. He looked at Mac, who shook his head and said, "It looks like her."

"Tell me, Dagan," Cooper said. "Is this woman…is her name Faith?"

"Aye, that be it," Dagan said with surprise on his face. They then told Dagan of the encounter with the highwaymen. Shaking his head, Dagan said, "Then it's glad I am to have met you. I will tell Gabe and Faith of our time."

"So you're going to Antigua," Cooper asked.

"Yes, I don't know how long I'll stay. My sister, Gabe's mother, is getting on in years. I may stay with her for a while if I can get a ship headed to Portsmouth."

"With Gabe an admiral, I don't see getting to Portsmouth being much of a problem," Mac offered.

"I don't think it will be if the war holds off," Dagan said.

"Do you really think there will be another war, Dagan?" Mac asked.

"Sir Robert Basnight does," Dagan admitted. "He is much opposed to the Royal Navy stopping American ships and pressing their seamen. He has argued with Parliament about it but feels they can't see beyond their purse."

"Is he going to England?" Mac asked.

"No, he's headed to Bermuda, but there are Royal Navy ships as well as merchants' ships leaving Bermuda for Antigua and Barbados every few weeks. So I'll find passage," Dagan said.

Let's have one more night out before we go our separate ways. It was hellish good luck meeting you," Cooper swore. "I have come to feel close to you, like maybe you were my father or uncle."

Dagan placed his hand on the young man's shoulder. "And I you, Cooper Cain, I can see squalls ahead for you, my friend, but brighter days after; if you keep your head and don't let your desire for revenge consume you. It's matured you, it's hardened you but don't let it be your undoing. The hangman doesn't care why you've done what you have, only that you've done it. I want to tell you one more thing, something for both of you. Mac, Gabe would see you commissioned again and put in a senior role, with a letter from me. It's yours for the asking. He would be most appreciative for your helping his family, likely saving their lives. But Gabe is a man who does his duty. Forget what Maddy or Faith said. Should one of his ships catch you in an act of piracy, he'd hang you. He'd not like it and it might cost him his marriage but he'd hang you. It's his duty. I hope he retires before another war starts, particularly if it's between our countries." Dagan looked saddened as he spoke. "Remember my words, my friends."

CHAPTER THIRTY ONE

THE WIND WAS FAVORABLE but the bay was slightly choppy. A misty rain hung in the air, creating a fog of sorts.

"I wish it'd rain or dry up," Banty moaned. "I hate this type of weather."

It was Sunday morning and the crew was making their way back aboard ship. Some of them were showing the effects of a rough night ashore. One had his arm in a sling from a gunshot wound.

"I told you she was in a bad mood," Moree said.

"Well, I didn't notice it until it was too late," his mate, Matt replied.

"The pistol in her hand was a dead giveaway, if you ask me," Moree exhorted.

In ones, twos, and groups, the men came aboard the ship until Johannes proclaimed they were all accounted for. After leaving Norfolk, *Raven* had sailed to Savannah. They'd spent a week there, and then sailed for Barataria. where Mac and Cooper had visited Cindy, ate their fill of Belle's home cooking, fished with Jumper and smoked Gus' cigars while he and Mac played music and sang.

LaFitte had been gone when the *Raven* had dropped anchor, but Dominique Youx said he'd planned to be back on Sunday. Dominque warned Cooper about the increasing number of British ships in the Gulf. Lafitte did return on Saturday afternoon. Cooper and Mac enjoyed the evening meal at LaFitte's house overlooking the tiny kingdom set up by LaFitte. Pirate, privateer, smuggler, whatever you labeled the man, he was also a leader and an organizer.

After the meal, Cooper told him that they had planned to set sail on the morning tide, weather permitting. As they shook hands in departing, LaFitte held Cooper's hand a bit longer as he spoke, "Eli Taylor is my friend. He set great store in you. By saving his life you have made me happy, as I do not wish harm to come to my friends. Therefore, I will extend to you, my young friend, the same courtesy Eli enjoyed. You bring your plunder or slaves to me and you will get the same deals Eli enjoyed." Cooper thanked LaFitte, and the men shook hands once more and headed to the *Raven*.

Once at sea, the misty rain increased to a drizzle and a moderate wind picked up with gray skies overhead. "A gloomy start," Johannes snorted.

Off to starboard the land faded away until the ship was alone… and alone they stayed. Not a single prize was sighted. After a quick meeting, the crew voted to give up on the Gulf. Mac and Johannes looked at the charts and decided to set a course to pass through the Yucatan Channel and into the Caribbean, rather than coming about and reverse the course they'd just sailed.

After weeks of zigzag in the Caribbean, they'd only taken one ship. It was a Spaniard that had little value except for fifteen slaves. The ship did have a good supply of wine, cocoa, and a few casks of rum. They sailed on to Saint Croix where the slaves were sold along with the wine and cocoa. Departing Saint Croix, they decided to sail the Atlantic coast up to Nova Scotia. If pickings were still poor, they'd head south.

"Slaves seem to be the biggest profit," Quang said. "Maybe we could head toward the Guinea coast and take a slaver."

"Might even look at the Indian Ocean," McKemie volunteered. "The Honest Johns should be making their voyages home soon."

So it was agreed, sail north but not to Nova Scotia, only to Savannah, spend a week ashore and then head south again. First to the slave routes and then the East India trade routes.

"DECK THAR! SOMETHING AFLOAT off the larboard side, two points off the bow."

It was a good hour after sunrise. The *Raven* was just north of Puerto Rico. They had passed well to seaward of the island with its huge fort and great guns. The crew rushed to the larboard side. It was a grate and a man clung to it. Diamond had a grappling hook cast out and snagged the grate, pulling it up to the side of the ship. Quang went down the battens at the entry port and got a rope around the man clinging so desperately he'd torn some of his fingernails off.

Aboard the ship, Dr. Cannington examined the man who looked more dead than alive. His back was sunburned, his face red, his lips were cracked and swollen. "Get a cup of water," Cannington ordered.

The man was coming around and grabbed at the offered cup. "Just a little at first," Cannington told him in a soft soothing voice. "We have plenty."

After a few sips, the man smiled, wincing at the pain in his lips. "I thought I was a goner." He lay back down and was then taken below.

Cannington had the gel squeezed from aloe plants in a jar. He rubbed it across the man's back, his face and lips.

"What's that?" Cooper asked.

"Aloe, they say the thick gel-like juice helps to heal burns," Cannington said.

"Where did you hear that?"

"A herb woman in New Orleans," Cannington replied.

"Herb woman?" Cooper asked.

"Yes, she was healing folks with her remedies long before I was born. Aunt Fanny, they call her. She is a Creole woman, says she's over a hundred years old. Regardless, I've found many of her herbs very useful," Cannington said.

"I hope it works," Cooper said. "He looks a shitten mess."

An hour later, McKemie knocked on the door of the captain's cabin. "Doc says you need to come down," he said, matter-of-factly.

The sailor was sitting up when Cooper made his way into the sick bay. Glancing up from his patient, Cannington said, "I think you need to hear this, Captain." Cooper was still trying to adjust to the new title.

"My name is Browne, sir, Brown with an e at the end."

"Alright," Cooper said, and then waited for the man to continue.

Browne with an e took a sip of water and then touched his lip. A spot of blood was on his finger. "I'll put more aloe on your lip after you tell the captain what you told me," Cannington said. "But hurry, he's got a ship to run."

"I was a mate on the merchant brig, *Mary Ann*. We were headed to Antigua." This caught Cooper's attention. "We were off the coast of Puerto Rico, when we were attacked by a pirate just before dusk. They killed the captain and crew right off. They took all the women passengers' prisoners and Lord Basnight. They will use the women and ransom Lord Basnight."

"How many women were there?" Cooper asked the man.

"Several, maybe ten or twelve, but two of them were Admiral Anthony's wife and daughter." Cooper now listened intently. "They don't mind using the women up and then..." Browne made the sign of slicing one's throat.

"I had heard you mention the admiral's wife and daughter," Cannington said to Cooper. "I thought you'd want to know."

"Thank you, Beau."

Cooper then turned back to Browne. "Did you by chance hear where they were going?"

"Yes sir, Culebra. It's a little island off the coast of Puerto Rico. They have a camp of sorts setup there."

"How did you manage to get away?" Cooper asked suddenly.

Browne looked embarrassed, "I was using the head, sir, so I just lay low. I saw them set a fuse to blow up the ship so I eased over the side. When the ship blew up, I spied the grate and latched on. You know the rest."

On deck, Cooper took a breath. He had to try to save the women. But he couldn't order the men to attempt the rescue. They were free men; part of the brethren of the coast. To attack other brethren just wasn't done. Well, if they wouldn't help, he'd have them put him ashore and he'd do what he could.

"Mr. MacArthur," Cooper called. "Put the ship about, and then call all hands for a meeting."

THE MEETING HAD GONE far better than Cooper had imagined. He quickly explained the events and then stretched it a bit by saying the Anthony women were good friends of his and Mac's.

"Aye, and don't forget I know the ladies as well," Beau Cannington said.

Cooper couldn't remember if the doctor had met Faith and Maddy or if it was a little white lie to add to the cause.

"Do you know who took them?" Bridges asked.

"No, only where," Cooper admitted.

"Probably El Diablo or one of his lieutenants," Spurlock volunteered. "These are his waters."

"Do we bargain for the two or just take the lot?" Robinson asked.

Spurlock answered the question, "There'll be no bargaining with his like, we take it or die trying, but there'll be no bargaining."

"Is it not against the code?" McKemie asked.

Diamond spoke with Johannes echoing his words, "The code don't mean shat to that bunch of rogues. They'd everyone slit your throat over the last swallow of rum in a bottle and then laugh about it."

A man named Johnson spoke up, "I don't like crossing swords with free men but if they's took the captain's friends I say let's be about getting them back and damn 'em to hell if they don't like it." Several men agreed.

Cooper looked at Johannes, who nodded and then shouted, "Then let's be putting it up for a vote. Them what's willing to go after the women, raise your hand." A quick glance told Cooper he had the vote. "No need counting, Captain, the crew is with you," Johannes said.

"Thank you, men," Cooper said.

Spurlock, Diamond, Johannes, and Mac all sat around the captain's table looking over a chart. Culebra looked to be about fifteen miles from the southeastern coast of Puerto Rico.

"This chart doesn't show much," Spurlock said. "But there are good beaches here, at this end of the island. The chart doesn't show it but there are a couple of smaller islands just off this coast. At the other end of the island is a good size cove or harbor. The water is deep enough to anchor in up close to the beach. It offers good protection from storms. The first beach I mentioned has the best landing spot for boats but from there to here is a good five to seven miles. Up and down hills and lots of sand and palmetto bushes; also a lot of plants with long thorns on them." Spurlock said this holding his thumb and index finger apart to emphasize the length. "They hurt worse than getting stabbed with a dirk."

"You been stabbed with a dirk?" Cooper asked.

"Aye, Captain, and the damn thorns as well," Spurlock answered. "They both hurt to hell and back." The man said it with such conviction; the little group couldn't help but chuckle.

After the men quieted down, Spurlock said, "Back your arse into one of the thorns and then we'll see who laughs." No one laughed this time. "I recommend we set a party ashore here, Captain, and come up on the camp from behind. At a set time, *Raven* can put into the harbor and if the blackhearts are anchored there, we can fire a couple of broadsides into their ship. Sink it then and there, and you'll not have to deal with it later."

Both Johannes and Diamond agreed. "Who knows," Diamond said, "we're likely to find more plunder than we've come across in weeks."

"Aye, but this ain't no stroll down the French Quarter," Spurlock said. "These are a tough bunch of rogues. Careful or not, some of us is not likely to make it back to the ship," he said in a solemn voice.

CHAPTER THIRTY TWO

IT WAS A THREE quarter moon, and the clouds were moving fast and would dim the moon's light on the beach for a few moments time to time. Three longboats had shoved off from the *Raven* and had just run up on the white sand.

"Probably rain in the morning," somebody volunteered, only to be hushed by a mate.

Once the boats could be seen safely ashore, *Raven* set sail. The plan was to anchor just off the entrance of the harbor until two a.m. or the alarm was given. Hopefully, it would be the first. Cooper, Mac, and Spurlock had each come ashore in a different boat and met up on the beach. Johannes and Diamond had stayed aboard and would bring *Raven* in at the time discussed.

The *Raven's* crew looked like a bloodthirsty lot with scarves around their waists, bandanas around their heads, pistols tucked into their waistbands, and cutlasses, blades gleaming in the moonlight, held in their hands. After walking up a narrow path to the top of a hill, the glow of campfires could be seen in the distance.

"Somebody's home," Spurlock said.

The group went down the hill and up another. At the top of this hill, parts of the harbor could be seen.

"I don't see a ship," Banty volunteered.

"Could be closer into shore," Mac said. "You can't see close in from here."

The beach was still a half mile off. They continued on until they could hear the surf as it washed ashore. Smoke from the fire floated on a slight breeze. The smell of the smoke mixed in with the smell of vegetation and the sea.

Banty shimmied up a palm tree and looked about. "There's a large palisade and you can see people moving about inside. Several huts are nearer the beach and a large tent is near the beach. It's a whitish color so it's probably made from sails. I count six fires, one by the tent and the rest in front of the huts. There are lanterns hanging along the palisade. Several men are walking about, some with women. It looks like there is a pig on a spit. Everybody seems to have a bottle or a mug." Banty paused and then added, "I don't see a ship. They's a shitten mess of the whoresons but no ship."

"Does it look like they're settling down for the night?" Cooper asked, hopefully.

"Not so's you can tell, Captain, much like it is at Barataria," Banty said.

Cooper nodded, not surprised. At Barataria, the men usually didn't start to go down until the sun started coming up.

"Let's move closer. If they're as drunk as you say, they ain't likely to notice us," Cooper said.

The palisade was similar to the one Gaspar had. Palmetto logs lashed together with ship's ropes. Only this one was poorly built. After watching for a bit, a guard was spotted making his rounds. He stopped at some place or another, grabbing some girl or woman who stood to close to the barrier. He'd grope her and make lewd, vulgar comments and then walk on. As he neared where Cooper and his men were hidden, Cooper motioned to Quang to eliminate the blackheart.

Quang didn't reply, but before he knew it the Oriental leaped out at the unsuspecting man and twisted his neck, snapping the spine before the man could speak. Robinson quickly pulled the man into the tree line.

Cooper took a chance and walked over to the enclosure. "Faith," he called, his voice just above a whisper. "Faith, it's me. Cooper Cain."

A girl with long black hair and torn clothes came over. "Who are you looking for?"

"Faith, Faith Anthony or her daughter, Maddy," he said.

"I will see if she's here, some have been taken out by the pirates," the girl told him.

"Oh God, please don't let it be either of them," Cooper prayed.

It seemed like forever when Faith walked up. Cooper had just about given up, not knowing when another guard might be making his rounds. Cooper put his hand out as Faith walked up.

"Thank God, it's you, Cooper." Tears flooded her face and her voice trembled as she tried to speak, anguish in her voice. "They took Maddy, Coop, to the big tent. You've got to help her."

"I will," he promised. "Keep the women quiet."

He went back to the edge of the trees and told the men what he had discovered. "Mac, you take half the men one way and Spurlock, you take the other half the opposite way. Quang, get inside the palisade and don't let anymore harm come to the women there. Banty, you go with him."

"Where you going, Coop?" Mac asked.

"To the big tent; I will attempt to keep things quiet but if I set off the alarm, you men give them hell. Make enough noise to bring the *Raven* in. It's just now one thirty, but I can't leave Maddy with the cutthroats another half hour."

The men drifted off like fog over the water. No one mentioned waiting. They just went to get in position. Quang and Banty cut a few ropes and squeezed in between the palmetto logs.

Cooper spoke once more to Faith, "I'm going after Maddy. Get the women on the ground if shooting starts."

Deciding a bold approach was best, Cooper pulled his hat down and walked past a fire where two drunken sailors were pulling pieces of overcooked pork from the spit. One of the sailors grunted a greeting. Cooper replied with a grunt. Seeing a discarded rum bottle, Cooper bent and picked it up. The men at the fire were watching him but when he picked up the bottle, their attention went back to the roasted pig.

The flap to the tent was on the ocean side. Cooper could hear voices inside, several voices. He recognized Maddy's quickly. It was the only woman's voice. She was cursing up a streak, calling the pirates names Cooper hadn't heard. This only made the pirates laugh. Another voice, a man's voice, begged the bastards not to hurt the girl.

Cooper had to duck back from the flap as a man walked over and cussed the person begging for mercy for Maddy. He could also hear chains rattle and then 'wham'. The begging man had received a blow. Was he dead? What was he hit with? Taking another look inside, Cooper couldn't believe his eyes. Maddy was stripped naked. Two pirates were holding her down, squeezing and pinching her breasts. *No way to do this quietly,* Cooper thought to himself. He grasp the neck of the rum bottle and threw it with all his might. It hit the pirate who'd positioned himself to rape Maddy at the base of the skull. Down he went, but for how long?

"What the hell," one of the rogues snapped.

Cooper pulled his pistols, praying Maddy would stay down and his aim would be true. Bang…bang, dead center. With surprise on their faces and curses on their lips, the men fell. Crimson poured from their chest wounds before they hit the sand. Cooper rushed over to Maddy but just as he got there, the pirate he'd hit with the rum bottle stood up. He blinked a time or two to clear his head, all the time drawing his sword. Instantly, Cooper pulled his from its scabbard, the blade making a rasping sound. Outside, the sound of gunfire seemed to be coming from all directions.

"So you've come to save the wench, have you?" the man spat. "I'll have your head and then pleasure myself with the tart while she stares at your headless body."

"Words," Cooper threw back. "Words from a sodomite so used to the windward passage of boys, he can't do proper service to a woman." What was it Jean-Paul had said? Anger your foe. Anger him so he makes mistakes.

The man was big…big and bald, with an earring in his ear. He'd taken his shirt off and the man's muscles stood out in the lantern light. If the brute chose, he could kill Maddy before Cooper could do anything. *I have to keep his attention and mind on me*, Cooper decided.

"No little boys around tonight. I'll show you a boy," the pirate said, as he charged.

The slash barely missed Cooper's head. It was so fast it almost ended the fight before it began. But Cooper was not without skill. His long hours with Jean-Paul were now to be tested. He'd never crossed swords with such a brute. Never had he faced an opponent so large and with so much strength. He realized he had no fear. After his foe slashed out, his weight carried him forward. Cooper whipped his sword about. The man had moved just enough that the strike was not true. Instead of cutting the man's carotid artery, he cut off the lower portion of his ear. The ear and its earring landed on the sand.

"There's one ear, now for the other," Cooper taunted.

This time his foe didn't rush. Blades clanged, the jolt went all the way down Cooper's arm. The pirate advanced. He beat at

Cooper's blade, and then thrust with his sword. Cooper parried each attack as steel grated on steel.

After the initial attack, the man slowed his pace. He gave up the bull-like rush, determined to save his strength. His anger was now in check. A smile crossed the brute's face. "You are smart," he said. "But Greekor is smart, too. I not fall for your tricks."

"You did once," Cooper responded. "Look at the blood running down your arm."

As Greekor looked at his arm, Cooper bore in. He attacked with a vengeance. Once again blades clashed; clang, clang, clang. Cooper thrust and then countered Greekor's riposte, and then thrust again. He was starting to tire but his blade had drawn blood in several places. None of the wounds were serious, but all were bleeding, and would soon cause his opponent to lose strength and let his guard down.

Seeing his many wounds, Greekor went on the offensive. He pressed Cooper hard, beating his blade with all his strength. Cooper parried and countered but Greekor kept pressing. Backing up, Cooper stepped in a spot where the sand was unlevel and almost lost his balance. Sensing victory, Greekor's eyes grew wide in triumph. He reared back and cut down with all his might. Cooper could feel the whoosh of air from Greekor's blade as he dove under and forward. Off balance now, Greekor was turning when Cooper thrust his blade. He felt it sink in and he shoved with all his might. The sword had gone in under the armpit and into the top of Greekor's lungs. The man fell, pulling the sword from Cooper's grasp. Blood and bubbles came from his nose and mouth as death took the man.

Exhausted, Cooper had to put his foot on the body of his enemy to pull his blade out. All his exhaustion seemed to be swept away as his gaze fell on Maddy. *Damn*, he thought, *this is one hell of a woman*. Different from Sophia, but where Sophia was exotic, Maddy was beautiful.

Her voice broke his revive, "Am I that hard to look upon that you must frown?"

"No, my beautiful lady," he responded. "Were I not a married man, I would fight a hundred such as him, if I thought it would gain me favor in your eyes."

Maddy smiled, "Well said, sir, but would it not be proper for you to find something to cover me. It would be embarrassing for Sir Robert to come to and see me like this."

Cooper took off his coat and put it on Maddy as she held out first one arm and then the other. Not knowing why, he took Maddy's hand and kissed it. "They didn't hurt you, did they, my beautiful lady?"

"No, you got here in time. It seems you always show up on time," Maddy replied.

The commotion outside was now sporadic. Most of the voices Cooper recognized as his men. Maddy and Cooper were freeing Sir Robert from his shackles when Faith, Mac, and several other men burst into the tent.

Maddy rushed to her mother, "You should have seen it, Mother. Cooper killed them all." Faith continued to hug her daughter, tears of joy running down her face. She mouthed 'thank you' to Cooper.

"But I don't understand," Sir Robert Basnight was saying. He'd been taken aboard *Raven* as soon as she anchored and boats were sent ashore. Beau Cannington had looked at his wounds, sutured up a scalp laceration, and advised Sir Robert that he'd be sore a few days but should have no lasting effects from his head trauma.

The doctor then turned his attention to the wounded crew. There were not that many and no deaths.

"Surprise was on our side," Spurlock had said.

"That and good rum," Banty added.

Sir Robert, Faith, Maddy, Cooper, Mac, and Johannes were all crowded into the captain's cabin. Sir Robert was doing his best to talk Cooper into providing passage for all those rescued, which Cooper agreed to do. He'd take them to Savannah. There, they could get another ship to transport them to Antigua or wherever they wanted to go. But time was of the essence to Sir Robert.

"I will pay you, sir. You will lose nothing if you provide passage, sir, you have my word on it."

"I can't," Cooper repeated.

"Sir, as a British gentleman, I implore you to do as requested."

"I can't."

"Why, sir, why after all you've done thus far, do you refuse?"

Cooper took a deep breath and blurted out, "Because, I'm not a British gentleman. I am a pirate. A bloody pirate, sir, that's why."

A silence filled the room. Mac was staring big-eyed at Cooper, not believing his friend had just admitted to being a pirate to a British lord. Surely, they were now all doomed for the gallows.

The silence was broken as Sir Robert let out a little laugh. "Damme, sir, but that was frankly said. As a British lord and as the next Governor of Antigua, I can promise you safe passage, not only to Antigua but your voyage home as well."

A discreet knock was heard at the door. Cooper walked over to it. When he opened the door, Spurlock was there. "All the supplies have been loaded and boats recovered, Captain. I'm thinking maybe we should set sail." By supplies, Spurlock meant all the plunder they had confiscated. His remarks meant they'd been lucky there was no ship in port to have to battle.

Now it was time to get the hell out of the area before one or more ships returned. In which case, they'd not get away with as much as they now enjoyed.

Speaking to the room at large, Cooper said, "We will speak of this later. Now, it's time we make our departure." As Cooper followed Mac and Johannes out of the cabin, Maddy brushed by him, as she passed she whispered, "Sir Pirate."

THE MARINE SENTRY KNOCKED on the door of the admiral's stateroom, "Flag captain, suh."

"Morning, David," the admiral greeted David, his friend since they were both midshipmen together.

"Did you hear the cannon go off, Sir Gabe?"

"Aye, Jake mentioned it was only one gun."

"Yes sir, that's all that was fired, but they have a signal hoisted. To flag, send barge," David said.

"Damnation," Jake Hex exclaimed. "Who's ordering Sir Gabe to send his barge?" Hex had been Sir Gabe's cox'n nearly thirty-five years. As such he came and went, and spoke when he pleased. You didn't mess with the admiral's cox'n, not if you enjoyed being in the Royal Navy.

"I wondered the same, Captain," David offered. "I then put my glass on the approaching ship. Seeing what I did, I ran right down."

"What did you see?" Admiral Anthony inquired.

"I believe Sir Robert Basnight is standing on the ship's quarterdeck. I wasn't totally sure, sir, but I'm one hundred percent sure it's Faith and Maddy standing next to him."

"Damnation, call out my barge," the admiral exclaimed.

"I have sir, and mine as well."

It was a rough looking lot that stood along the rails of the ship as the admiral's barge came alongside. Sir Gabe Anthony,

Vice Admiral, Royal Navy climbed out of his barge, up the battons and through the entry port. Protocol demanded he be greeted by the ship's captain before rushing his wife. Faith cared little for such things and rushed to meet her husband as soon as he stepped on the deck. His daughter followed her mother.

All the passengers had been treated well by the crew, but in the time it took to sail from Culebra to Antigua, Maddy had become the crew's favorite. She even asked to sign the articles so she could be part of *Raven's* crew. She was dressed in some seaman's clothes that were given to her by Banty. But right now, she was daddy's little girl.

After Gabe had been greeted by his family, Sir Robert stepped forward. "It's good to see you again, Sir Gabe."

"Aye, and you sir," Gabe replied.

"Thank you. Now let me introduce you to our rescuers," Sir Robert said.

"What was that?" the admiral asked.

"These men rescued us from a horde of cutthroats, like you never could imagine. We owe our lives and more to the good men of the *Raven*," Sir Robert replied. Introductions were made and invitations were extended.

"I'M SORRY, SIR, BUT we can't stay. We are overdue for Savannah," Cooper said.

"At least let me arrange to have payment for our passage brought to you," Sir Robert said to Cooper.

Shaking his head no, Cooper said, "There's no charge, Sir Robert, just that letter you mentioned would be fine."

"Yes, that you shall have right away. May we, the admiral and I use your cabin for a moment?" Sir Robert asked.

"Certainly," Cooper said.

After a few minutes, Jake Hex, who had followed the admiral down to the cabin, came on deck. He went down to the barge and handed one of the bargemen a note along with verbal instructions. In a little more than an hour, the *Raven* was underway with letters from Sir Robert and Admiral Anthony allowing them safe passage by any British ship.

As Faith and Maddy made ready to leave the ship, they both hugged and kissed Cooper and Mac. "Thank you for all you've done. We will always be in your debt."

"We'll not forget you," Cooper said, as the women made their way to the entry port. Maddy looked at Cooper and said, "I bet you don't forget me, Sir Pirate."

Chapter Thirty Three

The week in Savannah went by so quickly, Cooper and the *Raven's* crew had hardly started to enjoy the city's many wonderful delights. Beau Cannington went along with Cooper and Mac as they went hunting with Jonah Lee and Moses. Horse races were attended and of the five, Beau was the only one who showed any proficiency at the game of golf. Each day was filled with activities, some with Sophia, and some without, but the nights were all hers.

They attended a play and a concert given by local musicians as a fundraiser for some worthy cause. Cooper had told Eli, Debbie, and Sophia of the rescue, half expecting disapproval from his former captain and mentor.

"Aye, lad, it's a good deed you've done and I'd like to think I would have done the same. But if any of the blackhearts lived to hear your name or see the name of the ships, it's a marked man you are. Diabolita or Little Devil, as I've heard him called is one of the most violent men that sails the sea. Except for Roberto Confresi, I don't know of any others who associate with him, not even Gaspar. If he was not at Culebra he was either headed to Cuba to set up a sale for the women or perhaps setting up ransom for Sir Robert. He may have even gone to Mona Island. That's where Confresi makes his quarters."

After much discussion, Eli recommended a quick trip north towards Nova Scotia and if they didn't run into a British convoy to look at the triangular trade routes. "Just make sure any ship you take is not an American. The Don's have half a dozen ports where they take their cargo in South America. Most of those are on the eastern coast of Brazil but some will be headed to the West Indies and Cuba."

Captain Eli Taylor was not as successful as he was, without gathering knowledge during his entire career. Therefore if it was good enough for him, it was good enough for Cooper Cain.

Their last night at home, Sophia asked, "Have you thought of a name for our home?"

"Not really," Cooper admitted.

"I don't want it called the old Oxford place forever," Sophia said.

"Do you have a name in mind, dear lady?" Cooper asked.

Sophia sat up in the bed, letting the covers fall down to her waist. The moon shining through their bedroom window highlighted her chest, her hair, and her cream colored skin, and her perfect breasts. Cooper Cain couldn't have cared what she wanted to name their home, their land. Her beauty had him in a trance, hypnotized in awe. Her dancing eyes, her lips of fire, and her flashing smile. Truly, he was the luckiest man alive.

"Falcon's Trace. Coop…Coop. Did you hear me?"

"I'm sorry, Sophia, I'm intoxicated."

"You've not had that much to drink," she said.

"It's not the alcohol, my love, it's you. I'm drunk on your love."

Sophia laughed. "You've a glib tongue, Cooper Cain. You think you can lure me into your arms by being so…so flattering. Now do you like the name?"

It could have been sheep dung and Cooper would have said yes. Nodding, she smiled. "Do you really like it, Coop?"

"I do," he responded.

Sophia pushed him back and lay over on his chest. "I'm glad. I will have a sign made and hung across two poles at the gate. Falcon's Trace. Cooper and Sophia Cain's place."

"No, Sophia," Cooper whispered. "Falcon's Trace, Cooper and Sophia Cain's home; and one day the Cain family home."

"I like that," Sophia whispered in Cooper's ear as she inched over and lay on top of him. Her breasts crushing into his chest, the pulse of her heart beating against his. Two hearts beating together.

"Damn, I love you," Cooper vowed.

"Until I die," Sophia whispered in reply. "Until I die."

THE ATLANTIC WAS SHOWING its might and the heavy waves crashed against Raven as she climbed one huge wave and then fell into its trough. Water crashed over the bow and sluiced down the channels and out the scuppers. Overhead, the wind whistled through the rigging.

"Are we in for a storm?" Cooper asked Johannes.

Shaking his head and shouting to be heard; the quartermaster and former ship's master said, "No. This is not unusual for these waters. I think the wind will die down to a moderate breeze by sunset."

Johannes' words proved to be true and just before dusk the whistling in the overhead died down and the waves became little more than rolling white caps. They sailed north of Nova Scotia to the southeastern coast of Newfoundland. The *Raven* came about just off Cape Saint Francis, having found nothing entering or leaving Saint Johns. The weather continued to hold and *Raven* continued south.

Cooper opened the stern windows of his cabin and enjoyed a glass of Gus' brew. The last he'd brought aboard before they left Barataria. Mac was on deck. Quang, who acted as cabin servant, cox'n, and martial arts instructor handed a candle to Cooper so that he could light his pipe. Using his hand to shield the flame from the wind, Cooper turned the pipe sideways and puffed like he'd seen Eli Taylor do. "Keeps the wax from the tobacco and pipe," he had explained. Nothing like dripping wax to ruin your smoke. Once the pipe was lit, Cooper reclined back in his chair.

"We'll soon be off Sable Island," Quang said, breaking the silence. "It's called the graveyard of the Atlantic."

This caught Cooper's attention so he sat up. "Tell me about this."

Quang shrugged. "I only know what the quartermaster told a few of us. Hundreds of ships have wrecked on sandbars along the coast of the island. Johannes says it's a long narrow island. He also said that wild horses roamed the island. Nobody knows for sure how they got there, but they probably swam ashore when some ship struck a sandbar. Johannes says there are a lot of seals there as well."

"Well, damme Quang, but I learn something new every day," Cooper said.

"SAIL HO! DECK THAR! Sail ho!" The men aboard *Raven* had all but decided the voyage north was another failure when Banty's excited voice came down from the tops.

"Where away," Mac shouted.

"Off the larboard beam." Cooper had heard the cry as he was coming on deck.

"Sail to leeward," Mac volunteered as soon as he saw Cooper.

Picking up the speaking trumpet, Cooper called up, "What do you make of her, Banty?"

"She's a brig," Banty called down.

"Think she's British?" Cooper asked Mac and Johannes.

"Not sure," Mac replied. "But this far north, she's not likely to be an American."

"I agree," Johannes said, when Cooper looked his way.

"Coop, I'd alter course six points to larboard and clamp on all sails. If she is an American, we can wave as we go by, if not, we've a prize," Mac said.

Mac should be the captain, Cooper thought. *Damn little good I am when it comes to real seamanship*. The helm was put over and the deck canted as the wind filled the sails. The distance between the two ships closed quickly but still it was a three hour chase.

The *Raven* was less than a half mile and closing fast when Cooper called to Spurlock, "Put a shot across her bow if you will, Mr. Spurlock."

"Aye, Captain," the gunner answered and made his way forward.

Johannes was next to Cooper. "She ought to know she'll not escape," he said.

BOOM...The larboard forward bow chaser fired. A water spout appeared half a cable in front of the chase.

"That ought to get her attention," Johnson said. He and Moree were at the wheel.

"Bloody 'er bleeding nose, Spurlock," added Banty, who'd been called down from his lookout.

THE CAPTAIN OF THE brig was William Watson. He was a smallish fellow, who was neither pleasant nor offensive. He just stood at the quarterdeck with his hands behind him.

"Your ship is a prize of the *Raven*," Cooper offered. "Muster your men on deck and if there is no attempt to resist, I will leave you with your ship and your life." Watson nodded.

Within a few minutes, McKemie was on deck. "Ship is out of Newfoundland, Captain." Papers say he was carrying timber to the West Indies; and his return trip shows tobacco, rum, and sugar."

Johannes stepped over to Cooper, "Have Robinson and Bridges search the cabin. With a load of timber like the papers say she's setting too high in the water to have spent it all on trade goods. I'd have Banty and Johnson check the hole as well. Banty has a feel for things, he does, and Bridges and Robinson will sniff out a hidden compartment if there is one." It seemed like forever, until Banty came on deck with a smile on his face.

"Could you come with me, Captain?" Banty took Cooper to a hole full of fifty gallon rum barrels. "See those barrels, Captain? They all look alike, but look at these. There are four where the paint that says Saint Croix is newer, not as faded and stained." Handing a barrel stave to Cooper, Banty said, "Bang the side of that barrel." It had a dull thud. "Now, bang this one, Captain." It was different, more a solid sound.

Men were brought down and a hoist was rigged and the four barrels were brought on deck. The lids were removed and the barrels turned on their side. The clink of coin made an unmistakable sound. The captain of the ship looked most unhappy, "I'll see you in hell," he hissed to Cooper.

"You'll have to stand in line, I'm afraid," Cooper replied.

The coin was taken aboard *Raven*, and as an afterthought the ten barrels of rum. The rum would always bring a fair price. It was dusk when the *Raven* withdrew her grappling hooks and set sail.

"Fifteen thousand dollars and change, I believe," Johannes announced. It was his duty to count the coin. "Fifteen thousand and ten barrels of rum, a good voyage with little effort, I'd say. We got us another lucky cruise, Captain, I'd say."

Cooper grinned at the crew's enthusiasm, good luck indeed. They'd collected several thousand dollars in plunder on Culebra, when they'd rescued Faith, Maddy, and the others. Now, they'd made another good haul. Good luck, yes, they'd had some good luck but lady luck was a fickle mistress. She'd turn on you in a moment, she would…lady luck.

CHAPTER THIRTY FOUR

JOHN WILL ENTERED THE warehouse office. The man he had stationed atop of the warehouse had just informed him the *Raven* had been sighted entering the anchorage. "Jim Boy, quick, go fetch Captain Taylor like we planned. Hurry now, and don't spare that horse. If Captain Taylor's not back here by the time *Raven's* crew marches up the hill, he'll lay the cat to you."

Jim Boy had heard about the damage a cat-of-nine tails could do. He'd never had a whip touch his skin and he didn't want to start now, especially, not with the cat. As he rushed out the door, he ran headlong into Michael Brett. "Sorry, sir, Mr. John says to fly like my feet are on fire and my ass is catching."

Michael Brett wanted to smile at the boy's comment, but it dawned on him the reason for the boy's rush. Turning to John, he said, "*Raven's* been spotted."

John nodded, and slumped down into a chair. Finally, he said, "I'm glad that I'm not the one breaking the news."

"That's two of us," his friend and partner replied.

"DEAD…WHAT THE HELL DO you mean she's dead, Eli? Oh God, Eli, don't tell me such a thing. Oh God!!! Sophia…Sophia…God why'd you let her die? Why couldn't it have been me?" Eli Taylor looked on as his friend and protégé sobbed and fell apart over the news of Sophia's death.

They were sitting in the warehouse office. Taylor had made it to the office just as Cooper walked up the hill. Taylor took

Cooper into the office and as pre-planned, John Will went down to the ship to notify Mac and the crew. Mac and Johannes went ashore to be there for their captain, but no one else left the ship. How could they? Their captain came first. They'd wait to find out what was going to take place.

Taylor poured Cooper a stiff tumbler of rum which he gulped down. Taylor watched as he cried, with his head in his hands and then he pounded the desk with his fists. Taylor poured one more glass of rum…enough to settle his friend, but not enough to make him drunk. Finally, after a few minutes, Cooper looked up, "How…how did my Sophia die, Eli?"

Taylor swallowed hard and drank the rum he'd poured for himself. "We came into Savannah for a play. Debbie and Sophia were going to do some shopping the next morning so we stayed at the new Washington Hall Hotel. Our room and Sophia's room joined each other. We came back from the play and I went into our room while Debbie and Sophia chit-chatted about the next day's shopping. Debbie came in and undressed. That's when we heard a door slam and a scream. Debbie shouted to me, 'That's Sophia, Eli, hurry, get your pants on.' We heard another scream then. I had my pants on by then and grabbed a pistol. Sophia's door was closed so I kicked it open. I didn't notice the man at first, as the door to the balcony was open and I could see Sophia lying there. I checked her pulse, but she was gone. When I turned around, I saw him…D'Arcy. He was just sitting there in the chair by the vanity. He held a pistol in his hand. I was afraid we might have a go at one another. I asked him why."

He mumbled, "I…I saw her at the play. We were in town and who did I see…Sophia. I had to talk to her, to see her. I followed her here and watched." He paused for a while. People were now gathering outside the door.

"I saw Debbie and I shook my head, letting her know Sophia was gone. I told her to send for the law. D'Arcy poured himself a drink of water from the stand and started talking again."

He continued his story, "I knocked and Sophia answered the door. When she saw me, she slammed it shut but I kicked it open. 'Go away, go away,' she screamed. I have to see you, D'Arcy cried, I love you. 'No,' Sophia shouted back, 'I'm married, I love Cooper.' I went after her, D'Arcy had said. She bolted for the balcony. I grabbed her and pulled her to me. 'No! No!' she screamed, snatching away from me but fell, hitting the iron balcony rail. Oh God, I've killed her. I killed my brother and now I've killed Sophia. He stood up but then he sat back down," Eli continued, as he narrated the events.

"I'll kill the son of a bitch," Cooper swore. "God, I'll kill him, Eli."

"No, Cooper, there's no need. I watched the man, feeling something between hate and pity for him. He reached in his coat pocket for the pistol he'd placed there just a moment before. He started crying hard, making it hard to understand his words, but I heard him say, 'Tell father I'm sorry, but it was his entire fault.' Before I could react he put the pistol to his head and pulled the trigger. Since the door was open, several people saw and heard D'Arcy's words, I walked out."

The room was silent for several minutes. Eli swirled the rum around in his glass and watched it. Cooper sat with his head in his hands feeling lost, like his world had come apart and he didn't know where to turn or what to do. Yesterday, he was a happy man. Today, he was lost. His whole world had come apart. Everything he loved, everything he lived for, was gone. Like a candle flame when a door or window was opened.

"Where is she, Eli?" Cooper asked.

"She was partial to that oak tree overlooking the bluff. She said you'd put the bench there and that the two of you would sit in the shade of the tree and watch the river below. She told Debbie how the two of you sat and held hands without speaking, just enjoying each other. I laid her to rest there, Coop. I built a little fence around the grave and bench. There's a headstone with angels carved into it. We can move her if that's not to your liking."

"No," Cooper sniffed. "I can't think of a better spot, like you say, she loved it there. I want to go see her, Eli."

"Sure, Coop. I have a wagon outside. Coop, the men will want to pay their respects. What do you want to do?"

"I don't know," Cooper replied.

"Debbie said maybe a memorial service would be in order," Eli said.

"That's good. Tomorrow afternoon, just before sunset, that was her favorite time," Cooper replied.

LATER THAT NIGHT, ELI lay awake and talked to Debbie. "Did you tell him?" Debbie asked.

"Tell him?" Eli replied.

"Yes," Debbie said. "The reason we had to go shopping."

"No, and don't you breathe a word of it, either. It's one thing to tell a man his wife has been killed. I couldn't tell him she was with his child."

"He'd want to know, Eli."

"No, hell he wouldn't. Look at all the boy's lost. I'll not make him suffer more. I don't think I could stand it and I know he couldn't."

COOPER SPENT A LONG time on the bench looking at the grave. It had been a week since the memorial service at the graveside.

Colonel Lee had brought the local preacher with him. Jonah and Moses were also there, as were the entire crew of *Raven*. Pirates they might be, but they were good men with kind hearts. They showed that with the rescue of the Anthony women and they showed it with Sophia. There was not a man aboard who she'd not said a kind word to at some point or another.

She had been Banty's pet and he cried hard at the news. The men had gone back to the ship. Johannes was in charge. Mac had not wanted Cooper to be alone, so he had stayed. He gave his friend his privacy but he was always close by. Sophia had hired a cook and housekeeper, Rosa Palmer. She reminded Cooper of Belle with her cooking but, even though she was a black woman, she reminded him of his mother; her facial expressions, motions, and her peaceful ways.

He'd thought about closing the place but Rosa changed his mind. Sophia had hired her to help make the house a home. He'd not change that. David Gill had sent a couple of the slaves over and put her in charge. She'd keep them busy and she'd make sure Sophia's grave would be kept up.

The jingle of trace chains were audible before the horses and wagon appeared. The man driving pulled up and another man got off the wagon. The driver drove the team on up to the house.

"I've felt your pain, Cooper Cain." It was Dagan from Norfolk. James was the driver, Cooper realized. Cooper kept sitting but slid over as Dagan stepped through the tiny gate and sat himself beside Cooper, placing his arm around his friend's shoulders.

Dagan's kind act caused Cooper to break down again. "God, I loved her, Dagan."

"I know you did, Cooper. I could feel it in your words and actions back in Norfolk." Neither spoke for a while, both just allowing the other his own thoughts.

Finally, Cooper wiped his eyes and blew his nose. "I thought you were going to Antigua."

"I've already been," Dagan said.

"You decided not to go to England?" Cooper asked.

"Maria's decided to come here for a visit," Dagan replied.

"I'm glad you came, Dagan."

"I had to, Coop. You gave me energy again. I had to come support you."

Cooper turned and looked at Dagan, remembering his words; *I see squalls coming but better days ahead.* "You knew, didn't you, Dagan?"

"Aye, I had the feeling," he replied.

"Could I have changed it?" Cooper asked.

"No, my friend, you were given something few men ever experience, that true, unconditional love. Betsy and I shared it. You shared it with Sophia. It's better to have shared such a love and miss your woman, than to never have had it. But think, Coop, think about what you told me of Sophia's life before you came along. Do you think she'd regret a minute of it? You gave her not a contract but your love and your name. As humble as it may be," Dagan said this squeezing Cooper's knee gently, "being your wife, being Sophia Cain brought meaning into her life. You gave her something she'd likely not ever have had otherwise. You made her a woman, not a mistress. You made her a wife and gave her dignity. You can mourn her loss, for your sake, but rejoice in the knowledge that you took her away from the life she'd had."

Cooper stood up and hugged Dagan. "We were in Antigua not long ago."

"I know," Dagan said.

"You know, could you see that as well?" Cooper asked.

"You might say that. I was there when you brought Sir Robert, Faith, and Maddy home. Had you stayed a while, we could have had a wet. You also could have met Lord Anthony and Bart."

"To tell the truth," Cooper explained as the two walked toward the house. "It was one thing to rescue Faith and Maddy. The men looked upon that as an adventure of sorts. It's another to sail into a harbor full of warships knowing full well that given the slightest whim, they could sink you or hang you, whichever took their fancy."

"Aye, lad," Dagan said. "I can see where you are coming from. You've a letter from Faith and Maddy. James wants you to know he's got an overseer for the Beaufort Plantation and he's going to be here, so you will be neighbors."

"Are you going to stay long, Dagan?"

"Depends on how well you feed me," Dagan replied.

"Rosa will feed you well. I want you to meet some friends of mine."

Nodding, Dagan said, "I met the Lees today." Cooper laughed. *A good sign,* Dagan thought.

"That Moses is a fierce sight, is he not?" Cooper asked.

"Aye," Dagan agreed. "I'd not like to get crossways of either he or Jonah."

"You were going to say brother," Cooper said. "That's alright, it's the way they see things, and certainly the way Mama Lee sees it."

"I never did get her name," Dagan said.

"Sure you did," Cooper said with a smile. "It's Mama Lee. I've never heard her addressed any other way."

"Well, Mama Lee it will be," Dagan replied. "Now, let's see what Rosa has cooked. I'm ready to eat."

CHAPTER THIRTY FIVE

THE ROUTES TAKEN BY the slave ships were known as the 'Triangular Trade Route.' Ships from Europe would sail to Africa, buy or trade for slaves, and then sail to the Americas, West Indies, and on some occasions back to Europe.

The part of the voyage from Africa to wherever the slaves were to be sold was called the middle passage. Depending on the size of the ship, anywhere from one to seven hundred slaves might be chained together and packed into tiers, selling them was very profitable.

So the decision was made to head for the middle passage and prey on slavers. This would also keep the *Raven* from the Caribbean where Admiral Anthony's squadrons were patrolling.

LaFitte provided a ready market at discount, but fair prices and without any paperwork. Barataria was a lot closer to the slave route than Savannah, so the men of *Raven* voted to raid slavers. The easiest to raid were the Dons. Therefore, an area off the main slaving ports along the upper and lower Guinea coast became *Raven's* hunting ground.

A ship would be hit, the captain and crew put in boats not far from the coast and a mad dash made for Barataria. Before long, every man jack of the *Raven's* crew was wealthy beyond imagination. Slaves ships were sold at Trinidad and broken up for the wood; some of the ships in a poor state of repair were sunk or given away.

It was after several such hauls that LaFitte sent word for Cooper and Mac to visit him at his house. After a fine evening of lobster and steak, a better than average wine, dessert, and good cigars, LaFitte came to the point. "I can't take anymore slaves for a while. Buyers are coming from Texas, Memphis, Mississippi, and even Alabama and Georgia and we still have more slaves than we can sell. Prices have dropped and I'm catching hell from my own lieutenants that they can't sell their own cargo."

"Sounds like it's time to take some time off," Mac said.

"Aye, or change markets," Cooper said.

Mac continued, "We'll put it to a vote, but I think it's time to relax. We have been on one cruise after another since…for several months now."

"You were going to say since Sophia's been gone," Cooper explained.

Mac nodded his reply, "You needed to be kept busy but now the men need some time. Let's take a week or so off here, and go visit Cindy and her people. Maybe go into New Orleans, and see Otis and eat some decent food."

Smiling, Cooper said, "Belle will have some decent food. I need to see Mr. Meeks and we need to arrange things with the bank to transfer some funds to Savannah. It's decided then, we'll inform the crew."

Mac said, "You should spend the night ashore, Coop. You haven't slept off the ship…"

"Since Sophia died," Cooper said, finishing Mac's sentence again. "What are you going to do, Mac?"

"Humph, I thought I might find some strong rum and a weak woman," he said.

Cooper smiled and punched his friend. "Never let it be said that David, from clan MacArthur, let a willing lass go unattended."

CINDY AND HER CLAN were making ready to head to the Veigh Plantation outside of New Orleans, so Cooper and Mac followed along in their pirogue. The first night they camped on a medium sized cheniere. Cold cornbread fritters and catfish were served as the evening meal, washed down with cider.

Cindy and Cooper moved away from the fire so that they could talk in private, but stayed close enough so that the smoke helped keep the mosquitoes at bay. "Eli wrote me of your loss," Cindy volunteered. "For what it's worth, Sophia felt more loved and more like a person than all the years before you came along, Cooper. It's not our place to question God's ways or reasons. Just be grateful for the time you shared."

"You sound so much like another friend," Cooper said, and told Cindy about Dagan.

A sound of a short struggle was heard, followed by a loud splash. "A bull gator has just caught his supper," Jumper volunteered.

"I don't like it when they's gators about," his mother, Belle said with a shiver.

"Humph!" the boy snorted. "Watch this." He picked up a burning stick from the fire and held it out toward the dark bayou waters.

"Lordy me," Belle gasped.

"They is a thousand eyes out there, and all of 'em waiting on you, mama, thinking what a good supper you'd make," Jumper said, trying to scare her. "Ouch, what'd you do that for, Papa?"

"For trying to scare your mama," Gus replied firmly. "Next time, I might just throw you into them black waters, and see what kind of meal you'd make."

Jumper walked just out of Gus' reach and chirped, "Not as good as mama, she's got a lot more meat."

"Ah, that hurt." Jumper had stepped away from his daddy, but close to his mother, who smacked his rump with a wooden spoon. This caused everyone to laugh except Jumper, who was still recovering and rubbing his rear.

After everyone was talked out and getting ready to call it a night, Gus walked over to Mac and Cooper. "Must be in for some rain, there's more than the usual amount of gators and snakes. I saw two moccasins at the water's edge when I went to check on the boat lines. I think we need to take watches and keep a good fire going." Mac and Cooper nodded and Cooper took the first watch.

It was the afternoon of the third day when they pulled up at the dock of the Veigh Plantation. The river was several feet higher than the land so a dike had been built to keep the plantations along the river from flooding.

Gus had built a set of wooden steps up from the dock and over the dike. A path made from hauled in oyster shells went from the dock up to the house, winding its way through a stand of giant old oak trees. The huge, lower limbs from the oaks touched the ground in places.

"When I was little, I played on them oaks," Jumper told Cooper and Mac. "A couple places there, you could make like a limb was a horse and it would rock up and down with you."

As they neared the back of the house, which sat up on a rise, a gazebo with a swing set faced the river. "I love to sit in that swing and read," Cindy said, but looking at the sky. "I think we'll stay inside the rest of the day." She was right.

It started to sprinkle, and then turned into a steady rain but was gone the next morning. After breakfast, Cindy had Gus hitch up the carriage.

"I need to see Lawyer Meeks and we need a few supplies. I think since you needed to see him as well, we'll go into New

Orleans early and then get back before it starts raining again. This time of year it usually rains in the afternoon."

COOPER AND CINDY WENT to Meeks' office immediately after reaching New Orleans. Mac volunteered to go with Gus and get the needed supplies. Weather permitting, they'd see Otis and have lunch at Hotel Provincial.

Gus and Mac had just returned to Meeks' office when Cooper commented, "Were we at sea, I'd be looking for a safe anchorage." Overhead the sky had dark clouds that were moving from east to west.

"Storm clouds sure enough," Gus said and climbed into the carriage. By the time they'd traveled a few blocks the wind had picked up, causing store signs to sway back and forth making rusty hinges groan and squeak. Thunder could be heard in the distance by the time they made it to the hotel. Pulling around to the back, the first streak of lightening came down with a tremendous crack.

Otis must have seen them drive around the hotel as he dashed out with an umbrella for Cindy just as the rain started. There were just a few drops at first, and then a hard driving rain. Otis spoke to everyone as he rushed Cindy inside. Cooper and Mac helped Gus get the carriage full of supplies into the small barn and the horses into stalls. When they came out the barn door, the sky was almost black and the howling wind had the trees bent over.

"This ain't no afternoon thunder boomer," Gus said, concern in his voice. "We are in for a storm, maybe a hurricane."

Flashes of lightening were crashing down, one after another. Just before the three men made it to the hotel door, a big boom shook the ground and the sky was suddenly bright before turning dark again.

"Damn, that was close," Cooper swore.

It was no more than seventy-five feet from the barn to the rear entrance of the hotel, but the three men were drenched and dripping as they ducked through the door. Otis had a couple of workers there with towels and blankets.

"Dry off best as you can and we'll get you some dry clothes to put on," Otis offered.

A black maid was busy lighting hall candles, as the room was almost too dark to see anything. Outside the wind was now raging. Hotel guests were gathering around the windows of the main lobby, when someone screamed, "Look out!" A sign torn from its hinges was blown threw a window, breaking glass flying everywhere. A loud 'oomph' was heard as the sign hit a man in the chest, knocking him to the floor, his wife was calling for help for her dazed husband.

A large blanket was nailed over the opening but soon it was in tatters. A table was brought from the kitchen and put over the busted window. This was better than the blanket but water continued to come through, drenching the lobby's French carpet.

Outside on the street, a small oak tree was torn up by its roots and somewhere a great tearing sound was heard as the roof on a nearby store was blown away.

"I think we need…" CRASH!! Otis never finished his sentence as debris crashed through another window pane, sending a shower of rain and glass over everyone. Blood poured from a laceration on Otis' forehead. Cindy quickly put her hand to the wound to staunch the flow of blood. Mac snatched a cloth from a side table. He ripped it in half and Cindy used it to cover Otis' wound. Looking about, several of the people had small cuts.

"Let's move back," Cooper shouted to be heard above the wind. "Move back toward the kitchen."

"Shouldn't we go upstairs so we won't be standing in water," one man asked.

Thinking of the store roof that was just blown away, Cooper shook his head, "I wouldn't, not now with the wind blowing like it is."

As the group passed through the dining room toward the kitchen, Mac froze. A man had just been swept past the window. Once inside the kitchen, the sound was not so loud. Food sat on the stove and a few filled a plate and ate. Cindy tended to Otis' head wound, while Mac and Cooper stood by the kitchen door.

"Did you see what I saw?" Mac whispered.

"Aye," Cooper responded. Before long, it grew still and the wind died down to little more than a stiff breeze.

"Is it over?" a woman asked.

"Must be," her companion answered.

"No, not yet," Mac said. "We're in the eye of the storm. We may have a few minutes."

"I gotta go then," a woman said.

"Me too," another admitted.

"Quick, into the pantry and to the mud room," Otis ordered.

The men went to see the damage at the front of the hotel. The lobby was drenched and the carpet made a squishing sound as they walked over it. The dining room, which set to the side, was untouched except where the water had run in from the lobby. One gentleman pointed at the wine cabinets, "Let's get a few bottles before the storm starts up again."

"Go ahead," Cooper responded and then said, "Let's check things out upstairs, Mac."

The two bounded up the stairs two at a time. Everything was in order. Cooper stopped at the room he and Sophia had shared. He walked over to the bed and picked up the pillow she'd rested on and held it to his face as his eyes began to tear up. Outside, the sky began to darken again and the wind picked up.

"Coop! It's time to go down. Coop!"

"Leave me," Cooper said.

"No, let's go Coop," Mac said.

"Leave me, Mac."

"No Cooper, let's go."

"I'm not going, Mac."

"Alright, but look at me, Coop."

Cooper Cain never knew what hit him. As he turned, Mac hit him on the chin at full swing, knocking his friend unconscious. Mac tossed the pillow on the bed and scooped up his friend and was back in the kitchen as the storm raged outside.

"What happened to him?" a woman asked.

"He slipped on the wet floor," Mac lied. Cindy caught Mac's eye and gave him a knowing look.

CHAPTER THIRTY SIX

"SAIL HO!" THE LOOKOUT called down, creating excitement in the crew. "To the south," he called again. "Ten, no twelve sails it be, it's a bloody convoy."

Raven lay hove-to off Praia, Cape Verde. Cooper leaned forward, bringing the front legs of his chair down with a bang. He'd been daydreaming about their last day in New Orleans. After helping Otis get his head attended to, they went back to Cindy's plantation. She had been worried expecting the worst. But aside from dead limbs blown across the lawn, everything was as it had been when they left.

"Thank you, Lord," Gus had prayed. He'd been worried about Belle and Jumper. Belle exceeded all expectations that night. She made a soup with crawfish tails, corn, rice, and peppers in it. The peppers gave it a little kick but did not overpower it. After the soup, there was fried catfish that had an unusual lemony flavor. For dessert, she served what she called a tafia cake. It was a cake using the local rum, tafia, as an ingredient. The cake was accompanied by chicory coffee with a heavy cream and sweetened with sugar. Now that the thought of food was swept away by the convoy sighting, Cooper rushed on deck, his heart racing at the news.

Mac handed Cooper a glass and advised, "Look almost due south."

"Probably an Indiamen on the way home," Johannes volunteered.

"I can only make out two escorts at the front of the convoy," Banty said. Hearing the cry, he'd swiftly made his way up the shrouds and into the tops.

"Bound to be another to the rear," Diamond said.

"Aye, there's bound to be," Mac agreed.

"Prepare to make sail, Mr. MacArther," Cooper said, using the formal tone learned from Eli Taylor. "Mr. Spurlock, let's prepare our guns. Set a course to intercept yonder convoy, Mr. Ewers."

"Aye," Johannes replied, but smiling as he thought *if only Captain Taylor could see the boy now.*

"Deck thar."

"What is it, Banty?" Cooper called back.

"Two of the ships fly the yellow Finylson flag, Captain."

Now it was Cooper who smiled. "Banty has just named our targets, men. If we get the both of them, I'm buying when we get home." This created a cheer by the crew.

The *Raven* was overhauling the convoy fast. Cooper thought about getting the Royals on her, but Mac gave the slight nod that said, 'I wouldn't.' *Raven* tacked and then tacked again. Mac had recommended coming up on the windward side of the convoy.

"Deck thar," Banty cried down. "The frigate has worn ship."

"Too late," Diamond said. "Had we another ship, we'd cut out a few at the head of the column before she could come about."

Cooper looked along the deck at his men. "McKemie, you and Moree take twenty men with cutlasses and pistols and board yonder ship when we get alongside. We'll cover you with the swivels until you're aboard. Lay your men along the starboard gangway, lively now. Johnson, get a group of men ready with grappling hooks; smartly now. Lay us alongside, Mr. Ewers."

Raven slid up next to the Finylson ship and the grapnels shot out. A pistol shot was fired but didn't seem to hit anybody.

"Avast there or we'll blast ye," Moree shouted.

The boarding party was quickly over the side and Johannes had the helmsman steer a course for the next Finylson ship. Looking at the men still in the waist, Cooper called for Robinson and Bridges to lead the next boarding party over.

As they neared the next ship, the captain had the helmsman change his course. "Mr. Spurlock, put one across the bow and if she doesn't heave to, give her a broadside."

"Aye Captain," Spurlock said.

The forward gun roared and leapt inboard, straining at its ropes and tackles. The round shot skipped across the waves like a well thrown rock across a pond. Immediately, the chase dropped her sails. Without being told, Johnson had the grappling hooks heaved and the slack was taken up. The two ships came together without any offer of resistance from the prize's crew.

A rumble of gunfire caused Cooper to swear. "What the bloody hell?"

"It's the rear escort, Captain. Little more than a brig, but she's got her teeth bared."

"Put *Raven* about, Mr. Ewers. If she makes chase we'll give battle, but if she's content to let us escape with our prizes, we'll call it a day."

"Aye, I'm thinking she'll be content, Captain. But the insurance companies won't."

With all sail cracked on, *Raven* and her two prizes were soon distancing themselves from the convoy.

"Secure the guns, Mr. Spurlock."

"Aye, Captain."

"THE BILGE SUCKING SODOMITE doesn't want to cooperate, Captain."

The ship was the *Sir Phillip*. At five hundred tons, it was the larger of the two Finylson ships. Reading the ship's papers, Banty swore that some of the writing with no apparent meaning was in fact code. "That usually means specie, Captain, gold or silver coin."

Cooper had the crew lined up, twenty-four with two mates and the captain. "I'll ask you once and that's it," Cooper said. "If you fail to answer, you'll lose your ship. Now, where's the coin?" The ship's captain made a little snort and jerked his head to the side.

"You have just lost your ship, Captain. Banty, you take Johnson and chop the captain's cabin apart until you have our plunder."

"Aye," Banty replied, with a devilish smile.

The sound of hacking could be heard as teak paneling was chopped apart. Soon an excited shout was heard. Banty showed himself and called, "Come have a look see, Captain." He had been right, several bags were found. "I make it about eleven thousand English pounds, Captain, plus what's in her hole."

The second captain produced his papers and admitted to having eighteen thousand English pounds, but knew not where as it was stored in a sealed compartment while he was guarded on deck by Phillip's men. It took Banty no time at all to find the compartment and take the coin aboard *Raven*.

The cargo of tea, silk, rum, and teak was transferred aboard the larger Finylson ship. No one volunteered to serve aboard *Raven*, so both crews were sent aboard the second ship. As the *Phillip's* captain made to enter into the longboat with the rest of the crew, Cooper took out his sword and said, "I think not."

After the smaller Finylson ship sailed away with twice the crew but minus its cargo, Cooper called to the captain, "Had you been a gentleman, you would have sailed home with your ship. I intend to drop you off at Santa Maria, Cape Verde. You can get home the best way you can."

THE *RAVEN* DROPPED ANCHOR in the bay at Barataria. LaFitte would act as broker for the Finylson ship, putting a crew aboard it to sail it to Trinidad where his connection at the Port of Spain would make it a new ship. He also took the rum, giving a fair price for it.

As Cooper, Mac, and Johannes were leaving LaFitte's home, Vincent Gambi and Renato Beluche, two of LaFitte's lieutenants walked up. After a pleasant greeting, the fierce-looking Gambi said, "You have stirred up a hornet's nest, my young friend. No small nest, I might add. Your raid on Cobretta's plunder and captives at Culebra may well bring about your youthful demise." Cooper started to speak but Gambi raised his hand. "I have heard of your reasons and while I understand, you have endangered your ship and your men. Cobretta will not forget. You killed a trusted lieutenant and you stole from him a brethren. He will be out for your hide, Cooper. I hope the *Raven* is up to the fight that awaits you."

"We will be," Cooper replied.

"I hope so, my young friend, as it won't be just you. You are a marked man, Cooper Cain, but so is your ship and crew. Keep vigilant and trust no strange sail." Gambi then held out his hand to shake Cooper's. "If I'm around, I will lend you aid, as I have no love for the whoreson Cobretta myself."

A BRISK WIND DROVE *Raven* through the Gulf of Mexico and into the Caribbean. On a whim, they decided to search for prey in the Bahamas. They zigzagged through the numerous cays that made up the Exumas.

"I was told there were three hundred sixty-five islands and cays that made up the Exumas," Mac told several of the crew. "After America won its revolution with England, a good many British loyalists moved to the islands and set up a plantation style economy. The soil is so thin I was told it has about played out now, however."

"They still sell salt," Robinson volunteered.

"Aye," Bridges added. "I've seen the beacon."

Sailing past Georgetown, the *Raven* turned northerly, passing Rum Cay, Conception Island, and San Salvador, all on the starboard beam and Cat Island off the larboard side. They scared several local fishermen and tried to chase down a Bermuda sloop but it was much too fast. Smiling, Johannes seemed to enjoy the chase. Under full sail with a good wind, the sloop logged two miles for every mile *Raven* sailed.

"Fast ship," Johannes remarked. "They are made to make quick trips between the islands, and then to transport slaves. The British navy likes the sloops so much, they've started using them for dispatch vessels and chasing privateers."

"Aye," Mac agreed. "The *Pickle,* which carried the news of Trafalgar and Lord Nelson's death, was a Bermuda sloop. We'll have to keep our eyes open in these islands. *HMS Hunter* and *Rover,* both with sixteen guns, patrol between Bermuda and Antigua."

The name of the ship, Hunter, is that the one Maddy said her brother, Jacob, had just been assigned to? Cooper thought it was, but couldn't be certain. *Still it would not hurt to avoid them if possible. If possible…that was the key.* If they were seen, it would undoubtedly end up in a battle, as the fast sailing vessels would overtake *Raven*…not a pleasant thought.

Overnight, the air became much cooler and the sea picked up. Rollers crashed into *Raven's* bow, splashing spray inboard.

"It's a lively morning, is it not?" Mac offered.

"Aye, Mac," Cooper replied. He noticed either Mac or Johannes had put two helmsmen at the wheel.

"Sail ho, single ship off the starboard bow."

Picking up a glass, Mac climbed the shrouds to where he could get a better view. Satisfied it was a single ship, he climbed down the ratlines to the deck. "A single ship, alright, shall we alter course to intercept?"

"I see no reason not to," Cooper replied with a smile. "Send Banty to the tops," he added, his mind on the British sloops. "I don't want any surprises." In half an hour, the ship could be seen from the deck.

"She's not a fast sailor," Johnson, who was at the helm, remarked.

Moree, the other helmsman, smiled, "She must be loaded down."

Hearing the two men, Johannes walked over to Cooper, "She is sitting low in the water, Captain."

In another quarter hour, Banty called down, "She's flying your company flag, Captain." By that he meant the Finylson flag. Soon after, he called down again, "It's the *Bonnie Lass*, Captain… the *Bonnie Lass*."

"Damn," Mac said, smacking his fist into an open palm. "I thought that ship looked familiar." It wasn't long before they had nearly overtaken the ship.

"Send the hands to quarters, Mr. Diamond," Cooper ordered. "Mr. Spurlock, put one across her bow."

A cloud of smoke puffed out from the starboard chase gun, sending the acrid smell aft as the ball landed one hundred feet in front of the *Bonnie Lass'* bow. Sails came down immediately as the ship hove to. Standing on the quarterdeck, Cooper saw the familiar figure of the captain, which he was expecting. It was the other two that shocked him. It was Jessie and Josie, the twins.

"Mac, Johannes, Mr. Diamond, please attend me quickly," Cooper called. "I want Mr. Diamond to take the ship. Do not let on who is now *Raven's* captain. Should I need to speak with

Captain Nylinger bring him across. Also, those two ladies grew up with me. I will have them aboard this ship after we finish our business."

"Aye, Captain."

Cooper stood out of sight as he watched grapnel hooks fly across and hook on to the bulwark of the *Bonnie Lass*. No attempt to resist was given. Sooner, much sooner than expected, Johannes was back.

"It's a poor ship, Captain. There is two feet of water in the well with the ship being pumped every hour. I'd say she's made her last voyage. The captain requested to see you."

Nodding, Cooper said, "Send him over."

CHAPTER THIRTY SEVEN

SHIP'S BOATS WERE PUT out and Captain Nylinger and his crew of twenty-four men climbed down the battens into the waiting boats. It was early morning and the sky was cloudy with a drizzling rain. The sea had a slight chop but the row into Saint Augustine should not be too arduous. On deck in his tarpaulin, Cooper gave a slight nod to Captain Nylinger, who gave the briefest of nods back. Cooper Cain had saved the *Bonnie Lass'* captain from ruination. The bottom that had been suspect when Cooper and Mac were aboard was now leaking constantly. It was lucky she'd stayed afloat as long as she had. By taking what cargo that was not already ruined aboard *Raven*, the ship rose up somewhat, limiting her leak.

After telling Cooper where a chest was hidden containing eight thousand English pounds, they agreed to sail to Saint Augustine. There, they would put the captain and his crew ashore and then sail both ships out of sight. Cooper would then collect the chest and sink the ship.

He had allowed the crew of the *Bonnie Lass* to collect any personal belongings and had given Nylinger two hundred guineas. That would see the captain and crew through until they got back to England. Once there, he would tell the insurance company that the pirate, Robert Confresso, raided his ship. The men would all be witnesses. The Finylson Company could not fault the man. The insurance company would no doubt purchase him a new ship.

Captain Nylinger's passengers would likely be ransomed. He'd gotten the promise that no harm would come to the twins. He'd swear the pirates had not found the gold as far as he knew. The only thing was he now owed Cooper Cain a favor. A favor to be paid…when, where, and how was to be determined. Not a bad deal as he saw it.

Once off the Florida coast and in deep water, the *Bonnie Lass* was stripped of all that could be used but not traced. The gold was where the captain had said it would be. After everything was aboard *Raven*, Diamond and McKemie used one of the ancient brass cannons that the *Bonnie Lass* had used as armament and put a hole through her bottom. The ship soon sank from view as the dark Atlantic took her.

THE REUNION WITH JESSIE and Josie had been very enjoyable. The two had made their way into the captain's cabin with more than a little apprehension showing. Seeing Cooper, they squealed in delight. They ran to him and nearly smothered him to death with hugs and kisses. Jessie was the first to touch his scar and then she kissed it.

"That was because of us," she said, sorrow in her voice. "If only we hadn't been such tarts."

"No, it was because of Phillip," Cooper said. "He lied to Sir Lawrence."

"He's dead!"

This stopped Cooper abruptly. "Phillip's dead?"

"No," Jessie answered. "Sir Lawrence."

"He was not that old," Cooper said.

"Phillip did it to him," the twins said in unison. "He broke the old man's heart by being a sodomite and bringing his fancy boys to the estate. Soon the staff started leaving, including the kitchen staff. He'd invite others of his persuasion and have parties doing all sorts of unnatural things. Sir Lawrence walked in on one such party and tried to run everyone off but they just laughed at him. The next day he went to a lawyer and set up a trust of two hundred guineas per annum for each of us. He also set up a hundred guineas a year for your mother. This was done all perfect and legal. He was in the process of giving you back your father's land in Antigua when he died very suddenly. He was taking a glass of warm milk to help him sleep. The next morning, he was found dead in his bed. The glass of milk had fallen to the floor but did not break. A dead rat was found close by. While there was no proof, other than the dead rat, most felt Sir Lawrence was murdered before Phillip could be cut out of his will."

"It would not surprise me," Cooper hissed. "If I could get my hands on Phillip, he'd suffer."

"He already is," the twins chirped. "The loss in ships, cargoes, and revenue is hurting him badly. Gambling debts have caused him to sell off part of the estate. Your father's land is so debt ridden, that if payment is not soon received, it will be auctioned off."

"How much does he owe?" Cooper asked.

"We are not sure, but somewhere between fourteen and fifteen thousand pounds. Captain Nylinger was to sell his cargo in Bermuda and then take the money from it plus that in the chest and pay off the land, so that it could be used as collateral again."

Hmph, Cooper thought to himself.

The twins came to Cooper that night. "We heard about your wife, Coop. We are so sorry. Life has been so cruel to you." To his amazement, they dropped their gowns that they'd been wearing and nakedly slid into his cot.

Cooper started to protest, but one of the twins said, "Shh!" She then covered his mouth with hers. He was not sure when they left but he'd been completely vanquished by the vixens. It was surprising to him, when the next morning he found himself comparing their bodies, not to Sophia, but to Maddy. These thoughts made him feel guilty. He vowed to resist any further liaisons. The vow was taken in faith, but only lasted until that night. He and Josie were sated from their passion when it occurred to Cooper that the other twin was not there.

"Where is Jessie?" he asked.

"She's taken a liking to David, I believe."

"Mac?" Cooper questioned.

Josie was running Cooper's hands over her body; holding it to administer to her needs here and there, before moving on to other sensitive spots. "You don't mind, do you, Coop? I'm sure she'd come if I said you wanted us both." It was now Josie's hands doing the roaming.

"No," Cooper moaned, unable to say more as Josie went to work on his sensitive spots even more.

RAVEN SAT AT ANCHOR at the mouth of the Wilmington River, while barges were loaded with her cargo and taken to the warehouses by way of the Savannah River. John Will was overseeing the operation. Michael Brett was away in Charlestown. Captain Taylor had worked out the arrangements so that the unloading of cargo would not be seen by prying eyes in the Savannah harbor.

The following day, *Raven* would pull into the harbor and take on supplies. Mac would bring the ship in and then take a horse that would be waiting to Captain Taylor's place. A get together had been planned for the next day, a birthday party for Deborah. Afterwards there would be a private ceremony, one that Deborah didn't even know about.

Eli Taylor was somewhat of a romantic. He planned to marry Deborah after the birthday party, if she'd have him. It was a big to-do. Colonel Lee and Mama Lee were there, along with Jonah and Moses. Several people from surrounding farms were there also, as were some local businessmen. Even James Anthony was there. He and Cooper shook hands, each truly liking the other. Dagan had gone back to Norfolk.

Contests and games were set up. Some for the adults, but most of them were for the children. Jonah and Moses made it to the final round of a shooting competition, where Moses barely edged out Jonah to win.

A pig was roasted, as were several goats. The roasted kid was good but the fried chicken was what made Cooper and the twins sit up and take note. When Deborah finally made an appearance, she was not alone. Cindy Veigh was with her.

When Cindy finally had time to speak to Cooper, she whispered, "I have a letter from your mother for you."

The twins were a big hit. All the young gentlemen from around the countryside flocked to them. It was during the dancing that Cooper noticed Josie was taking a walk with James Anthony. He had to be several years older, but it was easy to see the two were smitten with each other. For some reason, Cooper couldn't explain why seeing the two together didn't bother him. Maybe someone like James would settle Josie down.

Later, when the three of them had a glass of punch, Josie said in a coy way, "Cooper and I grew up together. We are like brother and sister." The voice was sweet and innocent but the eyes begged, please don't say anything, Cooper. Well, he wouldn't and he wished them both the best. Jessie with Mac, and Josie with James, I guess I'll sleep along tonight; he decided and found that the thought didn't bother him.

The next morning Cooper woke up but not alone. He'd left the window ajar and the cook's cat had come in and laid on the pillow next to Cooper.

"Get," he snarled and pushed at the cat, who was in no hurry to give up its warm spot. The big yellow cat raised up, bowed its back and then stretched its front legs one at a time. Giving Cooper a go to Hades look, the cat jumped on a bedside chair and then out the window.

Cooper's head pounded as he sat up and his mouth tasted like an army had camped there the previous evening. Too much food, and corn whiskey followed by wine and cigars. No wonder he felt so bad. Once out from under the covers, the air had a chill to it. This caused a chill colder than the morning air to run through Cooper. It was this time last year that he and Sophia had come to Savannah for the first time. Damn how time had flown.

THE MOON WAS BRIGHT and reflected off the dark waters. Only a few of *Raven's* crew were on deck. One man moved forward toward the bow, probably to use the head with a degree of privacy offered by the night. Two men huddled together sitting on the deck leaning against the bulwark. The sweet smell of pipe tobacco drifted from where they sat forward to the quarterdeck. *Raven* was a good sailor but seemed to sail closer to the wind in the evening hours. The sound of the waves could be heard as they built up, crested, and then rolled away. The wake gave off a phosphorescent glow.

Staring down at the wake, Cooper's mind wondered. The letter from his mother told him much the same news as what the twins had told him. Phillip had met her and Jean-Paul as he was entering a fine dining establishment. He paused long enough to say he was looking into having the trust funds revoked on the grounds that his father had been a sick man and didn't know what he was doing. This was quickly dealt with. Jean-Paul, with the flick of his wrist, held a small sword in his hand with the tip against Phillip's companion's throat.

"I think not," he said. "You have ruined enough lives already. Should I hear another word on the matter, I will take matters into my own hands and you will find out how it feels to lose someone you care about."

The fancy dressed young man could barely speak with the sword point pricking his skin. "Surely, Phillip misspoke. Were he to see the trust revoked, it would only be to add to it a greater sum, I'm sure."

"I'm sure," Jean-Paul snarled. He withdrew his blade and took a silk handkerchief from fancy pants and touched the skin where the blade had been. A spot of blood stained the handkerchief. "Such a messy thing…blades, they do cause one to bleed."

Mother had gone on to say they would visit France for a few weeks and then return to England. The next thing that came to Cooper's mind was the twins. They had elected to stay behind. Captain and the new Mrs. Taylor had graciously invited them to stay at their home for a while, which the twins readily accepted. It was for the best so that Josie could see James Anthony. The last night ashore, Jessie had spent time with Mac.

Cooper had talked with Eli and the two decided it would be a good thing to sail to Antigua with enough specie to pay off the mortgage on the Cain's holdings. A letter from a local bank and one from a lawyer would be helpful but so would any help from the Anthonys or Sir Robert Basnight.

A shadow fell across Cooper. Turning, he saw Beau Cannington, the ship's surgeon. The two talked for awhile. Beau had been in the shooting competition and had easily been beaten by Moses, who won the prize. He had improved greatly though since they first met.

"I thought you had won with your last shot," Cooper said smiling.

"So had I," Beau admitted. "But Moses was a better shot, a true marksman. He was good competition."

They continued their conversation for a while longer and then Beau brought up Antigua. "Do you think it wise to sail into English Harbor?"

"We did it once," Cooper replied.

"Different circumstances," Beau said.

"You are right, of course. I think we will sail into Falmouth Harbor and take a wagon to English Harbor."

"It would make the crew less nervous," Beau responded.

"I have reminded them of the letters from Admiral Anthony and Sir Robert granting us safe passage."

"The letter has expired," Beau pointed out.

"Let's hope that they don't read that far," Cooper replied.

"You've had the luck of the Irish, so far," Beau said and then added, "I hope it lasts, Cooper. You've become a good friend."

IT WAS LATE AFTERNOON when the *Raven* dropped anchor in Falmouth Harbor. A boat was put ashore with Cooper, Quang, and Beau Cannington as passengers. Once ashore, Cooper asked for a carriage but settled for a wagon.

The wagon driver was a freed slave, who had lost more teeth than he'd kept. He had a stubble of gray, almost white, whiskers that stood out on his black face. He was a good-natured, old man and took the shillings pressed into his hands but swore there was no charge as he was headed to English Harbor anyway. Once they were off the wagon, the men dusted the road dust off their clothes as best they could.

"It's more-than-likely that both the admiral and Sir Robert will be at home at this time of day. We'll inquire as to where the two live and go see them."

At the nearest tavern, an officer was spied and so Cooper greeted him. "Good evening, Lieutenant. I am an American and friends with Admiral Anthony and Sir Robert Basnight. They encouraged Doctor Cannington and me to visit. Would you be so kind as to give us directions?"

"I could," the lieutenant replied. "However, if you walk down this street, you will come to the Saint George Inn. It's Bart's birthday, and they are there celebrating."

"Thank you, sir. I will mention you to the admiral."

"It's Fair, sir. Lieutenant Charles Fair."

The Saint George was a big inn, especially for an island. It was easy to see most of the clientele were the upper crust of the island's society. Not one jacktar could be seen. A dozen carriages waited on either side. The drivers were all decked out in whatever uniform their masters fancied, from black and white coats and tails to maroon or emerald green coats.

Cooper had worn a clean suit, but the least of the drivers looked better than he. "Quang, you'd better wait," Cooper told his big crewman. He would scare half the customers just by his Oriental looks.

It was much warmer here on Antigua than it had been in Georgia. Stepping into the inn with its candle chandelier's glowing made the heat intense. Cooper considered taking off his coat as he felt the sweat build and run down his spine.

"May I help you, sir?" the inn's maître d' asked.

"Yes," Cooper replied. "I'm friends with Admiral Anthony and I was told he was here."

"Do you mean Sir Gabe or Lord Anthony, sir?"

"Sir Gabe," Cooper snapped, not liking the man's attitude. "Now, lead me to him." The last let the man know he had no choice.

In a back room, a party was going on. You could hear loud voices and laughter before you even got to the room. When Cooper stepped into the room, the first to sight him was Maddy, who shouted, "Sir Pirate, you came back." The ensuing silence was eerie.

Heads turned and seeing Cooper, Sir Gabe whispered to his cox'n, "Damme, just damme." But being a proper host, Sir Gabe rose to greet his visitor, only to be brushed aside as Maddy rushed by him.

She hugged Cooper and gave him a kiss on his cheek. Faith followed Maddy, but her embrace and kiss was more reserved and ladylike. Sir Gabe was next. Shaking Cooper's hand, he said, "This is a surprise."

"Hopefully, not too inconvenient," Cooper said.

"We'll see, Cooper."

Introductions were made to Lord Anthony, Lady Deborah, Bart and Captain Davy, who smiled. "We've met," Davy said, shaking Cooper's hand. It was neither friendly nor unfriendly. At least he didn't call for the marines to arrest Cooper. Doctor Cannington was introduced. He too was sweating. Was it from the heat?

"A glass for our new guests," Bart ordered the waiter. "Would it be rum punch or rum?" he asked the guests.

Seeing the old seadog holding a bottle of each, Cooper said, "I'll take a man's drink if you don't mind."

"Aye," Bart said, pouring a full glass which Cooper gulped down and held out for Bart to refill. Cooper smacked his lips a bit and said, "Taste like real Cruzan rum." Bart smiled and set the bottle down.

Cooper really didn't know who made the rum, but for an inn of this caliber, they'd likely only carry the best. Eli Taylor had sworn that Cruzan was the best. It certainly wasn't Admiral Pusser's brand.

A seat was made by Maddy for Cooper, and Cannington was given a seat next to Lord Anthony. Lord Anthony had the doctor laughing in no time, telling him a story about one of Sir Gabe's friends, a surgeon, who had a monkey.

"Ape, it was an ape," Bart corrected him.

"At any rate, the animal had been allowed to get drunk and it ran amuck through the ship's rigging. The worst part was they'd been anchored next to *HMS Eagle*, which at the time was Lord Howe's flagship. I look back and wonder how I was ever able to raise my flag with all of Sir Gabe's and his friends exploits."

"Father, you never told me you had a friend with a monkey."

"Ape," Bart corrected again. "Come on down here, Maddy. I'll tell you some of your father's derring-dos." Smiling, Maddy made to rise.

"Keep your seat, young lady. I'd hate to shoot Bart on his birthday," Sir Gabe said.

"See, Maddy, see what old Bart tells ya. It's a wild side he has. Humph! Him threatening old Bart on his birthday. No respect, no respect I tell you. It's a good thing I'm retiring."

"Retiring!" Lord Anthony said with a laugh. "You've been retired these past ten years."

"Not so's you'd notice," Bart returned.

"What do you mean not so's you'd noticed?"

"Being keeper for the governor is a full time job."

"Humph," Lord Anthony snorted. "I ought to have you flogged."

"There you go. See Maddy, this is where Gabe gets it. It runs in the family, it does. No matter how hard I've tried over the years."

"Hush, Bart."

"I did."

Hearing the banter, Cooper couldn't help but chuckle.

Lord Anthony rose and held up his glass, "A toast. To the best cox'n and best friend a man could have. To Bart!" Everyone stood and toasted and the evening was soon over.

"Do you have a place to stay tonight?" Sir Gabe asked.

"No, we'd just arrived as Bart's party started."

"You shall then be our guests, you and Doctor Cannington."

"I have a man with me," Cooper said. "I will need to find lodging for him."

"Jake will see to that. We have space for him as well." Sir Gabe insisted that Cooper ride home in the carriage with him and Faith. As they pulled away, Sir Gabe came to the point, "Why are you here?"

"To buy back my father's property," Cooper said. He explained that the property was heavily in debt and he wanted to buy it before it was foreclosed on.

"Sir Robert can help with that," Jacob Hex volunteered. "Sir Gabe is in debt to you for saving his family but its best he is not involved in financial matters with…"

"You mean a pirate, don't you?" Cooper asked.

"I didn't say it, but yes. The admiral can't be seen having such dealings due to his position."

Cooper's temper was getting up when Faith laid her hand on Cooper's. "Tell Cooper about your family if you don't mind, Jake."

"My father was a front man for the Deal boatmen. You've heard of them, I'm sure."

"Indeed I have."

"Then you know there's not much difference in a smuggler and a pirate. I meant no ill feelings toward you, Cooper, but the fact is, our admiral cannot be involved. Tomorrow we will call on Sir Robert. He has the influence to back you without worry of recourse. He is soon to take over as Antigua's governor. Lord Anthony has asked to be relieved. I think he and Lady Deborah are ready to live out the rest of their life in peace, away from the navy and politics."

"Is Sir Jonathan Williams still the lieutenant governor?"

"Aye," Jake said, for the time being. "Do you know him as well?"

"Just his wife and daughters," Cooper said.

"He's not the gentleman Lord Anthony is. I'd steer clear of him, were I you. He's still angry for having to pay the ransom for his daughters. Had it not been for his wife, he might not have."

"I didn't take them," Cooper said. "In truth, I protected them."

"Don't test the waters, Cooper. He's mad that Sir Robert was made governor and not him. I'm sure he'll go back to England soon. Sir Robert has already informed him that he is being replaced."

MADDY SAT AT THE vanity brushing her hair and humming when her mother knocked and came in. Standing behind her daughter, Faith took the brush and brushed the back of her daughter's hair. "Your hair is getting long," she said.

"Do you like him, Mother?" Maddy asked.

"Like who?"

"Don't be coy, Mother, you know who I mean."

"Of course, I like Cooper, Maddy. He's saved our lives twice. Why wouldn't I like him?"

"Father said he was a rogue."

"That he is, dear, but a good rogue," Faith said.

"Uncle Jake was a rogue."

"Was, Maddy, there's a difference. He changed his ways. I will not hold his youth against him."

"Cooper is young, he could change his ways."

"I hope he does, Maddy. Think what would happen if he was raiding a ship and your father or brother happened along."

Maddy was silent for a moment, and then looking at her mother in the mirror, she confessed, "I love him, Mother."

"You love his derring do, sweetheart. He saved you from a fate worse than death. You are infatuated with a romantic, dashing, young rogue. I doubt its true love."

"It is, Mother, the kind that Nanny told me about. From the first time I saw him with his blonde hair blowing in the breeze and that ugly scar on his face, I knew he was the man for me." Maddy turned to face her mother and took her hand. "When he killed the pirate in that tent he turned and looked at me standing there with no clothes on and I felt no shame. In truth, Mother, I wanted him. He could have taken me then and there and I would have loved it. But he didn't. He handed me a coat and when I asked if I was so hard to look upon, he looked into my eyes, Mother, and said, 'Were I not a married man, my beautiful lady, I'd fight a hundred such as he if it would gain me favor in your eyes.'"

Faith pulled her daughter to her. "Our rogue is also a gentleman and an honorable one. Don't put him in an awkward position, Maddy. He's got two things going against a successful relationship." Maddy gave her mother a quizzical look. "Married *and* a pirate," Faith said, answering her daughter's look.

Maddy took a deep breath and sighed, "I can always hope and dream, Mother."

"Yes, my dear, that you can do."

Chapter Thirty Eight

SIR ROBERT BASNIGHT WAS sitting down to a plate of corned beef, eggs, and toast with coffee when he heard a carriage drive up. That was not unusual, but it was early. His doorman soon came to where he sat.

"The admiral's cox'n is here with a gentleman to see you on what the gentleman describes as a private matter."

"Jake Hex and a gentleman, you say. Did you get the gentleman's name, Charles?"

"I believe he said it was Cain, Sir Robert."

"Cooper Cain? Show them in at once and have the cook bring more cups."

"Yes sir."

Sir Robert stood and greeted his guest warmly. Coffee was poured and after a few pleasantries, Cooper came to the point.

"My uncle, Sir Lawrence is dead. His son, who is the reason for...my current status, has found himself heavily in debt. He's lost at the tables, he lived very high with his sodomite friends and he's had significant business losses."

"How do you know this?" Sir Robert asked.

Tempted to say he'd created much of the business loss, Cooper refrained and said, "From my mother and others I've known for years."

"I take it you don't want the land here on Antigua to be lost."

"The land here belonged to my father and mother. I would like to see it returned to its rightful owner," Cooper said.

"Did you not tell me your father was dead?" Sir Robert asked.

"My mother is not. I want to pay off the loans and put the plantation back in good order and restore it to her."

"You have the money to do this?"

When Cooper didn't speak, Sir Robert said, "Of course, you do, otherwise you wouldn't be here. It will take a few days to arrange things but I will get things started today. Do you know which bank holds the mortgage?"

"No sir."

"There are only two on the island. Do you have the money with you?"

"It's aboard my ship. I anchored in Falmouth Harbor."

"Humm…probably for the best," Sir Robert said.

"It would be helpful if I had a note from you vouching for my ship, Sir Robert."

"I will have my secretary see to it. I don't expect you to keep your crew on board ship, Cooper, but they need to be on good behavior while ashore. A man in his cups might, well say things, that would be embarrassing or worse."

"My crew are used to going ashore in Savannah where our… er…occupation is not known."

"Good, I will depend on their discretion," Sir Robert said.

"I will need the loan of a carriage or wagon to go get the money, Sir Robert."

"I will have a carriage and driver at your disposal while you are here, my friend."

"Thank you, sir. I, we, will take our leave now," Cooper said, looking at Jake, who nodded.

Then as an afterthought, Cooper pulled the letters from his inside coat pocket. "These are letters from our bankers and lawyer, Sir Robert."

"Very thoughtful, Cooper, they may come in handy. Are you staying at Sir Gabe's?"

"For now," Cooper replied.

"I will send a carriage there with a note for the authorities at Falmouth."

"CAN I GO, MOTHER, please? It's such a nice day." Cooper could see the indecision on Faith's face.

"It would not be proper to allow Maddy to go unchaperoned," Faith said.

"You could both go," he volunteered. "There will be plenty of room. There will only be Beau and I in the carriage, Quang would prefer to set topside, I'm sure."

"Of course, we'll go," Faith smiled.

The trip was much more comfortable in Sir Robert's carriage than it had been in the wagon. Cooper brought up seeing James at Debbie's birthday party and wedding. He even hinted his childhood friend, who was presently staying with the Taylors, seemed to have fallen for James while he seemed very infatuated with her in return.

After a few moments of discussing James, Faith asked, "How is your wife, Sophia, wasn't that her name, Cooper?"

Cooper flushed and clinched his fist. His lips trembled as he tried to keep his emotions in check. Faith and Maddy quickly realized this was not a subject that should have been broached. As Cooper kept his silence, unable to speak, Beau cleared his throat and spoke softly, "Captain Cain's wife is no longer with us."

"Oh, I'm so sorry," Faith and Maddy said. "Please accept our condolences."

Later, while waiting on a boat to take them to the ship, Beau had the opportunity to explain Sophia's untimely death. Later that night, Maddy thought to herself that one problem has been solved, though she wouldn't have wished it.

HMS Hunter, of sixteen guns, sailed along under easy sail. It was make and mend and the crew was occupied writing letters, and sewing up clothes that needed repair. Two men sat together doing scrimshaw and a little group was gathered forward, smoking and listening to the ship's fiddler.

Captain Wellington had just gone below and the deck belonged to Lieutenant Jacob Anthony. He could remember his father talking about his first command, *HMS SeaWolf*. Of course, there had been a war going on then. There was now too, with the French, but that was in Europe. Napoleon didn't send many ships to the Caribbean. Therefore, the chance for promotion and command was not what it had been in his father's younger days.

"Deck thar!" the lookout called down. "Two ships at battle, sir."

"Where away!"

"Fine off the larboard bow," the lookout responded.

"Mr. Woods!"

"Aye sir."

"Please inform our captain of the sighting."

"No need, Mr. Anthony. I was already on my way up when the lookout called down."

"Beat to quarters, Captain?"

"I think so, Mr. Anthony. It will take the better part of an hour to get within range but hopefully we can be of some assistance."

"To whom is the question," Anthony quipped.

"Right, Jacob."

Smiling, Lieutenant Anthony responded, "Aye, Captain."

The beat of feet drummed across the deck as personal items were quickly put aside and hands went to their battle stations.

The sound of gunfire was soon audible as it vibrated across the water. Lieutenant Anthony took a ship's glass and climbed up the shrouds. Captain Wellington was a man who liked a professional view of the situation. Knowing this, Anthony went up without being told. Standing on the ratlines, he wrapped his arm through and around a shroud to hold the glass steady. Focusing in, he saw they'd never get there in time to provide much assistance. The smaller ship carried a British flag. The larger ship didn't have a flag flying. A pirate, no doubt. Would they find anyone left alive?

"Fly *Hunter*," he said to himself. "Fly."

SIR ROBERT HAD SENT for Cooper Cain. "I have both good and bad news for you," he said when Cooper presented himself. "First the bank will sell you the mortgage. But it has to be under the terms of the original mortgage. What I mean by that is Phillip has until December to pay off the loan before it is considered in default. If the mortgage is not paid on the first of December, the land becomes the property of the bank or individual holding the mortgage. Should he present himself to the bank to pay off the note he will be referred to your agent. I am now your agent. Should he not present, my lawyer has already started the paperwork to assume ownership. Once that is done, the title will be placed in your mother's name and you will receive notification via your lawyer in Savannah. If this is acceptable, tomorrow morning we will go to the bank, and after paying sixteen thousand pounds the land will be in your hands."

"I thought it was fifteen thousand," Cooper said.

"It was, but there are certain administrative fees that have to be added to such a transaction."

He means bribes, Cooper thought to himself.

"What about funds to see the plantation up and running?" Cooper asked.

"Those should be entrusted to your agent to use when the property legally becomes your mother's," Sir Robert replied.

Nodding, Cooper asked, "Could I see the property?"

"I see no reason you shouldn't," Sir Robert said. "I think it will be a good outing but I was told, Cooper, that only a skeleton staff has been kept. Therefore, I'd not expect much."

"It was my father's," Cooper responded. "That's all that matters."

Two carriages made the trip inland to Cooper's birthplace. The property was located in the Parish of Saint Paul. The road was rutted, bouncing the carriage and the occupants inside. Maddy held onto Cooper longer than necessary, something neither Cooper nor Faith missed. Lady Deborah and Sir Robert smiled knowing smiles. They'd not missed Maddy's action either. The fields were overgrown, there was a hole in the stable roof and the fence around the main house was down. The slave quarters were ramshackle as well. However, the yard in front of the main house was swept clean and the house looked to be in a good state of repair, aside from needing painting.

Hearing the carriages pull up, a woman walked out of the house holding her hands over her eyes to see thru the sun's glare. Two children, a boy and a girl also came out. "That's your staff, Nettie and her two children," Robert said.

"Where's her man?" Cooper asked.

"Dead, some years now," Robert replied.

Nettie greeted everyone and introductions were made all around. "I'm sorry that I don't have anything for refreshments," she apologized.

"No need to be concerned, Nettie," Cooper said. "Until yesterday, we didn't know we were coming either."

This brought a smile from the black woman. She spoke to the boy to get water for the horses and the girl brought a gourd of water for the visitors.

After a look around, Lady Deborah approached Cooper, "The land needs a lot of clearing but the soil still looks rich and fertile."

Cooper had been astonished to see the women reach down and pick up a hand full of dirt as they walked over to a nearby field.

Lady Deborah continued, "Irrigation ditches will have to be dug again, and houses for the workers will have to be built. Better to tear down what you have and start over. A barn and blacksmith shop will come later. Water drainage from Table Hill and Green Hill will help keep the soil moist. Your father picked a good place, Cooper, some hillside but mostly flat growing fields. Should you decide to sell it, I will buy it."

Cooper found Lady Deborah's words very encouraging. As they departed the property, he left Nettie with ten pounds to spend on her family. "I have also set up funds with Sir Robert. Should you need anything, just let him know."

As they drove away, Nettie held her children to her and said, "Things are looking up, thank the Lord."

HMS Hunter SAILED INTO English Harbor an hour before the sun went down. No sooner had the anchor dropped than a signal from the flagship was hoisted, "captain repair on board." The return signal sent from *Hunter's* halyard simply said, "require assistance." The flagship responded immediately.

It was well known the admiral's son was the first lieutenant aboard *Hunter*. It was also noticable to the trained eye that *HMS Hunter* had been in a battle. The bulwark on the starboard side forward had a gap where a section was missing. The area where the forward gun should have been was scorched and ragged.

No gun was visible. The huge mainsail had been patched. As a number of boats pushed off from the flagship, the captain's barge was at the fore. One of its passengers was the admiral's cox'n, Jake Hex. Everyone knew Jake Hex's orders or recommendations were the same as those of his admiral. Therefore, the crew offered him the same respect they would have their captain or the admiral.

Once, alongside *Hunter*, Captain Davy grabbed the man-rope and quickly climbed the battens and through the entry port. Behind him were Hex and a surgeon. The bosun's pipe sounded and the stamp of muskets on the deck let him know at least someone was trying to maintain formality.

Jacob Anthony stood erect, arm in a sling and with a look of fatigue. The significance of this was that the captain was either dead or severely wounded. Behind Anthony, several people stood. Passengers! Hunter had likely come to the aid of a ship being attacked by pirates. Arrangements were quickly made to get the passengers ashore with what little personal belongings they were able to rescue. Jacob Anthony was then transported to the flagship, escorted by Hex.

Once aboard, he went directly to the admiral's stateroom. Since Hex was the only other person in the room, other than the admiral, Jacob said, "Father."

"Are you hurt, son?"

"Nothing serious, the surgeon says."

Admiral Anthony looked at his son's swollen arm. He had met a lot of good surgeons in his naval career but he'd also met some he considered lacking. He would see to it that his son was evaluated by his ship's surgeon or one at the hospital.

Hex went to the pantry and got three glasses and filled them with brandy. Once everyone was seated, Jacob made his report.

"We came upon a merchant vessel out of Bermuda headed for the Grand Cayman. They were being attacked by a pirate ship. Captain Wellington thought once they saw us, they'd bugger off. In fact, it seemed to me they delayed their departure. We fired at extreme range but still they lingered. Suddenly, their larboard gunports open and they fired every gun that came to bear. Captain Wellington was cut down by a ball right away. I had the forward guns fire. We hit the enemy ship with several balls but it did little damage. Our metal was nothing compared to theirs. As the ship set sail, two stern chasers fired, overturning the number one gun and killing its crew. As they sailed away a number of the blackhearts stood on the stern and jeered us. Had they decided to give more battle, I'm sure we wouldn't be here today. I did notice the name across the stern, *Cobra*. I counted sixteen gunports on her larboard side, so she's a thirty-two gun ship, probably an old frigate."

Admiral Anthony had kept silent and not interrupted his son's report. Now that he was finished, he asked, "The merchant ship?"

"The crew is all dead, slaughtered where they stood. A young woman was raped while her husband was made to watch. The granddaughter of the older couple was taken away, she was only fourteen. The ship was stripped of everything valuable and holed. I barely got the surviving passengers off before it sank."

Admiral Anthony nodded, "Let's go home to see your mother. We'll then go get that arm checked out."

As Hex called for his barge, Admiral Anthony couldn't help but think of Faith and Maddy's capture. Had it not been for Cooper Cain, Maddy would have been raped or worse. It was likely they'd both be dead right now. *God bless him, if only he'd give up being a sea robber. Damn him.*

CHAPTER THIRTY NINE

Cooper, Maddy, Faith, Lady Deborah, and Beau Cannington had just returned from viewing the property when Admiral Anthony arrived with his son and cox'n. Seeing her son climb out of the carriage, Faith ran to him, hugging her son as only a mother can. Maddy was next, calling him little Jake instead of Jacob. Introductions were made by Admiral Anthony.

Beau Cannington greeted the admiral's son, but with a professional eye. "I believe that arm needs to be looked at, young sir."

"We were going to have that done after I saw mother and Maddy," Jacob admitted.

"Let's go inside," Beau said, asking Cooper to get his bag. "Is this from a splinter?" he asked, once Jacob's coat had been removed and his shirt was off.

"Aye," Jacob replied.

"Did the surgeon open the wound or just extract the splinter?" Beau asked.

"He just pulled it out."

"Uh huh," Beau answered. The wound was very tender, a puncture wound that was red and hot to the touch already. "I think there's still something in there," Beau said. "The wound needs to be opened and explored." Looking at the admiral, he was very frank, "This needs to be done quickly, sir, or your son could lose his arm or worse."

"Where do you recommend?"

"We should go aboard your ship or possibly the hospital."

"My ship is probably cleaner, according to our surgeon."

"Let's be on our way then," Beau said.

As they made ready to depart, Admiral Anthony noted his wife had gathered her coat. The way she looked let him know there'd be no discussion on the subject. His only word was, "Maddy."

"I will stay with her, sir," Cooper volunteered. "I will be a gentleman. You have my word of honor."

"I've never doubted that, Coop," the admiral responded, realizing he meant it.

Aboard the flagship, they went directly to the sick bay. The surgeon was ashore but one of the mates was there. Seeing the admiral, he asked no questions, but got busy assisting Doctor Cannington.

Jacob was given something for the pain and laid back. A bite block was placed between his teeth and Faith took his hands. Beau poured brandy into the wound and was not surprised to see tiny bits of debris come out. It was dark material and looked like it was probably from Jacob's uniform coat. More brandy was poured into the wound until no further debris came out.

Beau then probed the wound and said, "Much as I thought." He then took a scalpel and opened the wound, making an incision to both sides of the puncture. With the help of the surgeon's mate, the wound was held open and an inch-long, thin splinter was removed. More debris was removed and brandy was used to wash out the wound. The incisions were closed and a drain was placed in the puncture. Sweat stood in beads across Jacob's forehead and his face was white. The bite block was removed and he gave a weak smile.

"I'd not move him tonight," Doctor Cannington advised. Admiral Anthony nodded.

"I will stay with him," Hex volunteered.

"We will all stay," Admiral Anthony said.

"Maddy," Faith said. "She'll want to know, she'll be worried."

"I'll send my flag lieutenant."

"No, I'll go," Hex said.

It suddenly became clear to Admiral Anthony that his cox'n, who was his son's namesake, needed to have something to do. He needed to be busy.

"Maybe that's best. Do you wish to accompany him, dear?"

"No," Faith said. "I will be fine until tomorrow."

COOPER WENT ABOARD *RAVEN*. The crew were getting restless and Johnson had gotten into a fight in Falmouth and had to be bailed out after damages had been paid.

"How much longer are we going to be stay anchored, Captain?" asked Johannes.

"I'm not sure," Cooper replied in earnest. He knew that they needed to depart but found it hard to leave Maddy. "Doctor Cannington is treating the admiral's son. As soon as he feels he's safe, we will go."

"There are other doctors on the island, Captain." Johannes said, speaking as the quartermaster, not as Cooper's friend.

"Doctor Cannington is the one who operated on the boy." Cooper looked up at the men who had gathered. "If the surgeon operated on one of you, would you want him to up and leave? Leaving you to just anybody, or would you want him to stay around until you were well?"

"We'd want him to stay," Banty said.

"Aye," McKemie seconded. The crew all agreed.

"Captain, you've bought yourself a few days," Johannes whispered.

Cooper nodded but didn't say anything. He walked over to the rail where Mac stood. "You are awful quiet," Cooper said to his friend.

"I saw Lucy. She was with some bullock major."

"Did she see you?"

"No, but it wasn't easy to not call to her."

Am I being selfish? Cooper wondered. We have been here nearly a month. My business has been handled, so why I am here? He knew the answer: Maddy. No matter how hard he tried to put her out of his mind, she wouldn't go. Was he being disloyal to Sophia? No, she was gone. He'd given her his all. If she were alive, he wouldn't be thinking about Maddy. But she was gone and Maddy was here…here and alive…very much alive.

Today was Friday. He made up his mind. "Mac, pass the word. We will sail with the tide on Monday."

Mac put his hand on his friend's arm. "Are you sure?"

"Yes." Cooper turned and went down the entry port to a ship's boat.

Beau Cannington was at the Anthony's home. Cooper went there to let him know their sailing date. He was surprised when he pulled up to find Lord Anthony's carriage there at this time of day. He climbed down the steps of Sir Robert's carriage and made a mental note to send him a thank you note for the loan of the carriage and driver.

Maddy saw him drive up and rushed out to him. Taking his arm in hers, she said, "Come in. Father has an announcement to make."

Walking inside, Cooper was glad to see Jacob was up and had most of his color back. Bart nodded as he went past. Lord Anthony shook his hand and Lady Deborah gave him a peck on the cheek. Jake Hex passed him a glass of what looked like sherry. Maddy held out her hand for one but got a smile instead.

Admiral Anthony spoke, "I'm sure everyone is aware by now the mail packet arrived today. The captain of the packet has hand delivered a letter to me from James. It seems he has found the right woman after all these years." Turning to Cooper, Anthony smiled. "It's your childhood friend. James and Josie are to be wed."

Oh shit, Cooper thought, *the vixen.* But thinking back, he thought, maybe she's been bitten by the same bug.

"It seems, sir," Lord Anthony said, speaking to Cooper, "that our lives continue to run a parallel course."

"When is the wedding?" Deborah asked.

"In December," Faith answered.

"Do you plan on going?"

"Of course, if we can get a ship," Faith replied.

"Oh, Mother," Maddy giggled. "Sir Pirate can take us."

"Damme," Lord Anthony snorted. "Maddy, will you ever learn to control your tongue?"

Maddy smiled and boastfully said, "Who knows, there might be a double wedding."

This time, everybody laughed except Cooper and Maddy's father. They both looked shocked. They were the only ones. Maddy had made no secret in regards to her feelings for Cooper.

Raven SAILED WITH THE morning tide on Monday morning as expected. What had not been expected was that she was carrying two passengers, Faith and Maddy. It was Jacob Anthony who had persuaded his father to approve the arrangements.

"I think it much preferable that Mother and Maddy sail in an armed ship with a trained crew, who know how to fight."

The alternative would have been for them to sail in a packet or some merchant vessel. Both of which would be easy pickings if the *Cobra* happened along.

"You condone their accompanying a pirate?" Anthony asked his son.

"Do you have proof of that?" Jacob asked.

"Only his confession in my cabin."

Jacob sighed. "Well, has there been any proof or charges placed against him?"

"No, none that I know of."

"It's up to you then, Father. A good pirate who's come to your family's aid more than once or send a ship to the colonies for some unspecified reason."

"You know I can't do that, Jacob."

"Let them sail with Cooper, then."

"Aye, I guess you are right." Anthony called for his cox'n. When he got there, Anthony filled up three glasses. "I thought you might like to give the news to little Jake."

Hex smiled, "Aye." Holding up his glass, he said, "To Lieutenant Jacob Anthony, the new captain of *HMS Hunter*."

Jacob smiled, he hadn't been called little Jake by anyone other than Maddy since he became a lieutenant. But this time he enjoyed it, especially coming from big Jake. "Thank you, Jake. Thank you, Father. When is it official?"

"As soon as you read yourself in. As I understand it, the *Hunter* has completed all repairs and is ready for sea."

"Yes sir, she is."

"Good, your new first lieutenant has been sent over by Captain Davy. You will sail Monday morning and resume your patrol from here to Bermuda. Should something happen and you find need to replenish your water, I'm sure the Americans would not deny you that."

"Father, you are the best."

Admiral Anthony said, "Lieutenant, this is your commander and chief speaking."

"Aye, sir. Is that how Uncle Gil used to do it?"

CHAPTER FORTY

FAITH AND MADDY WERE received by the crew as royalty. "There are women aboard," Johannes had said to the crew, "so watch your manners and watch your language. None of the dirty words. None of the dirty words, Banty, you hear me?"

Banty gave a sheepish smile, "No worries, quartermaster, my language will be that of a saint."

Johannes snorted, "There's nothing saintly about you, mate."

The morning was clear; the harbor had gulls and sea birds all about. A pelican sat on a rock at the water's edge and egrets walked about pausing to look into small pools looking for a tidbit of food. A sooty tern with its wide wingspan was headed out to sea.

"Eli Taylor told me a sooty tern will spend months at sea," Cooper volunteered to Faith and Maddy.

"It's a beautiful bird," Maddy offered, watching the bird until it was out of sight.

Mac had the *Raven* underway in a fluid, professional manner. Cooper had not wanted to appear lacking in front of Maddy so he had asked Mac to get the ship underway.

However, Maddy broached the subject, "You let your first officer weigh anchor and put the ship to sea?"

Swallowing, Cooper replied, "Mac is a much better seaman than I." Once he admitted that, the truth as he saw it flooded out of his mouth, "Maddy, I shouldn't be *Raven's* captain. I don't know why I am. Mac is a much better seaman and officer than I am. He's been at sea since he was twelve and I only have a year."

Maddy looked at Cooper and smiled. She touched his hand and said, "You had to show something, Coop, otherwise Captain Taylor would never have turned the ship over to you. I think you under estimate your abilities. Father told me when he was a young lieutenant and got his first command, the most important thing Uncle Gil did was make sure he had a good master, an old salt who knew ships and the sea. Father told me on more than one occasion the master had made quiet recommendations that kept him out of trouble. I'm sure by the time you've been at sea as long as Mac has been you will find your skills and seamanship will be as good as anybody."

Cooper suddenly had the urge to sweep Maddy off her feet and smother her with kisses. Damn, but she knew how to make a man feel good. However, with Faith standing close by he simply took Maddy's hand and kissed the back of it. "You are an angel," he said.

Maddy smiled now, "My parents and brothers would disagree with you."

"I think your father would agree but, regardless, the others see you in a different light."

"How would you define your light, Sir Pirate?"

"I think you know. If not, there's no hope."

Maddy put her hand on Cooper's arm. "I know, but still a woman likes to hear the words."

"I love you."

Maddy's reaction surprised Cooper. She literally jumped into his arms and kissed him long and hard. When she stopped, she stepped back but with her hands still on his chest. "Does that tell you how I feel, Sir Pirate?"

"Aye, your mother, me, and most of the crew," Cooper replied.

Maddy's hand went to her mouth as she smiled. She turned and saw a good many of the crew watching her. She gave a bow, which caused the crew to break out in cheers.

Cooper looked at Faith, "I'm sorry for that display, Madam."

Faith smiled slightly. "It is not your fault, Coop. Maddy is an impulsive and passionate girl. When she wants something, she goes after it. Just remember, Coop, you've made no secret of what you do. I don't want Maddy to be heartbroken with you being taken to the gallows. If you truly love Maddy, you need to give up this life as a pirate. My husband and son are duty bound. It's been engrained since they were born. How would you feel if Jacob happened to be on a ship you were chasing? Could you look down the barrel of one of your cannons and fire?"

"No, Madam, I couldn't."

Faith smiled, but her face took on a sad look, "Your men would. You might be shot or thrown over the side but they'd fight to keep from being captured. Think about it, Cooper, think what you might be doing to Maddy. If you love her, as you say, think about her future."

THE NIGHT WAS COOL with a slight breeze, and the moon looked big as it shined down. Occasionally, a cloud would pass in front to dim its glow for a few moments. Dinner had been served in Cooper's cabin. He had taken turns every night bringing one of the crew in to dine with him, Faith, and Maddy. Johannes set up a lottery system where a new hand's name was picked every night.

The crew enjoyed the meal and it helped quell the desire to sweep down on a likely prize when a sail was sighted. Other than Mac and Johannes, not a single crewman had ever sat down and dined with a lady. Some of the hands had even tried to bribe or pay another for his spot, knowing only a handful would have the pleasure of spending an evening with 'ladies of quality.'

Maddy had traded her dress for seaman's slops during the day, but at night, she dressed for dinner. After they had eaten a simple but tasty meal, they all came on deck. Mac was playing his guitar and singing with a group gathered around. The fiddler soon followed along.

Joining the group, Maddy was soon tapping her foot in time to the music. Seeing this, Mac and Moree, the fiddler, played an up tempo song. Banty jumped up, bowed to Maddy who took his outreached hand and the two danced to the delight of the crew. After Banty's dance, Robinson, Bridges, and McKemie all took a turn.

"Play something slower," Johannes said, as the last jig finished. As the music started, he asked Faith, "May I have the pleasure of this dance?" Faith gave a slight curtsey and the two danced an elegant dance. A side of Johannes, Cooper had never seen…a gentleman. Cooper then danced with Faith.

The last dance was with Maddy; a slow tune, a love ballad with Mac's voice soft and mournful. Maddy leaned in to Cooper and he felt her head on his chest, her warm body touching his. It was like they were in another world. When the music stopped they lingered together a moment. She looked up and Cooper kissed her, her lips were warm and sent a shock through him.

Taking a breath, he stepped back. "Thank you for such a wonderful dance, my love."

"You are most welcome, Sir Pirate."

"Sail ho!"

"Where away," Mac called.

"Dead ahead, straight off the bow."

The call did not generate the excitement as it usually did. Maddy, in her slops, was amidships watching Banty as he worked on a line, wrapping the end with sailcloth and tying it tightly. As he turned his head, the sun reflected off of his earring.

"Tell me, Banty, why do sailors wear earrings?" she asked.

Banty paused at his task. "Don't you know, Maddy, with you growing up with seamen?" Maddy shook her head no, so Banty continued, "Legend has it a man with gold in his ear will not drown."

"Humm, can't you swim, Banty?"

"No, my Cherie, most sailors can't. That's why they made ships, so we wouldn't have to learn."

This seemed odd to Maddy but she didn't say any more, mostly because the lookout called down again. "Yonder ship has come about."

This did create interest to everyone. Banty dropped what he was doing and went to the binnacle and took a glass from its rack. He glanced at Johannes, who gave him a nod, so up he went.

"Slide over, mate," he said to Johnson, once he reached the tops. Banty focused his glass and studied the ship. She was bearing down under full sail. As he watched, he saw her gunports open. There was no doubt what the ship intended. Down a backstay he went. He hit the deck and dashed to the quarterdeck. "She's a big bitch, a frigate I'd say and she's just opened her gunports. This ain't no social call."

Spurlock turned to his friend, Diamond, "I hope this doesn't mean I lose my turn to dine tonight."

Diamond punched his friend, "I'll stand in for you, mate."

The crew went to quarters and Mac touched Cooper's arm, giving a nod indicating Faith and Maddy. Quang was the closest sailor so Cooper called to him, "Take the women down to the sick berth. It's about the safest place they could be." As Quang gathered the women, Maddy turned to Cooper and mouthed, "I love you."

Cooper nodded and turned his attention to Mac and Johannes. "We can't trade ball for ball with that one. She's too big."

"What do you intend to do?" Johannes asked.

"We can't outrun her, correct?" Cooper asked.

"Never," Mac responded.

"The only option left, as I see it, is to board her and fight it out, blade for blade," he said. Both men nodded; Cooper was right.

"A word to the crew would be good, Captain." This was said just as smoke erupted from the forward guns of their foe.

"Men," Cooper shouted. "Yonder ship shows you no respect. They mean to take your ship, your plunder, and…your ladies." This caused the crew to roar. Cooper held up his hand. "They are bigger with more metal but not a man among them could even beat Banty." A laugh erupted from the crew. "I intend to lay us alongside and give them a taste of metal…this," Cooper said, raising and waving his sword in the air.

Standing at the hatch where they had paused, Maddy thought, *that's why you are the captain, Sir Pirate. That's why you are the captain.*

JOHANNES HAD AGAIN PLACED two men on the wheel. A ball had landed alongside with a dull thud and splashing water inboard.

"Johannes, I want to keep *Raven's* bow head on to yonder ship's bow," Cooper ordered. "If she changes course, as I'm sure she'll do, we will counter. I do not want yonder captain to have his way. We will offer as small a target as we can."

"Aye, Captain."

Quang was back from getting the ladies below. Seeing him, Cooper said, "Quang, go tell Spurlock to have his gunners to fire as they bear. Don't wait for my command, fire as the situation allows."

"Aye, Captain."

When the enemy ship turned to give a broadside, Johannes had the wheel put down, offering only the *Raven's* stern, a much smaller target. It was a risky target if the rudder was hit but the maneuver was worth the risk. When the other ship's captain laid his ship on a course to give chase, *Raven* was brought about with every gun firing as they bore on the other ship's bow. Cheers went up as the bowsprit fell and wood flew high in the air.

"Did you see the figurehead?" Mac asked Cooper. "It's a snake's head, that's the *Cobra*."

The *Cobra* tried one more time to give a broadside but Johannes was quick to change course again. Two balls hit the stern railing and sent wood high into the air this time.

"Too, too close," Mac snarled.

"We are dancing circles around the bugger," someone yelled.

For now, Cooper thought. As the distance grew, the *Cobra's* captain swung his ship around to give chase.

"Not the best ship handler I've seen," Mac commented.

Regardless, the advantage that they'd been given by the slow ship handling was soon to disappear.

"Do we have time to come about and meet yonder ship head on?"

"It will be close but we can try."

"Bring her about, Mr. Ewers."

"Aye, Captain." Formality was once again being used.

"Every shot they have fired has been with either the forward guns or the larboard side. Have you noticed that?" Cooper asked.

"Aye," both Johannes and Mac answered.

"If the *Cobra* continues on a collision course as we are now headed, I want you to change course at the last moment possible and lay us alongside her starboard beam. Mr. Diamond, have your sail handlers ready. Quang, go tell Spurlock what we are about. I want every gun and swivel we have loaded with a double shot of grape. Let's cut down as many of the whoresons as possible."

"Aye, Captain, I like yer way of thinking."

The *Cobra* continued to bear down. He must think I'm willing to trade broadsides, Cooper thought to himself. The ships continued to converge on each other. Another puff of smoke from the *Cobra's* forward guns and *Raven* took a glancing hit. The men were seasoned and did not have to be told to stay down behind the rails.

This time clouds of smoke bellowed out as *Cobra* fired. The shot was heard overhead as it passed through the sails, two pockmarks. Spurlock had *Raven's* guns going, getting two shots to one of the *Cobra's*. A cheer went up. Spurlock's last shot hit one of *Cobra's* forward guns, knocking it into the air. It must have been about to fire as it exploded as it came down. But still the ship came on, with the bow was looking larger and larger.

Fear went through Cooper as he thought about the women below. *Please God,* he prayed, *let us carry this day.*

CHAPTER FORTY ONE

THE *COBRA'S* CAPTAIN'S MINDSET must have been enough of this dancing around. Maybe, he thought, *Cobra's* heavier guns would end the battle with a broadside as *Raven* sailed past. Therefore, he continued on course. He did not tack and he did not come about. He didn't alter his course in the least bit. If the two ships continued, *Cobra's* starboard guns would erupt at pistol shot range. That's what Cooper wanted the blackheart to think. That's why he continued on course.

Mac stood next to Cooper, "We are going to be cutting it close, Coop."

Johannes looked at his captain anxiously, much longer and the *Cobra* would ram *Raven* as she made her cut.

"Now," Cooper ordered.

The helmsman spun the wheel as Johannes had instructed them in preparation for the maneuver.

"Mr. Spurlock, be ready," Cooper ordered. "Are the men ready with the grappling hooks, Mr. Diamond?"

"Aye, Captain."

The deck canted sharply as *Raven* responded to the wheel. Cooper, Mac, and Johannes had to grab hold of the fife rail to keep from falling. It seemed like they were holding on for ever when Johannes shouted for the change in course to lay *Raven* on *Cobra's* larboard side. The wheel spun again. This time it seemed like it took forever for the rudder to bite and *Raven's* new course set.

"Down with the sails," Mac called as pre-planned.

Instead of the usual evolution, lines were cut. This was life or death. The lines could be fixed if *Raven* took the day. If not, it wouldn't matter if all the lines were cut. They were almost alongside the *Cobra*.

Mac quickly took Cooper's hand and shook it, "Meet you on *Cobra's* quarterdeck." He then ran to meet his boarders.

In the fighting tops, the men were ready. The gunners stood by their cannons, which were filled with grape and set on maximum elevation. Mr. Diamond stood by the men with grappling hooks. *Raven* crashed into *Cobra's* side and bounced out with a loud thud, but came grinding back as the helmsman held the wheel over.

As the ships came together again the grappling hooks shot out and secured quickly. One, then two, and a third line snapped like a gunshot but more hooks were flying through the air. *Cobra* had not reduced sail so the first lines couldn't take the strain. But the bosun, Mr. Diamond, had every hook the *Raven* carried flying over.

Cobra felt the weight and tension now and slowed, but water came over *Raven's* stern. Would *Raven* be swamped? Overhead, the swivels banged away as they spit their load of grape down on men running to cut the grappling lines. The cannons roared and flames jumped forth as their deadly load flew across *Cobra's* deck.

Spurlock, a wise and experienced gunner, had foreseen the problem of *Raven's* possibly being swamped so he'd had every other gun captain concentrate on *Cobra's* mast and sails. Double-shotted with a measure of grape, the guns leaped as they were fired. The devastation to *Cobra's* mast and sails were felt at once as the air was rent with grape and ball. The sails were torn to pieces, tattered canvas flapping but unable to catch the wind.

Spars, tackles, and rope all crashed down on *Cobra's* crew. The foremast was leaning, its stays snapped.

"Boarders away," Cooper yelled. Mac and Diamond followed suit.

Overhead, the swivel gunner poured another load down on *Cobra's* crew. Men were down, kicking and screaming, but still *Raven's* crew were significantly outnumbered. A sharpshooter on *Cobra* fired his musket, striking the swivel gunner on the mainmast. He held to the handle on his gun and pulled the lanyard, his load cutting down several as he fell lifeless to the deck.

Seeing this, Johannes sent another man up to take the gunner's place. "Quickly now," Johannes urged the man.

Boarders from the *Raven* were climbing up *Cobra's* side, forward, amidship, and aft. Some of *Cobra's* men had opened gunports and were firing at the boarders, but they were quickly dispatched as several of *Raven's* men took advantage of the open ports and climbed through them. *No boarding nets*, Mac thought, as he was up and over *Cobra's* side. The captain would never make it in the Royal Navy.

As *Raven's* men made the deck, they were met with *Cobra's* crew. The men manning *Raven's* swivels continued to cut down on the odds. *Cobra's* captain finally sent someone to man their swivels, but *Raven's* aft swivel gunner cut him down with a load. The guns were now getting hot…too hot to risk another charge of powder. The bucket for the wet swabs was empty. It was sent down on a rope but for now the gun was useless.

On *Cobra's* deck, a fierce battle raged. Pistols were jammed into their foes' guts and fired. The pistol was then used as a club or discarded. Cooper had already fired the three pistols he'd brought. Now it was steel on steel. Someone fired a pistol next to his ear making him duck as the hot air scorched his neck, deafening him suddenly. However, ducking saved his life as a cutlass swooshed through the air, inches from where his head had been. He thrust his blade forward into the rogue who had tried to decapitate him. As he yanked his sword free from the man, he was attacked by two men; one with a cutlass and the other with a boarding pike.

Cooper quickly pulled his small sword and thanked Sir Lawrence for Jean-Paul's lessons. "You never know what or how many you will face," the fencing master had said. Therefore, Cooper was trained to be ambidextrous. The lesson came in handy as the two cutthroats realizing the victory they believed they had was no more than an illusion. Cooper blocked the pike's thrust with his sword, while deflecting the cutlass lunge with his small sword. The cutlass tore his shirt and sliced his shoulder but the blade did not impale his chest as the foe thought it would.

Cooper quickly stepped between the men, stabbing one of them in the kidney as he did so. "Ahhh!," the man cried, and then cursed as dark blood poured from his side. The small sword was nearly jerked from Cooper's hand as the man fell.

Cooper recovered just as the other foe wheeled around, swinging his boarding pike. Cooper blocked it with his blade but the blow numbed his arm. He took advantage of the foe's open guard and struck, driving the small sword into the man just below the breast bone. Dropping the boarding pike, the man grabbed Cooper's arm and pulled him to the deck as he fell. The man's eyes were wide open as he died. Cooper tried to rise but fell, slipping in the blood of the two men he'd dispatched. Scrambling to his feet, Bridges called to him, "Hurry up, Captain, no time to rest."

Glancing about, Cooper felt sickened and apprehensive. He'd never seen such savagery. He had fought and killed but never on such a magnitude. Men continued to fight, to curse, to cry in pain and to die. Was it worth all this? He then thought of Maddy.

Maddy and her mother, he'd fight to the death to keep these rogues from having their way with them.

Mac was still up, he could see him and he spied Diamond with Spurlock close at hand. They were mates. They would sail together, party together and if need be, die together. Cooper watched as a man pulled his pistol to fire at Banty, but Robinson brought his cutlass down with all his might, severing the arm. The hand still gripped the pistol handle as it fell.

Moree and Johnson were being pushed back by a group of *Cobra's* men when McKemie joined in, and wielding his cutlass cut through the men from the side. *Where's Quang*, Cooper thought, and then remembered he was the women's last defender. He'll guard the hatch leading down to the sick berth. Anybody trying to go through the hatch would face Quang's blade and pistols first.

The battle continued to rage. How long now? It felt like hours. Overhead, a swivel banged. Cooper realized it had been silent for some time. Were they winning? It was push forward and then forced back. *Cobra's* crew might be blackhearts, but they were fighters, every last one of them. But, so were the *Raven's* men. There was no give in them.

The air reeked with the foul stench of blood, body waste as men's bowels were loosened as they were killed, the smell of gunpowder as smoke from the swivels drifted down; the smell of death. The blades were now caked and darkened with blood. A man fell dead, almost knocking Cooper down. His or *Cobra's*... he didn't know. He was still off balance when he was faced by a larger man, taller than Cooper by several inches. His bald head was bleeding where it had been cut numerous times. The man's earring seemed to hang askew when Cooper realized the ear was partially severed. Was this the ship's captain? His eyebrows were thick and matched his coarse black beard. He had wild-looking eyes as he rushed Cooper.

BOOM! BOOM! BOOM! The *Cobra's* deck shook and vibrated. Where did that come from? The boom made the man pause. A snarl creased his face. "There goes your ship," he spat forth. Had it really? Cooper didn't know but now he was angry…a controlled anger.

Before him was the one who'd feel it. Not Sir Lawrence, he was dead. Not D'Arcy, he was dead. Phillip was hurt financially and his day might still come, but before him was the enemy. The man who had caused Maddy to be taken; and the man who'd pleasure himself with Maddy if he was not stopped. But he would stop him. This man would feel the wrath of Cooper Cain. Cooper had defended himself until now. He had counterattacked. But now, he attacked; his sword was quicker than the eye could follow. He lunged, he parried and then he thrust again. He cut his enemy's face, he nicked his arm, he sliced down on a shoulder and when the man rushed he parried, ducked and cut down on the man's unprotected back as he stumbled forward.

The man wheeled around and fear took him as he faced Cooper. Never had he faced a man so quick; a man who brought the battle to him and smiled as he did so. He did not back away as the others had. The rogue's eyes were still glaring; but now they glared at the face of death. This man meant to kill him. Why had he chosen such a life? Roaring, the man charged. If he had to die, he'd take his tormentor with him. He rushed and swung with all his might. Surely, he'd kill this devil but he missed. Where was he? He'd never missed before. His gut hurt, it burned, and it burned like fire. Looking down, he saw the hilt of a sword sticking out from his coat. He pulled on it, the pain, the burning. Smoke…did he smell smoke. Slumping to his knees he continued to pull the sword from his body. The smoke grew stronger.

He coughed and blood came from his mouth. Fire…he could feel the heat. Was this hell? It couldn't be, he wasn't dead yet, or was he. The blade was free now. He tried to rise. He had to get away from the smoke and the fire.

Someone took the blade from him. He looked up, "So you're the devil, you scar-faced imp." Falling forward then, he died. No more pain…just death.

CHAPTER FORTY TWO

THE SMOKE WAS GETTING thicker and the flames rose with an increasing heat. Turning, Cooper realized his path back to *Raven* was blocked by the burning inferno. He nearly panicked, recalling the stories he'd heard from Captain Taylor and others about ships burning at sea.

"Captain…Captain!" He could see several of *Raven's* crew rushing toward the *Cobra's* bow. Was it clearer forward? Cooper thought so.

Rushing forward, he realized it was clearer and he could breathe better. The flames were mostly amidships and back. Mac was nowhere to be seen. Spurlock and Diamond were there helping the wounded men from *Raven* cross over to their ship.

"Where's Mac," Cooper yelled.

"He was aft, Captain." This spoken by McKemie. "We better be getting across, Captain. If the wind changes, *Raven* will be in danger."

"Go ahead," Cooper ordered. "I'm going to find Mac."

"I'll come along," Moree volunteered. "If he's down, it may take two of us."

The two men crossed the deck and found several of *Raven's* men coming their way. Giving quick instructions, Cooper and Moree went further aft but had to stop as the flames were gaining and the smoke more dense.

"Think he's below?" Cooper asked.

"I wouldn't be below deck on a burning ship if I could help it," Moree replied.

Coughing, eyes burning, and skin starting to feel painfully hot, they had to turn away.

"Where is he?" Cooper shouted, trying to be heard above the roaring inferno.

Shaking his head, Moree gasped, "Don't know, but if he's down there, he's dead." Barely able to see, the two made their way back to the *Cobra's* bow.

"Hurry, Captain," someone shouted from the *Raven*. All of *Raven's* crew had crossed over; the grappling lines had either been burned or snapped as the tension grew. The two ships were drifting apart. Moree took a few steps back to gather speed. He ran, leaped over the side and landed in a heap on *Raven's* deck. Seeing Moree land on deck, Cooper took one more look around for his friend, his heart sinking.

"Hurry, Coop." Recognizing the voice, Cooper could see Mac already aboard *Raven*. Backing up to get a running start, Cooper ran as hard as he could, leaping when he got to the rail; but something was wrong. Something came down on him, something heavy…heavy and hot, pushing him down past *Raven's* side, down into the water below; deeper and deeper. He struggled but couldn't get loose. Blackness, the abyss. Somewhere his soul lingered between darkness and light. The darkness seemed to fade as the light grew stronger and brighter. He could feel his body being lifted but he couldn't speak. He could see forms and shadows, but no clear faces. *Was he dead?*

His head hurt, he hurt all over. Looking around, Cooper could tell he was aboard a ship, but not his ship, not his cabin. He was hungry. The sounds came to him, of a ship at sea. Voices, opening his eyes wider made his head hurt more. He closed them again. He heard a soothing voice, felt a soft, cool hand and then blackness again.

"Ahhh!" The cool hand again, and the soft voice. "Shh now. Take it easy." The light was bright, very bright. It hurt his face. He tried to rise but was pushed back down. He felt a rocking sensation, but not from the sea. Was he being carried? God, he felt sick. He retched. The movement stopped. He retched again, an awful sickening taste. The darkness then came again.

Cooper opened his eyes. The sun's rays filtered through the slats in the shutters. His head didn't hurt, but his stomach did. He was hungry, very hungry. Where was he? In someone's bedroom, that was obvious. The last thing he remembered was a burning ship and his jumping. He heard a door open and looked around. The face of an angel looked back at him.

"You decided to join the living again, I see." It was Maddy. She walked over and placed her hand, that cool, soft hand, on his head. "The fever is gone."

"I remember your hand," he said.

Maddy smiled and leaning over kissed him on the cheek. "If you'd died, I would have killed you," she swore.

Now that makes a lot of damn sense, Cooper thought. But that's Maddy.

"Welcome back, stranger," Faith said. "You had us all worried, you know."

"I'm sorry."

"Don't be."

"Coop, are you awake?" It was Mac. "So it seems. You had us worried."

Beau Cannington walked in the room then. "That's enough. Let me see to our patient. Time enough for talking later."

Everyone left but Maddy, who took a seat in a rocking chair. Beau looked at her and she glared back. A look that said I'm not going anywhere.

Doctor Cannington examined Cooper, smiling as he finished. "I wouldn't have bet a dollar against a hundred that you'd pull through, Cooper."

"What happened?" Cooper asked.

"The foremast fell as you jumped. Spurlock thought it'd been hit by a ball and then the fire. When all the supporting stays and riggings caught fire and burned into, down it came, right on top of you."

"How did I get out?"

"Quang jumped in after you. He grabbed up a rope and dove in. Mac jumped right after him. They grabbed you to keep you from sinking lower and then they held on until several men hauled you out, pulling on the rope. We thought you'd all drowned for a minute. You swallowed a lot of sea water."

"I remember being sick."

"All over me," Maddy told Cooper.

"Sorry," Cooper said.

"Would you like a little broth?" Cannington asked.

"I'd like a cow," Cooper replied with a smile. "Where's Quang? In Savannah?"

"Yes, they are in Savannah, we will send for them. The entire crew is anxious to see you." Cooper nodded. "Send in the broth," he said. "Send Mac in too, please."

Cannington shook his head but added, "Just for a few minutes."

"I'll keep it short," Maddy volunteered.

Mac came in with the broth and a cloth so none would spill on the bed linens. Maddy came over and fed Cooper one spoon at a time.

"Beau says if it was not for you and Quang, I'd be dead."

"Mostly Quang," Mac replied modestly.

"What caused the fire?" Cooper managed to ask between spoons of broth.

"*Cobra's* gunners were firing on us and one of our swivels fired down on them. I think it must have hit a charge of powder. There was an explosion and then the fire. We were lucky it didn't set *Raven* ablaze as well."

"Did we get back in time for James' wedding?" Cooper asked.

Maddy paused, holding the spoon in mid air, "The wedding was two weeks ago, Cooper. You have been out for a long time, my love."

Cooper's mouth fell open, "Two weeks ago."

"Yes, you sure ruined my chance at a double wedding, you rogue." Maddy shoved the last spoon of broth in Cooper's mouth as she said this.

Swallowing hard, Cooper looked at Mac and asked, "Are the men on board the ship or shore?" The way Maddy froze and turned pale, Cooper knew something was wrong. "What is it, Mac?"

"*Cobra* fired too many rounds into *Raven* before she caught on fire. Johannes had the pumps rigged and going even before we cast off from *Cobra*. But it was no use. Had it not been for Jacob seeing the smoke and coming along, we'd have been in longboats."

"I remember waking up on another ship. It was all a haze, but I knew it was not the *Raven*. How did the crew react to being rescued by a British warship?"

"At first, they were just glad to be aboard something that wasn't in danger of sinking. After that, I think the smell of the gallows crept in on a few. But Maddy and her mom set everyone at ease."

"Did anyone on the *Cobra* survive?"

"I truly don't know. I saw a few run below and others jumped over the side, but we didn't pick up anyone nor did anybody cross over with us. When you finished off their captain, the fight was over. I will never forget the big *Cobra* figurehead, it was eerie. The *Cobra* was from Cobretta, which was the captain's name. Maddy's brother, Jacob, told us he'd been able to discover this prior to departing Antigua." Seeing Cooper's eyes grow heavy, Mac stood up, "I'll talk to you soon. Captain Taylor will visit you tomorrow."

Putting the bowl on a side table, Maddy sat on the bed beside Cooper. She leaned in and gave him a passionate kiss. "I was worried to death about you, Sir Pirate."

Cooper reached out to embrace Maddy and realized he didn't have a shirt on. "I don't seem to be fully dressed."

"You're not dressed at all," she said.

Reaching his hands under the cover, he gasped, "Maddy! I'm naked."

"I know, you had bandages on you, silly. You were burned, cut, and bruised. You had to be bandaged up, but you are all healed up now."

"How do you know?" Cooper asked.

"How do you think? I looked! Maybe, I need to take another peak," she said, pulling at the covers. Cooper quickly grabbed them and pulled them to his chest. "Hush, Cooper, did I whine when you looked at me? Far longer than necessary, I might add."

"I...I gave you my coat."

"Only after you heard people coming. You got a good long look so don't try denying it, Cooper Cain."

Cooper pulled Maddy to him and this time it was he who gave her the passionate kiss.

EPILOGUE

THE CARRIAGE BOUNCED, HEAVING Cooper into his former captain and friend, Eli Taylor. David Gill, holding the reins loosely between nimble fingers, clucked to the horse, Lucy, as he glanced back at his passengers. Cooper still looked pale. It had been six weeks since he returned home in a British ship.

The sight of a war ship sailing up the Savannah River had created a stir. It had been several years since England and the United States had been at war, but everywhere you turned, it seemed like politicians were calling for another war. Something about sailor's rights among other things. Being a landsman, he did not understand all that the politicians were arguing about.

Tugging the reins to the left a bit, David tried to miss most of another hole. Still a bit of water splashed out. All the holes were full of water from the rain last night, but the road was not that muddy. Glancing back again, thinking that he should have called out a warning, David saw his passengers hadn't even noticed, wrapped up in conversation as they were.

Cooper had been brought home more dead than alive. Had it not been for Doctor Cannington and Maddy, he probably would have died. Just about the time it seemed Cooper was ready to be up and about, he had a relapse. He ran fever, coughed up foul-smelling stuff and even some blood. Doctor Cannington had said it was from a contagion from the sea water in Cooper's lungs that caused the ill humors. Cakes of brimstone were burned to fumigate the bedroom, leaving an odor, not unlike rotten eggs. A tea made from stripping the bark off of willow tree branches was made and this seemed to help with the fever. The cough was controlled by using a blackberry wine mixed with a spoon of opium. The bedrails and bedside table was washed with vinegar. Doctor Cannington, with the help of Maddy and Faith, did everything he could do to keep mortification at bay.

Finally, Cooper started to recover. Faith took passage on one of Taylor's company ships. Maddy flatly refused to go. A promise was made that once Cooper recovered, she'd live with her brother, James, and his new wife, Josie. The house would be crowded with Josie's sister, Jessie already living there. But, the two girls quickly became friends.

COOPER FELT THE SUN on his face and other than the potholes; the carriage ride was a blessing. He'd been cooped up in the farmhouse too long. He had come to love the openness one felt being at sea. His visitors had been few. Out of fear, mostly, of his illness. Therefore, when Doctor Cannington agreed to let him take a short ride with Eli Taylor, Cooper was elated.

The first part of the ride was filled with small talk. They talked about the weather, crops, and improvements to Eli and Debbie's place as well as Cooper's place.

Cooper finally found the courage to speak about the *Raven*. "Eli, I'm sorry I lost the *Raven*. She was a good ship. After the refit, she was perfect. I don't know what I can do to repay you, but I will." Taylor tried to hush his friend, but the floodgates were open. "If we hadn't raided Culebra, she'd probably still be afloat."

"If you hadn't raided Culebra, Maddy and Faith would probably both be dead or worse. Don't fault yourself, Coop, you took the right action. The same action I would have taken. We play a dangerous game, my friend. You have a talent for leadership. I recognized it the first time we met. Besides, fate deals us a strange hand at times. Had we not met the Anthony's on the road, there would not have been the need to attempt a rescue. You may have lost the *Raven* to a superior ship, I might add, but you took the ship. You have become not only a leader but a captain worthy of the title. The story of the battle will be told and retold again and again. Men will sign on because of it." When Eli finished his sentence, there was a lengthy pause.

"I'm...I'm not sure I want to go back to doing the same thing, Eli," Cooper said, with a tremble in his voice. He'd been trying to think of a way to tell his friend, his benefactor that his pirating days were over. How could he expect Maddy's father or mother to approve of her marrying a pirate?

"Do you want to give up the sea?" Eli asked.

"No, I've come to love the sea. It's in my blood now, I'll admit. I like the feel of a good ship beneath my feet. I love the challenge. In truth, I love being a raider. It provides more excitement than anything I've known thus far."

"I see," Eli said.

"Whoa! Whoa, now Lucy." David turned on his seat. "Down to the landing or to Mr. Watts' house?" he asked.

"To the landing, Robert Watts will not be at his home at this time of day," Taylor said.

David clucked to the horse, who after a gentle slap of the reins, took up the stress in the harness and moved on. After topping a hill, the boat works was laid out below. Men were busy and scaffolding was built up around a ship. Even at this distance, Cooper could see this was no merchantman. This was a war ship, a small frigate, larger than the *Raven*. She'd be a fast sailor.

"What you see before you is a raider," Eli said. "I have come to call her, *SeaFire*, but that can change. She was built similar to the British Enterprise class sixth rate frigate, which was so successful against us in our war for independence. The class has also been very successful in England's war with Napoleon. Of course, Mr. Watts, our trusty shipwright, has incorporated a few modifications that I feel will come in handy. She's one hundred and twenty feet long. That's twenty feet longer than the *Raven*. She'll go six hundred ton. Her beam is nearly thirty-four feet. When she's armed, her upper deck will carry twenty-four nine-pounders, four six-pounders will be on the quarterdeck. But that's not all. She'll carry four eighteen-pounder carronades on the quarterdeck and two more of the big bruisers forward. Mr. Watts has recommended fittings for twelve to fourteen swivel guns."

"Damn, Eli, what a ship," Cooper exclaimed, excitement in his voice.

"Care to go aboard?"

Aye, sir."

Eli stood back and let Cooper climb the makeshift stairs that lead to the entry port. Seeing Mr. Watts, Eli led the way over to the shipwright.

"Cooper, this is Robert Watts. His Yamacraw Shipyard will one day be famous. I have no doubt of this. Mr. Watts, this is Cooper Cain, the young man I told you about."

"Captain Cain," Watts said, extending his hand to Cooper. The man's grip was firm, his hand rough and calloused.

He not only designed the ship, Cooper thought, *he participated in its construction*. Watts gave Cooper a tour of the ship, pointing out modifications he'd made on the design.

"She should be faster. The new hull construction will be stronger and with a raised poop, the captain's cabin will be more comfortable than the British ships."

Some of the things Watts mentioned, Cooper understood the significance of. Others, Mac and Johannes could explain. He then felt a pang of guilt. All of this for him and he'd just decided to give up his life as a pirate. Would Mac take the ship? He was certainly a man who knew how to sail such a ship. The rest of the tour seemed a blur.

Finally, Eli said, "Mr. Watts, it seems I've had our captain out too long. He's showing signs of exhaustion."

Watts nodded, "I recall you'd mentioned the terrible ordeal Captain Cain has gone through." Turning his attention to Cooper, Watts said, "I wish you a full and speedy recovery, Captain."

Once they'd gotten back in the carriage and headed back toward Thunderbolt, Cooper broke his silence. "I've disappointed you, Eli."

"Nonsense," Taylor replied.

"You've had that raider built with me in mind."

"That's true, Cooper. You've said you love the sea and the feel of a good ship. You just don't want to be a pirate anymore. But what if you could do it legally?"

Cooper was all ears. "Legally?"

"That's what I said. Colonel Lee has it on good authority that we will be at war within the next few months. Should you decide to stand by us, meaning the United States, you can raid all the British shipping you desire. You can wipe out the Finylsons with no fear of reprisal. I have it straight from James Anthony's mouth that he will side with us Americans, so Maddy will undoubtedly do the same since her husband will be the captain of a privateer."

What will her father do? Cooper wondered. *There had been talk of retirement.* Cooper didn't know what to say. Smiling, Taylor continued, "The paperwork has already been completed. There are four investors who own *SeaFire,* John Will, Michael Brett, Colonel Lee, and myself."

"Captain Cain, within a week of war being declared, you will receive a Letter of Marque," Eli said, in an official tone. "May fortune be with you, my friend."

Notes from the Author

Having decided to write a trilogy on pirates, I wanted to avoid the arrr, avast matey, and shiver me timbers. Such language may be great for kids, but that was not my target. I wanted to focus on the older, adult audience. To write a book on pirates, certain subjects were such a part of a pirate's activities, writing a "G" rated book was impossible. However, I felt I could be authentic and entertaining without being "R" rated.

I chose to write on the last great period of piracy, the early 1800's. By doing this, I could incorporate characters from both my *Fighting Anthonys* series and my *War 1812* trilogy. This allowed the reader to have a sprinkling of characters they were familiar with.

The most prominent pirate of that period was Jean LaFitte. He was a gentleman, shrewd businessman, and was considered by many to be a man of prestige and honor. He never looted an American ship and he played a big part in Andrew Jackson's victory at the Battle of New Orleans. Therefore, Mr. LaFitte had to be prominent in my book.

For any story to be realistic and enjoyable requires research. Thanks to Cindy Vallar, a good deal of this research had already been done. Cindy has written more on pirates and piracy than anybody I know of. Contacting Cindy, I found a knowledgeable resource who was willing to answer numerous questions, offer advice, and wisdom. You can find anything you want to know about pirates in Cindy's articles and publications. She is the pirate lady.

Jim Nelson was also a big help with his recommendations of *"Under the Black Flag"* by David Cordingly, *"The History of Pirates"* by Angus Konstrom, and Time Life's *"The Pirates"* which was part of the *"SeaFares"* series. I also found *"LaFitte the Pirate"* by Lyle Saxon to be very helpful.

Chris and Jay at Bitingduck publishers have always been very supportive of Michael Aye. I was extremely happy when they decided to make *"Pyrate, the Rise of Cooper Cain"* my first hardback.

The front cover art for *"Pyrate"* was done by Johannes Ewers, specifically for this book. His continued support of Michael Aye has been very much appreciated.

The back cover art for *"Pyrate"* was done by Ruth Sanderon. While surfing the web looking for an image to base my character on, I came across Ms. Sanderon's painting. To me, it was the perfect image in which to base my pirate. He is Cooper Cain.

Cathy Vaught did the skull that is used at the beginning of each section. She is a very talented lady.

CPSIA information can be obtained at www.ICGtesting.com
Printed in the USA
BVOW11*0505080116

431631BV00020B/148/P

9 781938 463266